making babies!

Now she's pregnant, will he propose?

By Request

Praise for three best-selling authors—
Miranda Lee, Carole Mortimer
and Lucy Gordon

About Miranda Lee

"Miranda Lee…delivers seductive reading
with an intense conflict."
—*Romantic Times*

About Carole Mortimer

"Carole Mortimer delivers quality
romance with an exciting premise
and intense characters."
—*Romantic Times*

About *His Brother's Child*

"Lucy Gordon pens a highly emotional tale
with unique scenes."
—*Romantic Times*

making babies!

SIMPLY IRRESISTIBLE
by
Miranda Lee

AFTER THE LOVING
by
Carole Mortimer

HIS BROTHER'S CHILD
by
Lucy Gordon

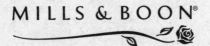

MILLS & BOON®

*MILLS & BOON and MILLS & BOON with the Rose Device
are registered trademarks of the publisher.*
Harlequin Mills & Boon Limited,
Eton House, 18-24 Paradise Road, Richmond, Surrey, TW9 1SR

MAKING BABIES!
© by Harlequin Enterprises II B.V., 2001

Simply Irresistible, After the Loving and *His Brother's Child* were first
published in Great Britain by Harlequin Mills & Boon Limited in
separate, single volumes.

Simply Irresistible © Miranda Lee 1993
After the Loving © Carole Mortimer 1987
His Brother's Child © Lucy Gordon 1997

ISBN 0 263 82770 4

05-0201

*Printed and bound in Spain
by Litografia Rosés S.A., Barcelona*

Miranda Lee is Australian, living near Sydney. Born and raised in the bush, she was boarding-school educated and briefly pursued a classical music career before moving to Sydney and embracing the world of computers. Happily married, with three daughters, she began writing when family commitments kept her at home. She likes to create stories that are believable, modern, fast-paced and sexy. Her interests include reading meaty sagas, doing word puzzles, gambling and going to the movies.

**Look out for MARRIAGE AT A PRICE
by Miranda Lee
in Mills & Boon Modern Romance™, April 2001**

SIMPLY IRRESISTIBLE
by
MIRANDA LEE

CHAPTER ONE

'WE'VE been accused of doing too many heavy stories lately,' Mervyn announced to his underlings seated around the oval table. 'From now on, one of the four segments we tape for each week's show is going to be in a lighter vein.'

Vivien looked up from where she was doodling on her note-pad, a sinking feeling in her stomach. As the last reporter to join the *Across Australia* team—not to mention the only woman—she just *knew* who would be assigned these 'lighter-veined' stories.

She hadn't long come off a *Candid Camera* style programme, and while it had been a huge success, she'd been relieved to finally have the chance to work on a television show that was more intellectually stimulating. At twenty-five going on twenty-six, she felt she was old enough to be taken seriously.

Ah, well, she sighed. One step forward and two steps backwards...

'And what constitutes lighter-veined?' demanded a male voice from across the table.

Vivien glanced over at Bob, widely known as Robert J. Overhill, their hard-hitting political reporter who wouldn't know 'lighter-veined' if it hit him in the left eye. Thirtyish, but already going bald and running to fat, he conducted every interview as a personal war out of which he *had* to emerge the victor. He had a sharp, incisive mind, but the personality of a spoilt little boy.

'I'm not sure myself yet,' Mervyn returned. 'This directive has just come down from the great white chief himself. I've only had time to think up a try-out idea to be screened on Sunday week. Ever heard of Wallaby Creek?' he queried with a wry grin on his intelligent face.

They all shook their heads.

'It's a small town out in north-western New South Wales just this side of Bourke, but off the main highway. Once a year, in the middle of November, it's where the Outback Shearers' Association hold their Bachelors' and Spinsters' Ball.'

Everyone rolled their eyes as the penny dropped. There'd been a current affairs programme done on a similar B & S Ball a couple of years before, which had depicted the event as a drunken orgy filled with loutish yobbos and female desperadoes. The only claim to dubious fame the event seemed to have was that no girl went home a virgin.

Vivien chuckled to herself at the thought that, from what she had seen, not too many virgins had gone to that particular ball in the first place.

'I'm so glad you find the idea an amusing one, Viv,' her producer directed straight at her, 'since you'll be handling it. The ball's this Saturday night. That gives you three days to get yourself organised and out there. Now I'm not interested in any serious message in this story. Just a fun piece. Froth and bubble. Right?'

Vivien diplomatically kept her chagrin to herself. 'Right,' she said, and threw a bright smile around the table at all the smug male faces smirking at her.

It never ceased to amaze her, the pleasure men got

from seeing women supposedly put in their places in the workplace, but she had always found the best line of defence was to be agreeable, rather than militant. She defused any antagonism with feminine charm, then counter-attacked by always giving her very best, doing such a damn good job—even with froth and bubble—that her male colleagues had to give her some credit.

'I hear they drink pretty heavily at those balls,' Bob said in a mocking tone. 'We might have to send out a search party of trackers to find Viv the next day. You know what she's like after a couple of glasses. Whew…' He whistled and waved his hand in front of his face, as though he was suddenly very hot.

Vivien sighed while the others laughed. Would she *never* live down the channel's Christmas party last year? How was she to know that someone had spiked the supposedly non-alcoholic fruit punch with vodka? She was always so careful when it came to drinking, ever since she'd discovered several years before at her first university party that anything more than two glasses of the mildest concoction turned her from a quietly spoken, serious-minded girl into a flamboyant exhibitionist, not to mention a rather outrageous flirt.

Luckily for Vivien on that first occasion, her girl-friend had dragged her home before she got herself into any serious trouble. But her hangover the next morning, plus the stark memory of her silly and po-tentially dangerous behaviour, had made her very careful with alcohol from that moment on.

The incident at last year's Christmas party had hardly been her fault. Vivien groaned silently as she recalled how, once the alcohol took effect, she'd actually climbed up on this very table and danced a wild tango, complete with a rose in her mouth.

Earl had been furious with her, dragging her down and taking her home post-haste. He'd hardly spoken to her for a week. It had taken much longer for the people at work to stop making pointed remarks over the incident. Now, her acid-tongued colleague had brought it up again. Still, Vivien knew the worst thing she could do would be to react visibly.

'Worried you might miss out on something, Bob?' she countered with a light laugh.

'Hardly,' he scowled. 'I like my women a touch less aggressive.'

'Cut it out, Bob,' Mervyn intervened before the situation flared out of hand. 'Oh, and Viv, I can only let you have a single-man crew. You like working that way anyway, don't you?'

'I'll get Irving,' she said. Irving was a peach to work with, a whiz with camera and sound. A witty companion, too.

But the best part about Irving was that he wasn't a womaniser and never tried to chat her up. In his late twenties, he had a steady girlfriend who adored him and whom he adored back. Fidelity was his middle name. Definitely Vivien's type of man.

'It goes without saying that you'll both have to drive out. *And* in the same car,' Mervyn went on. 'You know how tight things have been since they cut our budget again. I rang the one and only hotel in Wallaby Creek to see if they had any vacancies and, luckily enough, they did. Seems the proprietor is refusing to house any revellers for the ball after a couple of his rooms were almost wrecked last year. Might

I suggest you don't leave any valuable equipment in the car that night after you've retired? OK?'

'Sure thing, boss,' Vivien agreed. Maybe it wouldn't be so bad, she decided philosophically. She'd always wanted to drive out west for a look-see, having never been beyond the Blue Mountains. Not that she secretly hankered for a country lifestyle. Vivien was a Sydney girl. Born and bred. She couldn't see herself giving up the vibrant hustle and bustle of city life for wide-open spaces, dust and flies.

Not only that, but it would give her something to do this weekend, since Earl didn't want her to fly down to visit him. *Once again*, she reminded herself with a jab of dismay.

'Well, off you go, madam,' her boss announced before depression could take hold. 'Grab Irving before he's booked up elsewhere. That man's in high demand.'

'Right.' She smiled, and stood up.

'Phone call for you, Vivien,' the main receptionist called out to her as she passed through the foyer area on her way back to her office. 'I'll switch it back to your desk now. That is where you're heading, isn't it? It's STD, by the way. Your boyfriend.'

Vivien's heart skipped a beat. *Earl*? Ringing her during working hours? That wasn't like him at all...

She hurried along the corridor towards the office she shared with her three fellow *Across Australia* reporters, her heart pounding with sudden nerves.

Somehow she just knew this phone call didn't mean what she so desperately hoped it meant, that Earl wanted to say sorry for the way he'd been behaving, that he was missing her as much as she was missing him. Perhaps he'd finally given up trying to make her suffer for not dropping her career and following him to Melbourne the second he got his promotion and transfer six weeks ago.

Her heart twisted as she recalled the awful argument they'd had when he'd come home that night and made his impossible demand. She'd tried explaining that if she just quit on the spot she'd be committing professional suicide. But he hadn't been prepared to listen, his relentlessly cold logic being that if she loved him she would do what *he* wanted, what was best for *him*. If she wanted to marry him and have his children, then *her* career was irrelevant.

Although he had always shown chauvinistic tendencies, his stubborn selfishness in this matter had startled then infuriated her. She had dug in her heels and stayed in Sydney. Nevertheless, she had still been prepared to compromise, promising to look for a position in Melbourne in the New Year, which had been only three months away. To which idea Earl had sulkily agreed.

To begin with, Vivien had flown to Melbourne every weekend to be with him. These visits, however, had not been a great success, with the old argument inevitably flaring about her throwing in her job and staying with him. After three weeks of these bittersweet reunions, Earl had started finding reasons for her not to come, saying he was busy with one thing and another. Which perhaps he was... But underneath, Vivien believed he'd been exacting a type of revenge on her, being petty in a way he'd never been before.

She swept into the empty office and over to her corner, sending papers flying as she slid on to the corner of her desk and snatched up the receiver.

'Hello?' she said breathlessly.

'Vivien? That is you, isn't it?' Earl drawled in a voice she scarcely recognised.

Taken aback, she was lost for words for a moment. Where on earth had he got that accent from? He sounded like an upper-class snob, yet he was from a working-class background, just like herself.

'Oh—er—yes, it's me,' she finally blurted out.

His laugh had the most peculiarly dry note to it. 'You sound rattled. Have I caught you doing things you shouldn't be doing with all those men you work with?'

Now *that* was just like Earl. Jealous as sin.

She suppressed an unhappy sigh. He didn't have to be jealous. She'd never given him a moment's doubt over her loyalty from the moment she'd fallen in love with him two years before. Hadn't she even gone against her principles and agreed to live with him when he postponed their plans to marry till he was thirty?

'Don't be silly, darling,' she cajoled. 'You know you're the only man for me.'

'Do I? I'm not so sure, Vivien. And *you're* the one who's been silly. *Very* silly.'

Vivien was chilled by the tone in his voice.

'If you'd just come with me when I asked you to,' he continued peevishly, 'none of this would have happened.'

'None of w—what would have happened?' she asked, a sick feeling starting in the pit of her stomach.

'We'd probably be married by now,' he raved on, totally ignoring her tremulous question. 'The chairman of the bank down here likes his executives suitably spoused. You would have been perfect for the role of my wife, Vivien, with your personality and looks. But *no*! You had to have your own career as well, didn't you? You had to be liberated! Well, consider yourself liberated, my sweet. Set free, free of everything, including me.'

Vivien thought she made a choking, gasping sound. But perhaps she didn't.

'Besides, I've met someone else,' he pronounced with a bald cruelty that took her breath away. 'She's the daughter of a well-connected businessman down here. Not as stunning-looking as you, I admit. But then, not many women are,' he added caustically. 'But she's prepared to be a full-time wife, to devote herself entirely to *me*!'

Shock was sending Vivien's head into a spin. She wanted to drop the phone. Run. Anything. This couldn't be happening to her. Earl *couldn't* be telling her he'd found someone else, some woman he was going to *marry*?

Somehow she gathered herself with a strength that was perhaps only illusory. But she clung to it all the same.

'Earl,' she said with a quiet desperation, 'I love you. And I know you love me. Don't do this to us…not…not for the sake of ambition.'

'Ambition?' he scoffed. 'You *dare* talk to me of ambition? You, who put your career ahead of your so-called love for me? Don't make me laugh, sweetheart. Actually, I consider myself lucky to be getting out from under this…*obsession* I had for you. Any man would find it hard to give you up. But I'm cured now. I've kicked the habit. And I have my methadone at hand.' He laughed. 'Name of Amelia.'

Vivien was dimly aware that she was now in danger of cracking up on the spot. The hand that was clutching the receiver to her ear was going cold, shivers reverberating up her arm. She tried to speak, but couldn't.

'I'll be up this Saturday to get the rest of my things,' Earl continued callously. 'I'd like you to be conspicuously absent. Visit your folks or something. Oh, for pity's sake, say something, Vivien! You're beginning to bore me with this frozen silence routine. It's positively childish. You must have known the writing was on the wall once you refused to come with me.'

'I...I would have come,' she said in an emotionally devastated voice, 'if I'd known this would happen. Earl, please...I *love* you—'

'No, you bloody well don't,' he shot back nastily. 'No more than I loved you. I can see now it was only lust. I'm surprised it lasted as long as it did.'

Only lust?

Her face flamed with humiliation and hurt. She couldn't count the number of times sex hadn't been all that good for her. She'd merely pretended. For *his* sake. For his infernal male pride!

'No come-backs?' he jeered. 'Fine. I don't want to argue, either. After all, there's nothing really to argue about. You made your choice, Vivien. Now you can damned well live with it!' And he slammed down the phone.

She stared down at the dead receiver, her mind reeling as the reality of the situation hit her.

Earl was gone from her life.

Not just temporarily.

Forever.

All her plans for the future—shattered.

There would be no marriage to him. No children by him. No nothing.

Tears welled up behind her eyes and she might have buried her face in her hands and sobbed her heart out had not Robert J. Overhill appeared in the doorway of the office at that precise moment. Luckily his sharp eyes didn't go to her pale, shaken face. They zeroed in on her long, shapely legs dangling over the desk corner.

For the first time Vivien understood Bob's vicious attitude towards her. He *did* fancy her, her crime being that she didn't fancy him back.

With a desperate burst of pride she kept the tears at bay. 'Well!' She jumped to her feet and plastered a bright smile on her face. 'I'd better stop this lounging about and get to work. You wouldn't know where Irving might be, would you?'

'Haven't a clue.' Bob shrugged, his narrowed eyes travelling slowly back up her body.

'I'll try the canteen,' she said breezily.

'You do that.'

He remained standing in the narrow doorway so that she had to turn sideways and brush past him to leave the room, her full breasts connecting with his arm.

But she said, 'Excuse me,' airily as though it didn't matter, and hurried up the corridor, hiding the shudder that ran deeply through her. All of a sudden, she hated men. The whole breed. For they were indeed hateful creatures, she decided. Hateful! Incapable of true love. Incapable of caring. All they thought about or wanted was sex.

But then she remembered her father. Her sweet,

kind, loving father. And her two older brothers. Both good men with stable, secure marriages and happy wives and families. Even Irving was loyal and true, and *he* was in the television industry, hardly a hotbed of faithfulness. Was she asking for too much to want that kind of man for herself?

'Oh, Irving!' she called out, spotting the man himself leaving the canteen.

He spun round and smiled at her. 'What's up, Doc?'

'Got a job for you.'

'Thank the lord it's you and not Bob. I've had politicians up to here!' And he drew a line across his throat. 'So where are we off to this time?'

'Ever heard of Wallaby Creek?'

CHAPTER TWO

THE Wallaby Creek hotel was typical of hotels found in bush towns throughout Australia.

It was two-storeyed and quite roomy, sporting a corrugated-iron roof—painted green—and wooden verandas all around, the upper one with iron lacework railings—painted cream. It sat on the inevitable corner, so that any patrons who cared to wander out from their upstairs room on to the adjoining veranda would be guaranteed a splendid view of the main street below and an unimpeded panorama for miles around.

Vivien was standing on this veranda at six on the following Saturday evening, wiping the perspiration from her neck and looking out in awe at the incredible scene still taking shape before her eyes.

When she and Irving had driven into the small, dusty town the previous evening, tired and hot from the day-long trip west, they'd wondered where the ball would be held, since, at first glance, Wallaby Creek consisted of little else but this hotel, a few ancient houses, a general store and two garages.

They'd asked the hotel proprietor, a jolly soul named Bert, if there was a hall they'd missed. He'd given a good belly-laugh and told them no, no hall, then refused to answer their next query as to where the venue for the ball would be.

'Just you wait and see,' he'd chuckled. 'Come tomorrow afternoon, you won't recognise this place.'

He'd been right. In the short space of a few hours,

the sleepy hollow of Wallaby Creek had been transformed.

First, heavy-transport vehicles accompanied by utilities filled with men had descended on the place like a plague of locusts, and within a short while a marquee that would have done the Russian circus proud had mushroomed in a nearby paddock. Next came the dance-floor, square slabs of wooden decking that fitted together like giant parquet.

A car park was then marked out with portable fences, its size showing that they were anticipating an exceptionally large turn-out. This expectation was reinforced by the two long lines of porta-loos that stretched out on either side of the marquee, one marked 'Chicks', the other 'Blokes'.

Refreshment vans had rolled into town all day, with everything from meat pies to champagne to kegs of beer. Two enormous barbecues had been set up on either side of the front entrance to the marquee, complete with a multitude of plastic tables and chairs, not to mention plastic glasses and cutlery. Lessons had been learnt, it seemed, from accidents in previous years. Real glass was out!

Vivien had been kept busy all day, interviewing all sorts of people, from the members of the organising committee to the volunteers who helped put the venue together to the people who hoped to make a quick buck out of hot dogs or steak sandwiches or what have you.

She was amazed at the distance some of the men had travelled, though it had been patiently explained to her that Wallaby Creek was fairly central to most of the sheep properties around this section of New

South Wales and country people were used to covering vast distances for their entertainment. Every unmarried jackeroo, rouseabout, stockhand and shearer in a three-hundred-kilometre radius would be in attendance tonight, she was assured, together with a sprinkling of station owners and other assorted B & S Ball fans. Apparently a few carloads of young ladies even drove out from Sydney for such occasions, in search of a man.

If Vivien hadn't been so depressed inside, she might have been caught up in the general air of excited anticipation that seemed to be pervading everyone. But she couldn't even get up enough enthusiasm to start getting ready. Instead, she lingered outside, leaning on the old iron railing, staring at the horizon, which was bathed in the bold reds and golds of an outback sunset.

But she was blind to the raw, rich beauty of the land, her mind back in her flat in Sydney, where at this very moment Earl was probably taking away every single reminder she had of him. When she went back, it would almost be as though he had never existed.

Only he *had* existed, she moaned silently. And would continue to exist in her mind and heart for a long, long time.

Vivien's hands lifted to wipe moisture away from her eyes.

Damn, she thought abruptly. I can't possibly be crying again. There can't be any tears left! Angry with herself, she spun away and strode inside into the hotel room. 'No more,' she muttered, and swept up the towels off the bed for a quick visit to the bathroom. 'No more!'

And she didn't cry any more. But she still suffered, her heart heavy in her chest at having thought about Earl again, her normally sparkling eyes flat and dull as she went about transforming herself as astonishingly and speedily as Wallaby Creek had been.

By five to seven, the miracle was almost complete. Gone were the pale blue cotton trousers and simple white shirt she'd been wearing all day, replaced by a strapless ball-gown and matching bolero in a deep purple taffeta. Down was her thick black hair, dancing around her shoulders and face in soft, glossy waves. On had gone her night-time make-up, dramatic and bold, putting a high blush of colour across her smooth alabaster cheeks, turning her already striking brown eyes into even darker pools of exotic mystery, emphasising her sensually wide mouth with a coating of shimmering violet gloss.

At last Vivien stood back to give herself a cynical appraisal in the old dressing-table mirror. Now who are you trying to look so sensational for, you fool? And she shook her head at herself in mockery.

Still, the dressy dress was a must, since all patrons of the ball were required to wear formal clothes. And one did look insipid on television at night unless well made up.

There was a rapid knocking on her door. 'Viv? Are you ready?' Irving asked.

'Coming,' she said brusquely, and, slipping her bare feet into high-heeled black sandals, she swept from the room.

By ten the ball was in full swing, the heavy-metal band that had been brought up from Sydney blaring out its strident beat to a packed throng of energetic dancers. Vivien squeezed a path between the heaving, weaving bodies with her microphone and cameraman in tow, doing fleeting interviews as she went, as well as a general commentary that she probably wouldn't use except as a basis for her final voice-over.

Most of the merry-makers were co-operative and tolerant, and when she remarked to one group that some of the young people's 'formal' gear was not of the best quality she'd been laughingly told that 'experienced' B & S Ball attendees always purchased their tuxes and gowns from second-hand clothing establishments.

'Otherwise their good clothes might get ruined!' One young man winked.

'How?' she asked.

They all looked at her as though she'd just descended from Mars.

'In the creek, of course! Don't you city folks have creeks down in Sydney?'

'Er—well...' Hard to explain that one didn't go swimming in the Parramatta or St. George's River. Too much pollution. 'We do have the harbour,' she tried.

'Not as good as our creek,' someone said, and they all laughed knowingly.

They were still laughing as she moved on.

'I'm getting hot and tired, Viv,' Irving said shortly before eleven. 'I could do with a bite to eat and a cool drink.'

It was indeed becoming stuffy in the marquee and Vivien herself fancied a breath of fresh air. 'OK. Meet me back here, near the band, at midnight,' she suggested.

'Will do. Here. Give me the mike.' He rolled up the cord, slung it over his shoulder with his camera, and in seconds had disappeared, swallowed up by the throng.

Suddenly, despite being in the middle of a mêlée, Vivien felt incredibly lonely. With a weary sigh she glanced around, waffling over which of the various exits she would make for, and it was as her eyes were skating over the bobbing heads of dancers that she got the shock of her life.

For there was Earl, leaning against one of the tent poles, looking very elegant in a black evening suit, bow-tie and all.

She gasped, her view of him obscured for a moment. But when the intervening couples moved out of the way again she realised it wasn't Earl at all, but a man with a face and hair so similar to Earl's that it was scary.

She couldn't help staring at him, and as she stared his eyes slowly turned, drawn no doubt by her intense scrutiny. And then he was looking right at her.

The breath was punched from her lungs. God, but he was the spitting image of Earl! Facially, at least.

Perhaps she should have looked away, now that he was aware of her regard. But she couldn't seem to. It was as though she were hypnotised by this man's uncanny resemblance to the man who had been her lover for the past two years.

A frown formed on his handsome face as they exchanged stares, an oddly troubled frown. It struck Vivien that perhaps he thought he was getting the come-on and was embarrassed by her none too subtle stare.

But if he was, why didn't he just look away?

Suddenly, he moved—destroying his almost apparition-like quality—his spine straightening, his shoulders squaring inside his black dinner-jacket. His eyes never left her.

He was walking now, moving inexorably towards her, the gyrating crowd parting before him like the Red Sea had for Moses. Closer, he was still incredibly like Earl. The way his thick brown hair swept across his forehead from a side parting. The wide, sensuous mouth. And that damned dimple in the middle of a similarly strong square-cut jaw.

But he was taller and leaner than Earl. And his eyes weren't grey. They were a light ice-blue. They were also compellingly fixed on her as he loomed closer and closer.

Vivien's big brown eyes flicked over his elegant dinner suit. No second-hand rubbish for him, she thought, and swallowed nervously. Jackets didn't fit like that unless they were individually tailored. Of course, he was no callow youth either. He had to be at least thirty.

He stopped right in front of her, a slow and vaguely sardonic smile coming to his face. 'Care to dance?' he asked in a voice like dark chocolate.

'D-dance?' She blinked up at him, thrown by how amazingly similar that lop-sided, lazy smile was to Earl's.

His smile grew wider, thankfully destroying the likeness. 'Yes, dance. You know...two people with arms around each other, moving in unison.'

She blushed under his teasing, which rattled her even more than his looks. Good grief, she *never* blushed, having achieved a measure of fame around the channel for her sophisticated composure, her ability never to be thrown by anything or anyone. Which was perhaps why everyone had been so surprised by the wildly mad exhibition she had made of herself at that Christmas party.

'I…yes…all right,' she answered, her mind in chaos, her heart pounding away in her chest like a jackhammer.

He swept her smoothly into his arms and away on to the dance-floor, and once again there seemed to be miraculous room for him. She felt light as a feather in his arms. 'I don't disco,' he murmured, pulling her to him and pressing soft lips into her hair. 'I like my women close.'

'Oh,' was all she could manage in reply.

Good lord, she thought. What am I *doing*? I should have said no. He *had* to have got the wrong idea from my none too subtle staring, not to mention my tongue-tied schoolgirl reaction to his invitation.

Make your apologies and extricate yourself before things get awkward here, she advised herself.

Yet she stayed right where she was and said absolutely nothing, aware of little but the pounding of her heart and the feeling of excitement that was racing through her veins.

Somehow Earl's double invented a dance to the primitive beat of the music, even though it was more a rhythmic swaying than any real movement across the floor. People swirled back around them, shutting them in, making Vivien feel suddenly tight-chested and claustrophic. Someone knocked into them and her partner pulled her even closer, flattening her breasts against the hard wall of his chest.

'Put your arms up around my neck,' he murmured. 'You'll be less of a target that way.'

True, she thought breathlessly. I'll also probably

cease to exist as a separate entity, because if I get any closer I'll have become part of *you*!

But she did as he suggested, amazed at herself for her easy acquiescence. The whole situation had a weird, supernatural feel to it, from the man's uncanny likeness to Earl to her out-of-character reactions to him.

Or maybe they were *in* character, she thought dazedly. Maybe her body was simply responding to the same physical chemistry she felt when she was with Earl. Her responses were not really for this man. They were merely for a face, the face of the man she loved.

A moan of dismay punched which sounded more sensual than desolate from her throat and clearly gave her partner even more of the right—or wrong—idea.

'You feel it too, don't you?' he rasped, one of his hands sliding up under her bolero to trace erotic circles over her naked shoulder blades. 'Incredible...'

She tensed in his arms, appalled yet fascinated by her own arousal. She couldn't seem to gather the courage or common sense to pull away, to put a stop to what was happening between them. When he bent his head to kiss her neck, a betraying shiver of pleasure rippled through her. He groaned, opening his mouth to suckle softly at her flesh.

A compulsive wave of desire broke the last of her control and her fingers began to steal up into his silky, thick hair, fingertips pressing into his scalp.

'God...' he muttered against her neck.

The mindless depth of arousal in his voice plus an abrupt appreciation of where they actually were acted like a cold sponge on Vivien, snapping her back to reality.

'Dear heaven,' she cried, and, shuddering with shame, wrenched away from him.

He stared down at her, smouldering blue eyes still glazed with passion.

Her left hand fluttered up to agitatedly touch her neck where his mouth had been. The skin felt hot and wet and rough. There had to be a red mark. 'You shouldn't have done that,' she burst out. 'I...I didn't like it.'

A chill came into his eyes. 'Didn't you?'

'No, of...of course not!' she denied, her demeanour as flustered as his was now composed.

His eyes narrowed, his top lip curling with a type of sardonic contempt. 'So,' he said with a dry laugh, 'you're nothing but a tease. How ironic. How bloody ironic.'

For a moment she stared back up at him, confused by his words. But then she was angry. 'No, I'm *not*!' she retorted, chin lifting defiantly. 'And there's no need to swear!'

But when she went to whirl away his hand shot out to grab her arm, spinning her back into his body. 'Then *why*?' he flung at her in a low, husky voice. 'Why look at me the way you did? Why let me go that far before you stopped me?'

What could she say? I don't know? Maybe it wasn't *you* I was letting do that. Maybe it wasn't *you* I was wanting.

And yet...

She stared into the depths of the eyes, looking for answers, but finding only more confusion. For suddenly Earl was the furthest thing from her mind.

'You...you wouldn't understand,' she muttered.

'Wouldn't I? Try me.' And he gathered her forcefully back into his arms.

She gaped up at him. But before she could voice any bewildered protest he urged her back into their rocking, rolling rhythm, his hold firm, his eyes stubborn. 'Start explaining.'

For a second, her hands pushed at his immutable shoulders. But it was like trying to push a brick wall down with a feather.

'I deserve an explanation,' he said with maddening logic. 'So stop that nonsense and give me one.'

She glared up at him, knowing she should demand he let go of her, should tell him he had no right to use his superior male strength to enforce his will. Yet all she wanted was to close her eyes and melt back into him. It was incredible!

'I don't think I'm asking too much, do you?' he went on, disarming her with a wry but warm smile.

She groaned in defeat, her forehead tipping forwards on to his rock-hard chest. When he actually picked up her arms and put them around his neck, she glanced up at him, then wished she hadn't. He was too overwhelmingly close and too disturbingly attractive to her.

'So tell me,' he murmured. 'Why did you stare at me the way you did?'

Vivien tried to think of a plausible lie, but couldn't. How could she explain something she didn't fully understand herself? With considerable reluctance, she was forced to embrace the part she *could* grasp. 'When I first saw you I thought you were someone else. You... you look a lot like someone I know. *Used* to know,' she amended.

'An old boyfriend?'

'Sort of.'

He pulled back slightly and gave her a penetrating look. 'Would you like to be more specific?'

She sighed. 'Ex-lover, then.'

'How ex is ex? A week? A month? A year?'

'Three days. *No.*' She laughed bitterly. 'Three *weeks*. Maybe even longer. I just didn't know till three days ago.'

He stopped dancing. There was a strange stillness about his body.

'I see,' he finally exhaled, and began to move again.

'What about later?' he resumed casually enough. 'When we started to dance? What's your excuse for that?'

'I can't explain it,' she choked out.

'Neither can I,' he said, the hand on her waist lifting to hold the back of her head with surprising tenderness, forcing her face to nestle under his chin. 'I've never felt anything like it. Yet I don't even know your name.'

'Vivien,' she whispered, her lips dangerously close to his throat.

'Vivien what?'

'Roberts.'

'Mine's Ross. Ross Everton.'

'Are...are you a shearer?' she asked, trying desperately to get their conversation on to safe, neutral territory. Anything to defuse the physical tension still enveloping her.

'I *can* shear. But it's not my main job.'

She pulled her mouth away from his neck and looked up. 'Which is?'

'I manage a sheep station.'

'I would have thought you were an owner.'

He arched one of his eyebrows. 'Why's that?'

'You don't sound like a shearer or a jackeroo.' Which he didn't. He sounded very well educated.

He laughed. 'And what are they supposed to sound like? I'll have you know we had a jackeroo on our place last year who was the son of an English lord.'

'*Our* place? I thought you said you managed.'

'I do. My father's property. For the moment, that is.'

'You sound as if it's only a temporary arrangement.'

A black cloud passed over those piercing blue eyes. 'Dad had a serious stroke last month. The doctors say his chances of having another fatal one are high.'

'Oh. I...I'm sorry.'

'It's all right. You couldn't have known.'

There was a short, sharp silence between them.

'So tell me, Vivien Roberts,' he said abruptly. 'What television programme are you representing here tonight? No, don't bother asking. I spotted you earlier doing your stuff. Is it *Country Wide*? The *Investigators*, maybe? As you can see, we country folk can watch any station we like as long as it's the ABC.'

She laughed, and felt her tension lessen. 'Sorry, but I'm from a disgusting commercial station and the show's called *Across Australia*. And if you tell me you've never heard of it I'll be mortified.'

'I've heard of it,' he admitted, 'but never seen it. Do you think I'd forget you, if I had?'

Her stomach flipped over at the intensity he managed to put into what should have been a casual compliment.

'Ross,' she began hesitantly, 'this…this attraction between us. It can't go anywhere.'

Again she felt that stilling in his body. 'Why not?'

'It…it wouldn't be fair to you.'

'In what way?'

What could she say? Because you're not just *like* the man I've loved and lost. You're almost his mirror image. I'd never know if what I felt for you was real or not. Besides, you're from a different world from me, a world I would never fit into or want to fit into.

'I'm still in love with Earl,' she said, thinking that should answer all arguments.

Ross was irritatingly silent for ages before saying, 'I presume Earl is the man I remind you of, your ex-lover?'

'Yes,' was her reluctant admission.

His laugh sounded odd. 'Even more ironic. Tell me honestly, Vivien, if dear Earl walked back into your life this minute would you take him back?'

'Never!'

'That sounded promisingly bitter. Didn't he love you?'

'I thought he did. Apparently not, however. He's moved to Melbourne and found someone else.'

'I presume you're from Sydney, then?'

'You presume right.'

'And you're going to take your broken heart and enter a convent, is that it?'

Startled, she stared up at him. There was a mocking light in his eyes.

'Very funny,' she bit out.

'Yes, it would be. Somehow I don't think the woman I held in my arms a few minutes back would make a very good nun.'

She might have wrenched herself out of his arms and stalked away at that point if they hadn't been interrupted by a third party, a good-looking young man who tapped Ross on the shoulder with one hand while he held a can of beer in the other. By the look of him, it hadn't been his first drink of the night.

'Well, well, well,' he drawled with a drunken slur. 'I thought you were supposed to be here to watch over me, big brother. But *I've* been watching *you*. What would our dear father think of his God-like first son if I told him you spent this evening so differently from the rest of us mortal men, trying to get into some woman's knickers?'

Vivien gasped, then gasped again when Ross's fist flew out, connecting with his brother's chin. For a second, the young man merely looked shocked, swaying back and forth on his heels. But then his bloodshot eyes rolled back into his head and he tipped backwards, his fall broken by the quick reflexes of the man he'd just insulted.

'Well, don't just stand there, Vivien,' Ross grated out, looking up from where he was bent over his brother, hands hooked under his armpits. 'Pick up his feet and help me get the silly idiot out into some fresh air!'

CHAPTER THREE

No one seemed particularly concerned as Ross and Vivien carted the unconscious young man through the crowd towards the front exit.

'Too much to drink, eh?' was the only comment they received.

Vivien began to think one could murder someone here tonight and get away with it, by saying the corpse was 'dead' drunk as it was carried off for disposal.

'For a lightly built young man, he's darned heavy,' she complained once they made it out of the marquee and tried to prop him up in one of the plastic chairs. Vivien frowned as his head flopped forwards on to his chest. 'Do you think he'll be all right, Ross? Perhaps you hit him too hard.'

Ross made a scowling sound. 'He's lucky I didn't break his damned neck!'

'Why? He was only telling the truth.'

He flashed her a dry look. 'You do have a poor opinion of men at the moment, don't you? Look, if it was just casual sex I was after, I could have my pick of a hundred willing females here tonight. I certainly wouldn't attempt to seduce a sophisticated city broad who probably knows more counter-moves than a chess champion. Here, you pat his cheek while I get him a glass of water. But don't bat those long eyelashes at him if he comes round,' he added sarcasti-

cally over his shoulder as he strode off. 'He might
get the idea you fancy him!'

She squirmed inside, a guilty blush warming her
cheeks. But she busied herself doing as he'd asked,
trying to awaken the slumped body in the chair.
Tapping cheeks didn't work so she started rubbing
hands. His head jerked back and two bloodshot blue
eyes fluttered open just as Ross returned with a couple
of glasses in his hands.

'Wha—what hit me?' his brother groaned, then
clutched at his chin.

'What in hell do you think?' Ross snapped. 'Here,
drink this water and sober up a bit.' He turned to face
Vivien. 'This is for you,' he said, and pressed a fluted
plastic glass of champagne into her hands. 'Your re-
ward for helping me with lunkhead, here. I didn't
think water would be your style.'

'Oh, but I...no, really, I...' She tried to give him
back the glass, which brought a scoff of disbelief
from his lips. 'Good God, what do you think this is,
a ploy to get you drunk so that I can have my wicked
way with you? Hell, honey, you have got tickets on
yourself.'

Vivien stiffened with instant pique. She lifted the
champagne and downed it all in one swallow, rebelliously enjoying every bubbly drop, at the same time
reminding herself ruefully not to touch another single
mouthful that night. She plonked the empty glass
down on the littered table near by and looked Ross
straight in the eye. 'Even if I were plastered,' she
stated boldly, 'I wouldn't let you touch me!'

The young man sprawled in the plastic chair gave
a guffaw of laughter. 'Geez, looks like the legendary
Ross Everton must have lost his touch! Isn't she fall-

ing down on her knees, begging for your body, like every girl you give the eye to?'

Ross swung on his brother as though he was about to hit him again. 'Gavin, I'm *warning* you!'

'Warning me about what, big brother? What more could you possibly do to me? You've got it all now, everything I've ever wanted.' He struggled to his feet and managed to put a determined look on to his weakly handsome face. 'Let me warn *you*, brother, dear,' he blustered. 'Watch your back, because one day it's going to be *me* taking something that's *yours*! You mark my words.' And he lurched off back into the marquee, colliding with several people on the way.

'Will he be all right?' Vivien asked, worried.

'Tonight, you mean? I hope so. God knows why he has to get so damned drunk on these occasions. When he drinks to excess, he goes crazy.'

He's not the only one, Vivien thought, eyeing the empty champagne glass with a degree of concern. *I* don't even need to go to excess. My troubles start around glass number three.

She looked back at Ross, who was rubbing his temple with an agitated forefinger. She forgot about being annoyed with his earlier remarks, seeing only a human being weighed down with problems. And her heart went out to him.

But along with the sympathy she felt a certain amount of curiosity. Was his brother being sarcastic when he'd referred to him as legendary? And legendary in what way, for goodness' sake? His sexual prowess? Vivien's gaze skated over Ross's macho build. He was certainly virile-looking enough to be a womaniser.

There were other questions too teasing at her female curiosity. 'What did Gavin mean,' she asked in the end, 'when he said you've got everything he ever wanted?'

Ross shrugged. 'Who knows? The management of the property, maybe. Or Dad's good opinion. He thinks Gavin's an irresponsible fool. Though Gavin can only blame himself if Dad thinks that. He keeps acting like one. Last year, at this ball, he drove the utility into the creek and nearly drowned. You'd think by twenty-five he'd have started to grow up.'

'Twenty-*five*? He doesn't seem that old.'

'He *looks* his age. He just doesn't act it.'

'Is that why you came along tonight? To see he didn't do it again?'

He nodded. 'I don't think Dad needs any more stress right now.'

Vivien was impressed with his warm concern for his father. 'And your mother?' she queried. 'How's she coping with your father's stroke?' One of Vivien's uncles had had a stroke a couple of years previously and her aunt had almost had a nervous breakdown coping with his agonisingly slow recuperation.

'Mum's dead,' came the brusque reply. 'There's just Dad, Gavin and me.'

'Oh…'

'Yes, I know,' he muttered, and frowned in the direction of the marquee. 'You're sorry and I'm sorry. More than you'll ever know.' His head snapped back to give her a long, thoughtful look.

She squirmed under his intense gaze, especially when his eyes dropped to inspect her considerable cleavage, which the bolero wasn't designed to hide.

'Well,' he sighed at last, eyes lifting back to her face, 'I'd better go and check up on Gavin before he picks a fight with someone else, someone who won't know to pull his punches. Goodbye, Vivien Roberts. Time for you to go back to your world and me to mine.'

He went to move away, but couldn't seem to drag his eyes from her. 'Hell, but you're one beautiful woman. A man would have to be mad to get mixed up with you anyway. Still, I'd like to have a little more to remember than a mere dance!'

Before she realised what he had in mind, he pulled her into his arms and kissed her, his mouth grinding down on hers, his teeth hard. Only for the briefest second did his lips force hers apart, his tongue plunging forward with a single impassioned thrust before he tore his mouth away. Without looking at her again, he spun round and strode off, back into the marquee.

She stared after him, the back of her hand against her mouth. She wasn't at all aware of Irving coming to stand beside her, not till he spoke.

'Hey, Viv, what was that all about? Who *was* that guy?'

Vivien blinked and turned to focus dazedly on her colleague. 'What did you say, Irving?'

He frowned at her. 'Get with it, Viv. It's not like you to go round kissing strange blokes then looking as if you're on cloud nine. Aren't you supposed to be living with some chap back in Sydney? You're not getting swept up with the atmosphere of this Roman orgy, are you?'

She gathered herself with a bitter laugh. 'Not likely. And I'm not living with anyone any more, Irving. He tossed me over for someone else.'

Irving looked surprised. 'What is he, a flaming id-iot?'

Vivien's smile was wry. 'That's sweet of you, Irving. But no, Earl's not an idiot. He's a banker.'

Since Irving didn't socialise at the channel, he had never actually met Earl. Vivien only knew as much about Irving as she did because they had worked together before and he was quite a chatterer on the job.

Irving chuckled. 'Well, a banker's not much different from an idiot, judging by the state of the economy. You're probably well rid of him. But that doesn't mean you should encourage any of the males here tonight, sweetheart. They're all tanked up and ready to fly, yet most of them don't have a flight plan. It's gung-ho and away they go! You should see them out behind the marquee.' He rolled his eyes expressively. 'No. Come to think of it, *don't* go and see. Not unless you want to research a programme on the more adventurous positions from the *Kama Sutra*!'

Vivien was astonished. 'That bad, is it? I thought everything was fairly low-key, by city standards.'

'Gracious, girl! Where have you been this last half-hour? Things are really hotting up around here.'

'*Really*?' She wasn't sure whether to believe him or not. Irving's sense of humour included exaggeration.

He nodded sagely. 'Really. The only safe place now is *inside* the marquee, but, judging by the exodus to the nether regions down by the infamous creek, that'll be empty soon except for the band. Which reminds me—you haven't interviewed them yet. Maybe you could do that during their next break.'

'Good idea.'

Vivien, re-entering the marquee, doubted that it

would empty as Irving predicted, for there was still a huge crowd of fans standing around the band, clapping and singing, as well as dozens of couples dancing. She and Irving took up positions behind the bandstand to wait for the music to stop.

It didn't seem in a hurry to, one number following another. Vivien spotted Ross's tall head once, very briefly, and the sighting agitated her. She didn't want to think about him any more. She certainly didn't want to think about that disturbing kiss. It had sent sensations down to her toes that not even the longest, most sensuous kiss of Earl's could do, which was all very confusing.

Don't think about either of them, she kept telling herself. It's crazy. Futile. *Stupid*!

But to no avail. She couldn't seem to stop. She especially couldn't get her mind off Ross. He intrigued her, whether she wanted him to or not!

'Another glass of champagne?' a low male voice suddenly whispered in her ear.

She jumped and spun round, knocking an arm in the process and spilling some of the champagne Ross was holding.

'Oh, dear, I'm so sorry!' she gasped.

'So am I,' he said, and smiled with apologetic sincerity at her. 'I shouldn't have kissed you like that. Forgive me?'

She looked up into his quite beautiful blue eyes and felt a real churning in her stomach. It threw her into even more confusion.

'Oh, for Pete's sake, forgive him,' Irving drawled from beside her. 'And give me that damned mike. This band looks as if it's going to keep playing till the year 2000. I think I'll go off and take some sneaky bits down at the creek, all by myself. You go and do some flying, Viv. You deserve it if you've been banking all this time.'

'What did he mean by that?' Ross asked once he'd moved off.

'A private joke,' Vivien said, and struggled to smother a mad chuckle. Not since Earl's ghastly phone call had she felt like laughing about their breakup. And in truth, her perverse humour didn't last for long. Thinking about Earl only served to remind her that what she was feeling for Ross couldn't be real. It was an aberration. A cruel joke of nature.

'Have I said something wrong, Vivien? You look…distressed, all of a sudden.'

She gazed searchingly up into his handsome face, clinging to the various differences from Earl. But his features began to blur together and it was a few seconds before she realised tears had swum into her eyes.

'Here, drink this,' Ross urged, and pressed the plastic glass into her hands. 'It'll make you feel better.'

She hesitated, blinking madly till she had control of herself, all the while staring down into the glass, which was about three-quarters full. Perhaps it *would* make her feel better. Less uptight. Less wretched. There was no real danger. This drink wouldn't even bring her up to her two-glass limit.

'To absent bastards,' she toasted, holding the glass up briefly before quaffing the champagne down. 'Now, where's the fireplace?' she said, putting a forced smile on her face.

'*Fireplace*?'

'To smash the glass into. Oh, I can't,' she sighed, examining the glass in mock disappointment. 'It's plastic.' She looked up and flashed Ross what she thought was her most winning smile. Little did she know how brittle it looked, and how heartbreakingly vulnerable were her eyes.

'So is your Earl,' he murmured, 'if he let a girl like you get away.'

Vivien's whole throat contracted as an instant lump claimed it. 'I...I wish you wouldn't say things like that.'

'Why? Don't you believe me?' he asked gently.

'Does anyone believe in their own worth after rejection?'

'I should hope so.'

She gave him a bitter look. 'Then you haven't ever been rejected, Ross Everton. Perhaps if you had, you'd know how I feel. And how your brother feels.'

Vivien saw she had struck a nerve with her statement, and regretted it immediately. Ross might not be a saint, but she couldn't see him deliberately hurting his younger brother. Gavin was indeed a fool, trying to blame someone else for the consequences of his own stupid and irresponsible behaviour.

Before she could formulate an apology, Ross spoke.

'Gavin's passed out in the back of his station wagon. From past experience, he'll sleep till morning. Which leaves me free to enjoy the rest of the evening. I thought that perhaps you might...' He hesitated, his eyes searching hers as though trying to gauge her reaction in advance.

'Might what?' she probed, heart fluttering.

'Go for a walk with me.'

'W—where?' she asked, feeling a jab of real alarm. Not so much at his invitation, but at the funny tingling feeling that was spreading over her skin. And now she detected a slight muzziness in her head.

She frowned down at the empty glass in her hands. Perhaps the champagne had been a particularly potent brew... Or maybe on her empty stomach the alcohol had gone to her head, almost as if it had been shot straight into her veins.

Ross shrugged. 'Not many places to go. Down towards the creek, I suppose. It's a couple of hundred yards beyond the back of the marquee.'

'Irving said I wasn't to go down there,' she said with a dry laugh, though inwardly frowning at how hot she felt all of a sudden. Her palms were clammy, too.

There was no doubt about it. The alcohol had hit her system hard. A walk in some fresh air would probably be the quickest way to sober her up, but she wasn't ignorant of the dangers such a walk presented.

She lifted firm eyes. 'Just a walk, Ross?'

He settled equally firm eyes back on her. 'I'm not about to make promises I won't keep. You're a very lovely and desirable woman, Vivien. I'm likely to try kissing you again, and I won't be in such a hurry this time.'

His eyes dropped to her mouth and she gasped, stunned by the shock of desire that charged through her.

Don't go with him, common sense warned.

Before she could open her mouth to decline he took her free hand quite forcibly and started pulling her behind the bandstand. 'There's a flap in the tent we can squeeze through back here,' he urged. 'We'll go through the car park and down to the creek, but well away from the other carousers.'

Vivien quickly found herself outside, any further argument dying on her lips when the fresh air hit her flushed face. She breathed in deeply, sighing with relief as her head started to clear. 'Oh, that *is* better.'

'I was certainly getting stuffy in there,' Ross agreed. 'It's a warm night.'

'Is it ever anything else but warm in this neck of the woods?' She laughed.

'Too right it is. Some nights it's positively freezing. Come on. It'll be very pleasant down by the creek.' He took her hand again, which brought a sharp look from Vivien.

He smiled at her warning glare and quite deliberately lifted her hand to his mouth, kissing each fingertip before turning her hand over and pressing her palm to his mouth. Her eyes widened when his lips opened and she felt his tongue start tracing erotic circles over her skin.

One small part of her brain kept telling her to yank her hand away. The rest was dazed into compliance with the sheer sensual pleasure of it all.

'You...you shouldn't be doing that,' she husked at last.

He lifted his mouth away, but kept her hand firmly in his grasp. 'Why?' Dragging her to him, he dropped her hand to cup her face, all the while staring down into her startled brown eyes. 'You're a free agent, aren't you? Why shouldn't I kiss you? Why shouldn't you kiss me?'

'Because...'

His mouth was coming closer to hers and her heart was going mad.

'Because—' she tried again.

'Because nothing,' he growled, and claimed her

parted lips, his arms sweeping round her back in an embrace as confining as a strait-jacket.

When he released her a couple of minutes later, Vivien was in a state of shock. When he put his arm around her shoulder and started leading her through the car park in the direction of the creek, she was still not capable of speech.

Had Earl been able to arouse her so completely and totally with just a kiss? she was thinking dazedly. She didn't think so. When he'd made love to her, most of the time her desire had just been reaching a suitable pitch as he was finishing. Yet here…tonight…with Ross…

Perhaps she *was* tipsier than she realised. Alcohol did have a way of blasting her inhibitions to pieces.

'Are you always this silent when a man kisses you?' Ross murmured into her ear. He stopped then and turned to press her up against one of the parked cars, taking her mouth once more in another devastating kiss. She was struggling for air by the time he let her go, her heart going at fifty to the dozen. She was also blisteringly aware of Ross's arousal pressing against her. With great difficulty she ignored the excitement his desire inflamed in her, concentrating instead on the implication of what she was doing.

Truly, she could not let this continue. It wasn't fair to him. And, quite frankly, not to herself. She had never felt such desire, such excitement. In a minute or two, she wouldn't be able to stop even if she wanted to.

'Ross,' she said shakily as she tried to push him away, 'we have to stop this. We're both getting…excited, and I…I don't go in for one-night stands.'

'Neither do I,' he grated, stubbornly refusing to let her go.

'Ross, try to be sensible,' she argued, her stomach fluttering wildly. 'You're country. I'm city. After to-night we won't ever see each other again. I'm very attracted to you, but…' She shook her head, and care-fully omitted to add anything about his physical re-semblance to her ex-lover.

'Those problems are not insurmountable,' he said. 'Vivien, this doesn't have to stop at tonight. I often come down to Sydney to visit Dad in hospital and—'

She placed three fingers across his mouth and shook her head again, her eyes truly regretful. 'No, Ross. It won't work. Believe me when I tell you that. And please,' she groaned when he took her hand and started kissing it again, 'don't keep trying to seduce me. I…I'm only human and you're a very sexy man. But I don't really want you.'

He stopped kissing her palm then, lifting his head to peer down at her with thoughtful eyes. 'I don't think you know what you want, Vivien,' he said tautly.

'I know I don't want to act cheaply,' she countered, cheeks flaming under his reproving gaze.

His smile was odd as he dropped her hand. 'A woman like you would never be cheap.'

'Are you being sarcastic?' she flared.

He seemed genuinely taken aback. 'Not at all.'

'Oh…I thought—'

'You think too much,' he said softly, laying such a gentle hand against her cheek that she almost burst into tears.

She swallowed the lump in her throat and lifted a

proud chin. 'Better to think tonight than to wake up pregnant in the morning.'

His surprised, 'You're not on the Pill?' brought an instant flush. For of course she was. Earl had adamantly refused to take responsibility for contraception right from the start of their affair, claiming it was in *her* interests that she took charge of such matters. *She* would be the one left with an unwanted baby. Vivien could see now that it was just another example of Earl's selfishness.

'Actually, yes, I am,' she admitted. 'But there are *other* concerns besides pregnancy these days.'

'Not with me there aren't,' he bit out.

She viewed this statement with some cynicism. 'Really?' Her eyes flicked over his very male and very attractive body. 'I wouldn't have taken you for the celibate type, Ross.' His brother had implied just the opposite, Vivien remembered ruefully.

'One doesn't have to be celibate to be careful.'

'And would you have been careful tonight if I'd given you the go-ahead?' she challenged.

A slash of red burnt a guilty path across his cheeks. 'This was different,' he muttered, and lifted both hands to rake agitatedly through his hair.

Her laugh was scornful. 'I don't see how.'

His blue eyes glittered dangerously as they swung back to her. 'Then you're a fool, Vivien Roberts. A damned fool!'

For a second, she thought he was going to grab her and kiss her again. But he didn't. Instead, his mouth creased back into the strangest smile. It was both bitter and self-mocking. 'Look, let's walk, shall we? That's what you obviously came out here for. And don't worry your pretty little head. I won't lay a single finger on you unless I get a gold-edged invitation.'

He set off at a solid pace through the rows of cars, Vivien trailing disconsolately behind him. For she knew in the deepest dungeons of her mind, in the place reserved for unmentionable truths, that she didn't want Ross to lay a *single* finger on her. She wanted *all* his fingers, and *both* his hands. She wanted every wonderfully virile part of him.

CHAPTER FOUR

'CAN you slow down a bit?' she complained when the distance between them became ridiculous.

Ross had long left the car park and was almost at the tree-lined creek, while she was still halfway across the intervening paddock. If she'd tried to keep up with him she'd probably have fallen down one of the rabbit holes hidden in the grass. She'd already tripped a few times over rocks and logs and the like. Lord knew what her high heels looked like by now.

He stopped abruptly and threw a black look over his shoulder. Moonlight slanted across the angles of his face and she caught her breath as, for the first time, she saw little resemblance to Earl. His features suddenly looked leaner, harder, stronger. Yet they still did the most disturbing things to her stomach.

She slowed to a crawl as she approached, her eyes searching the ice-blue of his, trying to make sense of what she kept feeling for this man, even now, when he no longer reminded her so much of Earl. She couldn't even cling to the belief that she was tipsy, for the brisk walk had totally cleared her head.

His eyes changed as she stared up at him, at first to bewilderment, then to a wary watchfulness, and finally to one of intuitive speculation. They narrowed as they raked over her, his scrutiny becoming explicitly sexual as it lingered on specific areas of her body.

A wave of sheer sensual weakness washed through Vivien and she swayed towards him. 'Ross, I...I—'

He didn't wait for the gilt-edged invitation. He simply read her body language and scooped her hard against him, kissing her till she was totally breathless. 'God, I want you,' he rasped against her softly swollen mouth. 'I'll go mad if I don't have you. Don't say no...'

She said absolutely nothing as he lifted her up into his arms, carrying her with huge strides to the creek bank, where he lowered her on to the soft grass under a weeping willow. But her eyes were wide, her mind in chaos, her heart beating frantically in her chest.

'I won't ever hurt you, Vivien,' he whispered soothingly, and lay down beside her, bending over to kiss her, softly now, almost reverently.

Dimly she heard the sounds of distant revellers, their shouting and laughter. But even that receded as Ross's hand found her breast.

'You're so beautiful,' he muttered, and, pushing back the taffeta, he bent his mouth to the hardened peak.

Vivien closed her eyes and held his head at her breast, trying to take in the intensity of feeling that was welling up inside her. Briefly she remembered all that had happened to her over the last few days, and for a second she felt overwhelmed with guilt. She wasn't in love with Ross, couldn't possibly be. No more than he could be in love with her.

A tortured whimper broke from her lips.

'What's the matter, sweetheart?' Ross said gently, and returned to sip at her mouth. 'Tell me...'

'Oh, Ross,' she cried, her eyes fluttering open, raw pain in their depths. But as they gazed into his brilliant blue eyes, which were glittering above her with the most incredible passion in their depths, the most seductive yearning, she melted. He wanted her. He *really* wanted her. Not like Earl. Earl had never *really* wanted her.

An obsession. That's what he'd called his feelings for her. An obsession… An unhealthy, an unwanted need, one to be fought against, to be got over like something nasty and repulsive.

What she saw in Ross's eyes wasn't anything like that. It was normal and natural and quite beautiful.

She trembled as she clasped him close. 'Say that you love me,' she whispered. 'That's all I ask.'

He lifted his head to stare down at her, blue eyes startled.

'Oh, you don't have to mean it,' she cried, and clung to him. 'Just say it!'

A darkly troubled frown gathered on his brow and for a long, long moment he just looked at her. But then his hands came up to cradle her face and he gazed at her with such tenderness that she felt totally shattered. 'I love you, Vivien. I really, truly love you…'

She shuddered her despair at demanding such a pretence, but could no more deny the need to hear them than the need Ross was evoking within her woman's body.

'Show me,' she groaned. 'Make me forget everything but here…and now…'

At the first slightly vague moments of consciousness, Vivien was aware of nothing but a very fuzzy head and a throat as dry as the Simpson Desert. Her eyes blinked open to glance around her hotel room, and straight away she remembered.

With chest immediately constricted, she rolled over

and stared at Ross beside her, flat on his back, sound asleep, his naked chest rising and falling in the deep and even breathing of the exhausted.

Rounded eyes went from him to the floor beside the bed, where her beautiful taffeta dress was lying in a sodden heap. Her black lace panties were still hanging from the arm-rest of the chair in the corner where Ross had carelessly tossed them. Her bolero and shoes, she recalled, were still down beside the creek.

Oh, my God, she moaned silently, the night before rushing back in Technicolor. How could I have behaved so...so outrageously? To have let Ross make love to me on the river-bank was bad enough. But what about later?

Her face flamed as guilt and shame consumed her.

She should never have allowed him to talk her into going skinny-dipping in the moonlit creek afterwards. Naked, he was even more insidiously attractive than he'd been in his dashing dinner suit, his body all brown and lean and hard.

Vivien had been fascinated by the feel of his well-honed muscles. She'd touched him innocently enough at first, holding on to his shoulders to stop herself from tiring as she trod water in the deep. But her hands hadn't stayed on his shoulders for long. They had begun to wander. Once she had started exploring his body, one thing had quickly led to another and, before she knew it, Ross was urging her into the shallows, where he'd taken her again right then and there in the water.

Afterwards, he had carried her limp body back on to the bank where he'd dressed her as best he could, then carried her back to the hotel. Vivien could still remember the look on the hotel proprietor's face when Ross had carried her past his desk and up the stairs.

By this time her conscience had begun to raise its damning head, but Ross managed to ram it back down with more drugging kisses in her room, more knowing caresses. Before she knew it, he was undressing her again and urging her to further amazing new heights of sensuality.

Vivien blushed furiously to think of her abandoned response to his lovemaking.

I have to get out of here. Fast. I couldn't possibly face him. I'd die! God, I even made him say he *loved* me!

She cringed in horror, then even more so as she recalled how after the last time here on the bed she'd actually wept. With the sheer intensity of her pleasure, not distress. Ross's lovemaking had seemed to possess not just her body but her very soul, taking her to a level of emotional and physical satisfaction she had never known before.

At least…that was how it had *seemed* at the time…

Looking back now, Vivien realised it couldn't *possibly* have been as marvellous an experience as she kept imagining. Certainly not in any emotional sense. Ross was simply a very skilled lover, knowing just what buttons to push, what words to say to make a woman melt. After all, she'd only asked him to say he loved her once, but he'd told her over and over. There were times when a more naïve woman might have believed he really *did* love her—he sounded and looked so sincere!

She darted a quick glance over at his face, at his softly parted lips. And shuddered. There wasn't a sin-

gle inch of her flesh that those lips hadn't passed over
at some time during the night.

Once again, she felt heat invade her face. Not to
mention other parts of her body.

Thank God the bathroom is down the hall, Vivien
thought shakily. I'll get my things together and slip
out of this room and be gone before he opens a single
one of those incredible blue eyes of his. For if I wait,
I'm not sure what might happen…

A few minutes later she was knocking on Irving's
door. He looked decidedly bleary as he opened it
wearing nothing but striped boxer shorts.

'Viv?' He yawned. 'What are you doing up? I
thought you'd be out of it for hours.' He gave her a
slow, sly grin. 'Bert informed me that you were escorted back to your room at some ungodly hour by
someone he called the "legendary Ross Everton". I
presume he was the handsome hunk you were with
earlier in the night. Did he—er—cure you of the
banker?'

Vivien coloured fiercely, though her whirling mind
was puzzling again over that word 'legendary'.
Legendary in what way? Her colour increased when
she realised it probably meant Ross's reputation with
women. No doubt she had just spent the night with a
very well-known local stud. Why, even his own
brother had suggested Ross was a real ladies' man,
with an infallible success rate.

Squashing down a mad mixture of dismay and mor-
tification, Vivien gave Irving one of her most quelling
'shut-up-and-listen' looks. 'I need to be out of here
five minutes ago, Irving. Do you think you can get a
rustle on?'

'What's the emergency?'

'Shall we just say I don't want to see a certain "legendary" person when he finally wakes up?'

Irving pursed his lips and nodded slowly. 'Mornings after can be a tad sticky.'

'I would have used another word, like *humiliating*! You and I know this is not like me at all, Irving. I'm quietly appalled at myself.'

'You're only human, love. Don't be too hard on yourself. We all let our hair down occasionally.'

'Yes, well, I'd appreciate it if this particular hair-letting-down didn't get around the channel. Not all my colleagues are as good a friend as you, Irving.'

'Mum's the word.'

'Thanks. Look, I'll fix up the hotel bill and meet you at the car as soon as possible.'

'I'll be there before you are.'

Irving dropped Vivien outside her block of flats at seven that evening. She carried her overnight bag wearily up the two flights of stairs, where she inserted the key into the door numbered nine. She pushed the door open and walked in, switching on the light and kicking the door shut behind her in one movement.

Her mouth gaped open as she looked around the living-room in stunned disbelief. Because it was empty!

Well, not exactly empty. The phone was sitting on the carpet against the far wall, and three drooping pot plants huddled in a corner. Gone were the lounge and dining suites, the cocktail cabinet, the coffee-table, the television, the sound system and the oak sideboard, along with everything that had been on or in them. The walls were bare too, pale rectangles showing where various paintings had been hanging.

Vivien dropped the overnight bag at her feet and walked numbly into the kitchen. A dazed search revealed that she was still the proud owner of some odd pieces of chipped crockery and some assorted cutlery. The toaster was the only appliance still in residence, probably because it had been a second-hand one, given to them by her mother. The fridge was there too. But it had come with the flat. Vivien approached the two bedrooms with a growing sense of despair.

The main bedroom was starkly empty, except for her side of the built-in wardrobes. The guest bedroom shocked her in reverse, because it actually contained a single bed complete with linen.

'Oh, thanks a lot, Earl,' she muttered before slumping down on the side of the bed and dissolving into tears.

Five minutes later she was striding back into the living-room and angrily snatching the phone up from the floor. But then she hesitated, and finally dropped the receiver back down into its cradle.

There was no point in ringing Earl. Absolutely no point. For she hadn't paid for a single one of the items he'd taken from their flat. When she'd moved in, Earl, the financial wizard, had suggested *she* pay for the food each week while *he* paid for any other goods they needed. Over the eighteen months he'd bought quite a bit, but she'd also forked out a lot of cash on entertaining Earl's business acquaintances. He always liked the best in food and wine.

Now she wondered with increasing bitterness if he'd known all along how their affair would end and had arranged things so that he'd finish up with all the material possessions she'd assumed they co-owned.

A fair-minded person would have split everything

fifty-fifty. To do what Earl had done was not only cruel. It also underlined that all he'd thrown at her over the telephone was true. He had never loved her. He'd simply used her. She'd been his housekeeper and his whore! And he'd got them both cheap!

But then she *was* cheap, wasn't she? she berated herself savagely. Only cheap women went to bed with a man within an hour or two of meeting him, without any real thought of his feelings, without caring where it led, without…

'Oh, my God!' she gasped aloud, and, with the adrenalin of a sudden shock shooting through her body, Vivien raced over to where she had dropped her bag. She reefed open the zip. But her fumbling fingers couldn't find what she was looking for. Yet they had to be here. They *had* to!

A frantic glance at her watch told her it was almost eight, thirteen hours after she usually took her pill. In the end she tipped the whole contents of the bag out on to the floor and they were were!

Snaffling them up, she pressed Sunday's pill through the foil and swallowed it. But all the while her doctor's warnings went round and round in her mind.

'This is a very low-dosage pill, Vivien, and *must* be taken within the same hourly span each day. To deviate by too long could be disastrous.'

The enormity of this particular disaster did not escape Vivien. She sank down into a sitting position on the carpet and hugged herself around the knees, rocking backwards and forwards in pained distress. 'Oh, no,' she wailed. 'Please, God…not that…I couldn't bear it…'

Vivien might have given herself up to total despair

at that moment if the phone hadn't rung just then, forcing her to pull herself together.

'Yes?' she answered, emotion making her voice tight and angry. If it was Earl ringing he was going to be very, very sorry he had.

'Vivien? Is there something wrong?'

Vivien closed her eyes tight. Her mother… Her loving but very intuitive mother.

She gathered every resource she had. 'No, Mum. Everything's fine.'

'Are you sure?'

'Yes. Positive.' Smiles in her voice.

'I hope so.' Wariness in her mother's.

'What were you ringing up about, Mum?'

Vivien's mother was never one to ring for idle gossip. There was always a specific reason behind the call.

'Well, next Sunday week's your father's birthday, as you know, and I was planning a family dinner for him, and I was hoping you would come this time, now that Earl's in Melbourne. That man never seems to like you going to family gatherings,' her softhearted mother finished as accusingly as she could manage.

'Of course I'll be there,' she reassured, ignoring the gibe about Earl. Not that it wasn't true, come to think of it. Earl had never wanted to share her with her family.

She sighed. Perhaps in a fortnight's time she'd feel up to telling her mother about their breakup. Though, of course, in a fortnight's time she'd probably also be on the verge of a nervous breakdown, worrying if she was pregnant or not. God, what was to become of her?

'Do you want me to bring anything beside a present?' she asked. 'Some wine, maybe?'

'Only your sweet self, darling.'

The 'darling' almost did it. Tears swam into Vivien's eyes and her chin began to quiver. 'Oh, goodness, there's someone at the door, Mum. Must go. See you Sunday week about noon, OK?'

She just managed to hang up before she collapsed into a screaming heap on the floor, crying her eyes out.

CHAPTER FIVE

'I'M SORRY, Viv,' Mervyn said without any real apology in his voice. 'But that's the way it is. *Across Australia* has received another cut in budget and I have to trim staff. I've decided to do it on a last-on, first-to-go basis.'

'I see,' was Vivien's controlled reply. She knew there was no point in mentioning that fan mail suggested she was one of the show's most popular reporters. Mervyn was a man's man. He also never went back on a decision, once he'd made it.

'There's nothing else going at the channel?' she asked, trying to maintain a civil politeness in the face of her bitter disappointment. 'No empty slots anywhere?'

'I'm sorry, Viv,' he said once more. 'But you know how things are…'

What could she possibly say? If the quality of her work had not swayed him then no other argument would. Besides, she had too much pride to beg.

'Personnel has already made up your cheque,' he went on matter-of-factly when she remained stubbornly silent. 'You can pick it up at Reception.'

Now Vivien *was* shocked. Shocked and hurt. She propelled herself up from the chair on to shaky legs. 'But I'm supposed to get a month's notice,' she argued. 'My contract states that—'

'Your contract also states,' Mervyn overrode curtly, 'that you can receive a month's extra pay in lieu of notice. That's what we've decided to do in your case. For security reasons,' he finished brusquely.

She sucked in a startled breath. 'What on earth does that mean? What security reasons?'

'Come, now, Viv, it wouldn't be the first time that a disgruntled employee worked out their time here, all the while relaying our ideas to our opposition.'

'But…but you *know* I wouldn't do any such thing!'

His shrug was indifferent, his eyes hard and uncompromising. 'I don't make the policies around here, Viv. I only enforce them. If I hear of anything going I'll let you know.' With that, he extended a cold hand.

Vivien took it limply, turning on stunned legs before walking shakily from the room. This isn't happening to me, she told herself over and over. I'm in some sort of horrible nightmare.

In the space of a few short days, she had lost Earl, and now her job…

'Viv?' the receptionist asked after she'd been standing in front of the desk staring into space for quite some time. 'Are you all right?'

Vivien composed herself with great difficulty, covering her inner turmoil with a bland smile. 'Just woolgathering. I was told there would be a letter for me here…'

Vivien walked around the flat in a daze. She still couldn't believe what had happened back at the channel. When she'd arrived at work that morning, she'd thought Mervyn had wanted to talk to her to see how the segment at Wallaby Creek had gone over the weekend. Instead, she'd been summarily retrenched.

How ironic, she thought with rising bitterness. She had virtually lost Earl because of that job. And now…the job was no more.

Tears threatened. But she blinked them away. She was fed up with crying, and totally fed up with life! What had she ever done to deserve to be dumped like that—first by the man she loved, then by an employer to whom she had given nothing but her best? It was unfair and unjust and downright unAustralian!

Well, I'll just have to get another job, she realised with a resurgence of spirit. A *better* job!

Such as what? the voice of grim logic piped up. All the channels are laying off people right, left and centre. Unemployment's at a record high.

'I'll find something,' she determined out loud, and marched into the kitchen, where she put on the kettle to make herself some coffee.

And what if you're pregnant? another little voice inserted quietly.

Vivien's stomach tightened.

'I can't be,' she whispered despairingly. 'That would be too much. Simply too much. Dear God, please don't do that to me as well. *Please…*'

Vivien was just reaching for a cup and saucer when the front doorbell rang. Frowning, she clattered the crockery on to the kitchen counter and glanced at her watch. 'Now who on earth could that be at four fifty-three on a Monday afternoon?' she muttered.

The bell ran again. Quite insistently.

'All right, all right, I'm coming!'

Vivien felt a vague disquiet as she went to open the door. Most of her acquaintances and friends would still be at work. Who could it possibly be?

'Ross!' she gasped aloud at first sight of him, her heart leaping with…what?

He stood there, dressed in blue jeans and a white T-shirt, a plastic carrier-bag in his left hand and a wry smile on his face.

'Vivien,' he greeted smoothly.

For a few seconds neither of them said anything further. Ross's clear blue eyes lanced her startled face before travelling down then up her figure-fitting pink and black suit. By the time his gaze returned to their point of origin Vivien was aware that her heart was thudding erratically in her chest. A fierce blush was also staining her cheeks.

Embarrassment warred with a surprisingly intense pleasure over his reappearance in her life. My God, he'd actually followed her all this way! Perhaps he didn't look at the other night as a one-night stand after all. Perhaps he really cared about her.

And perhaps not, the bitter voice of experience intervened, stilling the flutterings in her heart.

'What…what are you doing here?' she asked warily.

He shrugged. 'I had to come to Sydney to visit my father and I thought you might like the things you left behind.' He held out the plastic bag.

Her dismay was sharp. So! He hadn't followed her at all. Not really. She wasn't deceived by his excuse for dropping by. The way he'd looked at her just now was not the look of a man who'd only come to return something. Vivien knew the score. Ross was going to be in town anyway and thought he might have another sampling of what she'd given him so easily the other night.

Her disappointment quickly fuelled a very real anger. She snatched the plastic bag without looking inside, tossing it behind the door. She didn't want to see her ruined bolero and shoes, not needing any more reminders of her disgusting behaviour the other night. Ross's presence on her doorstep was reminder enough.

'How kind of you,' she retorted sarcastically. 'But how did you find out my address? It's not in the phone book.'

His eyes searched her face as though trying to make sense of her ill temper. 'Once I explained to the receptionist at the channel about your having left some of your things behind at the Wallaby Creek hotel,' he said, 'and that I had come all this way to return them, she gave me your address.'

'But you didn't come all this way just to return them, did you?' she bit out. 'Look, Ross, if you think you're going to take up where you left off then I suggest you think again. I have no intention of—'

'You're *ashamed* of what we did,' he cut in with surprise in his voice.

Her cheeks flamed. 'What did you *expect*? That I'd be *proud* of myself?'

'I don't see why not... What we shared the other night, Vivien, was something out of the ordinary. You must know how I feel about you. You must also have known I would not let you get away that easily.'

'Oh? And how *does* the legendary Ross Everton feel about little ole me?' she lashed out, annoyed that he would think her so gullible. 'Surely you're not going to declare undying love, are you?' she added scathingly. 'Not Ross Everton, the famous—or is it infamous?—country Casanova!'

His eyes had narrowed at her tirade, their light blue

darkening with a black puzzlement. 'I think you've been listening to some twisted tales, Vivien. My legendary status, if one could call it such, has nothing to do with my being a Casanova.'

Now it was her turn to stare with surprise. 'Then what…what?'

He shrugged off her bumbled query, his penetrating gaze never leaving her. 'I *do* care about you, Vivien. Very much. When I woke to find you gone, I was…' His mouth curved back into a rueful smile. 'Let's just say I wasn't too pleased. I thought, damn and blast, that city bitch has just used me. But after I'd had time to think about it I knew that couldn't be so. You're too straightforward, Vivien. Too open. Too sweet…'

He took a step towards her then. Panic-stricken, she backed up into the flat. When Ross followed right on inside, then shut the door, her eyes flung wide.

'Don't be alarmed,' he soothed. 'I told you once and I'll tell you again: I won't ever hurt you. But I refuse to keep discussing our private lives in a damned hallway.' He glanced around the living-room, its emptiness clearly distracting him from what he'd been about to add. 'You're moving out?'

She shook her head. Somehow, words would not come. Her mind was whirling with a lot of mixed-up thoughts. For even if Ross was genuine with his feelings for her, what future could they have together? *Her* feelings for *him* had no foundation. They were nothing but a cruel illusion, sparked by his likeness to Earl.

'Then what happened to your furniture?' Ross asked.

She cleared her throat. 'Earl…Earl took it all.'

'*All* of it?'

Her laugh was choked and dry. 'He left me a single bed. Wasn't that nice of him?'

'Could win him the louse-of-the-year award.'

Vivien saw the pity in Ross's eyes and hated it.

Suddenly, the whole grim reality of her situation rushed in on her like a swamping wave, bringing with it a flood of self-pity. The tears she had kept at bay all day rushed in with a vengeance.

'Oh, God,' she groaned, her hands flying up to cover her crumpling face. 'God,' she repeated, then began to sob.

Despite her weeping, she was all too hotly aware of Ross gathering her into his strong arms, cradling her distraught, disintegrating self close to the hard warmth of his chest.

'Don't cry, darling,' he murmured. 'Please don't cry. He's not worth it, can't you see that? He didn't really love you...or care about you... Don't waste your tears on him... Don't...'

To Vivien's consternation, her self-pitying outburst dried up with astonishing swiftness, replaced by a feeling of sexual longing so intense that it refused to be denied. Hardly daring to examine what she was doing, she felt her arms steal around Ross's waist, her fingers splaying wide as they snaked up his back. With a soft moan of surrender, she nestled her face into his neck, pressing gently fluttering lips to the pulse-point at the base of his throat.

She felt his moment of acute stillness, *agonised* over it. Her body desperately wanted him to seduce her again. But her mind—her *conscience*—implored with her to stop before it was too late.

This is wrong, Vivien, she pleaded with herself.

Wrong! You don't love him. What in God's name is the matter with you? Stop it now!

She wrenched out of his arms just as they tightened around her, the action making them both stagger backwards in opposite directions.

'I'm s—sorry,' she blurted out. 'I...I shouldn't have done that. I'm not myself today. I...I just lost my job, and coming so soon after Earl's leaving... Not that that's any excuse...' She lifted her hand to her forehead in a gesture of true bewilderment. 'I'm not even drunk this time,' she groaned, appalled at herself.

Ross stared across at her. 'What do you mean? You weren't drunk the other night. You'd only had a couple of glasses of champagne. Not even full glasses.'

Her sigh was ragged. 'That's enough for me on an empty stomach. I have this almost allergic reaction to alcohol, you see. It sends me crazy, a bit like your brother, only I don't need nearly as much. I'm a cheap drunk, Ross. A *very* cheap drunk,' she finished with deliberate irony.

'I see,' he said slowly.

'I'm sorry, Ross.'

'So am I. Believe me.' He just stood there, staring at her, his eyes troubled. Suddenly, he sighed, and pulled himself up straight and tall. 'Did I hear rightly just now? You've lost your job?'

'Yes, but not to worry. I'll find something else.' She spoke quickly, impatiently. For she just wanted him to go.

'Are you sure?' he persisted. 'Unemployment's high in the television industry, I hear.'

'I have my family. I'll be fine.'

'They live near by?'

'Parramatta. Look, it…it was nice of you to come all this way to see me again, Ross,' she said stiffly, wishing he would take the hint and leave. She had never felt so wretched, and guilty, and confused.

'Nice?' His smile was bitter. 'Oh, it wasn't nice, Vivien. It was a necessity. I simply *had* to see you again before I…' He broke off with a grimace. 'But that's none of your concern now.'

He gave Vivien an oddly ironic look. Once again, she was struck by his *dissimilarity* to Earl. His facial features might have come out of the same mould. But his expressions certainly didn't. His eyes were particularly expressive, ranging from a chilling glitter of reproach to a blaze of white-hot passion.

Vivien stared at him, remembering only too well how he had looked as he'd made love to her, the way his skin had drawn back tight across his cheekbones, his lips parting, his eyes heavy, as though he were drowning in his desire. Immediately, she felt a tightening inside, followed by a dull ache of yearning.

Did he see the desire in her eyes, the hunger?

Yes, he must have. For his expression changed once more, this time to a type of resolve that she found quite frightening. His hands shot out to grip her waist, yanking her hard against him.

'I don't care if you were drunk,' he rasped. 'I don't care if you're still in love with your stupid bloody Earl. All you have to do is keep looking at me like that and it'll be enough.'

His mouth was hard, his kiss savage. But she found herself giving in to it with a sweet surrender that was far more intoxicating than any amount of alcohol could ever be.

The doorbell ringing again made them both jump.

'Are you expecting anyone?' Ross asked thickly, his mouth in her hair, his hands restless on her back and buttocks.

Vivien shook her head.

Their chests rose and fell with ragged breathing as they waited in silence. The bell rang again. And again.

Ross sighed. 'You'd better answer it.' His hands dropped away from her, lifting to run agitatedly through his hair as he stepped back.

Vivien ran her own trembling hands down her skirt before turning to the door, all the while doing her best to school her face into an expression that would not betray her inner turmoil. One kiss, she kept thinking. One miserable kiss and I'm his for the taking...

She was stunned to find Bob standing on the other side of the door, a bottle of wine under his arm, a triumphant and sickeningly sleazy look on his face.

'Hello, Vivien.' He smirked. 'I dropped by to say how sorry I was about the way Mervyn dismissed you today. I thought we might have a drink together, and then, if you like, we could...'

He broke off when his gaze wandered over Vivien's shoulder, his beady eyes opening wide with true surprise when they encountered Ross standing there.

'Oh...oh, hi, there, Earl,' he called out, clearly flustered. 'I thought you were in Melbourne. Well, it's good to know Viv has someone here in her hour of need. I—er—only called round to offer my sympathy and a shoulder to cry on, but I can see she doesn't need it. I...I guess I'd better be going. Sorry to interrupt. See you around, Viv. Bye, Earl.'

Vivien could feel Ross's frozen stillness behind her

as she slowly shut the door and turned. He looked as if someone had just hit him in the stomach with a sledge-hammer.

'Ross,' she began, 'I—'

'I'm not just *like* your ex-lover, am I, Vivien?' he broke in harshly. 'I'm his damned double!'

She closed her eyes against his pained hurt. 'Almost,' she admitted huskily.

'God…'

Vivien remained silent. Perhaps it was for the best, she reasoned wretchedly. At least now he would see that there was no hope of a real relationship between them and he would leave her alone. For God only knew what would happen if he stayed.

But what if you're already pregnant by him? whispered that niggling voice.

Vivien pushed the horrendous thought aside. Surely fate couldn't be that perverse?

'I want you to open your eyes and look at me, Vivien,' Ross stated in a voice like ice.

She did, and his eyes were as flat and hard as eyes could be. She shrank from the cold fury his gaze projected.

'I want you to confirm that the main reason you responded to me the way you did the other night is because I'm the spitting image of your ex-lover. You were fantasising I was this Earl while I was making love to you, is that correct?'

No, was her instant horrified reaction. *No! It wasn't like that*!

And yet… It had to be so. For if it wasn't, then what had it been? Animal lust? The crude using of any body to assuage sexual frustration? Revenge on Earl, maybe?

None of those things felt right. She refused to accept them. Which only left what Ross had concluded. Perhaps the reason she instinctively rejected that explanation was because her memory of that night had been clouded by alcohol. She recalled thinking the next morning that her pleasure in Ross's lovemaking could not have been so extraordinary, could *not* have propelled her into another world where nothing existed but this man, and this man alone.

'I'm waiting, Vivien,' he demanded brusquely.

'Yes,' she finally choked out, though her tortured eyes slid away from his to the floor. 'Yes…'

He dragged in then exhaled a shuddering breath. 'Great,' he muttered. 'Just great. I'll remember that next time my emotions threaten to get in the way of my common sense. Pardon me if I say I hope I never see you again, Vivien Roberts. Still…you've been an experience, one I bitterly suspect I'll never repeat!'

He didn't look back as he left, slamming the door hard behind him.

It wasn't till a minute or two later that Vivien remembered something that challenged both Ross's conclusion and her own. If her responses had really been for Earl, if her memory of that night had been confused by alcohol and her pleasure not as overwhelming as she had thought, then why had she responded with such shattering intensity to Ross's kiss just now? Why?

None of it made sense.

But then, nothing made sense any more to Vivien. Her whole world had turned upside-down. Once, she had seen her future so very clearly. Now, there was only a bleak black haziness, full of doubts and fears and insecurities. She wanted quite desperately to run

home to her mother, to become a child again, with
no decisions to make, no responsibilities to embrace.

But she wasn't a child. She was an adult. A grown
woman. She had to work things out for herself.

Vivien did the only thing a sensible, grown-up
woman could do. She went to bed and cried herself
to sleep.

CHAPTER SIX

'WHEN are you going to tell me what's wrong, dear?'

Vivien stiffened, tea-towel in hand, then slanted a sideways glance at her mother. Peggy Roberts had not turned away from where she stood at the kitchen sink, washing up after her husband Lionel's birthday dinner.

Vivien's stomach began to churn. There she'd been, thinking she had done a splendid job of hiding the turmoil in her heart. Why, she had fairly bubbled all through dinner, sheer force of will pushing the dark realities of the past fortnight way, way to the back of her mind.

Now, her mother's intuitive question sent them all rushing forward, stark in their grimness. She didn't know which was the worst: her growing realisation that she was unlikely to land a decent job in Sydney this side of six months, if ever; the crushing loneliness she felt every time she let herself back into her empty flat; or the terrifying prospect that her fear over being pregnant was fast becoming a definite rather than a doubtful possibility.

Her period had been due two days before and it hadn't arrived. Periods were never late when one was on the Pill. Of course, the delay might have been caused by her having forgotten one, but she didn't think so.

Just thinking about actually having a real baby— *Ross's* baby—sent her into a mental spin.

'Vivien,' her mother resumed with warmth and

70

worry in her voice, 'you do know you can tell me anything, don't you? I promise I won't be shocked, or judgemental. But I can't let you leave here today without knowing what it is that has put you on this razor's edge. The others probably haven't noticed, but they don't know you as well as I do. Your gaiety, my dear, was just a fraction brittle over dinner. Besides, you haven't mentioned Earl once today, and that isn't like you. Not like you at all. Have you had a falling-out with him, dear? Is that it?'

Vivien gave a small, hysterical laugh. 'I wouldn't put it like that exactly.'

'Then how would you put it?' her mother asked gently.

Too gently. Her loving concern sent a lump to Vivien's throat, and tears into her eyes. Forcing them back, she dragged in a shuddering breath then burst forth, nerves and emotion sending the words out in a wild tumble of awful but rather muddled confessions.

'Well, Mum, the truth is that a couple of weeks back Earl gave me the ole heave-ho, told me he didn't love me and that he had found someone else. I was very upset, to put it mildly, but that weekend I had to go out to that Bachelors' and Spinsters' Ball for work. You know, the one they showed on TV last week. And while I was there I met this man who, believe it or not, is practically Earl's double, and I…well, I slept with him on some sort of rebound, I suppose. At least, I think that's why I did it…'

She began wringing the tea-towel. 'But I also forgot my pill, you see, and now I think I might be pregnant. Then on the Monday after that weekend I was retrenched at the channel and that same day Ross came to Sydney to see me, hoping to make a go of things between us, but he found out how much he looked like Earl and jumped to all the right conclusions, which I made worse by telling him I was sloshed at the time I slept with him anyway. Not that I was, but you know what drink does to me, and I had had a bit to drink and…and…as you can see, I'm in a bit of a mess…'

By this time tears were streaming down her face.

To give her mother credit, she didn't look too much like a stunned mullet. More like a flapping flounder, holding stunned hands out in front of her, while washing-up water dripped steadily from her frozen fingertips on to the cork-tiled floor.

But she quickly pulled herself together, wiping her soapy hands on the tea-towel she dragged out of Vivien's hands, then leading her distressed daughter quickly away from potentially prying eyes into the privacy of her old bedroom.

'Sit,' she said, firmly settling Vivien down on the white lace quilt before leaning over to extract several tissues from the box on the dressing-table and pressing them into her daughter's hands. She sat down on the bed as well, then waited a few moments while Vivien blew her nose and stopped weeping.

'Now, Vivien, I'm not going to pretend that I'm not a little shocked, no matter what I said earlier. But there's no point in crying over spilt milk, so to speak. Now, I'm not sure if I got the whole gist of your story. Ross, I presume, is the name of the man who may or may not be the father of your child?'

'Oh, he's the father all right,' Vivien blubbered. 'It's the child who's a maybe or maybe not. It's a bit too soon to tell.'

Peggy sighed her relief. 'So you don't really know yet. You might not be pregnant.'

'Yes, I am,' Vivien insisted wildly. 'I know I am.'

'Vivien! You sound as if you *want* to be pregnant by this man, this…this…stranger who looks like Earl.'

Vivien stared at her startled mother, then shook her head in utter bewilderment. 'I don't know what I want any more, Mum. I…I'm so mixed up and miserable and… Please help me. You always know just what to say to make me see things clearly. Tell me I'm not going mad. Tell me it wasn't wicked of me to do what I did. Tell me you and Dad don't mind if I have a baby, that you'll love me anyway. I've been so worried about everything.'

'Oh, my poor, dear child,' Peggy said gently, and enfolded her in her mother's arms. 'You've really been through the mill, haven't you? Of course you're not going mad. And of course you're not wicked. But as parents we *will* be worried about you having a baby all on your own, so if you are pregnant you'll have to come home and live with us so we can look after you. Come to think of it, you're coming home anyway. You must be horribly lonely in that flat all on your own.'

'You can say that again,' Vivien sniffled.

'You must be horribly lonely in that flat all on your own…'

Vivien pulled back, her eyes snapping up to her mother's. Peggy was smiling. 'Mum! This isn't funny, you know.'

'I know, but I can't help feeling glad that you're not going to marry that horrible Earl.'

'You never said you thought he was horrible before.'

'Yes, well, your father and I didn't want to make him seem any more attractive than you obviously already found him. But believe me, love, I didn't like him at all. He was the most selfish man I have ever met. Selfish and snobbish. He would have made a dreadful father, too. Simply dreadful. He had no sense of family.'

Vivien nodded slowly in agreement. 'You're right. I can see that now. I can see a lot of things about Earl that I couldn't see before. I don't know why I loved him as much as I did.'

'Well, he could be charming when he chose,' her mother admitted. 'And he was very handsome. Which makes me think that maybe you never loved him. Not really.'

Vivien blinked.

'Maybe it was only a sexual attraction,' Peggy suggested.

Vivien frowned.

'This man you slept with, the one you said looks a lot like Earl—'

'More than a lot,' Vivien muttered.

'Obviously you're one of those women who's always attracted to the same physical type. For some of us it's blond hair and blue eyes, or broad shoulders and a cute butt, or—'

'Mum!' Vivien broke in, shock in her voice.

Peggy smiled at her daughter. 'Do you think you're the only female in this family who's ever been bowled over by a sexual attraction?'

'Well, I...I—'

'Your father wasn't my first man, you know.'

'*Mum!*'

'Will you stop saying "Mum!" like that? It's unnerving. I don't mean I was promiscuous, but there was this other fellow first. I think if I tell you about him you might see that what happened between you and this Ross person was hardly surprising, or wicked.'

'Well, all right…if you say so…'

Peggy drew in a deep breath, then launched into her astonishing tale. At least, Vivien found it astonishing.

'I was eighteen at the time, working as a receptionist with a firm of solicitors while I went to secretarial school at night. Damian was one of the junior partners. Oh, he was a handsome devil. Tall, with black hair and flashing brown eyes, and a body to swoon over. I thought he was the best thing since sliced bread. He used to stop by my desk to compliment me every morning. By the time he asked me out four months later I was so ripe a plum he had me in bed before you could say "cheese".'

'Heavens! And was he a good lover?' Vivien asked, fascinated at the image of her softly spoken, very re-served mother going to bed with a man on a first date.

'Not really. Though I didn't know that at the time. I thought any shortcomings had to be mine. Still, I went eagerly back for more because his looks held a kind of fascination for my body which I didn't have the maturity to ignore. It wasn't till his fiancée swanned into the office one day that my eyes were well and truly opened to the sort of man he was.'

'So what did you do?'

'I found myself a better job and left a much wiser girl. Believe me, the next time a tall, dark and hand-some man with flashing eyes set my heart a-flutter he had a darned hard time even getting to first base with me.'

'You gave him the cold shoulder, right?'

'Too right.'

'So what happened to him?'

'I married him.'

Vivien's brown eyes rounded. 'Goodness!'

'What I'm trying to tell you, daughter of mine, is that there's probably any number of men in this world that you might want as a lover, but not too many as your true love. When that chemistry strikes, hold back from it for a while, give yourself time to find out if the object of your desire is worth entrusting your body to, give the relationship a chance to grow on levels other than the sexual one. For it's those other levels that will stand your relationship in good stead in the tough times. You and Earl had nothing going for you but what you had in bed.'

'Which wasn't all that great,' Vivien admitted.

There was a short, sharp silence before Peggy spoke.

'I gather you can't say the same for the time you spent with this Ross person?'

Vivien coloured guiltily. There was no use in pretending any more that what she had felt with Ross that night had been anything like what she'd felt with Earl. Why, it was like comparing a scratchy old record to the very best compact disc.

Her mother said nothing for a moment. 'Have you considered an abortion?' she finally asked.

'Yes.'

'And?'

'I just can't. I know it would be an easy way out, a quick solution. Funnily enough, I've always believed it was a woman's right to make such a decision, and I still do, but somehow, on this occasion, it doesn't feel right. I'm scared, but I...I have to have this baby, Mum. Please...don't ask me to get rid of it.' She threw her mother a beseeching look, tears welling up in her eyes again.

Peggy's eyes also flooded. 'As if I would,' she said in a strangled tone. 'Come here, darling child, and give your old mother another hug. We'll work things out. Don't you worry. Everything will be all right.'

Vivien moved home the next day. Her pregnancy was confirmed two weeks later.

Once over her initial shock, her mother responded by fussing over Vivien, not allowing her to do anything around the house. Vivien responded by going into somewhat of a daze.

Most of her days were spent blankly watching television. Her nights, however, were not quite so uneventful, mostly because of her dreams. They were always of Ross and herself in a mixed-up version of that fateful night at Wallaby Creek.

Sometimes they would be on the creek bank, sometimes in the water, sometimes back in the hotel room. Ross would be kissing her, touching her, telling her he loved her. Inevitably, she would wake up before they really made love, beads of perspiration all over her body. Each morning, she would get up feeling totally wrung out. That was till she started having morning sickness as well.

Why, she would ask herself in the bathroom mirror every day, was she so hell-bent on such a potentially self-destructive path?

She could not find a sensible, logical answer.

A few days before Christmas, she made another decision about her baby, one which had never been in doubt at the back of her mind. All that had been in doubt was *when* she was going to do it.

'Dad?' she said that evening after dinner.

Her father looked up from where he was watching

a movie on television and reading the evening paper at the same time. 'Yes, love?'

'Would you mind if I made a long-distance call? It doesn't cost so much at night and I promise not to talk for long.'

Now her mother looked up, a frown on her face. 'Who are you ringing, dear?'

'Ross.'

Her father stiffened in his chair. 'What in hell do you want to ring him for? He won't want anything to do with the child, you mark my words.'

'You're probably right,' Vivien returned, the image of Ross's furious departure still stark in her memory. He'd made his feelings quite clear. He never wanted to see her again.

But a few months back, she had done a segment for television on unmarried fathers, and the emotional distress of some of the men had lived with her long afterwards. One of their complaints was that some of the mothers had not even the decency to tell them about their pregnancies. Many had simply not given the fathers any say at all in their decisions to abort, adopt, or to keep their babies. Vivien had been touched by the men's undoubted pain. She knew that she would not be able to live with her conscience if she kept her baby a secret from its father.

A dark thought suddenly insinuated that she might be telling Ross about the baby simply to see him again. Maybe she wanted the opportunity to bring her erotic dreams to a very real and less frustrating fruition.

Pushing *that* thought agitatedly to the back of her mind, she addressed her frowning parents with a simplicity and apparent certainty she was no longer feeling.

'He has a right to know,' she stated firmly, and threw both her father and mother a stubborn look.

They recognised it as the same look they'd received when they'd advised her, on leaving school, not to try for such a demanding career as television, to do something easier, like teaching.

'You do what you think best, dear,' her mother said with a sigh.

'It'll cause trouble,' her father muttered. 'You mark my words!'

Vivien recklessly ignored her father's last remark, closing the lounge door as she went out into the front hall, where they kept the phone. Her hands were trembling as she picked it up and dialled the operator to help her find Ross's phone number.

Three minutes later she had the number. She dialled again with still quaking fingers, gripping the receiver so tightly against her ear that it was aching already.

No one answered. It rang and rang at the other end, Vivien's disappointment so acute that she could not bring herself to hang up. Then suddenly there was a click and a male voice was on the line.

'Mountainview. Ross Everton speaking.'

Vivien was momentarily distracted by the sounds of merry-making in the background. Loud music and laughter. Clearly a party was in progress.

And why not? she reasoned, swiftly dampening down a quite unreasonable surge of resentment. Christmas was, after all, less than a few days away. Lots of people were having parties.

She gathered herself and started speaking. 'Ross, this is Vivien here, Vivien Roberts. I…I…' Her voice trailed away, her courage suddenly deserting her. It was so impossible to blurt out her news with all that racket going on in the background.

'I can hardly hear you, Vivien,' Ross returned. 'Look, I'll just go into the library and take this call there. Won't be a moment.'

Vivien was left hanging, quite taken aback that Ross's house would *have* a room called a library. It gave rise to a vision of an old English mansion with panelled walls and deep leather chairs, not the simple country homestead she had envisaged Ross's family living in. She was still somewhat distracted when Ross came back on the line, this time without the party noises to mar his deeply attractive voice. 'Vivien? You're still there?'

'Y…yes.'

There was a short, very electric silence.

'To what honour do I owe this call?' he went on drily. 'You haven't been drinking again, have you?' he added with a sardonic laugh.

'I wish I had,' she muttered under her breath. She hadn't realised how hard this was going to be. Yet what had she expected? That Ross would react to her unexpected call with warmth and pleasure?

'What was that?'

'Nothing.' Her tone became brisk and businesslike. 'I'm sorry to bother you during your Christmas party, but I have something to tell you which simply can't wait.'

'Oh?' Wariness in his voice. 'Something unpleasant by the sound of it.'

'*You* may think so.' Her tone was becoming sharper by the second, fuelled by a terrible feeling of coming doom. He was going to hate her news. Simply hate it!

'Vivien, you're not going to tell me you have contracted some unmentionable disease, are you?'

'Not unless you refer to pregnancy in such a way,' she snapped back.

His inward suck of breath seemed magnified as it rushed down the line to her already pained ears.

Vivien squeezed her eyes tightly shut. You blithering idiot, she berated herself. You tactless, clumsy blithering idiot! 'Ross,' she resumed tightly, 'I'm sorry I blurted it out like that. I...I—'

'What happened?' he said in a voice that showed amazing control. 'You did say, after all, that you were on the Pill. Did you forget to take it, is that it?'

She expelled a ragged sigh. 'Yes...'

Once again, there was an unnerving silence on the line before he resumed speaking. 'And you're sure I'm the father?' he asked, but without any accusation.

'Quite sure.'

'I see.'

'Ross, I...I'm not ringing because I want anything from you. Not money, or anything. I realise that I'm entirely to blame. It's just that I thought you had the right to know, then to make your own decision as to whether you want to...to share in your child's life. It's entirely up to you. I'll understand whatever decision you make.'

'You mean you're going to *have* my baby?' he rasped, shock and something else in his voice. Or maybe not. Maybe just shock.

'You don't want me to,' she said, wretchedness in her heart.

'What I want is obviously irrelevant. Does your family know you're going to have a baby?'

'Yes. I'm ringing from their place now. I moved back home a couple of weeks ago.'

'And how did they react?'

'They weren't thrilled at first, but they're resigned now, and supportive.'

'Hmm. Does Earl know?'

'Of course not!'

'Don't bite my head off, Vivien. You wouldn't be the first woman who tried to use another man's baby to get back the man she really wants. In the circumstances, I doubt you'd have had much trouble in passing the child off as his, since the father is his dead ringer.'

Vivien was shocked that Ross would even *think* of such a thing.

'Is that why you're having the baby, Vivien?' he continued mercilessly. 'Because you're hoping it will look like the man you love?'

She gasped. 'You're sick, do you know that?'

'Possibly. But I had to ask.'

'*Why*?'

'So that I can make rational decisions. I don't think you have any idea what your news has done to my life, Vivien.'

'What...what do you mean?'

'I mean that it isn't a Christmas party we're having here tonight. It's an engagement party. *Mine*.'

Vivien's mind went blank for a second. When it resumed operation and the reality of the situation sank in, any initial sympathy she might have felt for Ross was swiftly replaced by a sharp sense of betrayal.

'I see,' she bit out acidly.

'Do you?'

'Of course. You slept with me at the same time as

you were courting another woman. You lied to me when you came after me, Ross. You didn't want a real relationship. All you wanted was a final fling before you settled down to your real life.'

'I wouldn't put it that way exactly,' he drawled.

'Then what way would you put it?'

'Let's just say I found you sexually irresistible. Once I had you in my arms, I simply couldn't stop.'

Vivien was appalled by the flush of heat that washed over her skin as she thought of how she had felt in *his* arms. She couldn't seem to stop either. Once she might have fancied she had fallen in love with Ross. Now she had another word for it, supplied by her mother.

Chemistry, it was called, the same chemistry that had originally propelled her so willingly into Earl's arms. Though Earl had had another word for it. *Lust!*

Vivien shuddered. God, but she hated to think her mind and heart could be totally fooled by her body. It was demeaning to her intelligence.

Men weren't fooled, though. They knew the difference between love and lust. They even seemed capable of feeling both at the same time. Ross had probably kept on loving this woman he was about to marry, all the while he was lusting after *her*.

'Let's hope you don't run into someone like me after you get married in that case,' she flung at Ross with a degree of venom.

'I won't be getting married, Vivien,' he said quite calmly. 'At least…not now, and not to Becky.'

Vivien's anger turned to a flustered outrage. Not for herself this time, but for the poor wronged woman who wore Ross's ring. 'But…but you can't break your engagement just like that. That…that's cruel!'

'It would be crueller to go through with it. Becky

deserves more than a husband who's going to be the father of another woman's baby. I wouldn't do that to her. I've loved Becky all my life,' he stated stiffly. 'We're neighbours as well. I'm deeply sorry that I have to hurt her at all. But this is a case of being cruel to be kind.'

'Oh, I feel so guilty,' Vivien cried. 'I should never have rung, never have told you.'

'Perhaps. But what's done is done. And now we must think of the child. When can I come down and see you?'

'See me?' she repeated, her head whirling.

'How about Boxing Day? I really can't get away from here before Christmas. Give me your parents' address and telephone number.'

Stunned, she did as he asked. He jotted down the particulars, then repeated them back to her.

'Do me a favour, will you, Vivien?' he added brusquely. 'Don't tell your parents about the engagement. It's going to be tough enough making them accept me as the father of their grandchild without my having an advance black mark against my name. However, you'd better let them know about my remarkable resemblance to lover-boy. I don't think I could stand any more people calling me Earl by mistake.'

He dragged in then exhaled a shuddering breath. 'Ah, well...I'd better go and drop my bombshell. Something tells me this party is going to break up rather early. See you Boxing Day, Vivien. Look after yourself.'

Vivien stared down into the dead receiver for several seconds before putting it shakily back into its cradle. Normally a clear thinker, she found it hard to grasp how she really felt about what had just happened. Her emotions seemed to have scrambled her brains.

Ross, she finally accepted, was the key to her confusion. Ross…who had just destroyed the picture she had formed of him in her mind.

He was not some smitten suitor who had chased after her with an almost adolescent passion, ready to throw himself at her feet. He was the man she had first met, an intriguing mixture of sophisticate and macho male, a man who was capable of going after what he wanted with the sort of ruthlessness that could inspire a brother's hatred. He was, quite clearly, another rat!

No…she conceded slowly. Not quite.

A rat would have told her get lost. Her *and* her baby.

A rat would not have broken his engagement.

A rat would not be coming down to see her, concerned with her parents' opinion of him.

So what was he?

Vivien wasn't at all sure, except about one thing.

He was *not* in love with her.

He was in love with a woman named Becky.

Now why did that hurt so darned much?

CHAPTER SEVEN

'HE'S here,' Peggy hissed, drawing back the living-room drapes to have a better look. 'Goodness, but you should see the Range Rover he's pulled up in. Looks brand new. Can't be one of those farmers who're doing really badly, then.'

Lionel grunted from his favourite armchair. 'Don't you believe it, Mother. Graziers live on large overdrafts. Most of them are going down the tubes.'

'Well, I'd rather see my Vivien married to an overdraft*ee* than that overdraft*er* she was living with. Heavens, but I could not stand that man. Oh, my goodness, but this fellow does look like Earl. Taller, though, and fitter looking. Hmm… Yes, I can see why Vivien was bowled over. He's a bit of all right.'

'Peggy!' Lionel exclaimed, startled enough to put down his newspaper. 'What's got into you, talking like that? And don't start romanticising about our Vivien getting married just because she's having a baby. She's never been one to follow convention. Not that this Ross chap will want to marry her anyway. Young men don't marry girls these days for that reason.'

'He's not so young…'

'What's that?' Lionel levered himself out of his chair and came to his wife's side, peering with her through the lacy curtains. By this time, Ross was making his way through the front gate, his well-honed frame coolly dressed for the heat in white shorts and a pale blue polo shirt, white socks and blue and white striped Reeboks on his feet.

Lionel frowned. 'Must be thirty if he's a day.'

'Well, our Vivien *is* twenty-five,' Peggy argued.

'What on earth are you two doing?' the girl herself said with more than a touch of exasperation.

They both swung round, like guilty children found with their hands in the cookie jar.

The front doorbell rang.

Vivien folded her arms. 'If that's Ross why don't you just let him in instead of spying on him?'

'We—er—um…' came Peggy's lame mumblings till she gathered herself and changed from defence to attack.

'Vivien! Surely you're not going to let Ross see you wearing that horrible old housecoat? Go and put something decent on. And while you're at it, put some lipstick on as well. And run a brush through your hair. You look as if you've just got out of bed.'

'I *have* just got out of bed,' she returned irritably. 'And I have no intention of dolling myself up for Ross. He's not my boyfriend.'

'He *is* the father of your baby,' Lionel reminded her.

'More's the pity,' she muttered. Having been given a few days to think over the events surrounding that fateful weekend, Vivien had decided Ross was a rat after all. At least where women were concerned. He'd known she'd been upset about Earl that night, had known he himself had been on the verge of asking another woman to be his bride, one he *claimed* to have loved for years. Yet what had he done? Cold-bloodedly taken advantage of her vulnerability by se-

ducing her, making her forget her conscience and then
her pill!

'Vivien,' her mother said sternly, 'it was *your* idea
to call Ross and tell him about the baby, which was
a very brave and adult decision, but now you're acting
like a child. Go and make yourself presentable *immediately*!'

Vivien took one look at her mother's determined
face and knew this was not the moment to get on her
high horse. Besides, her mother was right. She was
acting appallingly. Still, she had felt rotten all day,
with a queasy stomach and a dull headache, as she
had the day before. She hadn't even been able to enjoy her Christmas dinner, due to a case of morning
sickness which lasted all day. If this was what being
pregnant was like then it was strictly for the birds!

'Oh, all right,' she muttered, just as the front doorbell rang for the second time. 'You'd better go and
let him in. Something tells me Ross Everton is not in
the habit of waiting for anything.'

She flounced off, feeling ashamed of herself, but
seemingly unable to do anything about the way she
was acting. On top of her physical ills, the news of
Ross's engagement had left her feeling betrayed and
bitter and even more disillusioned about men than she
already had. It was as though suddenly there were no
dreams any more.

No dreams. No Prince Charming. No hope.

Life had become drearily disappointing and utterly,
utterly depressing.

Vivien threw open her wardrobe and drew out the
first thing her hands landed on, a strappy lime sun-
dress which showed a good deal of bare flesh. For a
second, she hesitated. But only for a second. She had

always favoured bright, extrovert clothes. Her ward-robe was full of them. Maybe wearing fluorescent green would cheer her up.

Tossing aside all her clothes, she drew on fresh bikini briefs before stepping into the dress and draw-ing it up over her hourglass figure. With wry acces-sion to her mother's wishes, she brushed her dishev-elled hair into disciplined waves before applying a dash of coral gloss to her lips.

The mirror told her she looked far better than she felt, the vibrant green a perfect foil for her pale skin and jet-black hair. Yet when her eyes dropped to her full breasts straining against the thin cotton, Ross's words leapt back into her mind.

'I found you sexually irresistible…'

The words pained her, as Earl's words had pained her.

'It was only lust,' *he* had said.

Vivien couldn't get the dress off quickly enough, choosing instead some loose red and white spotted Bermuda shorts with a flowing white over-shirt to cover her womanly curves. The last thing she wanted today was Ross looking at her with desire in his eyes. Suddenly, she found her own sex appeal a hateful thing that stood between herself and real happiness.

Reefing a tissue out of the box, she wiped savagely at her glossed lips, though the resultant effect was not what she wanted. Sure, the lipstick was gone, but the rubbing had left her lips quite red and swollen, giving her wide mouth a full, sultry look.

'Damn,' she muttered.

'Vivien,' came her mother's voice through the bed-room door, 'when you're ready you'll find us on the back patio. Your father and Ross are having a beer together out there.'

Vivien blinked. Dad was having a beer with Ross? Already? How astonishing. He only ever offered a beer to his best mates. Perhaps he needed a beer himself, she decided. It had to be an awkward situation for him, entertaining Ross, trying to find something to talk to him about.

I should be out there, she thought guiltily.

But still she lingered, afraid to leave the sanctuary of her bedroom, afraid of what she would still see in Ross's eyes when they met hers, afraid of what she might *not* see.

Vivien violently shook her head. This was crazy! One moment she didn't want him to want her. Then the next she did. It was all too perverse for words!

Self-disgust finally achieved what filial duty and politeness could not. Vivien marched from the room, bitterly resolved to conquer these vacillating desires that kept invading her mind and body. Ross wanted to talk to her about their coming child? Well, that was all he'd ever get from her in future. Talk! She had no intention of letting him worm his way past her physical defences ever again.

She stomped down the hall, through the kitchen and out on to the back patio, letting the wire door bang as she went. The scenario of a totally relaxed Ross seated cosily between her parents around the patio table, sipping a cool beer and looking too darned handsome for words, did nothing for her growing irritation.

'Ah, here she is now,' her father said expansively. 'Ross was just telling us that he's not normally a sheep farmer. He's simply helping out at home till his father gets on his feet again. He flies helicopters for a living. Mustering cattle. Own your own business, didn't you say, Ross?'

'That's right, Mr Roberts. I've built up quite a clientele over the last few years. Mustering on horseback is definitely on the way out, though some people like to call us chopper cowboys.'

'Chopper cowboys... Now that's a clever way of putting it. And do call me Lionel, my boy. No point in being formal, in the circumstances, is there?' he added with a small laugh.

Ross smiled that crooked smile that made him look far too much like Earl. 'I guess not,' he drawled, and lifted the beer to his lips.

'But isn't that rather a dangerous occupation?' Peggy piped up with a worried frown.

'Only if you're unskilled,' Ross returned. 'Or careless. I'm usually neither.' He slanted Vivien a ruefully sardonic look that changed her inner agitation into an icy fury.

'Accidents do happen though, don't they?' she said coldly.

'Now don't go getting all prickly on us, love,' Lionel intervened. 'We all know that neither of you had any intention of having a baby together, but you *are*, and Ross here has at least been decent enough to come all this way to meet us and reassure us he'll do everything he can to support you and the child. You should be grateful that he's prepared to do the right thing.'

Vivien counted to ten, then came forward to pick up an empty glass and pour herself some orange juice out of the chilled cask on the table. 'I *am* grateful,' she said stiffly. 'I only hope no one here suggests that we get married. I won't be marrying anyone for any reason other than true love.'

She lifted her glass and eyes at the same time, locking visual swords with Ross over the rim. But she wasn't the only one who could hide her innermost feelings behind a facial façde. He eyed her back without so much as a flicker of an eyelash, his cool blue eyes quite unflappable in their steady regard.

'Believe me, Vivien,' came his smooth reply, 'neither will I.'

An electric silence descended on the group as Vivien and Ross glared at each other in mutual defiance.

'Perhaps, Mother...' Lionel said, scraping back his chair to stand up. 'Perhaps we should leave these two young people to have a private chat.'

'Good idea, dear,' Peggy agreed, and stood up also. 'Here, Vivien, use my chair. Now be careful. Don't spill your drink as you sit down.'

Vivien rolled her eyes while her mother treated her like a cross between a child and an invalid.

'Will you be staying for dinner, Ross?' Peggy asked before she left.

Ross glanced at his wristwatch which showed five to six. He looked up and smiled. 'If it's not too much trouble.'

'No trouble at all. We're only having cold meats and salad. Left-overs, I'm afraid, from yesterday's Christmas feast.'

'I love left-overs,' he assured her.

Once her parents had gone inside, Vivien heaved a heavy sigh.

'Not feeling well, Viv?' Ross ventured.

She shot him a savage look. 'Don't call me that.'

'What? ''Viv''?'

'Yes.'

'Why?'

She shrugged irritably.

'Did Earl call you that?'

'No,' she lied.

He raised his eyebrows, but said nothing.

'Look, Ross, I'm just out of sorts today, OK?' Vivien burst out. 'It isn't all beer and skittles being pregnant, you know.'

'No, I don't know,' he said with a rueful note in his voice. 'But I guess I'm going to find out over the next few months. Something tells me you're a vocal type of girl.'

She darted him a dry look. 'If by that you mean I'm a shrew or a whinger then you couldn't be further from the truth. It's just that I didn't expect to be this sick all the time. I guess I'll get used to it in time. Though I'm damned if I'll get used to my mother's fussing,' she finished with a grimace of true frustration.

'You're going to live here?'

'Where else? I had no intention of staying on in Earl's flat. Besides, I'm unemployed now and I wouldn't have enough money for the rent anyway, so I have to stay here. There's no other alternative.'

'You could come home with me,' he suggested blandly.

Her mouth dropped open, then snapped shut. 'Oh, don't be ridiculous!'

'I'm not being ridiculous. Dad wants to meet you, and I'd like to have you.'

'I'll just bet you would,' she shot at him quite nastily.

Both his eyebrows shot up again. 'You have a dirty mind, Vivien, my dear.'

'Maybe it's the company I'm keeping.'

Anger glittered in his eyes. 'Perhaps you would prefer to be with a man who used you quite ruthlessly then discarded you like an old worn-out shoe!'

Vivien paled. Her bottom lip trembled.

'God,' Ross groaned immediately, placing his beer glass down on the table with a ragged thud. 'I'm sorry, Vivien. Deeply, sincerely sorry. That was a rotten thing to say.'

'Yes,' she rasped, tears pricking at her eyes.

She stared blindly down into her orange juice, amazed at the pain Ross's words had produced. There she'd been lately, almost agreeing with her mother that she had never loved Earl. But she must have, for this reminder of his treachery to hurt so much.

Or maybe she was just in an over-emotional state, being pregnant and all. She had heard pregnancy made some women quite irrational.

With several blinks and a sigh, she glanced up, only to be shocked by the degree of bleak apology on Ross's face. He really was very sorry, it seemed.

Now she felt guilty. For she hadn't exactly been Little Miss Politeness since joining him.

'I'm sorry too, Ross,' she said sincerely, 'This can't be easy for you either. I won't pretend that I'm thrilled at finding out you only looked upon me as a "bit on the side", so to speak, but who am I to judge? My behaviour was hardly without fault. I was probably using you that night as much as you were using me, so perhaps we should try to forgive each other's shortcomings and start all over again, shall we?'

He stared at her. 'You really mean that?'

'Of course. You're the father of my baby. We should at least try to be friends. I can also see it's only sensible that I should come out to meet your family, though I really can't stay with you for my entire pregnancy. Surely *you* can see that?'

'Actually, no, I can't.'

She made an exasperated sound. 'It wouldn't be right. I've never been a leaner. I have to make my own way.'

'That might have been all right when it was just you, Vivien,' he pointed out. 'But soon you'll have a child to support. You have no job and, I would guess, few savings. And, before you jump down my throat for being presumptuous, I'm only saying that because you're not old enough to have accrued a fortune.'

'I'm twenty-five!'

'Positively ancient. And you've been working how long? Four years at most?'

'Something like that…'

'Women never get paid as much as men in the media. Besides, in your line of work you would have had to spend a lot on clothes.'

'Yes…'

'See? It doesn't take a genius to guess at your financial position. Besides, I have a proposition to make to you.'

This brought a wary, narrow-eyed glare. 'Oh, yes?'

'Nothing like that,' he dismissed. 'My father has just come home from a stay in hospital where he's been having therapy. I have engaged a private therapist who specialises in after-stroke care to visit regularly, but there are still times when he needs someone to read to him and talk to him, or just sit with him.'

'A paid companion, you mean?'

'Yes. Something like that. Do you think you might be interested? It would kill two birds with one stone. Dad would get to know the mother of his grandchild and vice versa. And you'd feel a bit more useful than you're obviously feeling now.'

'Mmm.' Vivien gnawed away at her bottom lip. 'I've applied for social security...'

'No matter. You can either cancel it or I'll put your wages into a trust fund for the child.'

She wrinkled her nose. 'I'd rather cancel it.'

'*You would.*'

She bristled at his exasperated tone. 'Meaning?'

'You're too proud, Vivien. And too honest. You must learn that life is a jungle and sometimes the good get it in the neck.'

'Are you saying you have no pride? That you're not honest?'

A shadow passed across his eyes, turning them to a wintry grey for a second. But they were soon back to their bright icy blue. 'Let's just say that I *have* been known to go after what I want with a certain one-eyed determination.'

She gave him a long, considering look, trying not to let his physical appeal rattle her thought processes. It was hard, though. He was a devastatingly sexy man, much sexier than Earl. Oh, their looks were still remarkably similar—on the surface. But Ross had an inner energy, a raw vitality that shone through in every look he gave her, every move he made. Even sitting there casually in a deckchair with his legs stretched out, ankles crossed, he exuded an animal-like sensuality that sent tickles up and down her spine.

'Have you thought up this companion job simply

to get me into a position where you can seduce me again?' she asked point-blank.

He seemed startled for a moment before recovering his cool poise. 'No,' he said firmly, and looked her straight in the eye. 'Believe me when I say there will *not* be a repeat performance of what happened that night out at Wallaby Creek.'

He sounded as if he was telling the truth, she realised with a degree of surprise. And disappointment. The latter reaction sparked self-irritation. If *he* had managed to bring this unfortunate chemistry between them under control, then why couldn't *she*?

'Are you two ready to eat?' her mother called through the wire door. 'It's all set out.'

'Coming,' they chorused.

Thank God for the interruption, Vivien thought as she and Ross stood up.

'Vivien?' he said, taking her elbow to stop her before she could walk away.

'Yes?'

'Are you going to take me up on the offer or not?'

She tried to concentrate on all the common-sense reasons why it was a good idea, and not on the way his touch was making her pulse-rate do a tango within her veins.

'Vivien?' he probed again.

Swallowing, she lifted her dark eyes to his light blue ones, hoping like hell that he couldn't read her mind. Or her body language.

'If you trust me in this,' he said softly, 'I will not abuse that trust.'

Maybe, she thought. But could she say the same for her own strength of will? She'd shown little enough self-control once she'd found herself in his arms in the past. What if he'd been lying earlier about why he wanted her in his home? What if he was lying *now*? Men often lied to satisfy their lust. Now that she was already pregnant and his engagement was off, what was to stop Ross from using her to satisfy his sexual needs? How easy it would be with her already under his roof...

'Vivien!' her mother called again. 'What's keeping you?' Her face appeared at the wire door. 'Come on, now, love. I've got a nice salad all ready. You must eat, you know, since you're eating for two. And I've put out the vitamins the doctor suggested you have. Ross, don't take any nonsense from her and bring her in here right away.'

'Sure thing, Mrs Roberts.'

He smiled at the pained look on Vivien's face. 'Well? What do you say? Will you give it a try for a few months?'

A few months...

Something warned her that was too long, too dangerous.

'One month,' she compromised. 'Then we'll see...'

Still looking into his eyes, Vivien would have had to be blind not to see the depth of Ross's satisfaction. Her stomach turned over and she tore her eyes away. What have I done? she worried.

As he opened the wire door and guided her into the large, airy kitchen, the almost triumphant expression on Ross's face sent an old saying into her mind.

'"Will you walk into my parlour?" said a spider to a fly...'

CHAPTER EIGHT

'WHAT did Mum say to you?' Vivien demanded to know as soon as the Range Rover moved out of sight of her waving parents.

Ross darted a sideways glance at her, his expression vague. 'When?'

'When she called you back to the front gate just now.' She eyed Ross suspiciously. 'She isn't trying to put any pressure on you to marry me, is she?'

'Don't be paranoid, Vivien. Your mother simply asked me not to speed, to remember that I had a very precious cargo aboard.'

'Oh, good grief! That woman's becoming impossible. God knows what she'll be like by the time I actually *have* this baby.'

'Speaking of the baby, are you feeling better today?'

'No,' she grumped. 'I feel positively rotten.'

'Really? You look fantastic. That green suits you.'

Vivien stiffened, recalling how she had argued with her mother over what she should wear this morning. In the end she had given in to her mother's view that she should dress the way she always dressed, not run around hiding her figure in tent dresses and voluminous tops.

But now Vivien wasn't so sure wearing such a bare dress was wise. She hadn't forgotten the way Ross had looked yesterday when she'd agreed to go home with him for a while. The last thing she wanted to do was be provocative.

'I thought you said that you wanted us to start all over again,' Ross reminded her, 'that we should try to be friends. If this is your idea of being friendly then city folk sure as hell are different from country.'

His words made Vivien feel guilty. She was being as bitchy today as she had been yesterday, and it wasn't all because she felt nauseous. When Ross had shown up this morning, looking cool and handsome all in white, she hadn't been able to take her eyes off him. Her only defence against her fluttering heart had been sharp words and a cranky countenance.

Vivien shook her head. Her vulnerability to this chemistry business was the very devil. It played havoc with one's conscience, making her want to invite things that she knew were not in her best interests. Maybe some people could quite happily satisfy their lust without any disastrous consequences. But Vivien feared that if she did so with Ross she might become emotionally involved with him.

And where would that leave her, loving a man who didn't love her back, a man whose heart had been given to another woman? It wasn't as though there was any hope of his marrying her, either. He'd made his ideas on that quite clear.

Still, none of these inner torturous thoughts were any excuse for her poor manners, and she knew it.

'I'm sorry, Ross,' she apologised. 'I'll be in a better humour shortly. This yucky feeling usually wears off by mid-morning.'

He smiled over at her. 'I'll look forward to it.'

They fell into a companionable silence after that, Vivien soon caught up by the changing scenery as they made their way up the Blue Mountains and through Katoomba. She had been the driver during this section when she and Irving had made the trip out to Wallaby Creek, and the driver certainly didn't see as much as the passenger. Oddly enough, the curving road did not exacerbate her slightly queasy stomach. In fact she was soon distracted from her sickness with watching the many and varied vistas.

Despite being built on at regular intervals, the mountain terrain still gave one the feeling of its being totally untouched in places. The rock-faces dropped down into great gorges, the distant hillsides covered with a virgin bush so wild and dense that Vivien understood only too well why bushwalkers every year became lost in them. She shuddered to think what would happen to the many isolated houses if a bush-fire took hold.

'It's very dry, isn't it?' she remarked at last with worry in her voice.

'Sure is. My father says it's the worst drought since the early forties.'

'How old *is* your father, Ross?' Vivien asked.

'Sixty-three.'

'Still too young to die,' she murmured softly. 'And you?'

'I'll be thirty-one next birthday. What is this, twenty questions?'

Vivien shrugged. 'I think I should know a little about your family before I arrive, don't you?'

'Yes. I suppose that's only reasonable. Fire away, then.'

'Who else is there at Mountainview besides you and your father and Gavin? I presume you three men don't fend for yourselves.'

He laughed. 'You presume right. If we did, we'd starve. We have Helga to look after us.'

'Helga… She sounds formidable.'

'She is. Came to us as a nurse when Mum became terminally ill. After she died, Helga stayed on, saying we couldn't possibly cope without her. I was twelve at the time. Gavin was only seven. He looks upon Helga as a second mother.'

'And you? Do you look upon her as a second mother?'

'Heaven forbid. The woman's a martinet. No, only Gavin softens that woman's heart. She'd make an excellent sergeant in the army. Still, she does the work of three women so I can't complain. Keeps the whole house spick and span, does all the washing and cooking and ironing, and still has time left over to knit us all the most atrocious jumpers. I have a drawer full of them.'

'Oh, she sounds sweet.' Vivien laughed.

'She means well, I suppose. She's devoted to Mountainview. The house, that is. Not the sheep.'

'Is it a big house? I got the impression it was on the phone.'

'Too damned big. Built when graziers were nothing more than Pitt Street farmers who used their station properties as country retreats to impress their city friends. We don't even use some sections of the house. Dad gets a team of cleaners in once a year to spring-clean. When they're finished, they cover the furniture in half the rooms with dust-cloths then lock the doors.'

'Goodness, it sounds like a mansion. How many rooms has it got?'

'Forty-two.'

Vivien blinked over at his amused face. 'You're pulling my leg.'

He glanced down at her shapely ankles. 'Unfortunately, no.'

'Forty-two,' she repeated in amazement. 'And you only have the one woman to keep house?'

'In the main. We hire extra staff if we're having a party or a lot of visitors. And there's Stan and Dave.'

'Who are they?'

'General farmhands. Or rouseabouts, if you prefer. But they don't live in the main house. They have their own quarters. Still, they do look after the gardens, so you're likely to run into them occasionally. Of course, the place is a lot busier during shearing, but that won't be till March.'

'March…' Vivien wondered if she would still be there in March. She turned her head slowly to look at Ross. In profile, he looked nothing like Earl at all, yet her stomach still executed a telling flutter.

'Do…do you think Helga will like me?' Vivien asked hesitantly.

'I don't see why not.'

Vivien frowned. Men could be so naïve at times. If Helga had been fond of Ross's Becky then she wouldn't be very welcoming to the woman who'd been responsible for breaking the girl's heart.

But *was* it broken? she wondered. Ross had confessed his long love for the woman he'd planned to marry, but Vivien knew nothing of the woman herself, or her feelings.

'Ross…'

'Mmm?'

'Tell me about Becky.'

He stiffened in his seat, his hands tightening around the wheel. 'For God's sake, Vivien…'

She bristled. 'For God's sake what? Surely I have a right to know something about the woman you were planning to marry, the woman you were sleeping with the same time you were sleeping with me?'

'I was not sleeping with Becky,' he ground out. 'I have *never* slept with Becky.'

Vivien stared over at him. 'But…but…'

'Oh, I undoubtedly would have,' he confessed testily. 'After we were properly engaged.'

Vivien could not deny that there was a certain amount of elation mixed in with her astonishment at this news. She had hated to think Ross had behaved as badly as Earl. Not that his behaviour had been impeccable. But at least he hadn't been sleeping with two women at the same time. Though, to be honest, Vivien did find his admission a touch strange.

'I'm not sure I understand,' she said with a puzzled frown. 'If you've always loved this Becky, then why haven't you made love to her? Why were you waiting till you were engaged?'

His sigh was irritable. 'It's difficult to explain.'

'*Try*,' she insisted.

He shot her an exasperated glance. 'Why do you want to know? Why do you care? You're not in love with me. What difference can it possibly make?'

'I want to know.'

'You are an incredibly stubborn woman!'

'So my mother has always told me.'

'She didn't tell *me* that,' he muttered.

'Didn't she? Well, what did she tell you, then? Were you lying to me back in Sydney whe—?'

'Oh, for pity's sake give it a rest, will you, Vivien?

We've a tiresome trip ahead and you're going on like a Chinese water torture. God! Why I damned well…' He broke off, lancing her with another reproachful glare. 'You would have to be the most infuriating female I have ever met!'

Vivien's temper flared. 'Is that so? You certainly didn't find me infuriating once you got my clothes off, did you? You found me pretty fascinating then all right!'

He fixed her with an oddly chilling glance as he pulled over to the side of the road and cut the engine.

'Yes,' he grated out, then thumped the steering-wheel. 'I did. Is that what you want to hear? How I couldn't get enough of you that night? How I wouldn't have stopped at all if I hadn't flaked out with sheer exhaustion?'

He scooped in then exhaled a shuddering breath, taking a few seconds to compose himself. 'Now what else do you want to know…? Ah, yes, why I haven't slept with Becky? Well, perhaps my reasons might be clearer if I tell you she's only twenty-one years old, and a virgin to boot. Convent-educated. A total innocent where men are concerned. Somehow it didn't seem right to take that innocence away till my ring was on her finger. So I waited…

'It's just as well I did, in the circumstances,' he finished pointedly.

Vivien sat there in a bleak silence, her heart a great lump of granite in her chest. Heavy and hard and cold. My God, he had really just spelt it out for her, hadn't he? *She* could be taken within hours of their first meeting. For *she* had no innocence to speak of, no virtue to be treasured or respected. She was little better than a slut in his eyes, fit only to be lusted after, to be *screwed*!

Not so this girl he loved. She was to be treated like spun glass, put up on a pedestal, looked at but not touched, not ruthlessly seduced as he'd seduced her over and over that night.

She pressed a curled fist against her lips lest a groan of dismay escape, turning her face away to stare blindly through the passenger window. Well, at least this would give her a weapon to use against herself every time that hated chemistry raised its ugly head. She would only have to remember exactly how she stood in Ross's eyes for those unwanted desires to be frozen to nothingness. She would feel as chilled towards him as she did at this very moment.

'Haven't you any other questions you want answered?' Ross asked in a flat voice.

'No,' was all she could manage.

'In that case I'll put some music on. We've a long drive ahead of us…'

They stopped a couple of times along the way, at roadside cafés which served meals as well as petrol. Each time she climbed out of the cabin Vivien was struck by the heat and was only too glad to be underway again under the cooling fan of the vehicle's air-conditioning.

Vivien stayed quiet after their earlier upsetting encounter, even though the scenery didn't provide her bleak wretchedness with any distractions. The countryside was really quite monotonous once they were out on the Western plains. Nothing but paddock after flat paddock of brown grass, dotted with the occasional clump of trees under which slept some straggly-looking sheep. Even the towns seemed the same, just bigger versions of Wallaby Creek.

They were driving along shortly after two, the heat above the straight bitumen road forming a shimmering lake, when Vivien got the shock of her life. A huge grey kangaroo suddenly appeared right out of the mirage in front of them, leaping across the road. Ross braked, but he still hit it a glancing blow, though not enough to stop its flight to safety.

Vivien stared as the 'roo went clean over the barbed-wire fence at the side of the road and off across the paddock. Within seconds it had disappeared.

'That's the first kangaroo I've ever seen, outside a zoo!' she exclaimed, propelled out of her earlier depression by excitement at such an unexpected sight. 'I'm glad we didn't hurt it.'

'It'd take more than a bump to hurt one of those big mongrels.' Ross scowled before accelerating away again.

'Why do you call it that?' she objected. 'It's a beautiful animal.'

'Typical city opinion. I suppose you think rabbits are nice, cuddly, harmless little creatures as well?'

'Of course.'

'Then you've never met twenty thousand of the little beggars, munching their way through acres of your top grazing land. The only reason the sheep stations out here haven't got a problem with them at the moment is because there's a drought. Come the rain and they'll plague up, as they always do. The worst thing the English ever did to Australia was import the damned rabbit!'

'Well, you don't have to get all steamed up about

it with me,' she pointed out huffily. 'It's not my fault!'

Suddenly he looked across and grinned at her, a wide, cheeky grin that was nothing like Earl would ever indulge in. She couldn't help it. She grinned back, and in that split second she knew she not only desired this man, but she liked him as well. Far too much.

Her grin faded, depression returning to take the place of pleasure. If only Ross genuinely returned the liking. If only she could inspire a fraction of the respect this Becky did...

'What have I done *now*?' he groaned frustratedly.

'Nothing,' she muttered. 'Nothing.'

'I don't seem to have to do anything to upset you, do I? What was it? Did I smile at you like Earl, is that it? Go on, you can tell me. I'm a big boy. I can take it!'

She shrank from his sarcastic outburst, turning her face away. What could she say to him? No, you remind me less and less of Earl with each passing moment...

'Don't you dare give me that silent treatment again, Vivien,' he snapped. 'I can't stand it.'

She sighed and turned back towards him. 'This isn't going to work out, is it, Ross?'

His mouth thinned stubbornly. 'It will, if you'll just give it a chance. Besides, what's your alternative—eight months of your mother's fussing?'

Vivien actually shuddered.

'See? At least I won't fuss over you. And neither will the rest of the people at Mountainview. They have too much to do. You'll be expected to pull your own weight out here, pregnant or not. That's what it's like in the country. You're not an invalid and you won't be treated like one.'

'Do you think that will bother me? I'm not lazy, Ross. I'm a worker too.'

'Then what *is* beginning to bother you? What have I said to make you look at me with such unhappy eyes?'

'I...I really wanted us to become friends.'

'And you think I don't?'

'Friends respect each other.'

He frowned over at her. 'I respect you.'

'No, you don't.'

'God, Vivien, what is this? Do you think I subscribe to that old double standard about sex? Do you think I think you're tainted somehow because you went to bed with me?'

'Yes,' she told him point-blank. 'If you didn't think like that, you'd have slept with Becky and to hell with her so-called innocence. Virginity is not a prize, Ross. It was only valued in the olden days because it assured the bridegroom that his bride would not have venereal disease. Making love is the most wonderful expression of love and affection that can exist between a man and a woman. Yet you backed away from it with the woman you claim you love in favour of it with a perfect stranger, in favour of a "city broad who probably knows more counter-moves than a chess champion". If that sounds as if you respect me then I'm a Dutchman's uncle!'

His face paled visibly, but he kept his eyes on the road ahead. 'That's not how it was, Vivien,' he said tautly.

'Oh?' she scoffed. 'Then how *was* it, Ross?'

'One day I might tell you,' he muttered. 'But for now I think you're forgetting a little something.'

'What?'

'The baby. *Our* baby. It's not the child's fault that he or she is going to be born. The least we can do is provide it with a couple of parents who aren't constantly at each other's throats. I realise I'm not the father you would have chosen for your child, Vivien. Neither am I yet able to fully understand your decision to actually go ahead with this pregnancy. I'm still to be convinced that it has nothing to do with my likeness to the man you're in love with.

'No, don't say a word!' he growled when she went to protest this assumption. 'You might not even recognise your own motives as yet. We all have dark and devious sides, some that remain hidden even to ourselves. But I will not have an innocent child suffer for the perversity of its parents. We're going to be mature about all this, Vivien. *You're* going to be mature. I want no more of your swinging moods or your wild, way-off accusations. You are to treat me with the same decency and respect that I will accord you. Or, by God, I'm going to lay you over my knee and whop that luscious backside of yours. Do I make myself clear?'

She eyed him fiercely, seething inside with a bitter resentment. Who did he think he was, telling her how to behave, implying that she had been acting like an immature idiot, threatening her with physical violence? As for dark and devious sides…he sure as hell had his fair share!

But aside from all that, Vivien could see that he *was* making *some* sense, despite his over-the-top threats. He even made her feel a little guilty. She hadn't really been thinking much about the baby's future welfare. She'd been consumed by her own ambivalent feelings for the man seated beside her. One moment she was desperate for him to like her, the next he was provoking her into a quite irrational anger, making her want to lash out at him. Right at this moment she would have liked to indulge in a bit of physical violence of her own!

Yes, but that's because you simply want to get your hands on him again, came a sinister voice from deep inside.

She stiffened.

'And you can cut out that outraged innocence act too!' he snapped, darting her a vicious glance. 'You're about as innocent as a vampire. *And* about as lethal! So I suggest you keep those pearly white teeth of yours safely within those blood-red lips for the remainder of this journey. For, if you open them again, I swear to you, Vivien, I'll forget that promise I made to you yesterday and give you another dose of what you've obviously been missing to have turned you into such a shrew. I'm sure you're quite capable of closing those big brown eyes of yours and pretending I'm Earl once more. And I'm just as capable of thoroughly enjoying myself in his stead!'

CHAPTER NINE

IT WAS dusk when Ross and Vivien finally turned from the highway on to a private road. Narrow and dusty, it wound a slow, steady route through flat, almost grassless fields where Vivien only spotted one small flock of sheep, but she declined asking where the rest of the stock was. She wouldn't have lowered herself to make conversation with the man next to her. She was still too angry with him.

How dared he threaten to practically rape her? He might not literally mean it, but she couldn't abide men who used verbal abuse and physical threats to intimidate women. It just showed you the sort of man Ross was underneath his surface charm. As for suggesting that she would actually enjoy it...

That galled most of all. Because she wasn't at all sure that she *wouldn't*!

Self-disgust kept her temper simmering away in a grimly held silence while she stared out of the passenger window, her lips pressed angrily together. Eventually, the flat paddocks gave way to rolling brown hills. One was quite steep, and, as they came over the crest, there, in the distance, lay some bluish-looking mountains. But closer, on the crest of the next hill, and surrounded by tall, dark green trees, stood a home of such grandeur and elegance that Vivien caught her breath in surprise.

'I did tell you it was big,' Ross remarked drily.

'So you did,' she said equally drily, then turned

flashing brown eyes his way. 'I'm allowed to talk now, am I? I won't be suitably punished for my temerity in opening my blood-red lips?'

His sigh was weary. It made Vivien suddenly feel small. What was the matter with her? She was rarely reduced to using such vicious sarcasm. She could be stubborn, but usually quietly so, with a cool, steely determination that was far more effective than more volatile methods. Yet here she was, flying off the handle at every turn. Snapping and snarling like a she-cat.

It had to be her hormones, she decided unhappily. God, but she was a mess!

She turned to look once more at the huge house, and as they drew closer an oddly apprehensive shiver trickled down her spine. Vivien knew immediately that she would not like living at Mountainview. If she stayed the full month, she would be very surprised. Yet she could not deny it was a beautiful-looking home. Very beautiful indeed.

Edwardian in style and two-storeyed, with long, graceful white columns running from the stone-flagged patio right up through the upper-floor wooden veranda to the gabled roof. An equally elegant white ironwork spanned the distance between these columns, for decoration alone downstairs, but for safety as well between the bases of the upstairs pillars.

Not that Vivien could picture too many youngsters climbing over that particular railing anyway. The house had a museum-like quality about it, enhanced possibly by the fact that only a couple of lights shone in the windows as they drove up in the rapidly fading light.

The Range Rover crunched to a halt on the gravel

driveway, Ross turning to Vivien with an expectant look on his face. 'Well? What do you think of it?'

'It's—er—very big.'

'You don't like it,' he said with amazement in his voice and face.

'No, no,' she lied. 'It's quite spectacular. I'm just very tired, Ross.'

His face softened and Vivien turned hers away. She wished he didn't have the capacity to look at her like that, with such sudden warmth and compassion. It turned her bones to water, making her feel weak and vulnerable. Instinct warned her that Ross was not a man you showed such a vulnerability to.

'You must be,' he said as he opened his door. 'I'll take you inside then come back for the luggage. Once you're settled in the kitchen with one of Helga's mugs of tea you'll feel better.'

It was only after she alighted that Vivien recognised the truth of her excuse to Ross. Yet she was more than tired. She was exhausted. Her legs felt very heavy and she had to push them to lug her weary body up the wide, flagged steps. When she hesitated on the top step, swaying slightly, Ross's hand shot out to steady her.

'Are you all right, Vivien?'

She took a couple of deep breaths. 'Yes, I think so. Just a touch dizzy there for a sec.'

Before she could say another word he swept one arm around her waist, the other around her knees, and hoisted her up high into his arms. 'I'll carry you straight up to bed. Helga can bring your tea to your room. You can meet Dad in the morning.'

Suddenly, Vivien felt too drained to protest. She went quite limp in Ross's arms, her head sagging against his chest, her hands linking weakly around his neck lest they flop down by her sides like dead weights. Her eyelashes fluttered down to rest on the darkly smudged shadows beneath her eyes. She felt rather than saw Ross's careful ascent up a long flight of stairs.

'You're very strong,' she whispered once in her semi-conscious daze.

He didn't answer.

Next thing she knew she was being lowered on to a soft mattress, her head sinking into a downy pillow. She felt her sandals being pulled off, a rug or blanket being draped over her legs. She sighed a shuddering sigh as the last of her energy fled her body. Within sixty seconds she was fast asleep, totally unaware of the man standing beside the bed staring down at her with a tight, pained look on his face.

After an interminable time, he bent to lightly touch her cheek, then to draw a wisp of hair from where it lay across her softly parted lips. His hand lingered, giving in to the urge to rub gently against the pouting flesh. She stirred, made a mewing sound like a sleepy kitten that had been dragged from its mother's teat. Her tongue-tip flicked out to moisten dry lips, the action sending a spurt of desire to his loins so sharp that he groaned aloud.

Spinning on his heels, he strode angrily from the room.

Vivien woke to the sound of raised voices. For a moment she couldn't remember where she was, or whose voices they could possibly be. But gradually her eyes and brain refocused on where she was.

Once properly awake, one quick glance took in the

large, darkly furnished bedroom, the double bed she was lying on, the moonlight streaming in the open french doors on to the polished wooden floors, the balcony beyond those doors. Levering herself up on to one elbow, she noticed that on the nearest bedside table rested a tray, which held a tall glass of milk and a plate on which was a sandwich, a piece of iced fruit cake and a couple of plain milk-coffee biscuits.

But neither the room nor the food was of any real interest to Vivien at that moment. Her whole attention was on the argument that was cutting through the still night air with crystal clarity.

'I don't understand why you had to bring her here,' a male voice snarled. 'How do you think Becky's going to feel when she finds out? You've broken her heart, do you know that? I was over there today and she—'

'What do you mean, you were over there today?' Ross broke in testily. 'You were supposed to be checking all the bores today.'

'Yeah, well, I didn't, did I? I'll do them tomorrow.'

'Tomorrow... You've always got some excuse, haven't you? God, Gavin, when are you going to learn some sense of responsibility? Don't you know that one day without water could be the difference between life and death in a drought like this? What on earth's the matter with you? Why don't you grow up?'

'I *am* grown-up. And I *can* be responsible. It's just that you and Dad won't give me a chance at any real responsibility. All you give me is orders!'

'Which you can't follow.'

'I can too.'

'No you bloody well can't! Just look at the bores today.'

'Oh, bugger the bores. We've hardly got any sheep left anyway. You sold them all.'

'Better sold than dead.'

'That was your opinion. You never asked me for mine. I would have kept them, hand-fed them.'

'At what cost? Be sensible, Gavin. I made the right business decision, the only decision.'

'Business! Since when has life on the land been reduced to nothing but business decisions? Since *you* came home to run things, that's when. You're a hard-hearted ruthless bastard, Ross, who'll stop at nothing to get what you want. And I know what that is. You want Mountainview. The land and the house. Not just your half, either. You want it all! That's why you were going to marry Becky. Not because you fell in love with her, but because you knew Dad was keen for one of us to marry and produce an heir before he died. That's why you dumped Becky and brought that other city bitch back here. Because she's already having your kid. You think that will sway Dad into changing his will all the sooner. Yeah, now I see it. I see it all!'

'You're crazy,' Ross snapped. 'Or crazy drunk. Is that it? Have you been drinking again?'

'So what if I have?'

'I should have known. You're only this irrational— and this articulate—when you're drunk.'

'Not like you, eh, big brother? You've got the gift of the gab all the time, haven't you? You can charm the birds right out of the trees. I'll bet that poor bitch upstairs doesn't even know what part she's playing in all this. You've got it made, haven't you? The heir you needed plus a hot little number on tap. A lay, laid on every night. I'll bet she's good in bed too. I'll bet she—'

The sounds of a scuffle replaced the voices. Vivien sat bolt upright, her heart going at fifty to the dozen, her mind whirling with all sorts of shocking thoughts. Could Gavin really be right? Was she some pawn in a game much larger and darker than she'd ever imagined? Were she and her child to be Ross's ace card in gaining the inheritance his brother seemed to think he coveted? It would explain why Ross had not made love to this Becky if he didn't really love her...

Shakily, she stood up and made her way out on to the balcony. The night air was silent now, the earlier sounds of fighting having stopped. The sky overhead was black and clear with a myriad stars, the moon a bright orb, bathing everything beneath in its pale, ghostly light.

Gingerly, Vivien looked down over the railing.

Ross was standing there on the driveway next to his Range Rover, disconsolate and alone. While she watched silently, he lifted his hands to rake back his dishevelled hair, expelling a ragged sigh. 'Crazy fool,' he muttered.

Vivien didn't think she made a move, or a sound. But suddenly Ross's head jerked up and those piercing eyes were staring straight into hers. Worried first, then assessing, he held her startled gaze for several seconds before speaking. And then it was to say only three sharp words, 'Stay right there.'

She barely had time to compose her rattled self before Ross was standing right in front of her, his big strong hands gripping her upper arms, his sharp blue eyes boring down into hers.

'How much did you hear?' he demanded to know.

'E—e-enough,' she stammered.

'Enough. Dear God in heaven. And did you believe what that fool said? *Did* you?' he repeated, shaking her.

Vivien could hardly think. 'I…I don't know what to believe any more.'

'*Don't* believe what my brother said, for Pete's sake,' Ross insisted harshly. 'He's all mixed up in the head at the moment. Believe what *I* tell you, Vivien. Your presence here has nothing to do with Mountainview. Nothing at all! You're here only because I want you here, because I…I… Goddammit, woman, why do you have to be so darned beautiful?'

And, digging his fingers into her flesh, he lifted her body and mouth to his, taking it wildly and hungrily in a savage kiss. For a few tempestuous moments, she found herself responding to his desperate desire, parting her lips and allowing his tongue full reign within her mouth. But when he groaned and swept his arms down around her, pressing the entire length of her against him, the stark evidence of a full-blooded male erection lying between them slammed her back to reality.

'No!' she gasped, wrenching her mouth from his. 'Let me go!' With a tortured cry, she struggled free of his torrid embrace, staggering back against the railing, staring up at him with wide, accusing eyes.

'You…you said this wasn't why you brought me here,' she flung at him shakily. 'You promised to keep your hands off.'

The sudden and shocking suspicion that he might have been using sex to direct her mind away from Gavin's accusations blasted into Vivien's brain, making her catch her breath. Dear heaven, he couldn't be that wicked, could he? Or that devious?

She stared at Ross, trying to find some reassurance now in his flushed face and heaving chest, as well as the memory of his explicit arousal. That, at least, was not a sham, she conceded. That was real. *Too* real.

But then his desire for her had always been real. That did not mean Gavin wasn't telling the truth. Ross could still be the ruthless opportunist his brother accused him of being, one who could quite happily satisfy his lust for her while achieving his own dark ends.

'I promised there would not be a repeat of what happened that night at Wallaby Creek,' he ground out. 'And there won't.'

'And…and what was that you were just doing if not trying to seduce me?' she blustered, still not convinced, despite his sounding amazingly sincere.

'That was my being a bloody idiot. But I was only kissing you, Vivien. Don't hang me for a simple kiss. Still, I will endeavour to keep my hands well and truly off in future. As for my reasons for bringing you here…I can only repeat it has everything to do with my child, but nothing to do with Mountainview. You have my solemn oath on that. Now go back to bed. You still look tired. I'll see you in the morning.'

Vivien stared after him as he whirled and strode off along the balcony and around the corner.

A simple kiss? There'd been nothing simple about that kiss. Nothing simple at all…

And there was nothing simple about this whole situation.

Though had there ever been?

Vivien lifted trembling hands to push the hair back

off her face. God knew where all this was going to end. Perhaps it would be best if she cut her visit short here, if she declined taking the position as companion to Ross's father. There were too many undercurrents going on in this household, too many mysteries, too much ill feeling.

Vivien wanted no part in them. Life was complicated enough without getting involved in family feuds. Yes, she would tell Ross in the morning that she wanted to go back home.

Feeling marginally better, Vivien made her way back into the bedroom, intending to drink the milk then change into some nightwear before going back to bed. But she found herself lying down again, fully dressed, on top of the bed. Soon, she was sound asleep again.

CHAPTER TEN

WHEN Vivien woke a second time, it was morning. Mid-morning, by the feel of the heat already building in the closed room. Her slim silver wristwatch confirmed her guess. It was ten-fifteen.

With a groan she swung her stiffened legs over the side of the bed and sat up, thinking to herself that she could do with a shower. It was then that she remembered her decision of the night before to go straight back home.

Somehow, however, in the clear light of day, that seemed a hasty, melodramatic decision. She'd been very tired last night. Overwrought, even. Perhaps she should give Ross and his father and Mountainview a few days at least.

As for Gavin's accusations that his older brother was a ruthless bastard intent on using Vivien and her baby to gain an inheritance... Well, that too felt melodramatic, now that she could think clearly. Ross might be a typically selfish male in some ways, but she had sensed nothing from him but true affection and concern for his family. She'd also been impressed by the way he'd handled things with *her* parents. Ross was not a cruel, callous man. Not at all.

Yes. The matter was settled. She would stay a while. A week, at least. Then, if things weren't working out, she would make some excuse and go home. She could always say she couldn't stand the heat. That would hardly be a lie, Vivien thought, as beads of perspiration started trickling down between her breasts.

Feeling the call of nature, she rose and went to investigate the two panelled wooden doors that led off the bedroom. The first was an exit, leading out on to a huge rectangular gallery. The second revealed an *en suite* that, though its décor was in keeping with the house's Edwardian style, was still obviously fairly new.

Vivien was amused by the gold chain she had to pull to flush the toilet, smiling as she washed her hands with a tiny, shell-like soap.

On going back into the hot room, she started unpacking, having spied her suitcase resting on the ottoman at the foot of the bed. A shower was definitely called for, she decided, plus nothing heavier to wear than shorts and a cool top.

Since everything was very crushed she chose a simple shorts set in a peacock-blue T-shirt material, with a tropical print of yellow and orange hibiscus on it. The creases would fall out if she hung it up behind the bathroom door while she had a shower. With the outfit draped over an arm, and some fresh underwear and her bag of toiletries filling both hands, Vivien made for the shower.

The hot water felt so delicious that she wallowed in it for ages, shampooing her hair a couple of times during the process, the heat having made her thick black tresses feel limp and greasy. Once clean, however, her hair sprang around her face and shoulders in a myriad damp curls and waves. In deference to the heat, Vivien bypassed full make-up, putting on a dab of coral lipstick, a minimal amount of waterproof mascara and a liberal lashing of Loulou, her favourite perfume.

Electing to leave her hair damp rather than blow-dry it, Vivien opened the door of the bathroom feeling refreshed but a little nervous. What was she supposed to do? Where should she go?

The unexpected sight of a large grey-haired woman in a mauve floral dress bustling to and fro across the bedroom, hanging Vivien's clothes up for her in the elegantly carved wardrobe, replaced any nerves with a stab of surprise. And a degree of dry amusement.

So this was Helga…

'And good morning to you too,' Helga threw across the room before she could say a word. 'High time you got up. Nothing worse than lying in bed too long. Bad for the digestion. I've straightened your bed and turned on the ceiling fan. Didn't you see it there? It's best to leave the windows and doors closed till the afternoon, then I'll come up and open them. We usually get an afternoon breeze. And leave your dirty washing in the linen basket in the corner.

'I'm Helga, by the way. I dare say Ross has told you about me. Not in glowing terms, I would imagine,' she added with a dry cackle. 'We never did get along, me and that lad. He's not the sort to follow orders kindly. Still, he's turned out all right, I guess. Loves his dad, which goes down a long way with me.'

She drew breath at last to give Vivien the once-over. 'Well, you certainly are one stunning-looking girl, aren't you? But then, I wouldn't expect any different from Ross. Only the best would ever do for him. Fancy schools in Sydney. Fancy flying lessons. Now a fancy woman…'

Vivien drew in a sharply offended breath, and was just about to launch into a counter-attack when Helga dismissed any defensive speech with a sharp wave of her hand.

'Now don't go getting your knickers all in a knot, lovie. No offence intended. Besides, there's no one happier than me that you put a spoke in Ross's plans to marry Becky. I presume you know who Becky is?'

Vivien found herself nodding dumbly. She'd never met anyone quite like Helga. Talk about intimidating! Ross had her undying admiration if he stood up to this bulldozer of a woman.

'Well, let me tell you a little secret about Miss Becky Macintosh,' Helga boomed on. 'She's always hankered after living at Mountainview, ever since she was knee-high to a grasshopper. She's no more in love with Ross than I am. But he's a mighty hand-some man and a girl could do worse than put her slippers under his bed every night. When Oliver had his stroke and Ross came back home, Becky saw her chance and set her cap at him. Lord, butter wouldn't have melted in her mouth around him all year. But it's not the man she wants. It's Mountainview!'

Helga snapped the suitcase shut and started doing the buckles up.

'Why are you telling me all this?' Vivien asked on a puzzled note.

A sly look came over Helga's plain, almost mas-culine face. 'Because I don't want you worrying that you might be breaking Becky's heart if you marry Ross. That little minx will simply move on to the next brother, which will be by far the best for all con-cerned.'

Vivien bypassed Helga's conclusion that she

wanted to marry Ross to concentrate on her next startling statement. 'You mean—'

'My Gavin loves her,' Helga broke in with a maternal passion that was unexpectedly fierce. 'He's loved her for years. But he's painfully shy around girls—unless he's been drinking. He can't seem to bring himself to tell her how he feels. Now, after this episode with Ross, he doesn't think he'll ever stand a chance. He's always felt inferior to his big brother. But if Ross moved far away...'

'I see,' Vivien murmured. 'Yes, I see...'

'You won't want to live here, will you? A city girl like you will want the bright lights. Ross likes action too, not the slowness of station life. You'll both be happy enough well away from here.'

Looking at Helga's anxious face, Vivien was moved to pity for her. She must love Gavin very, very much. As for Gavin... Her heart really went out to him. It couldn't be easy being Ross's brother. Even harder with the two brothers loving the same girl. That was one factor Helga had blithely forgotten. What of Ross's feelings in all this? Or didn't they count?

'I'm sorry, Helga,' she explained, 'but Ross and I have no plans to marry. We're not in love, you see.'

'Not in love?' Helga looked down at Vivien's stomach with a disdainful glower. 'Then what are you doing having his child? Not in love! Well, I never! What's the world coming to, I ask you, with girls going round having babies with men they don't love? It makes one ashamed of one's own sex!'

Vivien's lovely brown eyes flashed defiance as she drew herself up straight and proud.

'I would think you should feel more ashamed of

this Becky than me,' she countered vehemently. 'At least I'm honest about my feelings. She sounds like a shallow, materialistic, manipulative little witch, and I'm not sorry at all that Ross is not going to marry her. He deserves better than that. Much better. He's a...a... And what are you laughing at?' she demanded angrily when Helga started to cackle.

Again that sly look returned. 'Just thinking what similar personalities you and Ross have. Both as stubborn as mules. Lord knows what kind of child you're going to have. He'll probably end up running the world!'

'It might be a daughter!'

'Then *she'll* run the world.'

Helga grinned a highly satisfied grin, stopping Vivien in her tracks. Against her better judgement, she found herself grinning back. She shook her head in a type of bewilderment before a sudden thought wiped the grin from her face.

'Ross doesn't know about Gavin loving Becky, does he?' she asked.

'No,' the older woman admitted. 'Gavin made me promise not to tell him.'

'I see. So you told me instead, hoping I might relay the information. That way you'd keep your promise, but get the message across.'

Helga's look was sharp. 'There's no flies on you, lovie, is there? Now how about a spot of breakfast? You'll want a good plateful, I'll warrant, since you didn't eat the supper I left you. Remember, you're eating for two.'

Vivien only just managed to suppress a groan of true dismay as she slipped on her sandals and followed Helga from the room.

* * *

The kitchen was as huge as the rest of the house. But far more homely, with copper pots hanging over the stove, dressers full of flowered crockery and knick-knacks leaning against the walls, and an enormous table in the centre.

'Do you really look after this whole place by yourself?' Vivien asked whilst Helga was piling food on to the largest plate she'd ever seen. She already had a mug of tea in front of her that would have satisfied a giant.

'Sure do, lovie. Keeps me fit, I can tell you. Here, get this into you!' And she slapped the plate down in front of her. There were three rashers of bacon, two eggs, a lamb chop and some grilled tomato, not to mention two slices of toast.

Vivien felt her stomach heave. Swallowing, she picked up the knife and fork and started rearranging the bacon. 'Er—do you know where Ross is this morning?' she asked by way of distraction.

'Right here,' he said, striding into the kitchen and sitting down in a chair opposite her. Vivien looked down, thinking that she would never get used to the way her heart skipped a beat every time she saw him. Of course, it didn't help that he only had a pair of jeans on. Not a thing on his top half. Sitting down, he looked naked.

'You look refreshed this morning, Vivien,' he said, virtually forcing her to look back up at him. She did, keeping her gaze well up. Unfortunately, she found herself staring straight at his mouth and remembering how she had felt when he'd kissed her last night.

'I presume you want a mug of tea?' Helga asked Ross.

'Sure do. And a piece of that great Christmas cake you made.'

Helga threw him a dry look. 'No need to suck up to me, my lad. Your girl and I are already firm friends, aren't we, lovie?'

'Oh—er—yes,' Vivien stammered, which brought a surprised look from Ross.

'I see she appreciates your cooking as well,' he said, and gave Vivien a sneaky wink. She rolled her eyes at the food and he laughed. But laughter made the muscles ripple in his chest and she quickly looked down again, forcing a mouthful of egg in between suddenly dry lips.

'Where's Gavin?' Helga went on. 'Doesn't he want a cup too?'

'Nope. He's out checking bores. Won't be back till well after lunch.'

'Out checking bores?' Helga persisted. '*Today*? But it's going to be a scorcher. Why couldn't he go tomorrow?'

'Because he was supposed to have gone yesterday,' Ross informed her drily.

Helga looked pained and shook her head. 'That boy… Still, you have to understand he's been upset lately, Ross. He's not himself.'

'Well, he'd better get back to being himself quick smart,' Ross said firmly, 'or there won't be anything to do around here except have endless mugs of tea. Sheep don't live on love alone.'

A stark silence descended while Ross finished his tea and Vivien waded through as much of the huge breakfast as her stomach could stand. Finally, she pushed the plate aside, whereupon Helga frowned. Before her disapproval could erupt into words Ross was on his feet and asking Vivien if he could have a few words with her in private.

It was a testimony to Helga's formidable personality that Vivien was grateful to be swept away into Ross's company when he was semi-naked.

'Don't let Helga bully you into eating too much,' was Ross's first comment as they walked along the hallway together.

'I'll try not to. Where...where are we going?' she asked once they moved across the tiled foyer and started up the stairs.

He slanted her a look which suggested he'd caught the nervousness behind her question and was genuinely puzzled by it. 'I need to shower and change before taking you along to meet Dad,' he explained. 'I thought we could talk at the same time.'

He stopped at the top of the stairs, his blue eyes glittering with a sardonic amusement. 'Of course, I don't expect you to accompany me into my bathroom. You can sit on my bed and talk to me from there. Let me assure you the shower is not visible from the bedroom.'

Sit on his bed...

Dear heaven, that was bad enough.

Noting that he was watching her closely, Vivien lifted her nose and adopted what she hoped was an expression of utter indifference. 'I doubt it would bother me if it was,' she repudiated. 'I've seen it all before.'

His features tightened, but he said nothing, ushering her along the upstairs hall and into his bedroom, shutting the door carefully behind them. When he saw her startled look, a wry smile lifted the grimness from his face.

'You may be blasé about male nudity, Vivien, my dear, but Helga is not so sophisticated. Do sit down, however. You make me uncomfortable standing there with your hands clasped defensively in front of you. I had no dark or dastardly plan in bringing you up here, though I appreciate now that my idea of having a normal chat with you while I showered was stupid. Best I simply hurry with my ablutions and then we'll talk.'

Five minutes later he came out of the closed bathroom dressed in bright shorts and a loose white T-shirt with a colourful geometric design on the back and a surfing logo on the sleeves.

It was the longest five minutes Vivien had ever spent. Who would have believed the sound of a shower running could be so disturbing?

'You look as if you're ready to shoot the waves at Bondi,' she commented, mocking herself silently for the way she was openly feasting her eyes on him this time. But she couldn't seem to help herself.

'Dad likes bright clothes. They cheer him up.'

'That's good,' she said, and bounced up on to her feet. 'Most of my clothes are bright.'

'So I noticed.'

'You don't approve?'

'Would it matter if I didn't?'

'No.'

His smile was dry. 'That's what I thought. Shall we go?'

'But you said you wanted to talk to me.'

'I've changed my mind. I'm sure you'll handle Dad OK. You seem to have a knack with men. Follow me.'

She did so in silence, her thoughts a-whirl. What

was eating at Ross? Was it sexual frustration, or frustration of another kind? She seemed to be getting mixed messages from him. One minute she thought he admired her, though grudgingly. The next, he was openly sarcastic.

They trundled down the stairs and along a different corridor, towards the back section of the house.

'In here,' Ross directed, and opened a door into a cool, cosily furnished bed-sitting-room. She found out later that it had once been part of the servants' quarters, when Mountainview had had lots of servants. Ross had had it renovated and air-conditioned before his father came home from hospital.

'Dad?' Ross ventured softly. 'You're not asleep, are you?'

The old man resting in the armchair beside the window had had his eyes closed, his head listing to one side. But with Ross's voice his head jerked up and around, his eyes snapping open. They looked straight at Vivien, their gaze both direct and assessing.

'Hello, Mr Everton,' she said, and came forward to hold out her hand. 'I'm Vivien.'

Pale, parched lips cracked back into a semblance of a smile. 'So...you're Vivien...' His eyes slid slowly down her body, then up over her shoulder towards his son. 'Now...I understand,' he said, the talking clearly an effort for him. Vivien noticed that one side of his face screwed up when he spoke, the aftermath, she realised, of his stroke. 'They don't...come along...like her...too often...'

Vivien was slightly put out by his remarks. Why did men have to reduce women to sex objects?

'They don't come along like Ross too often either,' she countered, quite tartly.

The old man laughed, and immediately was consumed by racking coughs. Ross raced to pick up the glass of water resting on the table beside him, holding him gently around the shoulders till the coughing subsided, then pressing the water to his lips. Vivien hovered, feeling useless and a little guilty. She should have kept her stupid, proud mouth shut! The man meant no harm.

'You should let me call in the doctor, Dad,' Ross was saying worriedly. 'This coughing of yours is getting worse.'

'No…more…doctors,' his father managed to get out. 'No more. They'll only…put me…in hospital. I want to…to die here.'

Ross's laugh was cajoling. 'You're not going to die, Dad. Dr Harmon said that with a little more rest and therapy you'll be as good as new.'

'Perhaps,' he muttered. 'Perhaps. Now…get lost. I wish…to talk…to Vivien. *Alone*. You cramp…my style.'

'All right. But don't talk too much, mind?' And Ross lanced his father with an oddly sharp look. 'You'll find me in the library when he's finished with you, Vivien.'

'Call me…Oliver,' was the first thing Ross's father said once they were alone. 'Now, tell me…all about…yourself.'

For over an hour, Vivien chatted away, answering Oliver's never-ending questions. It worried her that he was becoming overtired, but every time she touched on the subject of his health he vetoed her impatiently.

It was clear where Ross had got his determination and stubbornness. Yet, for all his questions, Oliver never once enquired about her feelings for his son, or Ross's for her. He never asked her what she wanted for the future, either for herself or her baby. He wanted to know about her background, her growing-up years, her education, her job and her family. Finally, he sighed and leant back into the chair.

'You'll do, Vivien,' he said. 'You'll do...'

'As what, Oliver?'

His smile was as cunning as Helga's. 'Why...as the mother...of my grandchild. What else? Now run along... It's lunchtime... But tell Ross...I don't want...any.'

Vivien closed the door softly, her mind still on Ross's father.

Oliver Everton didn't fool her for one minute. He was going to try to marry her off to Ross. Not that she blamed him. Death was very definitely knocking at his door and he wanted things all tied up with pink bows before he left this world.

Gavin was accusing the wrong man when he said Ross was trying to manipulate his father. It was the father who was the manipulator, who had perhaps always been the manipulator at Mountainview. Maybe that was why Ross had chosen to follow a career away from home, and why Gavin hadn't. The stronger brother bucking the heavy hand of the father while the weaker one knuckled under.

Now, illness had brought the prodigal—and perhaps favoured—son home and the father was going to make the most of it. Vivien wouldn't put it past Oliver having been the one to insist Ross bring her out here, hoping that the sexual attraction that had once flared out of control between them would do so again, thereby making his job easier of convincing them marriage was the best course for all concerned.

And he'd been half right, the cunning old devil. That electric chemistry was still sparking as strong as ever. She could hardly look at Ross without thinking about that night, without longing to find out if the wonder of it all had been real or an illusion. How long, she worried anew, before her own body language started sending out those tell-tale waves of desire in Ross's direction? How long before his male antennae picked up on them?

He was not a man to keep promises he sensed she didn't want him to keep. He was a sexual predator, a hunter. He would zero in for the kill the moment she weakened. Of that she was certain.

So why stay? her conscience berated. Why tempt fate?

Because she had to. For some reason she just had to...

CHAPTER ELEVEN

'THERE you are!' Vivien exclaimed exasperatedly when she finally found the library. 'This house is like a maze.'

'Only downstairs,' Ross said, having glanced up from where he was sitting behind a large cedar desk in the far corner. With her arrival, he put the paperwork he was doing in a drawer and stood up. 'You must have really got along with Dad to stay so long.'

'Yes, I did,' she agreed, glancing around the room, which was exactly as she'd first imagined. Leather furniture, heavy velvet curtains and floor-to-ceiling bookshelves. 'I think he quite likes me.'

'I don't doubt it,' Ross muttered as he strode round the desk, his caustic tone drawing both her attention and her anger.

'Do you *have* to be sarcastic all the time?'

'Am I?' There was an oddly surprised note in his voice, as though he hadn't realised his bad manners.

'Yes, you are!'

'You're exaggerating, surely. I think I've been very polite, in the circumstances. Well? What did you think of Dad?'

Vivien sighed her irritation at having her complaint summarily brushed aside. What circumstances did he mean, anyway?

'He's a very sick man,' she commented at last.

'He's as strong as an ox,' came the impatient rebuttal.

'Not any longer, Ross. Maybe you've been away from home too long.'

'Meaning?'

She shrugged. 'People change. Things change.'

'I get the impression I'm supposed to read between the lines here.' Ross leant back against the corner of the desk, his arms folding. 'What's changed around Mountainview that I don't know about?'

Vivien frowned. This was not going to be easy, but it had to be done. 'Well, for one thing…did you know Gavin was in love with Becky?'

Ross straightened, his face showing true shock. 'Good God, he isn't, is he?'

She nodded slowly.

'Who told you that? It couldn't have been Dad!'

'No. Helga.'

He groaned, his shoulders sagging. 'Bloody hell. Poor Gavin…'

'Helga also says Becky doesn't really love you. She says the girl has always coveted Mountainview.'

Ross's eyes jerked up, angry this time. 'Damn and blast, what is this? You've been in this house less than twenty-four hours and already you know more about what's going on around here than I do. Why hasn't someone told me any of this? Why tell you? What do you have that I don't have?'

She looked past his anger, fully understanding his resentment. 'Objectivity, perhaps?' she tried ruefully.

'Objectivity?' His lips curled into a snarl. 'Oh, yes, you've got that all right, haven't you?'

She wasn't quite sure what he meant by that. Maybe he didn't mean anything. Maybe he just felt the need to lash out blindly. 'Ross, I…I'm really sorry.'

'For what?'

'For being the one to tell you that the woman you're in love with doesn't love you back.'

He stared at her, his blue eyes icy with bitterness. 'You don't have to be sorry about that, Vivien,' he bit out coldly. 'Because I already knew that. I've known it all along.'

'But...but—'

'You of all people should know that love is not always returned. But that doesn't stop you from loving that person, does it? Aren't you still in love with your Earl?'

'I...I'm not sure...'

'Real love doesn't cease as quickly as that, my dear,' he scorned. 'You either loved the man or you didn't. What was it?'

'I *did* love him,' she insisted, hating the feeling of being backed into a corner. But if he expected her to admit to not loving a man she'd lived with for nearly eighteen months then he was heartily mistaken. Yet even as she made the claim she knew it to be a lie. She had not loved Earl. Not really.

'Then you still do,' he insisted fiercely. 'Believe me. You still do. Now I must go and talk to my father. If what you say is all true then I have no time to waste. Things have to be done before it's too late.'

'Too late for what? What things?'

His returning look was cool. 'That is not your concern. You've done your objective duty. Now I suggest you go and have some lunch, then do what pregnant ladies do on a hot afternoon. Lie down and rest. Or, if that doesn't appeal, read one of these books. I'm sure there's enough of a selection here to satisfy the most catholic of tastes.'

'Ross!' she called out as he went to leave.

He turned slowly, his face hard.

'Please…don't be angry with me…'

The steely set to his mouth softened. He sighed. 'I'm not. Not really…'

'You…you seem to be.'

The slightest of smiles touched his mouth, but not his eyes. 'It's fate I'm angry with, Vivien. Fate…'

'Now you're being cryptic.'

'Am I? Yes, possibly I am. Let's say then that I'm angry with what I have no control over.'

'But you're not angry with me personally.'

'No.'

'Then will you show me around the house later, after you're finished with your father?'

He stared at her for a moment, his eyes searching. 'It will be my pleasure,' he said with a somewhat stiff little bow.

'I…I'll probably be here,' she said. 'I don't want any lunch. Oh, that reminds me. Your father said to tell you he didn't want any lunch either.'

A dry smile pulled at Ross's mouth. 'Helga *will* be pleased.' And, giving her one last incisive and rather disturbing glance, he turned and left the room.

Vivien stared after him, aware that her heart was pounding. Already, she was looking forward to his return, knowing full well that it wasn't the thought of a tour through this house that was exciting her. It was the prospect of being alone again with Ross.

A shiver ran through her. Oh, Oliver…you are a wicked, wicked man.

Ross returned shortly after two to find Vivien curled up in one of the large lounge chairs, trying valiantly to read a copy of *Penmarric*. The book was probably as good as everyone had told her it was, but she just hadn't been able to keep her mind on it.

Once the reason for this walked into the room she abandoned all pretence at finding the book engrossing, snapping it shut with an almost relieved sigh.

'Finished your business?' she said, and uncurled her long legs.

'For now. Come on, if you want to see the house.'

His tone was clipped, his expression harried. Clearly, his visit to his father had not been a pleasant one. Vivien wished she could ask him what it was all about, but Ross's closed face forbade any such quizzing. Instead, she put the book back and went to join him in the doorway, determined to act as naturally as possible.

But her resolve to ignore the physical effect Ross kept having on her was waylaid when he moved left just as she moved right and they collided midstream. His hands automatically grabbed her shoulders and suddenly there they were, chest to chest, thigh to thigh, looking into each other's eyes.

Vivien gave a nervous laugh. 'Sorry.'

Ross said absolutely nothing. But there was no doubting he was as agitated by her closeness as she was by his. After what felt like an interminable delay, his hands dropped from her shoulders and he stepped back. 'After you,' he said with a deep wave of his right hand and a self-mocking look on his face. See? it said. I'm a man of my word. I'm keeping my hands off.

But did Vivien want him to keep his hands off? So much had changed now. Becky didn't love him, and, while Ross might think he loved her, there was no doubting he was still very attracted to *herself*. And what of her own feelings for Ross? Had they changed too? Deepened, maybe?

She couldn't be sure, certainly not with the chemistry between them still sparking away at a million volts. Vivien would just have to wait a while longer to find out about her feelings. That was what her mother had told her to do. Wait.

'Oh, my God, *Mum*!' she gasped aloud.

Ross looked taken aback. 'What about her?'

'I forgot to ring her, let her know we arrived all right. She'll be worried to death, and so will Dad.'

'Worried?' His smile carried a wry amusement. 'About their highly independent, very sensible, grown-up girl?'

'Who happens to be on her way to being an unmarried mother,' was her droll return. 'That's really surpassing myself in common sense, isn't it? Now point me to a telephone, Ross, or you'll have my mother on your doorstep.'

'There's an extension in the foyer, underneath the stairs.'

Unfortunately, Ross sat on those stairs while she dialled the number, making her feel self-conscious about what she was going to say. The phone at the other end only rang once before it was swept up.

'Peggy Roberts here,' her mother answered in a breathless tone.

'Mum, it's Vivien.'

'Oh, Vivien, darling! I'm so glad you rang. I've been rather worried.'

'No need, Mum. I'm fine. Sorry I didn't ring sooner, but by the time we arrived last night I was so tired I went straight to bed and slept in atrociously late this morning. Then Ross wanted me to meet his father and we talked for simply ages.'

'Oh? And how is Mr Everton senior? Getting better, I hope.'

'Well, he—er—reminded me a little of Uncle Jack a few weeks after his stroke.'

'You mean just before he died?'

'Er—yes…'

'Oh, dear. Oh, how sad. Well, be nice to him, dear. And be nice to Ross. He's a sweet man, not at all what your father and I were expecting. We were very impressed with him.'

'So I noticed.'

'You don't think that you and he—er—might…' She left the words hanging. *Get married*?

Vivien knew what would happen if she even hinted marriage was vaguely possible. She'd never hear the end of it. Yet her mother's even asking the question sent an odd little leap to her heart. Who knew? If Becky didn't love Ross, there might be a chance. *If* she fell in love with him, and *if* he did with her.

That was a lot of ifs.

'Not at this stage, Mum.'

'Oh…' Disappointment in her voice.

'Give Dad my love and tell him not to worry about me. I know he worries.'

'We both do, dear. Do you know how long you'll be staying out there?' Now her voice was wistful.

'Can't say. I'll write. Tell you all about the place. Must fly. I don't like to stay on someone else's phone too long.'

'I'll write to you too.'

'Yes, please do. Bye, Mum. Keep well.'

'Bye, darling. Thanks for ringing.'

Swallowing, she replaced the receiver and walked round to the foot of the stairs. Ross was sitting a half-dozen steps up, looking rather like a lost little boy. Suddenly, Vivien thought of *his* mother. What had she been like? Did he still miss her? She knew she would die if anything happened to her mother. Much as Peggy sometimes interfered and fussed, Vivien always knew the interference and fuss was based on the deepest of loves, that of a mother for her child.

Automatically, she thought of her own baby, and a soft smile lit her face. For the first time, she felt really positive about her decision to have Ross's baby. No matter what happened, that part was right. Very right indeed.

'You look very pleased with yourself,' he remarked as he stood up. 'Anything I should know about?'

'No,' she said airily. 'Not really. Mum's fine. Dad's fine. Everything's fine.'

His eyes narrowed suspiciously. 'You look like the cat who's discovered a bowl of cream.'

Her laugh was light and carefree. 'Do I?'

'You also look incredibly beautiful…'

Her eyes widened when he started walking down the stairs towards her. Perhaps he interpreted her reaction for alarm for his expression quickly changed to one of exasperation. 'No need to panic, Vivien. I'm not about to pounce. I was merely stating a fact. You know, you look somewhat like my mother when she was young. No wonder Dad took to you.'

Vivien did her best to cool the rapid heating Ross's compliments had brought to her blood, concentrating instead on the opening he'd just given her. 'How odd,' she commented. 'I was just thinking about your mother, wondering what she was like.'

'Were you? That *is* odd. What made you think of her?'

'You wouldn't want to know,' she chuckled.

'Wouldn't I?'

'No,' she said firmly, and, linking her arm with his, turned him to face across the foyer. 'So come on, show me your house and tell me about your mother.'

Ross stared down at her for a second before moving. 'To what do I owe this new Vivien?' he asked warily.

'This isn't a new Vivien. This is the real me.'

'Which is?'

She grinned. 'Charming. Witty. Warm.'

'What happened to stubborn, infuriating and uncooperative?'

'I left them in Sydney.'

'You could have fooled me.'

'Apparently I have.'

'Vivien, I—'

'Oh, do stop being so serious for once, Ross,' she cut in impatiently. 'Life's too short for eternal pessimism.'

'It's also too short for naïve optimism,' he muttered.

His dark mood refused to lift, especially when he saw Vivien's reaction to the house. But she found it difficult to pretend real liking for the place. She favoured open, airy homes with lots of light and glass and modern furniture, not dark rooms surrounded by busy wallpaper and crammed to the rafters with heavy antiques. Still, she could see why a person of another mind might covet the place. It had to be worth heaps.

'You definitely do not like this house,' Ross announced as they traipsed upstairs.

'Well, it's not exactly my taste,' Vivien admitted at last. 'Sorry.'

'You don't have to apologise.'

'I like the upstairs better. There's more natural light in the rooms.'

The floor plan was simpler too, all the rooms coming off the central gallery and all opening out on to the upstairs veranda. There were ten bedrooms, five with matching *en suites* and five without. Any guests using the latter shared the two general bathrooms, Ross informed her. Finally, Vivien was shown the upstairs linen-room, which was larger than her mother's bedroom back home.

'My mother,' Ross explained, 'had an obsession for beautiful towels and sheets.'

Vivien could only agree as her disbelieving eyes encompassed the amount of Manchester goods on the built-in shelves. There was enough to stock a whole section in a department store.

'To tell the truth,' he went on, 'I don't think Mum liked this house any more than you do. Or maybe it was the land she didn't like. She was city, just like you.'

'Really?'

'Yes, really. Well, that's about it, Vivien,' he said as he ushered her out of the linen-room and locked the door. 'I must leave you now. I have to check on Gavin's progress with the bores. Perhaps you should have a rest this afternoon. You're looking hot. Dinner is at seven-thirty when we have visitors, and, while not formal, women usually wear a dress. I dare say I'll see you then. *Au revoir…*' And, tipping his forehead, he turned and strode away, his abrupt departure leaving her feeling empty and quite desolate.

Vivien shook her head, wishing she could come to grips with what she felt for this man. Was it still just sex? Or had it finally become more complicated than that?

There was one way to find out, came the insidious temptation. Let him make love to you again. See if the fires can be burn out. See if there is anything else left after the night is over...

Vivien trembled. Did she have the courage to undertake such a daring experiment. Did she?

Yes, she decided with unexpected boldness, a shudder of sheer excitement reverberating through her. Yes. She did!

But no sooner had the scandalous decision been made than the doubts and fears crowded in.

What if she made a fool of herself? What if her second time with Ross proved to be an anticlimax? What if—oh, lord, was it possible?—what if Ross *rejected* her?

No, she dismissed immediately. He wouldn't do that. Not if she offered herself to him on a silver platter. He'd admitted once he'd found her sexually irresistible. He wouldn't knock back a night of free, uncomplicated loving in her bed.

And that was what she was going to offer him.

There were to be no strings attached. No demands. No extracted promises. Just a night of sex.

Vivien shuddered with distaste. How awful that sounded. How...cheap.

Yet she was determined not to go back on her decision, however much her conscience balked at the crude reality of it. Life was full of crude realities, she decided with some bitterness. Earl had been one big crude reality. He'd made her face the fact that sex and love did not always go together. Now Vivien was determined to find out if her feelings for Ross were no more than what Earl had felt for her, or whether they had deepened to something potentially more lasting.

Maybe she wouldn't have been so desperate to find out if she weren't expecting Ross's baby. But she was, and, if there was some chance of having a real relationship with her baby's father, one that could lead to marriage, then she was going to go for it, all guns blazing. Married parents were a darned sight better for a baby's upbringing than two single ones.

Thinking about her baby's welfare gave Vivien the inner strength to push any lingering scruples aside. For the first time in weeks, she felt as if she was taking control of her life, making her own decisions for the future. And it felt good. Surprisingly good. She hadn't realised how much of her self-confidence had been undermined by what Earl had done to her. Losing her job hadn't helped either.

So it was with an iron determination that Vivien returned to her bedroom and set to pondering how one successfully seduced a man.

The practicalities of it weren't as easy as one might have imagined. She'd never had to seduce a man in her life before. Earl had made the first move. So had Ross. Neither was she a natural flirt, except when intoxicated.

Was that the solution? she wondered. Could she perhaps have a few surreptitious drinks beforehand?

It was a thought. She would certainly keep it in mind if she felt her courage failing her.

Of course, if she dressed appropriately, maybe Ross would once again make the first move. Vivien hoped that would be the case. Now what could she wear that would turn Ross on? Something sexy, but subtle. She didn't want to look as if there was a banner on her body which read: 'Here I am, handsome. Do your stuff!'

Vivien wasn't too sure what clothes she'd brought with her. Her mother had packed most of her clothes. And Helga had unpacked them. But she was pretty sure she'd spotted her favourite black dress in there somewhere when she'd rooted around for her toiletries.

Vivien walked over and threw open the wardrobe. First she would find something to wear, then she would have a bubble bath in one of the main bathrooms and then a lie-down. She didn't want to look tired. She wanted to be as beautiful as she could be. Beautiful and desirable and *simply irresistible*.

Vivien walked slowly down the huge semi-circular staircase shortly before seven-thirty, knowing she couldn't look more enticing. The polyester-crêpe dress she was wearing was one of those little black creations that looked simple and stylish, but was very seductive.

Halter-necked, it had a bare back and shoulders, a V neckline that hinted at rather than showed too much cleavage, and a line that skimmed rather than hugged the body. With her hair piled up on to her head in studied disarray, long, dangling gold earrings at her lobes and a bucket of Loulou wafting from her skin, a man would have had to have all his senses on hold not to find her ultra-feminine and desirable.

As Vivien put her sexily shod foot down on to the

black and white tiled foyer a male voice called out to her from the gallery above.

'Wait on!'

Nerves tightened her stomach as she turned to watch Ross come down the stairs, looking very Magnumish in white trousers and a Hawaiian shirt in a red and white print. It crossed Vivien's mind incongruously that Earl would not have been seen dead in anything but a business suit.

'Don't tell me,' she said with a tinkling laugh— one she'd heard used to advantage by various vamps on television. 'You've been to Waikiki recently.'

He gave her a sharp look. Had she overdone the laugh?

'No,' he denied drily. 'This is pure Hamilton Island.'

He took the remaining few steps that separated them, icy blue eyes raking over her. 'And what is that sweet little number you've got on?' he drawled. 'Pure King's Cross?'

Vivien felt colour flood her cheeks. Had she overdone *everything*? Surely she didn't really look like a whore?

No, of course she didn't. Ross was simply being nasty for some reason. Perhaps he'd been brooding about Becky and Gavin. Or perhaps, she ventured to guess, he resented her looking sexy when he was supposed to keep his hands off.

Some instinctive feminine intuition told her this last guess was close to the mark.

Knowing any blush was well covered by her dramatic make-up, she cocked her head slightly to one side and slanted him a saucy look. 'Been to the Cross, have you?'

'Not lately,' he bit out, jaw obviously clenched.

'Perhaps it's time for a return visit,' she laughed. 'You seem…tense.'

Vivien was startled when Ross's right hand shot out to grip her upper arm, yanking her close to him. 'What in hell's got into you tonight?' he hissed.

It was an effort to remain composed when one's heart was pounding away like a jackhammer.

'Why does something have to have got into me?' she returned with superb nonchalance. 'I felt like dressing up a bit, that's all. I'm sorry you don't like the way I look, but I won't lose any sleep over it. Now unhand me, please. I don't take kindly to macho displays of male domination. They always bring out the worst in me.'

Yes, she added with silent darkness. Like they make me want to strip off all my clothes and beg you to take me on these stairs right here and now!

'Sorry,' he muttered, and released her arm. 'I…did I hurt you?'

'I dare say I'll have some bruises in the morning. I have very delicate skin.'

'So I've noticed,' he ground out, his eyes igniting to hot coals as they moved up over her bare shoulders and down the tantalising neckline.

Vivien didn't know whether to feel pleased or alarmed by the evidence of Ross's obvious though sneering admiration. There was something about him tonight that was quite frightening, as though he were balancing on a razor's edge that was only partly due to male frustration. There were other devils at work within his soul. She suspected that it wouldn't take much to tip him into violence.

'Did Gavin check all the bores?' she asked, deliberately deflecting the conversation away from her appearance and giving herself a little time to rethink the situation. Suddenly, the course of action she'd set herself upon this night seemed fraught with danger. She wanted Ross to make love to her, not assault her.

'Yes,' was his uninformative and very curt answer. He glanced at the watch on his wrist. Gold, with a brown leather band, it looked very expensive. 'Helga gets annoyed when we're late for dinner,' he pronounced. 'I think we'd better make tracks for the dining-room.'

Vivien would never have dreamt she would feel grateful for Helga's army-like sense of punctuality.

Dinner still proved a difficult meal for all concerned. Gavin, who, unlike his brother, was dressed shoddily in faded jeans and black T-shirt, was sulkily silent. This seemed to make Helga agitated and stroppy. She kept insisting everyone have seconds whether they wanted them or not.

By the time dessert came—enormous portions of plum pudding and ice-cream—Vivien's stomach was protesting. Ross, in the end, made a tactless though accurate comment to Helga about her always giving people too much to eat. Vivien managed to soothe the well-intentioned though misguided woman by saying she would normally be able to eat everything, but that her condition seemed to have affected her appetite.

At this allusion to her pregnancy, Gavin made a contemptuous sound, stood up, and stomped out of the room, having not said a word to Vivien all evening other than a grumpy hello when she and Ross had first walked into the dining-room. Shortly, they heard his station wagon start up, the gravel screeching as he roared off.

'I…I'm sorry, lovie,' Helga apologised for Gavin. 'He's not himself at the moment.'

Vivien smiled gently. 'It's all right. I understand. He's upset.'

'He's not the only one who's upset,' Ross grated out. 'I'm damned upset that people around here chose not to tell me that my own brother was in love with the girl I was going to marry.'

He glowered at Helga, who stood up with an uncompromising look on her face. 'The boy made me promise not to tell you.'

'Then why didn't he tell me himself?'

'Don't be ridiculous!' Helga snapped. 'The boy has *some* pride.'

'Haven't we all,' he muttered darkly. 'Haven't we all…'

'Anyone for tea?' Helga asked brusquely.

'Not me,' Ross returned. 'I think I'll have some port in the library instead.'

He'd asked earlier—and with some dry cynicism, Vivien had noted—if she wanted some wine with her dinner. Vivien had politely declined, whereby Ross had still opened a bottle of claret, though he'd only drunk a couple of glasses. Gavin had polished off the rest.

'What about you, lovie?'

'Er—no, thanks, Helga.' She looked over at Ross, unsure of what to do. Swallowing, she made her decision. 'I might join Ross for some port after we've cleared up,' she said in a rush.

Ross's eyes snapped round to frown at her.

'If…if that's all right with you,' she added, battling to remain calm in the face of his penetrating stare.

He lifted a single sardonic eyebrow. 'I didn't think you liked port.'

'I do occasionally.'

Actually, she *did*, though she'd only ever indulged in small quantities before. Earl had always insisted she pretend to drink at their dinner parties, saying people hated teetotallers. She'd usually managed to tip most of her wine down the sink at intervals, but she'd often allowed herself the luxury of a few sips of Earl's vintage port at the end of the evening. It seemed to relax her after the tension of cooking and serving a meal that lived up to Earl's standards.

Vivien considered she could do with some relaxing at this point in time, while she made up her mind what she was going to do. Quite clearly, Ross wasn't going to make any move towards her. Any momentary interest on the staircase appeared to have waned. He'd barely looked at her during dinner.

'I'll see you shortly, then,' Ross said, leaving the room without a backward glance.

Vivien stood up to help Helga clear the table and then wash up. They had it all finished in ten minutes flat. Never had Vivien seen anyone wash up like Helga!

'Off you go now, lovie,' the other woman said, taking the tea-towel from Vivien's hands. 'But watch yourself. Ross is stirring for a fight tonight. I've seen him like this before. He can't stand not having what he wants, or not having things go his way. Oh, he's got a good heart but he's a mighty stubborn boy. Mighty stubborn, indeed!'

Vivien was still thinking about Helga's warning when she opened the library door. So she was startled to see Ross looking totally relaxed in the large armchair she'd been sitting in earlier in the day, his feet outstretched and crossed at the ankles, a hefty glass of port cradled in his hands.

'Close the door,' he said in a soft, almost silky voice. For some reason, it brought goosebumps up on the back of her neck.

She closed the door.

'Now lock it,' he added.

She spun round, eyes blinking wide. 'Lock it? But why?'

His gaze became cold and hard. 'Because I don't like to be interrupted when I'm having sex.'

CHAPTER TWELVE

VIVIEN froze. 'I beg your pardon?'

'You heard me, Vivien. Now just lock the door and stop pretending that your sensibilities are offended. You and I both know why you dressed like that tonight. You're feeling frustrated and you've decided once again to make use of yours truly. At least, I imagine it's me you've set your cap at. I'm the one who looks like your old boyfriend, not Gavin. Or are you going to tell me you've reverted to the tease I mistook you for that night at the ball?'

Vivien's first instinct was to flee Ross's cutting contempt. For it hurt. It hurt a lot. How could she not have realised her strategy could backfire on her so badly?

But she had faced many difficult foes during her television career. Belligerent businessmen...two-faced politicians...oily con men. She was not about to let Ross's verbal attack rout her completely, though she *was* badly shaken.

'You...you've got it all wrong, Ross,' she began with as much casual confidence as she could muster.

'In what way, Vivien?'

God, but she hated that cold, cynical light in his eyes, hated the silky derision in his voice.

'I...I did try to look extra attractive tonight, but I—'

His hard, humourless laugh cut her off. '"*Extra attractive*"? Is that how you would describe yourself tonight?' With another laugh, he uncurled his tall frame from the chair to begin moving slowly across the room like a panther stalking its prey, depositing his glass of port on a side-table on the way. Nerves and a kind of hypnotic fascination kept her silent and still while he approached. What on earth was he going to do?

Finally, he stood in front of her, tension in every line of his body.

'The dress could almost have been an unconscious mistake,' he said, smiling nastily. 'Despite the lack of underwear under it. But *not* when combined with those other wicked little touches. The hair, looking as if you'd just tumbled from a lover's bed...'

When he reached out to pull a few more tendrils around her face, she just stood there, as though paralysed.

'The earrings,' he went on, 'designed to draw attention to the sheer, exquisite delicacy of your lovely neck...'

Her mouth went dry when he trickled fingers menacingly around the base of her throat.

'The scarlet lipstick on your oh, so sexy mouth...'

Vivien almost moaned when he ran a fingertip around her softly parted lips. She squeezed her eyes tightly shut, appalled that he could make her feel like this when his touch was meant to be insulting.

But at least she was finding out the bitter truth, wasn't she? This couldn't be love—or the beginnings of love. This was raw, unadulterated sex, lust in its worst form, making her want him even while he showed his contempt. His own feelings for her were apparently similar, since he quite clearly hated wanting her nearly as much.

'Close your eyes if you like,' he jeered softly. 'I don't mind. I've already accepted I'm to be just a proxy lover. But believe me, I'm going to enjoy you anyway.'

Her eyes flew open in angry defiance of his presumption.

'You keep away from me. I don't want you touching me!'

His answering laugh was so dark that she shrank back against the door, one hand searching blindly for the knob.

'Oh, no, you don't,' he ground out, turning the key in the lock and pocketing it before she had a hope of escaping. 'And don't bother to scream. This room is virtually sound-proof, not to mention a hell of a long way from the servants' quarters.'

She froze when he coolly reached out to undo the button at the nape of her neck, then peeled the dress down to the waist. When he ran the back of his hand across her bared breasts her head whirled with a dizzying wave of unbidden pleasure and excitement. She didn't have to look down to know that her nipples had peaked hard with instant arousal.

'Bitch,' he rasped, before suddenly pulling her to him, *crushing* her to him, his head dipping to trail a hot mouth over her shoulders and up her throat. Vivien began to tremble uncontrollably.

She moaned when he finally kissed her, knowing that there was no stopping him now, even if she wanted to.

And she *did* want to stop him. That was the irony of it all. But only with her brain. Her body, she had already found out once with Ross, could not combat the feelings he could evoke in her, the utterly mind-less passion and need.

'No,' she managed once, when he abandoned her mouth briefly to kiss her throat again.

'Shut up,' was his harsh reply before taking pos-session of her lips again.

She felt his hands around her waist, then pushing the dress down over her hips. It pooled around her ankles with a silky whoosh. Now only a wisp of black satin and lace prevented her from being totally naked before him. It would have been a humiliating thought, if Vivien had been able to think. As it was she found herself winding her arms up around his neck and kiss-ing him back with the kind of desperation no man could misunderstand. Her naked breasts were pressed flat against his chest, her hips moulded to his, her abdomen undulating against his escalating arousal with primitive force.

Ross groaned under the onslaught of her frantic desire, hoisting her up on to his hips and carrying her across the room, where he lay her back across the large cedar desk in the corner. The cool hardness of its smoothly polished surface brought a gasp of shock from Vivien, almost returning her to reality for a mo-ment. But Ross didn't allow her mad passion any peace. His hands on her outstretched body kept her arousal at fever pitch till she was beside herself with wanting him.

His name fluttered from her lips on a ragged moan of desire and need.

'Yes, that's right,' he grated back with a satanic laugh while he removed the last items of clothing from her quivering body—her panties and her shoes. 'It's Ross. Not Earl. *Ross!*'

Vivien dimly reacted to his angry assertion, wondering fleetingly if he had been more deeply hurt over that Earl business than she'd imagined. But once he had access to her whole body, to that part of her that was melting for him, she forgot everything but losing herself in that erotic world of unbelievable pleasure Ross could create with his hands and lips.

'Yes...oh, yes,' she groaned when his mouth moved intimately over her heated flesh. She groaned even more when he suddenly stopped, glazed eyes flying to his.

'Say that you love me,' he demanded hoarsely as he stripped off his trousers.

A wild confusion raced through Vivien. Dazedly, she saw him smiling down at her, felt his flesh teasing hers. She didn't recognise the smile for the grimace of self-mockery it really was. All Vivien knew was that, quite unexpectedly, a raw emotion filled her heart with his demand, an emotion that both stunned and thrilled her.

'Go on,' he urged, his hands curving round her buttocks to pull her closer to the edge. And him. 'You don't have to mean it. Just say it!'

'I love you,' she whispered huskily and felt the emotion swell within her chest. The words came then, ringing with passion and truth. 'I really, truly love you, Ross.'

His groan was a groan of sheer torture. Quite abruptly, he thrust deeply into her. Vivien felt the emotion spill over into every corner of her body, felt it charging into every nerve-ending, sharpening them, electrifying them. She cried out, at the same time reaching out her arms to gather Ross close, to hold him next to her heart.

For she *did* really, truly love him. She could see it now, see it so clearly. She'd once believed Earl the real thing, and Ross just an illusion. But she had got it the wrong way round. Earl had been the illusion, Ross the real thing. He must have fallen in love with her too, to demand such a reassurance.

So she was startled when he took her hands in an iron grip, pressing them down over the edges of the desk while he set up an oddly controlled rhythm. It was only then that she saw the ugly lines in his contorted face.

Cold, hard reality swept into her heart like a winter wind. Ross was not making love to her. He was making hate, having a kind of revenge. That was why he'd demanded she tell him she loved him. It had been nothing but a cruel parody of what she had begged of him that first night.

'Oh, God…no,' she cried out in an anguished dismay, lifting her head immediately in a valiant but futile struggle to rid herself of his flesh.

'Oh, God…yes,' he bit out and kept up his relentless surging. '*Yes!*'

She moaned in despair when she felt her body betray her, felt that excruciating tightening before her flesh shattered apart into a thousand convulsing, quivering parts. Crushingly, her climax seemed to be even more intense than anything she could remember of that night at Wallaby Creek. She almost wept with the perverse pleasure of it all, but then she felt Ross's hands tightening around hers, and he too was climaxing.

She cringed even more under his violently shuddering body. He despised her and yet he was finding the ultimate satisfaction in her body. It seemed the epitome of shame, the supreme mockery of what this act should represent.

Tears of bitter misery flooded her eyes and she began to sob.

Ross's eyes jerked up to hers as though she had struck him. When he scooped her up to hold her hard against him, his body still blended to hers, she wanted to fight him. But every muscle and bone in her body had turned to mush.

'Leave me...be,' she sobbed. 'I...I *hate* you!'

'And I hate you,' he rasped, while keeping her weeping face cradled against his shirt-front. 'Hush, now. Stop crying. You're all right. It's just a reaction to your orgasm. It was too intense. Relax, honey. Relax...'

Vivien was amazed to find herself actually calming down under the soothing way he was stroking her back. When he moved over to sit down in the huge armchair, taking her with him, she didn't even object. Her legs were easily accommodated on either side on him, the deep cushioning allowing her knees and body to sink into a blissfully comfortable position.

Vivien even felt like going to sleep, which shocked her. She should be fighting him, hitting him, telling him he was a wicked, cruel man for doing what he had just done to her. She certainly shouldn't let him go on thinking that her pleasure had been nothing but sexual, that her crying was merely an emotional reaction to a heightened physical experience.

'You're not going to sleep, are you?' he whispered, his stroking hands coming to rest rather provocatively on her buttocks.

'No. Not quite.'

God, was that her voice? When had she ever talked in such low, husky, sexy tones?

'Tell me, Vivien,' he said thickly, 'was *any* of that for me, or is it still all for Earl?'

Vivien flinched, remembering how she'd momentarily thought during Ross's torrid lovemaking that his resemblance to her ex-lover had affected him deeply. He certainly did keep harping on it. Why care, if it was just vengeful sex he was after? If that were the case it shouldn't matter to him whom she was thinking about.

Vivien's heart leapt. If Ross wanted her to want him for himself, and not for his likeness to Earl, then that could only be because his feelings for her were deeper than just lust. He might not realise that himself yet—she could understand his confusion with Becky still in his heart—but one day soon...

First, however, she had to convince him that Earl was dead and gone as far as she was concerned, then that might open the way to Ross letting his feelings for her rise to the surface.

She lifted heavy eyelids to look up into his face, that face which, though so like Earl's, feature for feature, no longer reminded her at all of the man who'd treated her so badly.

Her hand reached up to lie against his cheek. 'What a foolish man you are, Ross Everton,' she said tenderly. 'You are so different from Earl in so many ways. When I look at you now, I see no one else but you. It was you I was wanting today, you I dressed for tonight, you I wanted to make love to me. Not Earl...' And, stretching upwards, she pressed gentle lips to his mouth, kissing him with all the love in her heart.

He groaned, his hands lifting to cup her face, to hold it captive while he deepened her kiss into an expression of rapidly renewing desire and need. When Vivien became hotly aware of more stirring evidence of that renewing desire, her inside contracted instinctively, gripping his growing hardness with such intensity that Ross tore his mouth away from hers on a gasping groan.

'Did…did I hurt you?' she asked breathlessly, her own arousal having revved her pulse-rate up a few notches.

He laughed. 'I wouldn't put it quite like that. But perhaps you should do it again, just so I can make sure.' And, gripping her buttocks, he moved her in a slow up-and-down motion, encouraging her internal muscles to several repeat performances.

'No.' He grimaced wryly. 'That definitely does not hurt.' He stopped moving her to slide his hands up over her ribs till they found her breasts.

'Lean back,' he rasped. 'Grip the armrests.'

She did so, her heart pounding frantically as he began to play with her outstretched body, first her breasts, then her ribs and stomach, and finally between her thighs, touching her most sensitive part till she was squirming with pleasure. He seemed to like her writhing movements too, his breathing far more ragged than her own.

'Oh, yes, honey, yes,' he moaned when she started lifting her bottom up and down again, squeezing and releasing him in a wild rhythm of uninhibited loving. 'Keep going,' he urged. 'Don't stop…'

After it was all over, and they were spent once more, they did sleep, briefly, only to wake to the sound of thunder rocking the house.

'A storm,' Vivien whispered, and shivered.

'Just electrical, I suspect. There's no rain predicted. You don't like thunder?' he asked when she shivered again.

'I'm just cold.'

He held her closer if that was possible, wrapping his arms tightly around her. 'Want to go up to bed?'

'Uh-huh.'

'I'll carry you upstairs.'

'You can't carry me out of the room like this!' she exclaimed in a shocked tone.

'Why not? No one's likely to see us. Dad's sleeping-pill will have worked by now and Helga will be busily knitting in front of the television. As for Gavin...he's playing cards and drowning his sorrows with the boys down in the shearing shed. Won't be back till the wee small hours.'

'You're sure we won't run into anyone?'

'Positive.'

'If we do, I'll die of embarrassment.'

'Me too. I haven't got any trousers on, remember?'

They didn't run into anyone, despite Vivien giggling madly all the way up the stairs. They both collapsed into a shower together in Ross's *en suite*, which revived them enough to start making love all over again. This time, it was slow and erotic and infinitely more loving, the touching and kissing lasting for an hour before Ross moved over and into her. They looked deep into each other's eyes as the pleasure built and built, Ross bending to kiss her gasping mouth when she cried out in release, only then allowing himself to let go.

Vivien lay happily in his sleeping arms afterwards,

feeling more at peace with herself than she had ever felt.

So this was what really being in love was like. She smiled softly to herself in the dark, pressing loving lips to the side of Ross's chest.

'And I think you love me too,' she whispered softly. 'You just don't know it yet…'

CHAPTER THIRTEEN

THREE days rolled by and Vivien was blissfully happy. Ross was sweet to her during the day, and madly passionate every night. With each passing day she became more and more convinced that he loved her, despite his never saying so. Her own love for him was also growing stronger as she discovered more about him.

Helga had been right when she'd said they had similar personalities. They also had similar likes and dislikes in regard to just about everything. They were both mad about travel and Tennessee Williams's plays and the Beatles and playing cards, especially Five Hundred. It was uncanny. With Earl, she had had to pretend to like what he liked, just to keep him happy. With Ross, there was no pretending. Ever. She'd never felt so at one with a person.

There was another matter that did wonders for her humour as well. She didn't have morning sickness any more. How wonderful it was to be able to wake and not have to run to the bathroom! Her appetite improved considerably once her stomach was more settled, which was just as well since Helga had decided she needed 'building up'.

Yes, Vivien couldn't have been happier. Even Oliver seemed a little better, though he still tired quickly. The couple of hours she sat with him each morning and afternoon were mostly spent with her reading aloud while he relaxed in his favourite armchair. Occasionally they watched a video which Ross brought out from town.

The only fly in the ointment was Gavin, who remained as sour and uncommunicative as ever. He'd hardly spoken a dozen words to Vivien since her arrival, but she refused to let his mood upset her new-found happiness.

He was only young, she reasoned. He would get over his love for this Becky girl, as Ross was obviously getting over his. Every now and then, Vivien found herself puzzling over exactly what sort of girl this Becky Macintosh was to command such devotion.

She found out on New Year's Eve.

Vivien had just finished her morning visit with Oliver. Ross and Gavin were out mending fences. She and Helga were sitting in the kitchen having a mug of tea together when suddenly they heard a screeching of brakes on the gravel driveway. Before they could do more than raise their eyebrows, a slender female figure in pale blue jeans and a blue checked shirt came racing into the kitchen, her long, straight blonde hair flying out behind.

'Where's Ross?' she demanded breathlessly of Helga.

'Down in the south paddocks, mending fences. What is it, Becky? What's happened?'

'There was a small grass fire on the other side of the river. Dad and I put it out, but not before the wind picked up and a few sparks jumped the river. Now the fire's growing again and heading straight for our best breeding sheep. I've rung the emergency bush-fire brigade number, but apparently all of the trucks are attending two other scrub fires. They said they'd send a few men along in a helicopter, one of those that can water-bomb the fire. The trouble is the only pilot available is a real rookie. I thought Ross might be able to help.'

'I'll contact him straight away,' Helga said briskly. 'They have a two-way radio with them. I won't be a moment. The gizmo's in the study. I'll send them straight over to your place.'

'Thanks, Helga, I'd better get back. Mum's in a panic. Not that the fire's anywhere near the house. But you know what she's like.'

'Can I help in any way?' Vivien offered. 'Maybe I could stay with your mother while you do what you have to do.'

Vivien found herself on the end of a long look from the loveliest blue eyes. There was no doubt about it. Becky had not been behind the door when God gave out looks. Though not striking, she had a fragile delicacy about her that would bring out the protective instinct in any man. Too bad they never saw the toughness behind those eyes.

'I presume you're Vivien,' she said drily.

Vivien stood up, her shoulders automatically squaring. 'Yes, I am.'

Those big blue eyes flicked over her face and figure before a rueful smile tugged at her pretty mouth. 'If I'd known the sort of competition I had, I would have given up sooner. What odds, I ask myself, of Ross meeting someone like you at that horrid ball? Still, I have more important things to do today than worry over the fickle finger of fate. Yes, you can come and hold Mum's hand. That'll free me to help outside.'

Helga bustled back into the kitchen just in time to be told Vivien was going with Becky. Oddly enough, the older woman didn't seem to think this at all strange. For all her earlier criticisms about the girl's behaviour with Ross, she seemed to like Becky.

It came to Vivien then that there was more worth in this girl than she'd previously believed. That was why Helga wanted her for Gavin—to put some fire in his belly. Becky had a positive attitude and energetic drive Vivien could only admire.

'So when are you and Ross getting married?' Becky enquired while she directed the jeep at a lurching speed down the dusty road that led back to the highway.

'I don't know,' came the truthful answer. 'He— er—hasn't asked me yet.'

Becky slanted a frowning glance her way. 'Hasn't asked you yet? That's odd. When he confessed to me that he'd fallen in love with someone else the night of the ball at Wallaby Creek, and that the girl in question was pregnant by him, I naturally thought you'd be married as quickly as possible.'

Vivien held her silence with great difficulty. Ross had said that? Back *then*? That meant he'd virtually fallen in love with her straight away.

Oh, my God, she groaned silently. My God…

Her heart squeezed tight at the thought of all she had put Ross through that night, especially making him tell her he loved her like that. It also leant an ironic and very heart-wrenching meaning to Ross's statement a few days ago that he had always known the girl he loved didn't love him back, but that didn't stop him loving her. Of course Vivien had thought he meant Becky. But he had meant herself!

Vivien felt like crying. If only she'd known. But, of course, why would he tell her? No man would, certainly not after that day when he'd followed her to Sydney, only to discover that he was the dead-ringer of her previous lover, the man she supposedly still loved. God, it was a wonder his love for her hadn't turned to hate then and there.

Maybe it almost had for a while, she realised, remembering the incident in the library.

But if only he had told her later that night that he loved her, instead of letting her think his feelings were only lust.

And what of you? a reproachful voice whispered. Have you told him you love him? Have you reassured the father of your child that your feelings for him are anything more than just sexual?

She almost cried out in dismay at her own stupidity.

Oh, Ross…darling…I'll tell you as soon as I can, she vowed silently.

'Of course I always knew he wasn't madly in love with me, or I with him,' Becky rattled on. 'But we go back a long way, Ross and I. Gavin too, for that matter. We've always been great mates, the three of us. We love each other, but I think it's been more of a friendship love than anything else To be honest, I wasn't at all desperate to go to bed with Ross. But then…I've never been desperate to go to bed with any man as yet.' She sighed heavily. 'Maybe I will one day, but something tells me I'm not a romantic at heart.'

Vivien only hesitated for a second. After all, nothing ventured, nothing gained. 'Has it ever occurred to you that you might have been looking for passion with the wrong brother?'

The jeep lurched to one side before Becky recovered. She darted Vivien a disbelieving glance. 'You're not serious!'

'Never been more serious. Helga says Gavin's crazy about you. He was simply crushed by your intention to marry Ross.'

'*Really*?'

'Yes, really. He's been as miserable as sin lately because he thinks you're suffering from a broken heart. He blames me and Ross.'

'But…but if he loves me, the stupid man, why hasn't he said so? Why hasn't he *done* something?'

'Too shy.'

'Too *shy*? With *me*? That's ridiculous! Why, we've been skinny dipping together!'

'Not lately, I'll bet.'

'Well, no…'

'Perhaps you should suggest you do so again some time. See what happens.'

Becky looked over at Vivien, blue eyes widening. 'You city girls don't miss a trick, do you? Skinny dipping, eh? Yes, well, I—er—might suggest that some time, but I can't think about Gavin right now. I have a fire to help put out.'

They fell silent as Becky concentrated on her driving. Not a bad idea, Vivien thought, since the girl drove as she no doubt did most things—with a degree of wild recklessness. Or maybe all country people drove like that on the way to a fire. Whatever, Vivien was hanging on to the dashboard for dear life.

Ross and Gavin must have gone across land, picking up Stan and Dave on the way, for all four men arrived at the homestead simultaneously with Becky and Vivien. A plump, fluttery lady raced out to greet them all with hysteria not far away.

'Oh, thank God, thank God,' she kept saying.

'Now, now, Mrs Macintosh,' Ross returned, patting her hand. 'Calm down. The cavalry's here.'

He turned to give Vivien a questioning look, but she merely smiled, hugging to herself the wonderful knowledge of his love for her. Later today, she would tell him of her own love. Not only would she tell him, but she would show him.

'There's the helicopter!' Becky shouted, pointing to the horizon. 'It's a water-bombing helicopter,' she explained to Ross, 'but the pilot's not very experienced. Do you think you might be able to help him?'

'Sure. I haven't exactly done that kind of thing myself before, but it can't be too difficult.'

The dark grey helicopter landed in a cloud of dust, forestalling any further conversation. It was all business. A side-door slid back to reveal several men inside. Stan, Dave and Gavin piled in with them. Ross climbed in next to the pilot, shouting back to Becky to collect some cool drinks and to drive down in the jeep.

Becky didn't look at all impressed at being given such a tame job to do, but in the end she shrugged resignedly. Within minutes of the helicopter taking off, she'd successfully filled two cool boxes with ice and drinks, refusing to let Vivien help her carry them to the jeep.

'You shouldn't be carrying heavy things when you're in the family way,' she was told firmly.

'Where will they get the water from to bomb the fire with?' Vivien asked as Becky climbed in behind the wheel.

'The dam, I guess, though there isn't too much water in it. Maybe the river.'

Vivien frowned. 'But wouldn't that be dangerous? The river's not very wide and there are trees all along the bank.'

'*Dangerous*? For the legendary Ross Everton?' Becky laughed.

'I've heard him called that before, but I don't know what it means.'

'It means, duckie, that you've got yourself hooked to the craziest, most thrilling-seeking chopper cowboy that ever drew breath. Ross prides himself on being able to fly down and hover low enough to open gates by leaning out of the cockpit. He'll heli-muster anything that moves in any kind of country, no matter how rough and wild. Cattle. Brumbies. Buffalo. He's a legend all over the outback for his skill and daring.' She gave Vivien a wry look as she fired the engine. 'Having second thoughts, are we?'

'Of course not!' she returned stalwartly, and waved Becky off.

But a type of fear had gripped her heart. Ross might be very skilled, but hadn't he just admitted he hadn't done this kind of job before? What if he made a mistake? What if the helicopter crashed?

Vivien felt sicker than she ever had with morning sickness. She felt even sicker an hour later while she and Mrs Macintosh stood together on the back veranda of the homestead, from where they had a first-class view of what was going on, both in the far paddocks and in the air. The helicopter had indeed scooped up a couple of loads of water from the dam, but clearly not enough. The grass fire was still growing. Now, the helicopter was being angled around to head for the river. Vivien just knew who it was at the controls.

'Oh, God, no,' she groaned when the machine skimmed the tops of trees in its descent to the narrow strip of water below.

She watched with growing horror when the helicopter dipped dangerously to fill the canvas bag, the rotor blades almost touching the surface of the water before the craft straightened and scooped upwards. 'I can't watch any more,' she muttered under her breath.

But she did, her heart aching inside her constricted chest as she watched Ross make trip after dangerous trip to that river then back to the fire. At last, the flames died, leaving nothing but a cloud of black smoke. Mrs Macintosh turned to hug her when, even from that distance, they heard the men's shouts of triumph.

Vivien couldn't feel total triumph, however. Fear was still gripping her heart. How could she bear Ross doing this kind of thing for a living? How could she cope with the continuous worrying? She wanted the father of her baby around and active when their child grew up. Not dead, or a paraplegic.

Her fears were compounded when the men came back to the house and Ross was laughing—actually laughing!—as the rookie pilot relayed tales of near-missed fences and trees. In the end, she couldn't bear it any more. She walked right up to him and said with a shaking voice, 'You might think that risking your life is funny, but I don't. I've been worried sick all afternoon, and I...I...' Tears flooded her eyes. Her shoulders began to shake.

Ross gathered her against his dusty chest. 'Hush. I'm all right, darling. Don't cry now...' He led her away from the others before tipping her tear-stained face up to him. 'Dare I hope this means what I think it means?'

'Oh, Ross, I love you so much,' she cried. 'I can't bear to think of you risking your life every day. Don't ever go back to doing that helicopter business. Please. I couldn't bear it if you had an accident.'

'I won't have an accident.'

'You don't know that. You're not immortal. Or infallible. No one is. If you love me even a little—'

'A *little*? My God, Vivien, I *adore* you, don't you know that?'

She stared up at him, stunned, despite what Becky had told her. It sounded so much more incredibly wonderful coming from Ross's actual lips. 'You... you've never actually told me,' she choked out. 'Not in words.'

'Well, I'm telling you now. I've loved you since the first moment I set eyes on you, looking at me across that crowded ballroom. You mean the world to me. But you don't understand. I won't have an accident because—'

Mr Macintosh's tapping him on the shoulder interrupted what Ross was going to say.

'Ross...'

Ross turned. 'Yes?'

'Er—Helga just called. I'm sorry, but I have some bad news.'

'Bad news?'

'Yes...your father...'

Vivien closed her eyes as a wave of anguish washed through her, for she knew exactly what the man was going to say. Fresh tears flowed, tears for the man who'd become her friend. More tears for the man she loved. He was going to take this hard.

Mr Macintosh cleared his throat. 'He…he passed away…this afternoon. I'm so sorry, lad.'

Ross's hold tightened around Vivien. Yet when he spoke, his voice sounded calm. Only Vivien could feel him shaking inside. 'It's all right. Dad's dearest wish was that he would die at Mountainview. He…he's probably quite happy.'

Oliver Everton was cremated, in keeping with his wishes, and his ashes sprinkled over the paddocks of his beloved Mountainview. They had a large wake for him at the house, again in keeping with his wishes, and it was towards the end of this wake that Mr Parkinson, Oliver's solicitor, called the main beneficiaries of his will into the study.

Mr Parkinson sat behind the huge walnut desk while Ross and Vivien, Helga and Gavin pulled up chairs. Vivien was perplexed—and a little worried—over what she was doing there. If she was to be a beneficiary, that meant Oliver had changed his will recently. She was suddenly alarmed at what she was about to hear.

'I won't beat about the bush,' Mr Parkinson started. 'It appears that Oliver saw fit to write a new will a couple of days ago without consulting me. Oh, it's all legal and above-board, witnessed by Stan and Dave. Helga had it in her safe keeping…'

Vivien stared at Helga, who kept a dead-pan face.

'But I have to admit that the contents came as a shock to me. I think they might come as a shock to you too, Ross.'

Vivien finally dared to look at Ross, who didn't look at all worried. It crossed her mind then that he knew full well what was in that will. She went cold with apprehension.

'Aside from Ross being left a couple of real estate properties around Sydney and Helga being left a pension trust fund to ensure she won't want for money for the rest of her life, it seems that Oliver has left the bulk of his estate, including the property Mountainview and all it contains, to his second son, Gavin.'

Gavin sat bolt upright in his chair, clearly stunned. 'But that's not fair. Mountainview is worth millions! *Ross*...' He swivelled to throw a distressed look at his brother. 'You must know...I had no hand in this.'

'I know that,' Ross replied equably. 'Dad told me what he was going to do. I fully agreed with his decision.'

Vivien almost gasped at his obvious twisting of the truth. It had been Ross, she realised, who had insisted on the change of will. This was what he had gone to see his father about a few days ago, before it was too late. He knew his father had actually left control of Mountainview to *him*. He had sacrificed his inheritance for love of his brother, for he knew his brother needed it more than he did, in more ways than one.

Gavin was looking even more stunned. 'You *agreed* with my having Mountainview?'

'Yes. I've been made an excellent offer for my fleet of helicopters and the goodwill of my business. I'm going to take it. Believe me, Gavin, I won't be wanting for a bob, if that's what's worrying you. And don't forget about those Sydney properties Dad left me.'

'But they'd be nothing compared to Mountainview!'

'That depends on the point of view. One of them is that penthouse unit at Double Bay Mum inherited. It's hardly worth peanuts. The other is a substantial acreage Dad bought years ago just outside Sydney on the Nepean River. I've always had a dream to set up an Australian tourist resort, catering for people who want to experience typical Australian country life without having to actually travel out there. That piece of land on the Nepean would be the ideal site.'

'You've never mentioned this before,' Gavin said, clearly still worried.

Ross gave him a ruefully affectionate smile. 'We don't always talk about our dreams out loud, do we, little brother? I thought my duty lay here till I saw you had more heart for this place than I ever would.'

'And what will this tourist resort have in it, Ross?' Vivien joined in, intrigued by the thought of it all.

Smiling widely, he turned to her. 'Lots of things. There'll be a miniature farm with examples of all our animals, shearing exhibitions, sheep-dog trials. Individual cabins for people to stay in. Restaurants that serve typical Australian food. Barbecue and picnic facilities. Souvenir shops. All sorts of things. I think it could be a great success, especially if my wife joins in and helps me. She's a whiz with people…'

She stared back at him, having only heard the word—'wife'. He bent over and kissed her before turning back to face his brother.

'So don't worry about Dad leaving you Mountainview, Gavin. He's put it in the best of hands. And I think there might be a girl somewhere around here who might like to help you and Helga look after the place.'

'Gosh, I don't know what to say.'

Neither did Helga, it seemed. Tears were streaming down her face.

Vivien reached out to take Ross's hand. 'You are a wonderful, wonderful man,' she murmured. 'Do you know that?'

'Yes,' he said, and leant close. 'You will marry me, won't you?'

'You know I will.'

'That's what your mother told me that day. She said if I were patient you'd come around. She said you loved me, but you just didn't know it yet.'

Vivien was astonished. 'Mum said that?'

'Sure thing. She told me her daughter didn't go round having babies with men she didn't love. I should have believed her sooner.'

A lump filled Vivien's throat. Dear heaven…her mother knew her better than she knew herself. But she'd been so right. So very right.

Mr Parkinson coughed noisily till they were all paying attention to him again. 'I have one more bequest to read out. It seems the late Mrs Everton had a sizeable amount of very valuable jewellery which has been kept in a bank vault in Sydney all these years. Mr Everton senior left it all to the mother of his first grandchild, Miss Vivien Roberts. To be worn, his will states. Not locked away. He says it could only be enhanced by Miss Roberts's beauty.'

Vivien tried not to cry, but it was a futile exercise. The tears had already been hovering. She began to sob quietly, Ross putting an arm round her shoulder to try and comfort her. Helga stood up abruptly and left the room, returning quickly with a tray full of drinks. She passed them all around.

'I wish to propose a toast to my employer and friend, Oliver Everton.'

They all stood up.

'May I?' Ross asked thickly.

Helga nodded.

'To Oliver Everton,' he said. 'He was a good father and a good friend. He was a good man. They don't come along like him too often…'

CHAPTER FOURTEEN

'IRVING! What do you think you're doing?' Vivien remonstrated. 'I asked you to film just the christening, but you've been following me around all afternoon with that darned camera. I came out here on my own back patio to catch a breath of fresh air and up you pop like a bad penny.'

Irving continued filming as he spoke. 'Now, Viv, sweetie, I don't often have such a gorgeous-looking subject to film. You're looking ravishing today in that white dress, especially with that pearl choker round your lovely neck. Have pity on me. I've been doing nothing but film sour old politicians for the channel lately. Of course, if a certain lady journalist would heed her old boss's pleas to return to work then I might get assigned some more interesting jobs…like that one out at Wallaby Creek.'

Vivien's laughter was dry. 'Mervyn can beg till he's blue in the face. I have no intention of ever returning to work for a man who's so stupid. Fancy keeping Bob on instead of me. No intelligence at all.'

'Didn't I tell you? Bob's moved to Western Australia. He's decided the politicians are more interesting over there.'

'Oh, so that's it! Now Mervyn has a hole in his staff and he thinks he can fill it with yours truly. No way, José. I'm very happy helping Ross build this place.' And she swept an arm round to indicate the mushrooming complex. Already their own house was finished on a spot overlooking the river. So was the gardener's cottage. The foundations of the restaurant and shops had been poured that week.

'That's what I told him,' Irving said. 'But he's a stubborn man.'

'Who's a stubborn man?' Ross remarked on joining them. Vivien thought he looked heart-stoppingly handsome in a new dark grey suit. And very proud, with his six-week-old baby son in his arms.

'Mervyn,' she explained. 'You know he keeps asking me to go back to work for him.'

'Why don't you?'

Vivien blinked at her husband. 'But you said—'

Ross shrugged. 'I always believe in letting people do what they want to do, regardless. If you're missing work then by all means go back. You know your mother's dying to get her hands on Luke here, and since your father agreed to quit the railways and take on the job as chief gardener you've got a built-in baby-sitter. Your parents will be living only a hundred yards away.'

Vivien could hardly believe her ears. That was one aspect of Ross's character that never ceased to amaze her: his totally selfless generosity. So different to Earl, who'd been greedily possessive of her time. He'd hated her working.

Thinking about the differences between Ross and Earl brought a small smile to her lips, for they were more different now than ever. Her mother had shown her a picture in a women's magazine the other day, of a couple at the Flemington races. Vivien had not recognised the man till she'd read the caption below the photograph:

Mr and Mrs Earl Fotheringham enjoying a day at the races.

She had stared at the photograph again, then had difficulty suppressing a burst of laughter. For Earl was not only grossly overweight, but he was going bald. In less than a year, he looked ten years older, and nothing like Ross at all. She'd shown the picture to Ross, who'd looked at it, then stared at her.

'And *this* is who I'm supposed to look like?' he said.

'Once upon a time,' she said, trying to keep a straight face.

When Ross had burst out laughing she had too. But from relief, rather than any form of mockery, for now Ross could put Earl's ghost to rest once and for all.

Vivien's father opened the sliding glass doors and popped his head out. 'Is this a private session, or can anyone join in?'

'By all means join us, Lionel,' Ross said warmly. 'Get Peggy out here too and we can have a family shot.'

Lionel looked sheepish. 'Well, actually I was told to bring you all back inside. Your mother says it's getting late, Vivien, and you should be opening the baby's presents.'

They all were soon gathered in the large living area of the modern, airy house, Vivien sitting down on the white leather sofa to begin opening the gifts and cards that were piled high on the coffee-table, while everyone looked on. Irving kept happily filming away. Vivien decided to ignore him as best she could, and began ripping off paper with relish.

There were all the usual christening presents from toys to teddies, clothes to engraved cups, all beautiful and much gushed over by everyone. Gavin, who had become ecstatically engaged to Becky the previous month, had already sent down their excuses at not being able to attend, since they were in the middle of shearing. He'd posted down the cutest toy lamb Vivien had ever seen. The card attached had a small note from Becky.

'What does she mean,' Ross asked, 'about how she's been practising her swimming a lot lately?'

Vivien felt her lips twitching. 'I—er—told her the only way to get good at anything was to practise it.'

Ross frowned. 'Becky practising swimming? That's silly. She's a fantastic swimmer. Why, we used to go…' His voice trailed off as suspicion dawned in his eyes. He gave Vivien a narrow-eyed stare. She busied herself with another present by way of distraction.

'Here's one from Helga,' she announced, feeling it all over before opening it. 'I wonder what it is.' It was quite bulky, but soft.

Ross groaned. 'I have an awful feeling of premonition that Helga's been knitting again.'

Vivien ripped the paper off and everyone just stared. It was, she supposed, a rug of some sort, knitted in the most ghastly combination of colours she had ever seen, not to mention different ply wools. Now she knew why Ross's jumpers had never seen the light of day. Who would think to combine mauve with orange with black with red with purple in a series of striped and checked squares that had no regular pattern? On the card was the following explanation:

I began this before I knew whether your baby would be a boy or a girl, so I decided that neutral colours would be best.

These were *neutral* colours? Vivien stared down at the rug, unable to think of a thing to say.

'What…what is it?' Vivien's mother finally asked.

'A horse blanket,' Ross stated with a superbly straight face. 'For Luke's first pony. Helga's horse blankets are quite famous. Horses love them.'

'Oh,' Peggy said.

'We'll put it in a drawer for him, sweetheart,' Ross said to Vivien. 'Perhaps we should put a special drawer aside in which to save up all of Helga's marvellous gifts.'

'Yes, dear,' she returned with an even better poker-face. 'I think that would be best.'

They were lying in bed that night after Luke had finally condescended to go to sleep, chuckling over the incident.

'I almost died when I first saw it,' Vivien giggled.

'Don't you mean ''almost died laughing''? And now, madam, would you like to tell me in the privacy of our bedroom what decadent advice you gave Becky?'

'Decadent advice? Who, me?'

'Yes, *you*, city broad.'

She laughed. 'That's for me to know and you to find out.'

'I think I already have…'

'Then why are you asking? Besides, it worked, didn't it? They're engaged and happy.'

'Not as happy as we are,' Ross insisted, pulling her close.

Vivien lifted her mouth to his in a tender kiss. 'No one's as happy as we are.'

'Too true.'

'Which is why I'm not going back to work.'

'You're not?'

'No. I'm happy doing what I'm doing, looking after Luke and helping you. Maybe some day I might want to go back to television, but not right now. I want to be right here when Luke cuts his first tooth, says his first word, takes his first step. Let Mervyn find someone else,' she went on without any regret. 'I can see I'm not going to be available for at least ten years, till our last child has gone to school.'

Startled, Ross propped himself up on his elbow and stared down at her. 'Our *last* child? How many are we going to have, for heaven's sake?'

'Oh, at least four. Kids these days need brothers and sisters to stick up for them. It's a tough world.'

He shook his head in a type of awed bewilderment. 'You never cease to amaze me, Mrs Everton. First, you bravely went ahead and had my baby when most women in your shoes wouldn't have. Now, after you've just been through a rotten long labour, you tell me you want a whole lot more! I'm beginning to wonder if you're a glutton for punishment or just plain crazy.'

'I'm crazy,' she said, and with a soft, sexy laugh pulled him down into her arms. 'Crazy about you...'

Carole Mortimer says: 'I was born in England, the youngest of three children—I have two older brothers. I started writing in 1978, and have now written over 90 books for Mills & Boon®. I have four sons, Matthew, Joshua, Timothy and Peter, and a bearded collie dog called Merlyn. I'm in a very happy relationship with Peter senior; we're best friends as well as lovers, which is probably the best recipe for a successful relationship. We live on the Isle of Man.'

**Look out for TO BECOME A BRIDE
by Carole Mortimer
in Mills & Boon Modern Romance™, March 2001**

AFTER THE LOVING
by
CAROLE MORTIMER

**For John,
Matthew and Joshua.**

CHAPTER ONE

'CONGRATULATIONS, Bryna,' Frank Stapleton beamed at her. 'By my calculations you're just nine weeks pregnant.'

The fingers that had been rebuttoning her blouse after the examination began to shake. Pregnant? My God, she thought, that possibility hadn't even occurred to her when she had made the appointment to see the man who had been her doctor ever since she came to London eight years ago. *Pregnant?* She couldn't be!

'I'll give you an initial prescription for the usual vitamins,' her doctor continued briskly. 'I'm sure you can be relied upon to be sensible during these early weeks—good diet, a healthy amount of exercise, are very important at this stage. You——'

'Are you sure?' Her voice broke with the tension his diagnosis had put her under. 'I meant,' she hurried on at his frowning look, 'I always thought— well, I wouldn't want to—to tell anyone unless I'm one hundred per cent sure.' She hoped she didn't look—or sound—as anxious as she felt to have him tell her he couldn't be *completely* sure that his diagnosis was the right one. At any other time in her life she would have been overjoyed with the news, and she knew Frank was aware of that, but she *couldn't* be pregnant *now*.

Frank gave her a reassuring smile. 'Believe me,

Bryna, there's no doubt. It's amazing how many women ask me the same thing when I tell them the good news,' he teased. 'Even though they're usually pretty certain of what my diagnosis will be before they come here.'

The last was said cajolingly, but she *hadn't* known, hadn't even guessed that the results of the tests the doctor had taken the previous week would reveal that this was the reason her body had decided to play tricks on her. All the experts claimed that emotional tension could cause the same result, and God knows she had been through enough of that recently!

'Now as soon as you can I want you to get along and see a good obstetrician,' her doctor advised. 'I can give you the name of one if you would prefer——'

'There's no rush, is there?' She was still too numb to think about things like that.

'I shouldn't leave it too long, Bryna,' the doctor smiled, moving to sit on the edge of his desk. 'You and the baby will need the best of care during the next seven months.'

Pregnant. It still didn't seem real to her. It couldn't be happening to her *now*!

She studiously finished buttoning her blouse so that the doctor shouldn't see that he was more pleased by the news than she was, and picked up her bag ready to leave once she was fully dressed, a blush darkening her cheeks as the doctor raised surprised brows. She gave him a quick smile. 'Unlike those other ladies who came to you, I have to admit to being a little—surprised,' she revealed shakily. 'You must realise why.' She looked at him dazedly.

'Of course I do,' he patted her hand. 'And as soon as you're feeling a little less shocked I want you to give me a call so that we can talk about that. The only thing you need to know now is that you're in excellent health and I'm sure you're going to have a perfectly normal pregnancy.'

Nothing had been normal in her life the last few weeks, and her pregnancy could only make things worse. Its existence already did that.

'Thank you.' She swallowed hard. 'I am a little dazed,' she admitted tremulously. 'I—I'll call you later today,' she added shakily, clutching her bag in front of her. As if a few hours were going to make any difference to the shock she had just received!

Frank nodded, smiling warmly. 'I'm sure you're bursting to tell someone your good news.'

By 'someone' she knew he meant the baby's father. And that was where the problem lay.

'Yes,' she gave a tight smile. 'Well, thank you, and——'

'Don't thank me, Bryna,' he gave her a teasing smile. 'I had nothing to do with this miracle, you and the baby's father managed this all on your own!'

The trembling hadn't stopped by the time she had walked through the reception area and waiting-room, across the car park, unlocked her car door, and sat inside, her head resting on the steering-wheel.

Pregnant! Years ago she had dreamt about this day, of knowing her child was growing inside her.

Then her parents had broken the news that, owing to an emergency operation during puberty, she would probably never be able to have a child of her own.

It had been a bitter blow, days of crying, weeks of cursing fate for doing this to her, months of self-recrimination as she tried desperately to convince herself she was still a woman worth loving, years of telling herself she could still live a full life, her years as a model doing a lot for her self-esteem. And now, somehow, when she had only fleetingly glimpsed the happiness she could have, she found she was pregnant. With Raff's child.

Raff. He was the last person she could tell about the life they had created between them.

She put her hand protectively on her stomach. Her child.

Dear God, how she wanted it!

But she would lose Raff if she had the baby.

She was losing him anyway.

The last thought came unbidden, but she knew it was the truth even as she tried to deny it. Each day Raff faded a little more away from her, until eventually he would tell her it was over between them. She was only surprised he hadn't already done so; she had lasted much longer than his affairs usually did.

It still surprised her to realise she was the mistress of Raff Gallagher, a man who wielded much power in the City, both monetarily and personality-wise. The first moment she had seen him she had known he was a power to be reckoned with. But she certainly hadn't expected to become his mistress within a matter of days!

He wouldn't want this child she carried, she had no doubt of that. Raff had made it clear from the first that he was offering her no more than any of the other women he had had in his life the last ten years: passion and consideration, and the truth when he no longer felt either of them for her any more.

How could she tell the man who had made it clear he offered no commitment that they had made the biggest commitment of all, that of forming another life from their desire for each other? Once again she acknowledged that she couldn't tell him. Which gave her only a matter of weeks with him before the child physically began to show on her slender figure.

Why bother to count in weeks when she knew Raff could end it in days? Maybe even today.

'So will you talk to Daddy about it?'

Bryna blinked at the pretty girl who sat opposite her at the restaurant table. Lunch had been the last thing she had felt like after leaving the doctor's surgery, but she had promised to have lunch with Kate, and somehow she had managed to drive herself to the restaurant. How, she didn't know, not recalling the drive here at all, but she had already been seated at the table when Kate had breezed into the room five minutes ago, her hair a mass of glossy black curls, grey eyes gleaming with determination.

It was that gleam of determination that warned Bryna she had better be more on her guard and pay

closer attention to what Kate was saying; this young
lady could be deviously charming when she chose to
be! And lack of attention when Kate's eyes were
gleaming like this could have dire results. This
young lady could be every bit as manipulative as her
father when she was set on a course of action.

'Talk to him about what?' Bryna prompted
guardedly, listening intently now.

Irritation flickered in the dark grey depths.
'What's the matter with you today, Bryna? You
haven't heard a word I've said since I arrived!'

Bryna gave a half-smile as Kate displayed
another characteristic of her father: impatience
with anyone who didn't pay complete attention to
what concerned them at any given moment. In the
father it was part of his strength of character, in this
eighteen-year-old girl it appeared merely petulant.
But she didn't doubt Kate would be every inch the
matriarch in her later years.

'Sorry. I—I've had a busy morning,' she dismissed with a shrug.

'Hm,' Kate gave her a censorious look. 'Well, I'd
like you to talk to Daddy on my behalf about the
idea of my sharing a flat with Brenda next term.'

Bryna's brow cleared at the explanation. 'I
thought you'd already discussed it with your father
and he'd said no,' she returned drily, knowing all
about the conversation between father and daughter, also knowing the outcome would be inevitable.

'Not a definite no-more-discussion-on-the-
subject no.' Kate sat forward eagerly. 'I'm sure that
if you told him you think it's a good idea he might be
more—open-minded.'

Bryna wasn't sure she did think it was a good idea. Oh, she understood Kate's wish to leave the home she had shared with her family the last eighteen years, but she wasn't altogether sure Kate was up to setting up home on her own just yet, especially with Brenda Sanders.

Kate had become friends with the other girl when she had started college the previous term, but Brenda seemed to have a different boy in tow each time they met, and the one time Bryna had been to the flat Kate proposed sharing it had been very untidy, with a sleepy-eyed, completely naked young man emerging from Brenda's bedroom. That way of life might be Brenda's choice, but for all her outward sophistication she was sure Kate was still very much an innocent. And her father would like her to remain that way a little while longer!

'I don't think my opinion, favourable or otherwise, would make the slightest difference to his decision,' she told the younger girl coolly, sipping her mineral water, having realised just in time before she ordered her drink from the waiter that she shouldn't really drink alcohol in her condition.

'Oh, but I'm sure—— Oh,' Kate broke off as realisation dawned. 'You aren't saying that your affair with Daddy is almost over?'

Candour, cruelly blunt or otherwise, was something neither of the Gallagher children lacked, neither Paul at twenty, or his young sister Kate. It was something Bryna had been made aware of the first time Raff had introduced her to his two children from his very young marriage and they had asked why she and Raff didn't just live together and have an open affair, assuring them that they were both adult enough to accept the situation.

They might well be, but neither she nor Raff had wanted that close a relationship, she because she liked having her own home and independence, Raff because he never became that intimate with the women he was involved with, and both of them were happy to continue as they were. Or they had been.

'I don't believe it,' Kate dismissed before she could answer her. 'You and Daddy have been together for over six months now; that's at least three months longer than any of the others!'

Tact and diplomacy seemed to be traits the Gallagher children *hadn't* received when virtues were being given out!

Bryna was well aware of the fact that her affair with Raff had lasted twice as long as they usually did, just as she had been aware of his increasing irritability the last month or so, knowing it was only a matter of time now before he ended things between them.

Until today, until an hour ago, she had been grateful for each extra *day* she had lasted than his other women; now she knew she would have no choice but to end things herself if he didn't do it soon.

'All the more reason for him to feel enough is enough,' she gave a tight smile.

'I don't believe it,' his daughter scoffed. 'Paul and I have been laying bets on how soon he would marry you!'

Bryna gave the younger girl a pitying look. 'You

should both know better than that.'

Grey eyes, so much like her father's it was unnerving, looked Bryna over speculatively. 'I somehow never expected the woman to turn *Daddy* down when he finally decided to take the plunge again.'

She turned away. 'One has to be asked in order to give a refusal.'

'You're so beautiful, Daddy is sure to ask you soon,' the younger girl said with certainty.

As if beauty had anything to do with it! Oh, she was well aware of her own looks, she had to be in the profession she had chosen to enter on leaving school eight years ago. She knew how well her long mane of white-blonde straight hair and wide, dark-lashed, violet-coloured eyes photographed, not to mention the slender length of her body.

Her looks had been her stock-in-trade for six years, and could have continued to do so for many years after that, but two years ago she had decided to open her own modelling agency, where her looks and appearance were still very important, but she no longer had to watch everything she ate, or look anxiously in the mirror each morning as she searched for those tell-tale lines on her face that would tell her the choice was no longer hers to make.

It had been a successful move, both financially and personally, and she had also met Raff through the agency. But while her beauty might have attracted his attention initially, it certainly wasn't enough to hold his interest for any length of time; there had been too many beautiful women before her for her to ever believe that.

'I don't think so, Kate,' she dismissed as gently as she could, liking the young girl for all her brashness. How could she not like the daughter who looked so much like the man she loved!

No ties, no commitment, they had said at the start of their affair, and Bryna had meant to keep to those rules. But it had been impossible for her not to fall in love with Raff, although she had taken care not to let him even guess at the emotion, knowing it would precipitate the end of their relationship. She had broken all the rules, but Raff had kept to every one of them, and she had no illusions why.

Would the child she carried look like him as Kate did? They were both tall, so the child was sure to inherit that trait from one of them, but Raff was so dark against her blondeness, and surely that would be the more dominant of the two. How strange to look at her child and see Raff in every glance!

'Bryna? Bryna!' Kate repeated impatiently at her second lapse into unattentiveness. 'Are you sure? I mean——'

'I'm sure. And I accept it,' she huskily assured the young girl. 'Now let's order lunch, shall we?' she added briskly as the waiter approached their table. 'It hasn't happened yet, and until it does we can enjoy each other's company.'

She was well aware that when her affair with Raff ended he wouldn't be the only one to leave her life, that, fond as she had become of Kate and Paul, they could hardly keep up a friendship with one of their father's ex-mistresses!

Kate gave her a frowning look once they had

ordered their meal. 'You don't seem exactly heartbroken.'

Bryna gave rueful grimace. 'Would it do any good if I screamed and shouted?'

'Well ... no,' Kate admitted moodily. 'But it might make *you* feel better.'

'Believe me, it wouldn't,' Bryna drawled.

'You're always so cool and controlled,' the girl rebuked. 'Don't you care for Daddy at all?'

Her heart felt heavy at the irony of that. 'I don't think you really want me to answer that——'

'But I do,' Kate insisted earnestly. 'Daddy tells me that I shouldn't even think about going to bed with someone unless I'm absolutely sure I'm in love with them, and yet Daddy isn't in love with the women he goes to bed with.'

Bryna picked uninterestedly at the prawns she had chosen as her appetiser. 'It doesn't seem very fair, does it?' she acknowledged, her cheeks pale beneath their light dusting of blusher.

'He told me there's a certain type of woman a man would never contemplate marrying,' Kate added with a bitchiness unusual for her.

Bryna swallowed hard, recognising the accusation for what it was. Except that she knew Raff didn't mean her. He had been her first and only lover.

After her parents had told her she could never have a child she had deliberately set out to attract men to the sensuous sway of her body, always drawing back before any physical commitment had been made, believing they would realise she wasn't a complete woman if they ever made love to her. By

the time she realised that wasn't true she had earned
herself the reputation of being icy and aloof. And
the ice hadn't begun to melt until she met Raff. If he
had been surprised to find her virginity intact he
had never said so.

The bitchy comment hadn't been worthy of Kate,
with her forthright manner and lack of guile. Bryna
guessed that the girl was fond of her too, and would
miss her when the time came.

'He was right,' she told the younger girl.

Only six years separated them in age, and yet at
eighteen Bryna had already been mature beyond
her years, scarred by what she believed to be her
inadequacy. God, how she wished she could share
the life growing within her with someone! Prefera-
bly Raff.

But that was out of the question. Her parents,
then. She didn't doubt for a moment that they
would be overjoyed by the news, whether she had a
husband or not; as Bryna was an only child they had
given up any idea of ever becoming grandparents.
Maybe instead of telephoning them she would go up
to Scotland at the weekend and tell them in person;
the look on their faces might be worth the long
journey!

'I'm sorry, Bryna.' Kate gave a self-disgusted sigh
at her intention to wound. 'You aren't what Daddy
meant at all.' She picked up her fork to eat her
salmon. 'I'm disappointed, that's all,' she grimaced.
'I thought you would make a great stepmother.'

Raff had lost his wife, and Kate and Paul their
mother, over ten years ago, but Raff gave the
impression that the marriage he had entered into at

only eighteen had ceased to be a complete success years before that. But both parents were devoted to the children, and while their marriage didn't exactly sparkle it hadn't been unpleasant either.

Paul and Kate obviously had very warm memories of their mother, and it warmed Bryna to know that Kate, at least, would have had no objection to her taking that place in her father's life. If the situation had ever arisen. Which it never would.

'Thank you,' she accepted briskly. 'Now, as a friend, would you hurry up and eat your lunch; I have to get back to work.' She smiled brightly in the face of Kate's pain at the deliberate snub; she couldn't allow Kate to live under the misapprehension that there would ever be a happy-ever-after between Raff and herself. Raff was thirty-nine years old, with a grown-up family, and the thought of having to go through night-time feeds, teething, crawling, walking, the terrible-twos, and so on and so on, with another child, would throw even the self-confidently arrogant Raff Gallagher into a panic! It threw *her* into a panic!

Who would have guessed when she had walked into a restaurant very similar to this one six short months ago that this would happen?

She had been meeting Courtney Stevens, to discuss the use of six of her models to promote a new line he was introducing to his chain of fashion stores throughout Europe and America for the winter. He had proved every bit as charming as the advertising agency she was working with had told her he was.

Or warned her. She and Janet Parker had worked together before, and when the cynical Janet described a man as 'charming' it was like any other woman saying he was lethally attractive!

Courtney Stevens—or Court, as he had insisted she call him as they introduced themselves—was a blond giant of a man with a devilish charm glinting in deep blue eyes that were guaranteed to seduce even the most hardened of women. Bryna was charmed almost from the first moment, almost forgetting what she was there for as he deftly centred the conversation on her rather than the business she had come here to discuss.

'We have to decide what models you would like to use,' she had finally laughingly protested.

'Well, we're going to use the family pile,' he dismissed drily. 'For some reason my father bought himself a manor house in Kent and left it to me in his will; I've never had reason to use it until now. So as it means the crew will have to stay overnight down there, how about making one of the models a tall violet-eyed silver-blonde?' He looked at her expectantly.

She couldn't possibly feel insulted by the intimacy of the suggestion, and she laughed huskily. 'I no longer work as a model myself.'

'Couldn't you make this the exception?' His large hand covered her much slenderer one.

Her eyes glowed. 'I'm afraid not.'

'No?' He looked as if she had dealt him a wounding blow. 'Then how about joining me for——'

'Would you like to introduce us, Court?' interrupted a harshly rasping voice.

Court frowned his irritation up at the other man.

'Not now, Raff,' he protested.

'Exactly now,' the other man drawled.

'Bryna, Raff Gallagher. Raff, Bryna Fairchild,'
Court made the introductions in a disgruntled
voice. 'A friend of mine,' he told the other man
pointedly.

'I'm glad to meet you, Miss Fairchild.' The man,
who until that moment had only been a dark blue
tailored suit, she could see out of the corner of her
eye, and a rasping voice, lowered himself into the
chair beside her.

For some reason just the sound of his voice as he
cut in on their conversation had made her reluctant
to look at him before, and as she glanced at him now
she knew the reason why; it was like the moon
eclipsing the sun. Court was the sun, open and
uncomplicated, and Raff Gallagher was the moon,
dark with secretive depths he allowed no one to
enter.

She told herself she was being imaginative, and
yet piercing grey eyes seemed to look into her very
soul and see all that was Bryna Fairchild.

Raff couldn't be called handsome, his features
were too rugged for that, and yet he had something
else that was even more effective, a compelling
quality that overshadowed and obliterated every
other man but him.

He appeared to be the same age as Court, in his
late thirties, and yet the years had left their mark in
the cynical twist of his mouth, the hardness of his
eyes, and the grey wings of hair over each temple.

And from the moment she looked at him Court

Stevens ceased to be anything but an attractively pleasant client.

'Mr Gallagher,' she greeted him coolly.

'Please call me Raff,' he invited gruffly. 'I have every intention of calling you Bryna.'

Whether she liked it or not! she acknowledged ruefully. Of course she realised who he was now; anyone who was in business and hadn't heard of Raff Gallagher was either a fool or doomed to fail. And she hoped she was neither of those things. This man was Midas, anything he touched, from property to industry, turning to gold.

'Raff, why don't you get lost?' Court invited irritably. 'Bryna and I have some business to discuss. Not that sort of business, you fool,' he admonished as the other man raised disbelieving brows in Bryna's direction. 'Bryna runs the Fairchild Agency.'

The dark brow cleared. 'I've heard of it,' Raff drawled, turning to Bryna. 'I apologise for the assumption I made just now.'

Being a model, Bryna had received her fair share of insults over erroneous assumptions of what her profession actually entailed, but never before had a man presumed *that* about her without knowing a thing about her!

She turned to Court Stevens with frosty eyes. 'I really do have to go,' she snapped. 'Perhaps you could give me a call and we could get together to discuss this another time.' She was probably walking away from a contract that could mean even bigger things for her agency if Court Stevens was pleased with the work they did for him this time, but she wasn't going to stay around and be insulted by a man who acted as if he owned half of London—and probably did!

'Now look what you've done!' Court turned accusing eyes on the other man. 'Will you just get out of here?'

It was testament to how deep the friendship was between the two men that Raff Gallagher didn't take exception to the way Court had been trying to get rid of him ever since he had interrupted them. But at that moment Bryna was too angry to care how close the two men were, as she stood up to leave.

'Please stay, Miss Fairchild,' Raff Gallagher drawled as he stood up, the formality deliberate, she was sure. 'And please accept my apology for interrupting the two of you. Game of golf tomorrow, Court?'

'OK,' Court sighed unenthusiastically. 'But you're starting with a handicap.'

'Don't I always,' the other man mocked. 'Miss Fairchild,' he nodded dismissively before strolling across the restaurant to join two men at a table who had obviously been waiting for him.

'He always wins, too,' muttered Court. 'Sit down, Bryna. Please,' he persuaded.

She did so slowly, pointedly turning her chair so that she didn't have to look at Raff Gallagher.

'We became friends in our first week of boarding school after he bowled me out at cricket and I hit him with my cricket bat in the changing room,' Court sighed. 'I broke his nose.'

Bryna had noticed that slight bump on the

hawklike nose, laughing softly now as she envisaged the two little boys glaring at each other across a cricket bat, both taking their aggression at being away from home out on the other. 'Stranger meetings have formed just as strong a friendship, I'm sure,' she teased.

Court smiled, his eyes brimming with laughter. 'It wasn't the fight that caused the friendship,' he assured her. 'What did that was the fact that Raff told everyone he'd fallen over and hit his nose. If he hadn't I would have been expelled in my first week of school!'

Two little boys who had bonded a lifetime friendship through resentment and pain. Maybe Raff Gallagher did have some redeeming qualities after all. One just had to dig deep to find them!

She made a point of not looking his way as she and Court got down to the serious business of discussing the models. Nevertheless, she was aware of the exact moment Raff Gallagher stood up to approach their table before leaving.

Grey eyes delved into her soul a second time. 'We'll meet again, Miss Fairchild,' he murmured as he bent over the hand he had lifted to his mouth, his lips cool and yet moist.

'Give me a chance, Raff!' Court complained.

His friend chuckled huskily. 'The choice will be Bryna's,' he said softly, meeting her gaze once again with compelling intensity before taking his leave.

'It's a no contest,' groaned Court resignedly. 'It always is.'

'I can assure you Mr Gallagher holds no interest for me,' Bryna dismissed primly.

When she got back to her office a box containing a single red rose lay on her desk. There was no card with it, but she guessed that it wasn't from Court; he was the type of man who would sign his name with a flourish to the accompanying card if he found a woman attractive enough to send her flowers.

Half an hour later two more roses arrived, half an hour after that another three, then another three, and another three, until by four-thirty she had the round dozen.

Her secretary/receptionist, Gilly, was agog to know who had sent them. When the man himself arrived at five o'clock neither woman was in any doubt as to who the sender had been. When Raff courteously invited Bryna out to dinner she had breathlessly accepted, her earlier antagonism forgotten; she had never met anyone quite like this man before.

She still hadn't met anyone like him, and even when he was long gone from her life, she knew she would never meet anyone like him again.

CHAPTER TWO

'KATE tells me the two of you had lunch together today,' Raff said enquiringly as he sat down opposite her.

Bryna met his gaze guardedly, her heart skipping its usual beat as she looked at him, still affected, even after six months of knowing him intimately, by that compelling power that surrounded him. Tonight, dressed in black evening suit and snowy white shirt, he appeared even more devastating than usual.

'That's right, we did,' she confirmed coolly, wondering where the conversation was leading to.

Raff gave an inclination of his head, his mouth twisted into a rueful smile. 'She seems slightly annoyed with you.'

She and Kate had parted a little stiffly outside the restaurant, the younger girl seeming to blame Bryna for the fact that her father hadn't fallen in love with her!

Bryna shrugged. 'She hoped I would talk to you about her moving in with Brenda next term,' she told him truthfully.

His eyes became suddenly flinty. 'And what did you tell her?'

She maintained her calm poise in the face of his obvious displeasure. 'What do you think I told her?' she drawled.

Raff relaxed slightly, his long length stretched out comfortably in the armchair. 'I think you agree with me, that young lady is *not* the choice of flatmate I want for Kate.'

And what Raff wanted he invariably got, Bryna had found these last months. She was a prime example of that, in the past having been able to freeze off even the most ardent of men, and yet she and Raff had been lovers within days of their meeting. And far from feeling inadequate as she had always imagined she would, she had felt complete for the first time in her life! It had been the same every time they made love.

'Perhaps not Brenda,' she agreed. 'But I think Kate is determined to get a place of her own, and she is over eighteen——'

'I think I know what's best for my children, Bryna,' he bit out cuttingly, standing up abruptly. 'We should be going now,' he added curtly. 'At the moment we're politely late, any later and we may as well not bother!'

Despite the fact that the dig about their lateness was aimed at her she wanted to say 'then let's not bother!' She wanted to be in his arms tonight, close to him in the only way he allowed any woman to be close to him. She had long ago ceased to be upset by the way he cut her out of showing any interest in his children's activities; it was far from the first time he had done so. To her it only served to emphasise the transient role she played in his life.

And because of the child she herself carried inside her she didn't suggest they miss the party, but slipped her arms into the coat he held out for her, the suede soft and supple against her body. 'I'm sure Court won't mind our tardiness,' she shrugged lightly.

She wished he would smile, because it completely transformed his face when he did, alleviating some of the harshness, lending warmth to eyes the colour of slate, the harshness of his mouth softening as deep grooves were etched into the leanness of his cheeks.

Instead he nodded tersely. 'After all these years Court has come to expect my rudeness,' he said drily. 'I wouldn't want to disappoint him!'

The two men were still the unlikeliest couple to have found such an enduring friendship that Bryna had ever met, Raff being hard where Court was gentle, Raff blunt to the point of rudeness where Court was always kind. Bryna had even wondered, when loving Raff hurt too badly, why it couldn't have been Court she fell in love with that day. But she hadn't, and so the two of them had become friends instead.

'What did the doctor say?'

Her smile faded as she looked up at Raff with startled eyes. 'Sorry?' she frowned, her hands shaking slightly as she held her coat around her as they braved the icy-cold early December winds to go out to the waiting Jaguar, the sudden chill not leaving her body even as Raff turned on the ignition and the burst of warm air filled the interior.

'You told me last night that the doctor was going to tell you the results of your tests today,' he explained raspingly. 'You did keep the appointment, didn't you?' The lights on the dashboard illuminated his frown.

'Yes, of course.' Bryna huddled down into the collar of her coat, the chill seeming to have permeated her bones.

She inwardly bemoaned the fact that the intimacy of their relationship told Raff without words exactly when her body had failed her. She had assured him that it occasionally happened, although he had been aware that it never had in their previous four months together. When it happened again he had been the one to urge her to consult a doctor.

'I'm anaemic, that's all,' she evaded. 'It can have that effect. The doctor has given me some vitamins,' she added truthfully.

Raff gave her a probing look. 'You do look a little pale,' he conceded.

She looked pale because she was still suffering from the shock of knowing she was pregnant; even the call to her parents telling them she would be home for the weekend hadn't made the baby she carried seem more real to her. She was sure there would be visible signs of it soon enough, but at the moment, with her body still so slender, and no ill-effects such as morning sickness to cope with, she couldn't help questioning the accuracy of the doctor's diagnosis.

Except that she felt different emotionally, filled with a tranquillity and inner peace she had thought never to know. Maternal instinct had previously only been an expression to her, but now she knew exactly what it was, the completely unselfish love for a human being you just *knew* was inside you despite there being no visible signs of its existence.

'Warmer now?' Raff cut in on her musings. 'You seem a little distracted this evening,' he frowned as she raised questioning brows. 'You shivered earlier, I wondered if you were warmer now,' he explained.

'Fine,' she gave him a dreamy smile. 'Isn't it a lovely evening?'

'It's been raining most of the day and they forecast sleet for tonight,' he drawled derisively.

Bryna blushed self-consciously. 'I happen to like rain,' she defended, her golden bubble firmly burst.

'And sleet?' Raff arched dark brows.

She realised it was ridiculous to expect Raff Gallagher to act like a giddy lover, but sometimes she wished he wasn't quite so controlled and cynical all the time. It would be nice to sometimes relax with him completely and show him how much she cared.

But it was impossible with a man as armoured against the softer feelings as Raff was, and she knew it was only the child she carried inside her that made her hunger for that closeness now.

'No,' she conceded ruefully. 'But maybe this bad weather is an indication that we're going to have a white Christmas this year.'

'And then you wouldn't be able to get to your parents' house for the holiday,' he rasped.

'No.' She was tempted to tell him she wouldn't mind that too much as she was going home this weekend anyway, but on their way to a party didn't seem the appropriate time to tell him that.

'Of course you're welcome to spend Christmas

with us if anything goes wrong with your plans,' he
invited smoothly.

If he had issued that invitation a few weeks ago
she would have been tempted to accept no matter
how out of place she felt at the time, but he hadn't
suggested it before, neither had he shown any sign
of displeasure that they wouldn't be spending the
holiday together. 'I don't think so, thank you,' she
refused lightly. 'Christmas is a time for families,
isn't it?'

His jaw tightened. 'Yes, I suppose so.'

The drive from Raff's house to Court's apartment
was a short one, and Bryna was relieved to escape
the suddenly icy atmosphere that had developed in
the car after her refusal. She didn't know what Raff
was so annoyed about—his invitation had lacked
warmth, to say the least! And it was also a little late
in coming, when he knew she had made her plans
weeks ago.

'My favourite lady!' Court greeted her warmly as
soon as they were admitted to his apartment,
kissing her lightly on the lips as he took her coat
himself. 'I thought you were never going to get
here,' he grinned at her. 'It's Raff's fault you're late,
of course——'

'Of course,' the other man drawled coolly.

'Only because you knew the sole reason I
arranged this party at all was so that I could ask
Bryna to dance and hold her in my arms for a
while!' Court challenged firmly. 'Bryna?'

'I'd love to dance,' she accepted laughingly. The
lounge of Court's apartment was completely cleared
of furniture, a dozen or so couples moving sensuous-

ly together in there to the sound of a romantic love song.

'You look lovely tonight.' Court looked down at her appreciatively.

Raff had told her the same thing earlier about the purple dress that made her eyes appear the same colour, but somehow Court's compliment seemed less perfunctory. Or maybe tonight she was just looking for faults in her relationship with Raff; the pity of it was it was so easy to find them!

Court looked at her searchingly. 'There's a sort of glow to you ... Oh God, I haven't stepped in with my size tens, have I?' he groaned as a blush darkened her cheeks.

'Raff and I came straight here, if that's what you mean,' she told him. 'I'm afraid it was *my* fault we got here late; I arrived late at Raff's.' Because of the telephone call to her parents, both of them concerned—if delighted!—at her sudden need to go home for the weekend. It had taken her some time to convince them that nothing had gone drastically wrong in her life to warrant the visit.

Court shook his head. 'I'm surprised Raff hasn't told you you work too hard.'

'He has,' she smiled. 'But as he wouldn't tolerate interference in his business neither will I!'

His friend chuckled softly. 'No wonder he finds you so fascinating; all his other women were quite willing to forgo their own plans to pander to his whims!'

'I sometimes wonder if you two love or hate each other!' she mocked.

'Love, of course,' Court drawled. 'Although if

looks could kill I'd be dead now!' he groaned as he glanced over Bryna's shoulder. 'Unless it's you he's upset at? Maybe he really didn't like your being late earlier.'

He hadn't seemed too worried at the time, but from the way he was glaring at the two of them now something had upset him! Perhaps he was still annoyed about Christmas?

He stood beside the bar in the adjoining dining-room, a drink remaining untouched in his hand as Rosemary Chater did her best to attract him to her fiery-haired beauty. For all the notice Raff took of her she might not have been wearing the most low-cut gown Bryna had ever seen, or been wearing that look of open invitation on her beautiful face. Raff's gaze was fixed on Court and Bryna as they moved slowly to the music.

Maybe he really was angry about her refusal to spend Christmas with him and Kate and Paul, but with Christmas only two weeks away he had left the invitation late enough!

She smiled at Court. 'No, I think it's you he's angry with,' she teased him.

'Well, I did beat him at golf today . . . !'

'You didn't!' she laughed disbelievingly; Court had been trying to win a round of golf against Raff ever since she had known the two of them.

'I did,' Court grinned triumphantly. 'Of course his mind didn't seem to be altogether on the game,' he admitted with some reluctance. 'But who's to say I haven't always lost in the past because of pressures of work?'

'I didn't think Raff had any pressures of work

now,' Bryna frowned. Raff had employed a very capable assistant four months ago, and while she might not like Stuart Hillier very much, and found his smooth charm more than a little overpowering, she knew he was good at his job, and that he had taken over a lot of the pressure of the solitary reign over his business empire that Raff had previously refused to relinquish. Everything had seemed to be going so smoothly in that direction the last four months.

Court shrugged. 'How should I know how well it is or isn't going? He never discusses business with me. Maybe it wasn't business worrying him at all, but he certainly had something on his mind.'

Her, and the fact that, despite their agreement that when the affair was over for one, or both, of them, they would admit that honestly, Raff seemed to be having trouble breaking the news to her. Maybe he did care for her in his own distant way and didn't want to hurt her. He might even have guessed at some of the love she felt for him. But she was soon going to have to decide if she walked away from him with some of her pride intact, or if she waited the short time until he ended things once and for all.

'Hey, have I said something I shouldn't?' Court frowned down at her concernedly.

Bryna shook off her mood of depression, knowing he had only confirmed for her what she already knew, smiling brightly to dispel his concern. 'Shall we go and join him before Rosemary falls out of her dress completely?' she suggested drily as the music came to an end.

Court groaned. 'I'm afraid she had herself lined up as next in line to share his bed before he met you.'

And like a vulture the other woman was now circling, waiting for the affair to end, trying to give it a helping hand if she could! And she was certainly going all out to do that at the moment.

From the first Bryna had found the world of cynicism, bitchiness, and self that Raff inhabited a little overwhelming, although she was hardened to a certain degree herself from her years as a top-class model. But almost every woman she met clearly let her, and Raff, know that they wanted him too, only the fact that he showed no interest in returning their attraction giving her comfort during the last months.

Until now. Raff had ceased to look bored by Rosemary Chater, in fact as Court and Bryna moved to join the other couple he led the other woman on to the dance floor, seeming to enjoy the way her body instantly melded to every contour of his.

'She can only cause trouble if you let her,' Court spoke quietly at Bryna's side, also watching the other couple with narrowed eyes.

Bryna turned to him with a grateful smile. 'Then I won't let her.'

He raised blond brows. 'Is it as easy to dismiss as that?'

Easy? She *hated* the way the other woman moved against Raff with deliberate seductiveness, but what could she do about it when Raff was enjoying it? She wasn't a fool, to make a scene about what was, for all the sensuousness of movement, just a dance; she knew that would be the surest way to drive Raff away from her. He hated scenes—he had once told her his wife had caused several before the two of them decided to live together but go their separate ways, to have their own lovers.

'No, it isn't easy,' she gave Court a tight smile. 'Why don't we go through and help ourselves to some of that lovely supper you've laid out in the other room?' It was almost ten o'clock and she hadn't eaten anything since lunchtime. So much for the doctor's confidence that she would maintain a healthy diet!

'Is everything okay between you and Raff?' Court eyed her curiously as she nibbled uninterestedly on a sandwich.

Her eyes were overbright as she looked up at him. '"The Queen is dead. Long live the Queen."' She looked pointedly at Rosemary Chater as she said the latter, too numb to even sound bitter.

Court looked much older when the boyish humour deserted his face. 'Are you sure?'

Her heart was breaking, the tears threatening to cascade down her cheeks—and she was incongruously trying to work out how she could bite into the cold chicken leg she held in her hand, without choking on it! 'Have you ever known him to behave like *that* in front of me before?' She felt sick as she watched Raff nuzzle against the other woman's silky throat.

'Hell!' muttered Court furiously as he followed her stricken gaze. 'I'll go and break them up——'

'No.' Her hand on his arm stopped him. 'Would

you please just get my coat and call a taxi to take me home?'

'I'll take you——'

'This is your party, Court,' she reminded him huskily, no longer able to look at Raff with the other woman. 'The host shouldn't walk out on his guests.' She tried to sound teasing, but to her dismay she just sounded forlorn.

Court's mouth tightened. 'None of this lot cares about that, half of them wouldn't even know I'd gone!'

'I'd really rather go on my own, thank you,' she refused as gently as she could, sure that if she didn't get out of here soon she was going to make an absolute fool of herself.

Court looked as if he were about to argue again, but the pleading in her eyes silenced him. Bryna kept her face averted from the couple dancing as she and Court moved through to the entrance hall to collect her coat.

Raff had done to her what they had always agreed wouldn't happen, publicly humiliated her by turning to another woman when the two of them had arrived here together.

Court put his hands warmly on her shoulders as he came to stand in front of her after helping her on with her coat. 'If you ever need a shoulder to cry on . . .' he told her affectionately.

'I know I can call you,' she gave him a wan smile. 'You——'

'Where do you think you're going?' rasped a harsh voice Bryna recognised only too well.

She took a second to regain control before turning

to face Raff, blinking a little uncertainly as she saw
the fury blazing in the depths of his eyes. 'I was just
about to leave——'

Cool grey eyes turned to Court. 'You too?' Raff
bit out coldly.

Court met the challenge in his friend's gaze
unflinchingly. 'I wanted to go with her, but Bryna
insisted I stay here.'

Raff's mouth twisted. 'Running out on me,
Bryna?' he taunted.

'I——'

'Good God, man, what did you expect her to do?'
Court exploded. 'Tap you on the shoulder while you
were making love to Rosemary to tell you she was
leaving!'

'I wasn't making love to her, damn it,' Raff
ground out, his hands clenched into fists at his sides.

'Then you were doing a good job of acting as if
you were!' his friend accused heatedly.

Grey eyes flickered coldly. 'Bryna?'

She swallowed hard, not enjoying being the bone
of contention between the two friends. 'I really
think it would be best if I left——'

'Then I'm coming with you,' rasped Raff.

'—and you stayed,' she finished dully. 'There's no
point in our both ruining our evening. "The night is
still young," and all that,' she added brittlely.

Raff strode purposefully across to grasp her arm
in his hand. 'I said I'm coming with you!'

'Maybe she doesn't want to go with you?' Court
told him caustically.

His mouth tightened. 'She came with me, she'll
leave with me.'

Bryna frowned up at him. Why was he doing this? Couldn't he see this was a perfect way out for him, why drag out their parting any longer than they had to? But she could see by the inflexibility of his jaw that he was determined to leave with her.

'Thank you, Court,' she squeezed his arm reassuringly. 'Raff will take me home.'

'I'll call you tomorrow,' Raff told the other man gratingly.

'Make sure that you do, and that it's nice and early. Otherwise I'll be the one to call you,' Court warned in a controlled voice.

The heating system in the Jaguar was blasting out hot air, and yet Bryna still felt cold. Why was Raff continuing with this? Unless he was going to tell her now that they were finished? As if she didn't already know that!

He accompanied her up to her apartment, neither of them having spoken a word since they left Court's home, Raff's expression harshly forbidding each time she had dared a glance in his direction.

She turned to him once she had unlocked her door. 'I don't think there's any point in your coming in——'

'Of course I'm coming in, Bryna,' his voice was huskily soft, as he pushed the door open for her to precede him inside and closed the door firmly behind him.

Bryna felt nervous in his company, as if this were their first date and they were only a couple of inexperienced teenagers, her hands shaking slightly as she faced him across the lounge. 'Rosemary will be waiting for you——'

'No one is waiting for me,' he told her gruffly, noiselessly crossing the lounge to stand in front of her. 'It's you I want, Bryna.'

Her eyes were wide with disbelief. 'No—you can't mean——'

'I need your fire and passion tonight, Bryna,' he groaned as his head lowered to hers.

'But earlier——'

'I was angry,' he dismissed. 'But I'm not angry any more. Now I just want to feel your silken legs wrapped about me while I bury myself in you!'

Their lovemaking was always different, sometimes fierce, sometimes gentle, sometimes so slow it drove the two of them insane, other times fiercely out of control. And tonight she knew Raff wanted it to be the latter, for both of them to be mindlessly lost in their passion for each other. And she wasn't sure, after what had happened earlier, that she could give him the response he seemed to need.

She swallowed hard. 'Raff, I don't know if I can. I don't——'

'Of course you can.' He melded his body against hers, moving against her provocatively.

Yes, she could, because this would be their farewell. She couldn't go through the pain he had made her endure earlier again, and so they would have this one last night together and then she would tell him it was over between them.

'All right, Raff,' her arms curved up about his neck as she relaxed against him, 'make love to me.'

Asking Raff to make love to her was like standing in the way of a tidal wave, knowing it would knock her completely off her feet, cloud her brain until she couldn't think or feel anything but him!

He was a man who rarely, if ever, lost control, and it took her breath away when he began to throw off their clothes as they stood together in her lounge. Usually they both had a leisurely shower, either apart or together, and then they would go to bed together. She had never known this wildness from him before.

But if he felt differently about their lovemaking tonight so did she, the child inside her, and the knowledge that this would be their last time together, making her own responses as wild as his.

He had a magnificent body, strong and lithe, with not an ounce of superfluous flesh anywhere. And as he stripped off the last of his clothing Bryna was able to see he was already fully aroused.

His hands entangled in her hair as he kissed her deeply, and she squirmed with delight as one of those hands moved to cup the fullness of one of her breasts. She had wondered at the increased sensitivity of her breasts in recent weeks, but now she knew they were making ready for her baby, and as Raff's dark head moved down to allow him to capture one aching nipple into the moist cavern of his mouth she felt as if her child already suckled there.

But the flicking of his tongue and the sharp sting of his teeth were not the movements of a child nourishing, and her legs buckled weakly beneath her, drawing the two of them down on to the carpeted floor.

'Don't move,' Raff instructed gruffly as she would have caressed him.

What followed was the most erotic and tortuous experience of her entire life. Raff kissed her from the top of her head to the soles of her feet, discovering pleasure spots that took her again and again to the edge of the sensual abyss he refused to let her enter, always drawing her back before she could attain release.

Finally she could stand no more, moving above him to take them *both* over the edge as she moved her body in rhythm with his, her nipples knowing the tug of his teeth as she bent above him.

The explosion inside her was greater than anything she had ever known before, and for a brief moment she felt blackness enshroud her, still feeling dizzy as Raff stood up to carry her through to her bedroom.

'That was for us,' he murmured as he gently laid her down between the covers. 'Now this is for you.'

She had barely recovered from the previous onslaught when she felt him intent on arousing her a second time.

He was trying to drive her insane, she decided minutes later, her body writhing and sweat-dampened as she silently begged him to release her from the tortuous frenzy he remorselessly drove her to.

He poised above her, his expression fierce. '*Now* do you believe I want you?' he rasped.

'Yes,' she almost sobbed. 'But please, *please*, Raff,' she let out a shuddering breath of need.

She had been made for him, she decided for what had to be the hundredth time, knowing even as the silken length of him thrust inside her that he would fit perfectly, that he always had.

And then she couldn't think at all, her hips arching to meet his throbbing rhythm, groaning her own shuddering release at the exact moment she felt his warmth inside her.

As partings went, it had to be one of the most soul-shattering on record!

Raff was already in the bathroom showering and shaving when Bryna woke the next morning, falling back against the pillows with a relieved groan as she realised it was Saturday, and her flight wasn't scheduled until later that morning.

Last night had been frightening in its intensity, Raff taking her once more before he allowed her to sleep, and her rest finally that of the almost unconscious, and this morning her body ached from the force of those fierce caresses.

Last night they had been closer than ever before, and Bryna dreaded having to tell Raff she thought it best if they didn't see each other any more. But what real choice did she have?

He was smiling when he came out of the bathroom, freshly shaved, wearing only the black trousers to his suit, although they were a little creased from where they had been left forgotten on the lounge floor all night. His chest was bare and golden, the dark hair there sprinkled even more liberally with grey than at his temples.

He sat on the side of the bed, smoothing back her ice-gold tangle of hair. 'I thought you were going to sleep all day,' he teased indulgently.

She longed to turn her face into that hand, to

shower kisses over his palm, to tell him how much she loved him, of his child that she carried inside her. Instead she drew back from him. 'I'm going up to Scotland today to stay the rest of the weekend with my parents.' It was an effort to keep her gaze on a level with him when his darkened angrily. 'I think we should take that time to accept that it's over between us,' she added in a rush of emotion.

Raff drew in a harsh breath, his hand dropping back to his side. 'What do you mean, it's over?' he rasped abruptly.

Bryna sighed. 'We've both known it for weeks, Raff, so why fool ourselves any longer?'

He stood up forcefully, grey eyes blazing. 'When did you decide this?' he demanded.

She shrugged, sitting up against the pillows. 'I've realised for some time——'

'I meant, when did you decide to visit your parents?' he ground out.

'I telephoned them yesterday afternoon and made the arrangements——'

'So you knew when we met to go out last night?' he accused.

She blinked. 'Yes. But——'

'Then what was last night all about?' His voice rose angrily.

Bryna swallowed hard. 'Goodbye?'

'Good——?' His face darkened thunderously as he grabbed hold of her arms and pulled her up to him so that her face was only inches away from him. 'Look at me and tell me you don't want me any more,' he ordered harshly.

For the sake of her pride she had to do it; she

knew she would never be able to face their child if she allowed their relationship to deteriorate to the stage where they were no longer equal but she was just someone Raff came to when he wanted a willing woman in his arms.

She met his gaze steadily. 'I no longer want you,' she lied.

'Damn you!' he grated forcefully, releasing her so suddenly she fell back on the pillows, watching numbly as he pulled on his clothes. 'Damn you,' he said again before slamming out of the apartment.

With a shuddering sob Bryna's body began to heave in racking waves of agony.

CHAPTER THREE

'ARE you sure, darling?' her mother choked through her tears of happiness. 'The doctors seemed so sure——'

'Mine is just as sure I'm pregnant,' Bryna told her laughingly. Her parents' reaction to her news, the one she had expected from them, had been pure joy! At last she had been able to tell someone, and the happiness of sharing her child with them was all she had thought it would be.

'It's just so incredible!' Her father hugged her, tears in his own deep blue eyes. He was tall and muscular, with hair that was grey now but that had once been the same colour as Bryna's.

'I know,' she laughed again. 'Yesterday I was still too shocked by the news to be able to take it in myself, but before I left this morning I called my doctor and asked him if he could be absolutely certain I was pregnant. I mean, he knows my medical history as well as I do! But he's almost certain the doctors told you there was always the possibility I could conceive, even if that possibility was a remote one.' She looked at them questioningly.

Her mother frowned thoughtfully. 'They seemed pretty convinced you wouldn't——'

'Well, he also said that they know more nowadays than they did then, and that perhaps they really did

believe I couldn't conceive. But they were wrong,'
she told them happily. 'Because my doctor also told
me I should start thinking of names!'

'Oh, darling!' Her mother was crying in earnest
now, small and dark, with a plump figure Bryna's
father had always maintained was cuddly!

Bryna had only arrived half an hour earlier, but
she had been too excited to contain her news until
after they had all eaten. She came home to see her
parents regularly in the home she had known all her
life. Her father owned and ran a ski-school in this
lovely part of north-east Scotland.

'No more tears,' she instructed briskly, her face
glowing. 'Let's have dinner before it spoils.'

'We should have some wine to celebrate,' her
father decided, hesitating suddenly. 'Can you drink
wine?' he asked curiously.

'One glass occasionally,' she nodded, smiling.
'And I think this is definitely an "occasion"!'

By the time they were halfway through the meal
her father was discussing which schools her unborn
child should attend! Bryna just smiled at him
indulgently, knowing how much he was enjoying
himself in his role of grandfather.

'Really, James,' her mother admonished lightly.
'That will be for Bryna and Mr Gallagher to decide.'

A shadow darkened Bryna's eyes to purple. 'Raff
and I are no longer together,' she announced flatly.

She had told her parents all about Raff and the
part he played in her life after their first week
together, never having kept secrets from them, and
knowing they respected the fact that she was old

enough to make her own decisions—and her own mistakes, if need be.

Her father frowned. 'I'm not old-fashioned enough to believe, or imply, that the two of you should get married because you're pregnant, but surely he'll want to take some interest in his own child?'

'It's my child, Dad——'

'You haven't told him,' he reproved gently. 'Isn't that a little selfish, lass?'

She blushed. 'He already has two children, why should he want mine?'

'Because——'

'Now, James, this isn't the night for an argument,' her mother cut in determinedly. 'I'm sure Bryna knows what she's doing.'

'But, Mary——'

'Not tonight, James!' her mother bit out, her brown eyes flashing warningly. She might be small and cuddly, but when the occasion warranted it she had a fiery temper that even her husband was in awe of!

Bryna gave a rueful smile, as her father, almost twice her mother's size, subsided into silence.

She hadn't meant to cause any friction between her parents, but she didn't want to talk of Raff this weekend, not when she had managed to avoid thinking of him since setting out for Scotland this morning.

It was a pleasant evening for all of them, making plans, laughingly suggesting the most outrageous names they could think of. A boy's name was already decided in her mind—Rafferty James, after its father and grandfather, but a girl's name was a little harder to decide upon. Maybe because she was already convinced she carried Raff's son.

Once she was alone in the single bed in the room that had remained hers, even though she had left so long ago, it was impossible to banish Raff from her mind any longer, and she allowed the tears of desolation to fall unheeded down her heated cheeks.

Was he with Rosemary, or someone like her, tonight, having put from his mind and his life the woman who had dared to end their affair?

God, how she would love his child, she vowed protectively.

Home to her would always be Scotland, Bryna realised the next day as she trudged through the thick snow with her father to the ski-lodge, greeting several of the ski-instructors by name as they entered the building, most of them having been with her father for years.

She had skied almost from the time she could walk, and she longed now to join the skiers on the white slopes. But she wouldn't selfishly risk her child no matter how she ached for the freedom being on skis gave her, having a feeling very much like flying when the skis moved beneath her and the wind whipped through her hair. Almost like making love to Raff. Almost . . .

'I hope you aren't even thinking about it,' rasped a coldly harsh voice from behind her.

Bryna turned so suddenly the ground tipped on its axis and the image of Raff moved in and out of her focus until there was only darkness.

When she returned to consciousness she found she was lying on the leather couch in her father's office.

Only her stricken gaze moved, her breath catching in a pained gasp as she saw the man standing with his back to the room as he stared out of the window at the mountains. He was dressed more casually than she had ever seen him before, in a thick black sweater and fitted denims, and yet she would know that thick dark hair anywhere, the powerful width of his shoulders, tapered waist, and strong thighs.

Raff really was here, and not a figment of her tormented imagination after all!

She moved to sit up, and the movement attracted Raff's attention; his narrowed grey eyes levelled on her. Bryna determinedly withstood that censorious gaze. 'My father?' she prompted abruptly.

Raff's mouth twisted. 'He had to organise some ski-instructors,' he dismissed. 'Once we'd established that you'd merely fainted he seemed quite happy to leave you in my care.'

No doubt her father saw this as the ideal opportunity for her to tell Raff about their baby! But she wasn't going to take it. 'You introduced yourselves?' She swung her legs to the floor, sitting up properly against the back of the sofa.

Raff turned to her fully, his hands thrust into his denims' pockets. 'It's the usual practice when one man finds another man holding his unconscious daughter in his arms!' he scorned.

A blush darkened her cheeks. 'What are you

doing here?' she snapped, still feeling slightly lightheaded.

'I've thought over what you said yesterday,' he told her. 'And I've decided I don't *want* to accept that it's over between the two of us.'

Bryna frowned warily at the silky softness of his tone. 'I told you, I don't want you any more.'

'So you did,' he nodded. 'But I believe our child *will* want me,' he added harshly.

Bryna paled. 'What on earth are you talking about?' She stood up agitatedly. 'What child?'

His eyes were steely. 'The one you're carrying. My child.'

She regained enough control to be able to give a scornful laugh, although his announcement had badly shaken her. 'I don't know what you're talking about——'

'I called your doctor, Bryna,' Raff interrupted softly. 'He confirmed my suspicions.'

'I don't believe you,' she shook her head. 'A doctor doesn't break a patient's confidence, no matter what the provocation.'

'And I'm sure yours wouldn't have done so this time if he hadn't thought I was already aware of the fact that I'm going to be a father again,' Raff ground out. 'I telephoned him and asked him if he thought your pregnancy was going well; he was only too happy to assure me it was,' he added hardly.

Bryna breathed hard in her agitation. 'What on earth made you call him and ask him such a question in the first place?'

His eyes narrowed. 'You seem to have forgotten

that I've been a father twice before, that I know the signs.'

'What signs?' she challenged.

He shrugged. 'Your extreme tiredness, a sudden aversion to the smell of fish. The fact that——'

'Why didn't you ask me?' A deep blush darkened her cheeks. 'Why call my doctor?'

'I just did ask you,' he rasped. 'You know the answer I got!' he scowled. 'I waited for you to tell me, Bryna, but instead you came up here!'

'Why on earth would you be interested in any pregnancy of mine?' Her agitation deepened.

Raff's eyes narrowed. 'Why wouldn't I?'

Her head went back in challenge. 'Maybe this baby isn't yours!' She didn't care that she was admitting her pregnancy by asking the question; it was useless continuing to deny it when her doctor had already assured him of its existence. It hadn't even occured to her that because Raff had been through two pregnancies with his wife he would know and recognise her own symptoms!

He relaxed slightly. 'I know that it is, Bryna,' he told her quietly.

She gave a pained frown, swallowing hard. 'What do you intend doing about it?'

'What do *you* intend doing about it?' he returned, silkily soft.

'Me?' She gave him a startled look, anger darkening her expression as his meaning became clear. 'How dare you think that I——'

'Bryna!' Her father burst into the room, looking her over anxiously. 'Thank God you're all right!'

She gave him a reassuring smile as she squeezed

his arm, controlling her burning anger towards Raff with effort. 'I'm fine,' she assured him.

'She's just been working too hard,' Raff cut in smoothly, his brows arching slightly as her father gave him a questioning look. 'I'll take her for a walk out in the fresh air.'

'Bryna?'

'Maybe that would be a good idea, Dad.' She gave him a bright smile, her heart skipping a beat as Raff helped her on with her thick anorak before taking his own leather jacket off the back of her father's chair. 'It's a little warm in here,' she excused lightly.

'I'll drive her back to the house afterwards.' Raff's tone dared either of them to dispute his right to do that.

Bryna gave her father's arm another squeeze as he looked at her uncertainly. 'I'll see you lunchtime.'

'He knows, doesn't he,' Raff stated as they walked at the foot of the panoramic mountains, dozens of skiers already on the slopes.

She gave him a brief glance before again watching her footing. 'They both do,' she nodded.

His eyes were steely. 'And yet your mother was polite enough to me when I called at the house, and your father didn't seem too concerned either. I'd want to kill any man who got Kate pregnant when they weren't married!'

'My parents love me too,' she defended resentfully. 'They just know I'm mature enough to handle this on my own.'

'You haven't told me how you feel about "this"

yet,' Raff prompted drily. 'Although it's obvious from your reaction earlier, and the fact that you've told your parents, that you don't intend having an abortion.'

'No, I don't,' she snapped. 'Look, Raff, why should I tell you anything?' She stopped to glare at him. 'I meant what I said yesterday; it's over between us.'

His hands moved to tightly grip her arms. 'Our child doesn't think so.'

'Raff, you already have two children, you don't need mine,' she reasoned warily.

'Do you want this child?' He shook her none too gently, his expression fierce.

'Yes!' she shouted at him, tears glistening in her darkened eyes.

'Well, so do I,' he told her softly.

'But why?' She wrenched away from him. 'You can have children with any woman, whereas I——'

'Yes?' he prompted harshly as she broke off abruptly.

She breathed deeply to calm herself. 'This baby is mine——'

'Ours,' he corrected abruptly. 'A sister or a brother for Kate and Paul.'

She had never thought of it from quite that angle before; she had imagined her child looking like the attractive pair, but never thought that her child would have them as a sister and brother.

But as she did realise it she also recognised that *either* of them was old enough to be the parent of her baby. Raff *couldn't* want another baby around him at this stage in his life, just as Kate and Paul wouldn't; he just didn't like to be thwarted.

'That changes nothing,' she dismissed. 'And I wouldn't stop either of them seeing the baby if they wanted to.'

'And what about me?' snapped Raff. 'When would I get to see my child—once a month, two weeks in the summer, and alternate Christmases if I'm lucky?' His disgust with that arrangement was obvious!

'Our lawyers could work something out——'

'They won't "work anything out" because no matter what other plans you may have made you're going to marry me!'

Raff could be arrogant, domineering, even downright unreasonable, but Bryna had never seen him actually lose his temper enough to shout before; his anger was usually cold and controlled. But he was shouting now, and Bryna flinched in surprise. 'Do you really want to start another marriage with a child born only six months after the wedding day?' she reasoned gently.

On one of the warm summer evenings they had spent together in her bed Raff had told her that the reason he and Josey had married so young was because Josey was already pregnant with Paul at the time. They were in love, had taken risks, and they had paid for it with a teenage marriage that could have succeeded despite that, and yet somehow hadn't. She was sure Raff couldn't want a repeat of that.

His mouth twisted. 'It seems I'm destined to get my wives that way,' he derided. 'God, Bryna, there's no comparison!' he dismissed impatiently.

'I'm thirty-nine now, not eighteen. And you are hardly a child either!'

She shook her head slowly. 'I don't want to marry you.'

'Because you no longer want me physically?' His eyes were narrowed to steely slits.

She looked at him unflinchingly. 'That's right.'

A nerve pulsed in his cheek. 'That's easily settled; I won't touch you in a physical way again.'

Bryna looked at him as if he had gone insane right before her eyes, but she could tell by his set expression that he meant every word he said. 'Easily settled'? Could he really stand there and decide in that calm way that he no longer desired her either? It seemed that he could. And wasn't it what she had suspected in their relationship the last month or so? But for the sake of their child he was determined to marry her, no matter what he had to do to get her to agree. And much as her parents loved her and would want to help her, could any of them defy one of the richest men in England, possibly the world? Where could she go that he wouldn't find her!

'I can't give you an answer now, Raff,' she told him tremulously. 'I need time to think.'

He looked pointedly at the flatness of her stomach that would soon swell with his child. 'Time is something we don't have too much of,' he rasped.

Her eyes flashed. 'A few days isn't going to make that much difference!'

'All right,' he gave an abrupt inclination of his head. 'You have a few days.'

And after that he would make the decision for

her, he seemed to be telling her without actually saying the words!

Bryna, of all people, knew how charming Raff could be when he chose to be, and over lunch with her parents he wanted to be very much, talking freely about their life together in London, answering questions about Kate and Paul.

She knew her parents respected the fact that it was her decision what the future held for her and her unborn child, but as Raff solicitously saw to her every need during the meal she could see them both shooting her questioning looks as to why *she* had decided she and Raff were 'no longer together'; it was obvious from Raff's behaviour that it hadn't been his decision to end things! And her parents knew that she loved him, that she would never have become his lover if she hadn't been in love with him from the first.

Their first evening together Raff had deliberately set out to seduce her, with an expensive dinner eaten by candledlight, romantic music playing softly in the background, with a slate-eyed Raff sitting across from her. She hadn't wanted to be seduced, had found his domineering attitude of earlier disquietening, even if she couldn't help but be attracted to him.

She had expected him to take her home by car from the restaurant, instead he had suggested picking his car up later and walking through the park to her home. Her scepticism with this idea turned to enchantment as she realised that no mugger in his right mind would argue with Raff, and that the scent of early summer flowers was even

more heady than the wine they had consumed
during their meal.

The biggest surprise of the evening had come
when he refused her invitation to come into her
apartment for coffee, and instead gave her a
lingering goodnight kiss on her doorstep before
taking his leave. That single kiss had been enough
to tell her she was more attracted to him than to any
other man she had ever known.

When Court telephoned her the next day and
invited her out to dinner with him that evening it
wasn't too difficult to refuse him, knowing she was
keeping her evening free just in case Raff called.
She knew she was behaving like a teenager waiting
for a call from her first boyfriend, but she couldn't
help herself!

He didn't call, and she spent the evening washing
and drying her hair instead, cursing herself for
turning down an invitation from such a nice man as
Court Stevens on the offchance that a rat like Raff
Gallagher might deign to call.

She was still angry with herself the next day, her
mood one of snapping irritation. How could she
have been so gullible as to have been taken in by a
man like Raff Gallagher! He had proved his point,
that they had indeed 'met again', and that like all
the other women in his life she hadn't been able to
resist him!

'Wishing that pencil were my neck?' drawled a
coolly confident voice.

Bryna looked up at Raff Gallagher with a start as
he stood unannounced in the doorway to her office;
she would have a word with Gilly about this

oversight later, *after* she had evicted Raff Gallagher from her office!

'I didn't think you were the violent type,' he raised dark brows as he strolled fully into the room, closing the door softly behind him.

She glanced down at the broken pencil in her hands with some surprise; she hadn't even realised she had snapped it in two. 'I'm not.' She dropped the two halves of the pencil into the bin beside her desk. 'I don't believe we have an appointment, Mr Gallagher.' She looked at him with cool enquiry.

He bent his long length into the chair opposite hers. 'Do you have any coffee? I'm in need of waking up.'

Bryna's eyes flashed angrily. 'Then maybe you should have stayed in bed longer!' How dared he come here demanding she give him coffee after spending the night with one of his women!

He leant his head back in the chair, closing his eyes briefly. 'I haven't been to bed——'

'Mr Gallagher——'

'I must be getting old,' he drawled ruefully, straightening in his chair, just that few seconds' relaxation with his eyes closed seeming to have revived him a little. 'A couple of years ago I would have been able to take flying to the States, working through their evening—our night—and then flying back to England when my business was finished, without any ill-effects.' He shook his head. 'Now I just feel exhausted.'

'Well, of course you do,' scolded Bryna, having listened in horror as he related his gruelling schedule of the last twenty-four hours; no wonder he hadn't called her, he hadn't had time! And she knew how shattering jet-lag could be too. 'You'll kill yourself working that hard!' She stood up to pour him a cup of coffee from the percolator across the room.

He drank the strong black brew gratefully. 'I couldn't give Court the opportunity to move in on the woman I so badly want for myself,' he said softly, watching her over the rim of his cup as he drank some more coffee. 'Now could I?' He looked at her warmly.

A sophisticated lady, used to any amount of male attention during her years as a model, and she blushed! 'Maybe you should have taken the time to telephone me before you left so that I knew you felt that way,' she snapped.

His eyes narrowed. 'Does that mean I'm too late, and Court has called you?'

Was this man ever too late, had any woman ever denied him? Could *she*? 'I think you should go home to bed now, and——'

'Come with me,' he invited huskily, his tiredness completely gone now.

Bryna swallowed hard at the directness of his approach. 'And if you still want to see me again you can call me later,' she finished firmly, resisting with effort the temptation she had to go home with him right now. If he asked again she might not have resisted, but instead he stood up to leave.

'I'll call you later,' he told her throatily.

She faced him across the room; she hadn't returned to her seat behind her desk after pouring him his coffee. 'Fine,' she acknowledged nervously.

Nervous? The woman who had been called icy and distant? Incredible!

'Bryna,' Raff murmured huskily before taking her in his arms and kissing her lingeringly on the mouth. 'I'll definitely call you later,' he told her ruefully as he straightened reluctantly. 'And next time I have to go away on business unexpectedly I'll make sure I call and let you know,' he promised softly.

Next time? Bryna pondered over the statement all afternoon. He seemed to be implying that their relationship was going to be a lengthy rather than short one, and knowing about him what she did she knew that any lengthy relationship she had with Raff Gallagher would have to be a physical one. And before she saw him again she would have to decide if that were what she wanted with him.

If the romantic dinner and the moonlit stroll through the park had come as a surprise to her two days ago when arranged by such a cynical man as Raff Gallagher, then spending the evening at his home with his two children came as even more of one!

Raff had telephoned just before she was due to leave her office for the day, something she was relieved about because she didn't think he knew her home telephone number and so she had been contemplating sitting at her desk waiting for him to call. Even if it took all night!

When he had invited her out to dinner but advised her to dress casually she still hadn't been alarmed. The suspicion had only begun when they turned into the long driveway to his home!

Raff gave a derisive smile at her accusing look. 'I didn't manage to get to bed this afternoon,' he drawled. 'And the thought of sitting in a restaurant and possibly falling asleep in the company of the most beautiful woman I've ever met is not something I relish!'

Her mouth quirked at his self-derision. 'Your reputation would be shot to pieces!' she acknowledged.

He raised dark brows. 'Don't believe everything you hear—or read—about me,' he said drily, opening her car door for her.

She turned from admiring the Georgian-style house situated in Royal Berkshire to smile at him. 'You mean you don't drink champagne for breakfast and wear silk pyjamas?' she mocked one of the articles she had once read about him, although the thought of the latter against the velvet hardness of his skin sent a shiver of pleasure down her spine.

'No,' he grinned.

'No to which one?' Bryna raised blonde brows curiously.

'No, I don't drink champagne for breakfast, and no, I don't wear any sort of pyjamas. But I'm willing to reconsider the first if you'll join me one morning,' he added huskily.

A blush darkened her cheeks. 'Did you say something about dinner . . .?'

'Coward!' he taunted as he clasped her arm lightly in his hand as they entered his home.

The presence in the lounge of the pretty dark-haired girl and a young man as tall and dark as Raff, if not quite as muscular, that he introduced as his children, Paul and Kate, instantly took her aback. She had thought Raff had brought her to his home for the sole purpose of trying to seduce her into his bed, and as she glanced at him she could tell by his expression that he had known exactly what she had thought.

The fact that Kate and Paul obviously intended spending the evening at home with their father, no matter who he had with him, threw Bryna into a state of nervous tension.

'Relax,' Raff advised softly as he sat down beside her on the sofa after handing her the glass of sherry she had asked for. 'My children don't bite!'

They didn't bite, but they were so forthright that they made her more uncomfortable than ever with the bluntness of their questions.

At twenty Paul was very like Raff must have been at that age, and he saw no reason to hide the fact that he found her as attractive as he presumed his father did!

Kate was more interested in discussing fashions with her, and she grabbed on to the subject gratefully. Nevertheless, she felt exhausted by the time Paul left to return to his flat in town and Kate went up to her room to listen to a new cassette she had bought that day.

'What did you think of them?' Raff arched mocking brows as she relaxed for what had to be the first time that evening.

Bryna took her time answering, formulating her opinion now that the pressure was off her. His children—although their ages precluded them actually being that!—were both friendly and without affectation, and it was a reflection on their father, with all the wealth he had at his disposal and the fact that he had been a single parent for the last ten years, that they had turned out as nice and uncomplicated as they were. It was obvious that he loved them very much, and that the protective emotion was more than returned.

But she had found Kate's candour a little unnerving, and Paul had flirted with her endlessly.

Raff gave a brief laugh at her continued silence. 'They don't usually have the effect of leaving people speechless!' he assured her. 'Over the years I've been told that they're brash, rude, inquisitive, and spoilt brats.'

'I don't agree with that,' she instantly protested. 'Kate is just brutally honest, and Paul is—well, he's——'

'I'll talk to him tomorrow about his behaviour towards you tonight,' rasped Raff, his mouth tight.

'Oh no,' she protested again. 'He was only— only——'

'Trying to steal the woman I want.' Raff drew her determinedly into his arms. 'No one, least of all my twenty-year-old son, takes something I want away from me,' he told her arrogantly before his head bent to hers.

Looking at him now, as he chatted amiably with her parents, Bryna couldn't help wondering what she thought she was doing trying to refuse him something he wanted as badly as he seemed to want her child!

CHAPTER FOUR

'YOU'RE very quiet.'

Bryna opened her eyes to look across the luxury of the personalised jet Raff had insisted she join him on during her return flight to London. 'I'm just tired,' she shook her head.

She wasn't just physically tired, but mentally too; she had been fighting a battle with herself all day, talking herself in and out of agreeing to marry Raff as he wanted her to do. She still had no solution to the question he demanded she answer soon.

'Just relax, Bryna,' he rasped. 'No one is going to force you into anything.'

He never had forced her, and she had no doubt that he didn't intend to start now. He had never *needed* to use force with her, just as he hadn't that night they made love after she had remained a virgin for the twenty-four years of her life.

It had seemed strange spending the evening with his children on only their second date, but neither they nor Raff had seemed bothered by the fact, and so she had told herself she didn't care either. Despite her protests that she could get a taxi home, because he had to be feeling exhausted by now, Raff had insisted on driving her home himself.

She turned to him as he parked the car outside her apartment building. 'I won't invite you in because——'

'Invite me in, Bryna,' he urged huskily.

'—you're tired, and——' she broke off as she realised what he had said. 'You want to come in?' She blinked her surprise.

'More than anything,' he nodded, his expression intent.

'But you're tired, and——'

'Bryna, I'm wide awake, and I want you to invite me in!'

What could she say to a forceful request like that? She shrugged her shoulders. 'All right,' she agreed a little dazedly. 'If that's what you want . . .'

'It is,' he said somewhat grimly, following her into the building.

Bryna eyed him warily across the width of the lift as it ascended to her floor, aware that the moment of truth had come quicker than she had thought it would, the evening spent with his children having lulled her into a false sense of security where their own physical relationship was concerned.

Raff was broodingly silent, filled with a tension of his own, and she knew by just looking at him that he would never settle for the basically platonic relationships she had shared with the other men she had dated over the years. As they entered her apartment she knew now was the time to make up her mind what she wanted from him.

'What are you thinking about?'

Raff's harsh voice cut in on her memories, and once again she opened her eyes to look across the width of the plane at him. 'What do you think?' she scorned irritably.

He gave an impatient sigh. 'I thought you were

sleeping until I saw your eyes moving under your lids!' he bit out. 'Why bother to fight it, Bryna; you know you'll have to agree in the end.'

'Is that really the sort of marriage you want?' she flared. 'Two people who don't love each other tied together because of a child they accidentally created! Didn't the failure of your first marriage tell you anything about that sort of arrangement?' she scorned.

'My first marriage didn't fail,' he snapped. 'Josey and I were too young, too idealistic about our feelings, to survive all the pressures we had put on us. But we did respect each other.'

'But it wasn't enough, was it?' Bryna reasoned forcefully.

'This time it will have to be,' he grated. 'You talk as if your pregnancy were my fault,' he snapped. 'We may have created that child, Bryna, but I don't believe it was *my* "accident".'

She felt her cheeks pale. 'I wondered when you would get around to blaming me——'

'I'm not blaming you for anything,' he gave a weary sigh. 'But you did tell me you would take care of birth control. I just presumed that you had.'

As she had presumed nature had done for her years before! She had seen no reason for either of them to use birth control when there was no possibility of her becoming pregnant, although she hadn't chosen to tell Raff that. 'I thought I had,' she told him gruffly, not quite able to meet his gaze.

He shrugged. 'Then you did what you could, and it happened anyway.' He pushed away his seat-belt, crossing the cabin to come down on his haunches in front of her. 'Bryna, we've been lovers for six months, we aren't strangers who stumbled into bed together, with your pregnancy the result of that night. Would marriage to me really be so terrible?' he encouraged, gently holding her hands within his own.

She looked at him searchingly, wishing she could believe that a marriage of necessity to him wouldn't be the nightmare she thought it would be. Maybe if they were strangers it *could* have worked, at least then she wouldn't hunger for his love the way she did now. But to live in the same house with him, be married to him, and know she was only the mother of his child, would be purgatory! And to be married to him and have him make love to her out of duty would be pure hell! She couldn't win whatever she did, not now that Raff knew about her child.

Her head went back proudly. 'I've already told you that the only way there would *be* a marriage is if we led separate lives.'

His expression darkened as he released her hands to straighten and drop into the seat beside her. 'I believe *I* said separate beds, Bryna,' he rasped. 'I have no intention of entering another marriage where we each have our own sexual partners.'

The colour came and then went in her cheeks. 'That wasn't what I meant at all,' she gasped, the thought of him leaving her in the evenings to go to another woman making her feel ill. And yet he was a sensual man; what else could she expect him to do in the circumstances? 'I—I suppose I could learn to live with the fact that you—you have other women——'

'I couldn't accept your having other men,' he grated. 'If you marry me you'll occupy no one's bed but your own! And if I ever find out you've broken that agreement our marriage will be at an end and I'll do everything in my power to get custody of my child.'

Bryna was very pale, not doubting for a moment that he meant what he said—or his ability to carry it out. It was only because she was so aware of the power he wielded that she was even considering agreeing to his proposal.

His eyes were narrowed grey slits. 'You can carry on working, you can hire a nanny to care for the child, you can do what you damn well please, but you won't give any other man what you deny me!'

He was like a child refusing to let anyone else play with his toy even though he didn't want it himself! Because that was all she would be if she married him, a beautiful ornament for his home.

'Can't you see that it wouldn't work, Raff?' she tried reasoning with him.

'I would make sure that it did work,' he told her arrogantly.

She sighed. 'I'm a person, Raff, with feelings of my own, not some business deal you're putting together!'

'I'm well aware of the fact that you have feelings,' he bit out. 'Which is why I offered you a normal marriage.'

So that she could be a charity case, with Raff making perfunctory love to her so that she didn't need to go to other men! God, she couldn't exist that way. 'The pregnancy is my problem, Raff, why don't you just let me handle it?' she urged forcefully.

'The child,' he harshly emphasised the word, 'is mine. And I want it.'

Again she acknowledged that Raff was never denied anything he wanted badly enough. She was like a caged bird trying to escape the bars, even though those bars were made out of gold. A lot of people would say she was being ridiculous by wanting to escape, but then those people didn't love the man who had the key to the door of the golden cage. Besides, she didn't need his money, she was financially secure herself, although she had nothing like the wealth Raff controlled.

'How do you think Kate and Paul are going to react to this cuckoo in their nest?' she demanded.

His expression darkened. 'This child will be as much mine as they are,' he rasped. 'So they'd better learn to accept it!'

Bryna had run out of arguments for the moment, knowing that the only real one she had was that she loved Raff and he didn't love her. She had no doubts about his ability to be a good and loving father to her child, she knew that with her inexperience in the role he had more reason to doubt her capabilities as a mother!

She closed her eyes. 'All right, Raff,' she sighed, 'I'll marry you. On the condition that I have my own bedroom, and that you never enter it,' she added the last quickly as she saw the blaze of triumph in his eyes, making them appear almost silver.

He nodded calmly, looking nothing at all like a man who had just fought a major battle and won. Maybe because there had never been any doubt in his mind that he would be the victor! 'Agreed,' he bit out. 'But I meant it about there being no other men' he watched her with narrowed eyes. 'If you want to make love then come to me!'

Heat burnt her cheeks. 'That won't be necessary,' she told him coldly. She would rather suffer the agony of unfulfilment for the rest of her life than beg him to make love to her!

Raff's mouth twisted angrily. 'You don't think you'll ever be that desperate, hmm?'

'No!' she snapped defensively, her eyes flashing deeply purple.

He shrugged. 'The offer is there if you want it. We never did get around to drinking champagne together for breakfast,' he taunted. 'But I don't suppose it really matters,' he dismissed, turning away.

It was strange that he should remind her of that night when it had already been so much on her mind today.

The minute her apartment door had closed behind them that night she had known that she wanted him as he so obviously wanted her. And yet her inexperience made her shy, the uncertainty she still harboured about being able to satisfy any man. Physically, outwardly, she was sure she was the same as other women, but Raff was a man who had made love to a lot of women over the years; would he be able to tell that she lacked something inside her that made her into a real woman? There was only one way to find out, she decided, taking a deep breath.

'I've been imagining doing this all evening,' he

groaned as his hands threaded through the softness of her hair to cradle the back of her head as he bent to claim her lips.

That single kiss of the night before hadn't prepared her for the sensual onslaught of the second drugging kiss, Raff's body curved into hers, holding her against him only by his hands entangled in her hair.

Not that she wanted to move away from him, straining against him for closer contact as the pleasure of his touch washed over her in waves, her lips parting beneath the pressure of his, moving together moistly.

Every other thought but Raff and what he was doing to her went out of her head, and she arched her throat as his lips caressed her there with insistent passion, their breaths a ragged rasp in the silence.

'Is it all right for you tonight, Bryna?' he pressed urgently.

She gave him a startled look. 'All right? But——' Colour suffused her cheeks as his meaning became clear to her. 'Yes, I—I'm fine,' she assured him awkwardly.

'Can we spend the night here?' His gaze was intent on her flushed face. 'I would have invited you to stay on at the house with me, but with Kate there . . .'

'I understand,' she cut in hastily. God, was this the way it was done—a mutual desire, and they just spent the night together? Probably it was, she was just such a novice when it came to these relationships, and if she hadn't already realised she was falling in love with Raff she wouldn't even be contemplating entering into one of them now. And she didn't want Raff to think she was a complete fool. 'It will be much more convenient if we spend the night here,' she said lightly, throwing her clutch-bag down into a chair, wondering what it had still been doing in her hand in the first place, belatedly realising she could have hit Raff around the head with it as they kissed. Well, from now on she was going to appear a little more sophisticated! 'The bathroom is through there,' she pointed to the rose-coloured door. 'Maybe you would like to use it first,' she invited, congratulating herself on how blasé she sounded as she evasively told him she didn't intend sharing it with him.

'Bryna——'

'I have to remove my make-up and all those other going-to-bed things, anyway,' she added brightly. 'But maybe I should just tell you,' she continued haltingly as he just stood there looking at her. 'That my—experience won't be anywhere near as extensive as your own, and I——'

His hard kiss silenced her. 'I don't want to talk about our pasts or the other lovers we've known,' he said harshly. 'For the moment there's only this,' his kiss was lingeringly thorough. 'We can talk later,' he promised. 'When I don't need you quite as badly as I do now,' he added self-derisively.

Fool! Bryna berated herself agitatedly. Of course he didn't want to discuss the extent of her experience—or lack of it—now. Just as she didn't want to know about the other women he had had in his life. 'Take your time in the bathroom' she invited abruptly, making a hurried escape to her bedroom.

God, she hoped Raff didn't realise just *how* inexperienced she was by her fumbling display of so-called sophistication!

If he had he certainly didn't show it, sitting back against the pillows in her three-quarter-size bed when she emerged from the bathroom after her own shower, the sheet draped across his thighs revealing that he was completely naked beneath its flimsy covering. And she was buttoned up from neck to ankle in a towelling robe! She also felt like a gauche teenager without her make-up, while he managed to look more devastating than ever, less awe-inspiring with the dark swathe of his hair falling over his forehead, but just as overwhelmingly attractive.

She suddenly felt more shy than ever, wondering what she was doing contemplating making love with this stranger that she believed she was falling in love with.

And then Raff threw back the sheet to get out of the bed, magnificent in his golden nakedness, and Bryna was too bemused by him to notice as he deftly unbuttoned her robe before letting it fall to the floor.

Her lack of experience didn't seem to matter as they kissed and caressed each other; she reacted to him instinctively, knowing a fierce longing to touch him in the same way he was touching her.

They made love slowly, tantalisingly, with Bryna wild for his possession when he finally parted her thighs to move between them, all thoughts of inadequacy pushed to the back of her mind as she

felt that brief pain followed by the most wonderful
feeling of completion she had ever known, meeting
the fierce thrusts of his thighs as he drove them both
to, and over, the edge of fulfilment.

Bryna had never felt so free, as if she was
completely weightless as she flew on a soft, downy
cloud of hazy pleasure.

But as she looked up at Raff as he still lay joined
to her some of the happiness faded from her eyes,
knowing that for him it had just been another sexual
encounter. 'I did try to warn you I'm a bit of a
novice at this type of thing.' She couldn't quite meet
his gaze, only inches away from her own.

'Novice?' he echoed gruffly. 'It was more than
that, you were——'

'Very clever to choose someone as skilful as you
for my first lover,' she cut in lightly. 'And
admittedly I may not be very experienced, but I'm
sure we both know the rules well enough——'

'What rules?' he echoed softly, suddenly still as
he looked down at her watchfully.

She smiled, still not quite meeting his gaze. 'No
ties, no commitments, we can just enjoy each other!'

'Of course,' he agreed flatly, moving away from
her to lie at her side.

Bryna looked at him searchingly. Had she been
too hasty, could she have been mistaken about the
pleasure he had found from their lovemaking? She
was discussing the two of them having an affair,
and he hadn't even given any indication that he'
wanted to see her again!

'Unless tonight was all you wanted——'

'It wasn't,' Raff cut in harshly. 'I have a hunger

for you that won't be satisfied with just one night!'
He kissed her fiercely as he began making love to
her a second time.

And so they had had their affair, but although
their lovemaking always gave her that feeling of
completion, as if Raff were the other half of herself,
it had never been quite as emotionally fulfilling as it
had that first night; the last month or so it hadn't
even made her feel close to Raff any more.

And now she had given up even the little she did
have, to become his wife.

CHAPTER FIVE

CHRISTMAS Eve sounded a romantic day for a wedding, and this wedding had had it all—the breathless bride in her gown of flowing white chiffon and lace, attended by four beautiful bridesmaids, one of them the groom's daughter from his previous marriage, the other three all close friends of the bride, the groom himself looking very handsome and distinguished in his grey morning-suit.

The church had been packed with guests, the bride was given away by her proud father, the vows were exchanged with quiet intensity. The wedding of Bryna Fairchild to Raff Gallagher had lacked nothing.

Unless you looked beneath the fairy-tale veneer and realised the reason the bride was so breathless was because the wedding had all been arranged within a matter of two weeks rather than the months such a lavishly perfect occasion would normally take to organise.

Raff had done all the organising, of course, from insisting she wear a white gown, despite her protest that she really shouldn't, to asking her to choose several other bridesmaids to attend her after she had told him Kate would be enough, to inviting so many guests to the church, and the ballroom of this prestigious hotel for their wedding reception, that after greeting them at the door as they arrived she doubted she would see most of the guests again tonight!

Everyone agreed that it had been a beautiful wedding and now reception, that the bride looked beautiful if a little pale—but then what woman wouldn't have been a little pale when she had just become the wife of that magnificently rich and handsome creature?—she had heard one of her female guests murmur bitchily to her companion.

Raff hadn't been about to deny or confirm the rumours going around during the two weeks before their wedding that the reason for the haste was the expected arrival of the 'third Gallagher heir', as one newspaper had put it. But before too many weeks had passed everyone was going to know that was the reason his bride had looked so pale!

Raff had insisted on telling Kate and Paul about the baby and marriage as soon as they got back from Scotland, and although Bryna hadn't even been able to guess what their reaction would be to either piece of news she was pleasantly surprised by Kate's unreserved pleasure, although Paul seemed to feel slightly embarrassed at the thought of having another sister, or perhaps brother, at his age. But neither of them had openly rejected the baby, which was more than Bryna could have hoped for in the circumstances.

Paul had been his father's best man, of course, with Court waving away Raff's explanations as to why he had chosen his son over him, with the laughing comment that he had already been his best man once and that had been enough, only willing to face the embarrassment of the speech he had had to give after the ceremony once in his life. He had chosen to give Bryna a congratulatory kiss instead.

'Would you care to dance, Mrs Gallagher?'

Hearing herself called that gave her a slight jolt, and her smile was a little shaky as she turned to a teasing Court.

His expression darkened with concern as he saw how strained she looked. 'Maybe you should sit down instead and I'll get you something to eat; you look as if you're about to faint!'

'It's this headdress and veil,' she sighed, easing her scalp where the weight of the diamond tiara held her veil in place. Raff had given her the tiara as part of her wedding present, the matching earrings and necklace being locked away in the family safe for her. The tiara demanded that she have her long hair styled beneath it, but she had insisted that it not be twisted and curled into some style that would just feel tortuous by the end of the day. But the pins that secured the tiara in place dug into her flesh instead.

'Take it off,' Court suggested. 'There's no reason why you shouldn't now. I'll help you,' he smiled, his actions matching his words as he searched for the hidden pins.

'No,' she put a hand up to stop him, looking anxiously about the crowded room in case Raff was watching her. He stood across the room talking with Penny and Janine, two of her bridesmaids, and their partners for the evening. But he was looking straight at her, his eyes cold and condemning. 'Raff wouldn't like it,' she told Court a little desperately.

'Don't be silly,' he frowned down at her. 'Raff isn't the one who's uncomfortable.'

'Please don't worry about it,' she assured him quickly. 'The bride can't walk around without her veil!'

'I don't see why you can't now,' Court dismissed. 'If you——'

'Why don't we have that dance?' and forget about the damned veil! Raff had been determined that *nothing* should go wrong with the wedding, and she knew he included her own behaviour in that.

'But——'

'Don't you want to dance with the bride?' she teased. 'Maybe you're frightened that some of the confetti will give you ideas yourself?' she taunted.

'Not me,' he grinned as he swept her deftly around the dance floor. 'I'm what's known as a "crusty old bachelor"—and determined to stay that way!' he added firmly.

Bryna gave him a scathing glance. 'In that case leave my fourth bridesmaid alone!'

'I happen to find Alyson a very stimulating conversationalist,' he returned in a reproachful voice.

'Of course you do,' Bryna laughed softly. 'That's why you suggested the two of you book into a room here for the night!' She arched mocking brows.

'I was only trying to be helpful by offering an alternative to the journey to her home late at night,' he defended.

Bryna chuckled. 'She only lives half a mile away!'

'That's right, mock my generosity!' Court sound-ed as if she had offended him, but the twinkle in his eyes belied the emotion. 'Women,' he muttered. 'They can't keep anything to themselves!'

She smiled at him. 'If it's any consolation, Alyson was almost tempted to accept!'

'That's the story of my life,' he bemoaned with a sigh. 'Women are always *almost* tempted.'

'From what Raff has told me about you it isn't always almost!' she reproved.

Court gave a self-satisfied grin. 'We "crusty old bachelors" need companionship occasionally, you know.'

Bryna shook her head. 'No wonder you and Raff are such good friends.'

He sobered. 'Raff hasn't looked at another woman since the two of you started seeing each other. Well—except Rosemary the other week,' he amended awkwardly. 'And that doesn't really count.'

'It doesn't?' she frowned, wondering if he knew something she didn't, because as far as she was concerned that night still smarted very much.

'Well, he should never have let it go that far, of course, but he did have that business deal on his mind, and——'

'Is that what he told you?' she scorned disbelievingly. She had never actually asked Raff what excuse he had given to his friend for his behaviour that night, and Raff hadn't offered to tell her, but now she knew he had told a deliberate lie. Why not just tell the truth, that he was tired of her and looking for a way out?

Over the last two weeks he had consulted her on the finer points of the wedding, overridden her where he didn't agree with her opinion, making her wonder why he had bothered to consult her in the first place. And he had kept to his promise that he wouldn't touch her in a physical way again.

As an example of what their married life was going to be like she learnt just how miserable she was going to be, but as a testament to how well Raff could keep his promise his behaviour had been unimpeachable!

Court frowned. 'You mean it isn't what really happened?'

She looked up at him searchingly. 'Court, Raff did tell you that we're only getting married because of the baby?'

'What baby?' He looked perplexed, his brows disappearing beneath his hair-line at the same time as his gaze lowered disbelievingly to the high-waisted gown she wore, the swelling of the baby barely perceptible beneath its Regency-style lines. 'You're pregnant?' He frowned his disbelief.

Now it was Bryna's turn to look puzzled. 'You mean Raff *didn't* tell you? She had thought that he would at least trust his best friend with their secret.

'You mean you *are* pregnant?' Court stopped dancing to stare down at her, tightly gripping her arms.

'Yes,' she confirmed simply, tears glistening in her eyes.

'There have been rumours, because of the suddenness of the wedding,' he said slowly, still looking dazed. 'But Raff never gave a hint—My God, I never guessed!' His face darkened angrily. 'The stupid——'

'It wasn't Raff's fault,' she cut in quickly. 'I'm afraid I was in charge of that, and I—goofed.'

'And from the look of you he's obviously been making your life hell because of it,' he scowled, scouring the room for the other man. 'How could he do this to you? He——'

'Court, please!' She put a hand of entreaty on his muscle-tensed arm, conscious that they were attracting considerable attention as they stood in the middle of the ballroom while the other couples danced around them. 'Let's go somewhere and talk,' she encouraged. 'I——'

'Stuart has been longing to dance with you, Bryna.' A harsh-faced Raff appeared at her side, his assistant firmly in tow. 'You seem to have concluded your dance with my wife, Court,' he told the other man firmly.

Court looked set to argue that point, but Bryna evaded the scene that would ensue if he did by moving lightly into Stuart Hillier's arms.

As she moved instinctively to the music she was barely conscious of her dancing partner as she watched Raff and Court leave the dance-floor to go into a room together off the main area where all the guests were gathered.

'Your parents seem to be having a good time.' Stuart Hillier's abrupt statement brought her attention back to him, although she couldn't stop feeling anxious about what was transpiring between the two friends behind that closed door.

She glanced across the room to where her mother and father were once again dancing together, returning to the table they shared with Raff's more

elderly parents during the short resting periods
between dancing. They had always enjoyed dancing
together, and as her father had laughingly teased,
what better occasion to dance than at their only
child's wedding?

Having met Raff, and liked him, they were
pleased she had decided to marry him, and she
hadn't had the heart to tell them how much this
marriage distressed her. They only wanted her to be
happy, and they believed Raff could make her that;
they could have no idea of the bargain she had made
with her new husband.

'Yes,' she turned back to Stuart Hillier. 'I hope
you're enjoying yourself too.' She looked at him
enquiringly.

'Of course,' he returned stiltedly.

His manner was unfriendly to say the least, and
after months of finding him overly familiar, if
anything, she couldn't help wondering if he had
been warned off by Raff's attitude towards Court a
few minutes ago. She hoped so.

She didn't know why she disliked this man, he
was always polite, sometimes too much so, and yet
for some reason she felt uneasy in his presence. He
was reasonably tall, although not as tall as either
Raff or Court, with dark hair and deep brown eyes
that should have been warm but somehow weren't.
He made Bryna feel uncomfortable every time she
was with him.

'Good,' she gave him a bright smile as the music
ended, turning to walk away, only to have him clasp
her arm. 'Yes?' she turned to him enquiringly.

'Raff asked me to—look after you, until he

returns,' Stuart told her challengingly.

'Indeed?' She gave him a look of haughty disdain. 'I don't believe I need "looking after" at my own wedding, thank you!'

'Nevertheless——'

'Mr Hillier,' she cut in icily, 'at this moment I intend talking to one of my cousins, and I certainly don't need your company to do that!'

How dared Raff tell his assistant to watch over her as if she were a child who could step out of line and embarrass him if left alone! He had never acted in that autocratic way with her before, never given the impression she wasn't to be trusted if left on her own. Maybe he expected her to get up on a table and announce to all their guests that they were to be parents in just over six months' time! *That* was going to be obvious soon enough anyway, and she certainly wouldn't embarrass *her* parents by even thinking about doing such a thing!

She was chatting absently with her cousin and her fiancé when she saw Court leave the room he and Raff had entered together, quickly excusing herself to cross the room towards him, a perplexed frown marring her brow as he turned to leave the reception room without a second glance, his expression thunderous.

Bryna hurried after him. 'Court——'

'Don't!'

The pain of having her wrist cruelly grasped was as nothing to the ache in her chest as she looked up into Raff's coldly furious face. He actually looked as if he hated her in that moment! He had never seemed so much a stranger.

She wrenched her gaze away from his cold one, looking towards the door. 'But Court——'

'Had to leave unexpectedly,' Raff bit out in harsh reply.

Bryna turned back to him slowly, frowning her bewilderment. 'You asked your best friend to leave our wedding,' she said disbelievingly.

'No,' Raff grated softly. 'He chose to leave.'

Bryna faced him accusingly. 'Because you made him,' she realised disgustedly. 'What on earth do you think you're doing ——'

'I think I'm trying to avoid causing a scene, but if you're intent on one——!' He nodded in the direction of the room he and Court had so recently vacated. 'Let's go in there,' he instructed between gritted teeth.

Bryna went willingly. She had been woken by her mother at seven o'clock this morning, been hustled and bustled about all morning dealing with all the last-minute details, been married to a man who was now a stranger to her, and for the last four hours she had tried to put a happy face on that marriage in front of their families and friends. It felt good to at last have a respite from that, although she wished it could have been in happier circumstances.

The room turned out to be a small lounge, even a small fire burned in the grate; the room was obviously provided for people who found the festivity in the ballroom a bit much. Bryna wished she had known about it earlier; four hours earlier!

She turned to Raff. 'Why are you being so arrogantly unreasonable?' she demanded.

He looked at her coldly. 'I consider my behaviour

very reasonable,' he snapped. '*You're* the one who insisted on making an exhibition of yourself!'

Her cheeks coloured at the accusation. 'I was only dancing with Court——'

'Forgive me, but when I interrupted you certainly weren't dancing,' rasped Raff, thrusting his long capable hands into his trouser pockets. 'The two of you were drawing attention to yourselves by that mere fact alone, and minutes earlier dozens of our guests witnessed the way he caressed your hair——'

'He wasn't caressing my hair,' she defended heatedly. 'He was trying to take off my veil!'

Grey eyes narrowed. 'Why?'

'Because he's kind.' Tears glistened in her violet-coloured eyes. 'Because the veil was making by head ache!'

'If it makes your head ache why didn't you just remove it yourself?' he challenged.

Because she had known it would displease him! My God, she thought, in the space of just two weeks she had become one of those women she despised, in awe of her husband instead of the independent woman she had always been, fearing his disapproval to the slightest move she made.

She was a successful businesswoman, for goodness' sake, with a mind and will of her own, not some simpering simpleton afraid of her own shadow. Consideration for the feelings of others was one thing, but in Raff's case she had taken it too far!

'I thought I was supposed to keep up appearances,' she told him caustically, deftly removing the pins from her hair, at once feeling the pressure ease.

'But I think four hours is enough for any bride!' She put the tiara and veil down on a small table in front of her, shaking her hair just to feel its freedom. 'Now I intend enjoying what's left of my wedding reception, you can act as watchdog if you want to!' She turned to leave.

'What's that supposed to mean?' he grated harshly, his mouth tight.

Bryna spun around. 'Do you think I'm a fool, Raff?' she scorned. 'I know you've been watching my every move since I agreed to marry you. Why, I have no idea, but I think even you can trust I wouldn't do anything stupid at my own wedding!'

His mouth was taut and unremorseful. 'You've already caused quite a lot of talk by your behaviour earlier with Court——'

'What behaviour?' she demanded impatiently. 'I only danced with him!'

'And told him about the baby,' Raff bit out accusingly.

'He's your best friend, I would have thought you would have already told him!' she retaliated, her eyes blazing deeply purple.

'Why should I have done?' he challenged.

She frowned. 'Because—well, because——'

'It's none of his damned business,' Raff told her coldly.

Bryna gave a weary sigh, her head starting to pound again. 'Look, I don't want anything I've done to be the cause of friction between you and Court——'

'Don't you?' he scorned. 'I thought all women liked men to fight over them.'

Whatever Court had had to say to Raff about her pregnancy, it had obviously caused a rift between the two men. 'You and Court have no reason to argue because of me,' she dismissed impatiently. 'It's ridiculous, and I don't like it——'

'That's just too bad,' her husband snapped. 'Because I have a feeling it's something you're going to have to get used to!'

'But why?' Bryna reasoned intensely. 'Court is just upset with you at the moment for not confiding in him about the baby. He'll come around——'

'But I won't,' Raff warned softly. 'Now we'll rejoin our guests together,' he instructed coldly. 'I think it's time they started to leave anyway; you need to get some rest.'

She was surprised he had noticed how fatigued she was, only having seemed concerned with keeping up appearances until now. But maybe that was it, a new bride should be glowing with vitality and love for her husband, not just look exhausted!

Luckily some of the guests had decided it was time for them to depart; if they hadn't she felt sure Raff would have somehow persuaded them it was time to go—politely, of course!

Ordinarily, as the bride and groom, they could have escaped hours ago, but as it was Christmas the next day they had decided not to go away on a honeymoon but to spend the holiday period at the house with their families. As she should have been spending Christmas with her parents Raff had invited them to spend Christmas with them instead, and Raff's parents would be joining them all for the day too. As honeymoons went it had to be one of the strangest! Not that she had any wish to be alone anywhere with Raff in the stange mood he had been in since she first agreed to marry him.

It was gone midnight by the time the last of the guests left, Paul taking his girl-friend home before returning to the house later, Kate being driven home by Roger Delaney, a rather pleasant young man she was at college with whom she had decided to invite at the last minute. Raff's parents had chosen to stay at their home in London and drive down to join them for the festivities tomorrow, so that only left Raff, Bryna, and her parents to drive home together.

She awoke as Raff carried her up the long staircase to her room; she must have fallen asleep almost as soon as she got in the car, because she certainly remembered nothing of the journey.

Raff glanced down at her as he sensed she was awake. 'Your parents said to say goodnight,' he told her.

Flatly, uncompromisingly, totally unapproachable. 'You can put me down now.' She twisted in his arms.

His arms tensed as his grip tightened. 'We're almost there now,' he dismissed abruptly.

Despite the fact that they had been married today the gap between them was widening by the minute, and if they were to be even tolerably happy in this marriage it couldn't be allowed to continue. 'Raff, I didn't realise you hadn't told Court about the baby,' she explained regretfully. 'And when I did——'

'You told him anyway.' He pushed open the bedroom door with his foot.

'He's your best friend——'

'And the baby you're carrying is ours, and anything to do with it, *anything* at all, should be decided by us jointly!'

'But—— This is your bedroom,' she realised in alarm; the austere green and cream décor was nothing at all like the warm peach of her own bedroom further down the hallway. She knew exactly what her bedroom should look like, having moved all her things into it yesterday. She was also familiar with Raff's bedroom through the bathroom that connected their two rooms, the housekeeper having given her a detailed tour of the house after she had unpacked. And the room he had brought her to was definitely his!

Raff slowly lowered her to the floor, their bodies moving against each other before Bryna moved abruptly away.

'I'm well aware of whose room this is.' He pulled his tie undone, leaving it dangling about his throat as he unbuttoned the stiff collar of his white shirt. 'It's been a long day, Bryna,' he said wearily. 'Use the bathroom and let's get to bed.' He sat down on the side of the bed to take off his shoes.

The action drew her attention to the king-size bed he had only ever previously occupied alone. None of his women had ever stayed the night in his home. Raff refused to expose his children to that; all their previous nights together had been spent at her apartment.

Bryna moistened suddenly dry lips. 'You said we would have separate rooms——'

'We have separate rooms.' He stood up forcefully to continue undressing.

'But——'

'Bryna, we have guests in the house,' he bit out tautly. 'My son and daughter too. What do you think they'll make of our sleeping apart on our supposed honeymoon?'

She blinked. 'I wouldn't have thought you cared what other people thought.' He never had in the past!

His eyes glittered angrily. 'Your parents believe you wanted this marriage, and when they leave in three days' time I don't want anything we've said or done to have disturbed their peace of mind. My children's feelings are also important to me, but they will also be gone in three days. And until they are we will share this room and this bed if nothing else, at least give an outward impression of normality. If any of them find out the truth later on we can tell them that it's more comfortable for you, and the baby, if you sleep alone,' he added grimly.

Bryna had also dreaded the idea of her parents realising her marriage to Raff had been a matter of compulsion rather than choice. But she now understood Raff's sudden change of mind about Kate moving into Brenda's flat with her; if his daughter stayed here she would realise how estranged her father and Bryna really were.

'Raff, don't make a decision about Kate's future that you'll later regret. I'm sure we can work something out if you——'

'Kate is eighteen, and it's time she realased there's a whole harsh world out there,' he dismissed.

Bryna shook her head, knowing that wasn't the way he really felt. 'You'll regret it if anything happens to her.'

His brows rose. 'What could happen to her?'

She looked down pointedly at her own body. 'I was once a sophisticated innocent, remember?' she reminded him.

His expression darkened and he looked at her coldly. 'Are you saying I'm forcing my daughter out of her home and risking her becoming pregnant?' he rasped.

'No, of course not! I was only—— Oh! She closed her eyes as a wave of dizziness washed over her, and would have fallen if Raff's arms hadn't closed about her. 'I'm sorry,' she shook back her hair, blinking up at him dazedly.

'You're exhausted!' His expression was grim as he sat her down on the bed, turning her slightly away from him to begin undoing the row of pearl buttons down her spine. 'Don't argue,' he warned as she gave a murmur of protest. 'I told you I wouldn't touch you, and I won't. This is just helping an overtired woman, who's eleven weeks pregnant, into bed where she belongs!'

She wanted to protest that she didn't 'belong' in this particular bed, but she didn't have the strength to argue, not when Raff was already slipping the gown from her shoulders. She was too tired to fight him, and sat docilely while he sponged the weariness from her body, returning again and again to the bathroom to moisten the sponge, until he was satisfied that every part of her felt refreshed. She wondered at this thoughtfulness from the man who

had been so coldly aloof from her all day, but she
was too weary to question it. She didn't even object
as he gently sponged the perspiration from the
valley between her breasts, although she did
murmur a protest as he moved towards her thighs.

'All right.' He straightened, moving to take her
nightgown from the chair where he had draped it, a
thoughtful maid having laid it out on the bed for her
earlier, indication that the staff expected them to
share this room tonight too, at least.

Raff dropped the floaty creation of the white
nightgown over her head before settling her back on
the pillows and pulling the bedclothes up to under
her chin as she sighed her comfort.

Bryna had never felt so tired, and she saw Raff's
movements through a haze, her lids refusing to obey
her command for them to open. But she did know
that he removed his own clothes without sparing
her a second glance, going through to the adjoining
bathroom, the sound of the water being run telling
her he intended taking the shower she had longed
for.

She fell asleep to the sound of the water falling in
the shower.

And she awoke to the caress of Raff's hand on her
body.

At first the shought it was a dream; she was too
tired to wake up for anything! But her body knew its
master, and she returned to consciousness with the
sure knowledge that Raff *was* touching her.

She was turned on her side in the bed, but she
could feel the warmth of Raff's body inches away
from her back and legs, knew he would be

completely naked, that he always slept that way. And his arm rested against her hip as one of his hands trailed over her stomach, and lower.

It was exquisite torture to let him continue, and yet it would cause her even more pain to make him stop. But finally it was the former she feared the most, deciding physical discomfort was preferable to the mental anguish if she let him continue.

She moved abruptly away from him, her eyes accustomed to the darkness as she turned to face him. 'Raff, you promised——'

His eyes glittered silver. 'And I kept my promise,' he rasped.

Her eyes widened. 'But——'

'I wasn't touching you, Bryna,' he denied harshly.

'I felt your hands on my body,' she protested, willing herself to be unmoved by the bronze smoothness of his naked chest as he leant up on his elbow beside her, knowing she was failing as her hands longed to touch him, her body still aroused by his caresses.

'I was touching my child,' he bit out harshly. 'We made no agreement about my not doing that!'

Bryna stared at him disbelievingly. It was true, his hand hadn't strayed anywhere but over the slight curving of her body that was his child. But even so——

'Did we?' he demanded forcefully.

No, there had been no mention of him not touching his child; it was her misfortune that she happened to be carrying the child at the moment!

She felt the awakening of sensual pleasure she had known at his touch shrivel and die.

'Get used to the idea, Bryna.' He lay flat against the pillows beside her. 'I intend to be as close to this child as I am to Kate and Paul, and I'll touch it any time I damn well please!' The closing of his eyes and the evenness of his breathing told her that as far as he was concerned the discussion was at an end, whether she chose to dispute his claim or not.

How could she dispute what was, after all, his right?

What father didn't long to touch his unborn child in its mother's womb, to know the wonder of that life before it was born?

The six months left of her pregnancy promised to be a living hell for Bryna.

CHAPTER SIX

CHRISTMAS had always been a time of joy and laughter in Bryna's family, with a visit to church on Christmas morning, a happy closeness as they all prepared the lunch together, sitting around a glowing fire together after they had eaten the sumptuous meal, occasionally dozing in front of its warmth as the food and peace of the day washed over them.

Never having spent Christmas with Raff and his family before, Bryna was a little uncertain about what to expect, although she soon realised that even Raff became caught up in the festivity of the day, the two of them being rudely awakened by an exuberant Kate at only seven o'clock in the morning.

'Time to get up,' she announced cheerfully, wearing her nightgown and robe, looking very young with her face free of make-up and her hair a tumble of glossy black curls.

The transition of shielding their affair from Raff's children to having one of them burst in on them the day after their wedding was a difficult one for Bryna, and she looked awkwardly at Raff as she burrowed under the bedclothes.

Raff looked younger with his hair falling darkly across his forehead, blinking sleepily, a dark growth of beard on the firmness of his chin. 'Shouldn't you have knocked, young——'

'I did,' his daughter told him happily, perched on the end of their bed. 'You didn't answer.'

'Obviously because we were still asleep,' he drawled, moving to sit back against the headboard. 'And if we hadn't been sleeping we *certainly* wouldn't have welcomed the interruption,' he taunted.

Embarrassed colour darkened Kate's cheeks as she stood up. 'Really, Daddy, you shouldn't make too many of those sort of demands on a woman in early pregnancy,' she told him reprovingly.

He scowled as she neatly turned the tables on him. 'How the hell do you know that?'

Kate gave him a derisive look before giving Bryna a conspiratorial smile. 'Maybe now that he's actually going to *have* a baby in the house he'll realise I'm not one any more,' she mocked with a cheeky grin. 'Now do hurry up and come down-stairs, Daddy, I want to open my presents.' She abandoned her air of sophistication at the thought of the gifts waiting under the tree for them all, hurrying downstairs to wait for them—and prob-ably to prod and poke about her own parcels until they arrived!

Bryna gave an indulgent smile, feeling closer to Raff than she had for weeks as he returned the smile.

'In one breath she tells me how grown up she is, and in the next moment she looked eight years old again,' he shook his head ruefully.

'We all like to open presents,' she smiled, the fatigue of the night before completely erased after a good night's sleep. She wished the same could be said of the memory of Raff's hand caressing her body.

'Do we?' he frowned. 'I seem to recall you insisted I *didn't* give you any presents during the last six months,' he added harshly.

'That was because I was your mistress, and not your wife,' she reasoned.

'You weren't my mistress,' he rasped. 'That implies dependency of some kind, and we both continued to live our own lives. We were lovers. And I certainly wouldn't have objected if you had bought *me* presents. In fact, I would have welcomed the knowledge that you thought of me at other times than when we were in bed together.'

The shadow in their depths made her eyes purple. 'Raff, please let's not argue——'

'No,' he grated, shifting in the bed so that he leant over her. 'Happy Christmas, Mrs Gallagher.'

'Happy Christmas,' she barely had time to murmur before his lips merged with hers.

After days of knowing only his cold remoteness she blossomed to the sensual search of his lips like a flower opening to the sun, wrapping her arms about his neck to draw him down to her, returning his passion with a fierce longing of her own.

'Dad, are you—— Don't you know you should treat a woman with extreme gentleness during the early months of pregnancy?' a concerned Paul burst out, his cheeks colouring with a ruddy hue as both Raff and Bryna turned to look at him in surprise. 'Well, you should,' he muttered uncomfortably, wearing a robe over his rumpled pyjamas, his dark hair tousled. 'I read it somewhere,' he added resentfully.

Raff gave a strangled groan as he rolled over on to his back, glowering at his son. 'I was only kissing Bryna, not making love to her,' he bit out irritably. 'What chance do I have of doing that when you and Kate keep bursting in here unannounced?'

Paul shifted uncomfortably. 'I did knock, but——'

'We didn't hear you,' his father acknowledged wearily. 'We are on our honeymoon, Paul.'

'I know, and I'm sorry,' he sighed. 'But if you don't come downstairs soon Kate's going to open everyone's presents!'

Bryna laughed softly once her stepson had gone back downstairs. 'Why do I get the impression that for all their sophistication the rest of the year Kate and Paul become children again at Christmas?' she said drily.

'Probably because they do.' Raff threw back the bedclothes to get out of bed, strolling unselfconsciously across the room to get his dark bathrobe. 'And Paul isn't joking about Kate opening all the presents; one year Josey and I only just got downstairs in time to stop her opening Paul's things; she'd already opened her mother's and mine besides her own! I think we'd better join them now before they come to blows!'

Bryna had seen Raff naked dozens of times the last six months, had even shared in that nakedness, but in the light of their arrangement she felt a little embarrassed about the longing she had to just look and look at him, knowing she was only torturing herself with what could never be.

She turned away abruptly. 'Actually, I think it's a good sign that Paul is taking an interest in the welfare of the baby.'

'You've noticed he's been less than enthusiastic?' Raff sounded troubled.

Bryna gave him a reassuring smile. 'Put yourself in his place, Raff, and see how you feel!'

'Hm,' he grimaced ruefully. 'I suppose it is awkward for him.'

As she watched Kate and Paul dive into their presents under the ten-foot tree that they had all decorated together the previous weekend it was difficult to imagine there would be much of an age gap between her child and them! They were as enthusiastic over the small gifts she and Raff had chosen for them together as they were over the gold watches they also received, and they were obviously truly touched by the thoughtfulness that had gone into the purchase of the books they received from their new grandparents.

Her parents had taken to their new role with gusto, and had already decided that Kate and Paul would be as much their grandchildren as the new baby would be, and Bryna had been delighted to help them choose gifts for both them and Raff, knowing how much he would love the silk tie of pale grey.

She deliberately kept to the background as she watched the rapport between her new family and her parents, relieved beyond words that they were all getting along so well together, giving a start of surprise when Kate dropped a pile of parcels in her lap. She had completely forgotten her own presents.

Her parents had bought her a range of her

favourite perfume, from bath-oil to body lotion, and she smiled at them gratefully. Kate had bought her some books on pregnancy and childbirth, and the two of them shared a smile of understanding. Paul looked a little sheepish about his gift, and she understood why as the rather large box revealed a maternity nightgown.

'Kate helped me pick it out for you,' he put in quickly as his father looked at him with raised brows.

His sister grinned. 'What he means is that he sent me in to buy it and approved it afterwards!' she mocked.

Paul shot her a glowering look. 'Well, I wanted to give her the books, but you insisted that was your gift, and——'

'I love both my presents, thank you.' Bryna kissed them both on the cheek, knowing by the mischievous twinkle in Kate's eyes that she was enjoying teasing her brother about their expected sibling.

'And now mine.' Raff placed a small parcel in the palm of her hand.

She frowned up at him. 'But you've already given me so much, the necklace and——'

'They were wedding presents,' he cut in arrogantly. 'Besides, you bought me a Christmas present,' he reminded her abruptly.

And she knew that he genuinely liked the sculpture she had given him. It was by a relatively unknown English sculptor who they had both agreed would one day be very much in demand. Unfortunately, as with all the greats, it would probably be after his death.

Her fingers shook slightly as she unwrapped the

parcel, the small box revealing an even smaller box inside, and Bryna gasped her stunned delight as she flipped open the lid to reveal a ring. Not an engagement ring, as she had suspected once she saw the size of the box, but a thin gold band topped by seven diamonds. An eternity ring. She looked up at Raff questioningly, but his expression revealed none of his thoughts.

'It's lovely, Daddy!' Kate was the one to enthuse.

It was lovely, and like the wedding band Raff had placed on her finger only yesterday, it was a perfect fit.

Bryna still looked up at him uncertainly, not understanding the significance of the gift. 'It's beautiful, Raff, thank you.'

He nodded abruptly. 'I'm glad you like it. Now I suggest we all get dressed and have some breakfast before my parents arrive and we have to leave for church.'

Because she preferred it, and because she knew her parents felt the same way, Bryna had asked Raff if she and her mother couldn't do the catering for at least Christmas Day, knowing the housekeeper had a sister in Kent she would like to spend the day with. Surprisingly he had agreed to her suggestion, and the cosy family atmosphere increased as the four men talked in the lounge while the four women prepared the meal in laughing camaraderie.

The day passed very much as it would have done at her parents' home, a late lunch of turkey and all the trimmings, *she* being the one to doze off in front of the fire, Raff insisting he and the children would prepare the supper while the rest of them sat down and chatted together. Bryna had been unsure how

Raff's parents would react to the marriage, especially once they knew there was a baby on the way, but they couldn't have been nicer.

Only one thing happened to mar the perfection of the day.

They had finished supper and were clearing away when Kate gave a sudden frown. 'In all the excitement I've only just realised that Uncle Court didn't join us for the day.'

Anger, cold and biting, flickered in Raff's eyes before it was quickly masked. 'He had other commitments,' he shrugged.

Kate wasn't satisfied with that answer. 'But he always spends Christmas Day with us.'

'And after twenty years don't you think he's entitled to a change?' her father demanded.

'But——'

'Kate, we aren't his only friends,' Raff cut in, his tone brooking no further argument.

The subject was dropped, sulkily by Kate, determinedly by Raff, and yet Bryna knew that, in some way she didn't completely understand, she was the one who had caused the friction between the two men that now meant Court no longer even felt welcome in his friend's home.

She felt guilty without really knowing what she had done. It didn't seem possible that Raff could be so angry just because she had told Court about the baby, neither could she accept that it had been because she had danced with Court at the wedding. She had danced with him dozens of times before at parties, and Raff had never objected then. He was behaving unreasonably; she only hoped he soon realised that!

Nevertheless, the incident ruined the rest of the day for her slightly, and she couldn't help wondering if Kate had connected her father's remarriage with Court's absence today, and resented her for it. The girl gave no indication she felt that way, but Bryna couldn't help feeling uncomfortable about the situation. She felt somewhat uplifted by Raff's mother before she left later that night.

'I can't tell you when we've enjoyed a Christmas more.' She kissed Bryna on the cheek; she was a tall woman, as imposing as her son, until you saw her eyes, warm blue eyes that smiled as she talked.

Raff had inherited his grey eyes from his tall and still-handsome father, although in the older man they had mellowed and warmed. 'We had a lovely time, my dear.' He kissed her too.

Michael Gallagher had been a force to be reckoned with himself until his retirement from the business world, and as she watched father and son shake hands Bryna couldn't help thinking what a formidable pair they must have once made.

Raff looked so handsome today, casually dressed in a grey shirt and black fitted trousers, the gold band that perfectly matched her own glinting on his left hand, the watch she had bought him as a wedding gift strapped to his wrist.

Last night she had been too tired to care about their sleeping arrangements, but tonight, despite feeling weary, she was all too aware of them, as she picked up her nightgown to go through to the adjoining bathroom.

No one had guessed at the strain between Raff and herself today, she felt sure, and she knew that was mainly due to Raff and the way he had cared for her in a way that didn't smother her. Was it only because he was concerned about the health of his child, or did he genuinely care about her welfare? The answer to that question was all too obvious—and painful.

She had turned on her side and was pretending to be asleep when he came back from the bathroom and climbed into bed beside her, turning to face her as he had the previous night, his hand moving to rest possessively on the baby.

The heat began between her thighs and radiated outwards, the warm ache making her tremble.

'Are you cold?' Raff questioned gruffly.

Cold—she was on fire! The trembling increased, her breathing becoming ragged, the instructions her brain passed to her body to calm down were completely ignored. How *could* she calm down when she wanted him so much!

'Do you want me, Bryna?' he huskily voiced her pained longing.

To say yes would be to completely abandon her pride, to accept the charitable lovemaking he offered. And she couldn't do that.

'I'm sure you're perfectly well aware from your first wife's pregnancies that women often feel highly—emotional during pregnancy,' she dismissed curtly, remaining rigidly turned away from him.

'Highly sexed, you mean,' he amended bluntly. 'I told you, Bryna, you only have to ask.'

She closed her eyes in pain, gritting her teeth in an effort to resist the impulse she had to turn into his arms and *plead* for his lovemaking. 'I'm really not in the mood, Raff,' she lied, the ache as intense as ever. 'Did you ask Court not to come here today?' she abruptly changed the subject, hoping talking about Court would help her forget the ache.

The hand that had been moving rhythmically across her stomach stopped for a moment, before continuing more determinedly. 'No, it was his own decision,' Raff returned harshly.

'Because of yesterday?'

'Among other things,' he bit out.

'What other things?' she queried tensely, blinking in the darkness.

'I don't want to talk about this just now.' His hand was removed as he turned to lie on his back.

With that intoxicating hand removed she felt able to turn and face him. Raff was making no effort to go to sleep, his eyes clearly open as he stared up at the ceiling. 'It's important to me, Raff,' she began.

'I know that,' he scorned, his eyes glittering dangerously in the darkness.

Bryna's cheeks were flushed. 'Kate and Paul will resent me if they think I had anything to do with your argument with Court,' she snapped.

His mouth twisted. 'I'm sure Kate's and Paul's opinion is very important to you.' he sneered.

'Of course it is,' she defended heatedly. 'Also I don't like to be the cause of a rift between you and Court when there's no reason to be.'

'No reason?' Raff loomed up out of the darkness as he moved to a sitting position, anger in every taut line of his body, the politeness of the day obviously over. 'You flaunted your affair with Court at *our* wedding and you simply expected me to accept it without retaliation?' He sounded incredulous—and furious.

The ringing in her ears made her head spin. Affair with Court—? Raff couldn't be serious!

But as he viciously flicked the switch on the bedside lamp, the cold fury in his face unmistakable, she knew that he was perfectly serious. But why? She had never given him cause to think such a thing

'Raff, how could I have been having an affair with Court when I was already having an affair with you?' she reasoned in bewilderment.

His mouth thinned. 'I admit, being unfaithful to a lover is a little unique?'

'And untrue,' she claimed incredulously. 'What on earth made you think such a thing? I——'

'I didn't just *think* it, Bryna,' he rasped. 'I have proof.'

She became suddenly still, wondering if she could possibly have fallen asleep without realising it and this was all a nightmare. But as she pinched herself and felt the pain she knew she was wide awake, that this was all very real. 'What proof?' she asked dazedly.

'You were seen having lunches together, cosy little dinners for two——'

'I told you about them,' she defended.

'Not all of them,' he grated.

'Most of them.' Guilty colour darkened her cheeks. Her decision not to discuss her business with Raff in an effort to make him realise how he shut her out was backfiring in a way she could never have envisaged! 'They were business meetings.'

'Your contract with Court ended weeks ago,' Raff dismissed coldly.

'I was trying to interest him in using several of my models again,' she told him heatedly.

'Of course you were,' Raff said with obvious scepticism.

'But I was! I—have you spoken to Court about any of this?' she asked exasperatedly.

'Of course,' he nodded abruptly. 'He denies that the two of you are having an affair.'

'There you are——'

'But of course he would,' Raff insisted unrelentingly. 'But you're married to me now, expecting my child, and I don't have to pretend ignorance any more.'

'If you really believe that we had an affair behind your back how do you know this isn't his child?' Bryna challenged, hurt and confused by the unexpectedness of his attack.

'That's the one thing I can be sure of.' He looked at her coldly as he climbed out of the bed. 'You see, Court is sterile!'

Bryna knew she must have paled, but the irony of Court's tragedy after years of believing herself incapable of ever having a child made it too unbearable to contemplate his torment.

But it didn't diminish the fact that as far as Raff was concerned the only thing he could be sure of was the paternity of her child!

It also explained his threats to force her into marriage with him. Maybe he had thought, knowing of Court's sterility, that the other man would be more than glad to marry her himself once he knew she carried a child. She realised now that it was probably also the reason he hadn't told Court about the baby.

Oh, now she understood what he had meant that day in Scotland when he had told her he 'didn't care what other plans she had made, she was marrying him'! He couldn't take the risk that Court would welcome her pregnancy with open arms.

My God, she thought, was the affair he believed her to have been having with Court the reason he had been acting so coldly towards her the last couple of months, the reason he had been so unreasonable and hurt her by flirting with Rosemary the night of Court's party, before making love to her so exquisitely?

If that were so, did it also mean that he hadn't tired of her at all but had believed she was being unfaithful to him?

She looked at him with wide eyes as that last thought occurred to her, realising for the first time that he was in the process of dressing, black trousers already fitted to his narrow hips and legs, a cream shirt unbuttoned down his chest. 'Where are you going?' she asked in dismay; he couldn't walk out on her now, not without discussing this further!

'Out,' he rasped.

'But——'

'Don't worry, Bryna, I'll be back before morning,' he bit out derisively. 'And I'll think of a good excuse for you to move back into your own bedroom tomorrow night!'

'Raff, we have to talk——'

'It's too late for that,' he grated, thrusting his shirt into the waist of his trousers. 'It was too late the

moment you decided to take Court as your next
lover!'

'But I didn't——'

'Was he as experienced as me, Bryna?' he
demanded coldly. 'As "skilled"? Of course he was,'
he answered disgustedly. 'But no other man, not
even one I once called friend, is going to bring up a
child that I know is mine!'

'Raff!' Bryna cried out as he reached the door.
'Raff, it isn't true,' she pleaded. 'None of it's true!'

'I told you, you were seen together,' he rasped
contemptuously. 'And even if you hadn't been, do
you think I can't tell when a woman changes
towards me in bed? My God, I've had one wife who
preferred another man to me, so I should know!' he
scorned.

She drew in a ragged breath. 'If I did change it
was only because——'

'Yes?' he prompted harshly.

'Because *you* changed,' she accused, standing up
agitatedly. 'Oh yes, you did,' she insisted at his
sceptical expression. 'I thought you were getting
tired of me. I thought——'

'You would line up another lover for when our
affair was over,' he finished disgustedly. 'What's
the matter, Bryna, now that you've discovered the
"joys of sex" can't you do without it for even the
length of time it would have taken you to find my
replacement once our affair was over?'

'Stop twisting things to suit your own warped
accusations,' she cried. 'You've got it all wrong,' she
insisted emotionally. 'Court isn't, and never will be,
my lover!'

'The past I can't do anything about, but you're

right about the future,' Raff told her grimly. 'No other man is going to know your body but me in future. And now that I know how much you like to make love I don't expect I'll have to wait long before you come begging me to take you!'

Bryna stared at the door he had closed forcefully behind him without actually slamming it and waking up the rest of the household.

Did he really believe all that he had accused her of? Of course he did, he wouldn't be acting this way if he didn't!

Court and her? How could he have come to such an erroneous conclusion? She and Court were friends, yes, and Court flirted with her endlessly, but surely no more than he did with every other female he came into contact with.

Proof, Raff had said, but surely he couldn't count a few meals together where they discussed business as that? He did, she knew he did, and it seemed there was nothing she could say to change his mind.

No wonder his cold indifference had actually seemed to turn to hate since he had found out about the baby and he had forced her into marriage!

Only now he was making no secret of that hate—or the reason for it.

CHAPTER SEVEN

BRYNA was glad when the holiday period was over and she could get back to work, away from the oppression of living with Raff.

As promised, he had let her move back into her own bedroom, but he had arrogantly offered no explanation to anyone who might be curious about this abrupt estrangement between husband and wife.

Her parents had gone back to Scotland, Paul had returned to his flat, and she had helped Kate move in with Brenda, still having misgivings about the advisability of the latter. But Raff made it obvious he didn't wish to discuss his daughter, or anything else, with her.

They were living like complete strangers only ten days after their wedding, not bothering to make polite conversation even over dinner now. In fact, the strain at the dinner table had been so intense that the last two evenings Bryna had asked for a tray in her bedroom. As far as she was aware Raff hadn't even noticed her absence!

'Get me Mr Stevens on the telephone, Gilly,' she requested as soon as she walked into her office on her first day back at work.

She leafed listlessly through the mail Gilly had left on the desk for her attention as she waited for the call to come through. She had been longing to speak to Court, to see what he made of Raff's ridiculous accusations, ever since Raff had hurled them at her, but she knew that if she had called him from the house and Raff found out about it—! Well, there was enough friction between them already.

She snatched up the receiver as soon as the telephone rang. 'Court?' she said breathlessly.

'Bryna?' He sounded surprised to hear from her.

Which wasn't surprising if Raff had launched the same accusations at him that he had at her! 'Court, we have to talk,' she told him without prevarication.

'My God, he didn't upset you with his fantasies in your condition, did he?' he returned disgustedly.

'I can't seem to convince him they are fantasies,' she confirmed shakily, feeling like crying after the last days of tension.

'Bryna, he—he hasn't hurt you, has he?' Court demanded concernedly.

'No, of course not,' she protested the suggestion. Raff was a very physical man, who could display displeasure as easily as he could give pleasure, but she was sure he would never use violence on a woman. 'I just need to talk to someone who understands how I feel.'

'Thank God for that,' said Court with obvious relief. 'Okay, Bryna, how about lunch?'

They made the arrangement to meet at the restaurant before Bryna rang off to get caught up in the rush of the day; she had plenty to do after the long Christmas and New Year break. She was glad of the hectic pace of the morning, she had felt as if her life had plummeted completely out of control since the night Raff had accused her of having an affair with Court. With any luck she could continue to work until the day the baby was born!

Court gave her a searching look when she joined him at their table. 'I know you're supposed to tell a pregnant woman how radiant she looks, but you don't look at all well, Bryna,' he frowned as they both sat down.

She knew the truth of that; she rarely slept and had a complete lack of appetite, knowing that both things showed in her lacklustre hair and shadowed eyes. Her pregnancy was becoming very noticeable as she lost weight and the baby inside her grew, the loose dress she wore doing little to hide that fact.

'It's Raff and this stupid idea he has that we had an affair,' she sighed, shaking her head when the waiter enquired if she would like a drink, her fingers moving nervously against the tablecloth.

'When did he tell you about that?' All the laughter had been erased from Court's face and eyes, his own strain very evident.

She shrugged. 'When we got to bed after spending Christmas Day with our families. He——'

'Trust Raff to at least take his damned wedding night before alienating you!' he said disgustedly.

'But he didn't! I mean, we didn't,' she amended with a blush. 'We have this agreement, you see——'

'What sort of an agreement can a newly married couple have that involves them not making love on their wedding night?' Court looked dumbfounded.

Bryna signed. 'The sort of agreement where the father wants complete rights to his as yet unborn child.'

'And that's the only reason he married you?' Court realised incredulously.

Her gaze lowered to the snowy white tablecloth, absently realising that she had badly creased the crisp linen with the constant pleatings of her restless fingers. 'The only reason,' she confirmed huskily.

Court leant back in his chair with an angry sigh. 'You would have been better off fighting him for custody in court!'

'I think that's the reason Raff married me so quickly and then didn't tell me what he believed about the two of us until I was safely his wife,' she told him dully.

'The damned fool,' said Court angrily. 'Why on earth is he throwing your relationship away?'

Bryna shook her head. 'He says he has proof, that the two of us were seen dining together.'

'Business meetings,' he claimed instantly.

'I told him that, but——'

'He didn't believe you,' Court bit out. 'Telling me about his suspicions at the wedding was one thing, but I had no idea he was going to make you unhappy with them too. I would have come to the house even though I wasn't welcome, if I'd known.'

Her mouth twisted ruefully. 'He would have thrown you out, literally. But Kate asked after you——'

'I've seen her,' he nodded grimly.

'You have?' Bryna looked at him in surprise; Kate had come home for dinner three nights ago— the last time Bryna had eaten with Raff—and she had given no indication that she had seen her Uncle Court.

He shrugged. 'She telephoned me and we had dinner together last night. Don't look so worried, Bryna,' he drawled. 'Raff may not want to know me any more, but I've known those kids so long that sometimes I feel as if they're mine!'

Knowing what she did about him she could understand how he felt about the children of his best friend. 'They're very fond of you too,' she nodded.

He gave an indulgent smile. 'Kate is enjoying sharing a flat.'

'Raff doesn't approve,' Bryna frowned. 'He only agreed to let her go so that she shouldn't realise we were living in the same house but apart.'

'The fool!' rasped Court. 'What the hell is the matter with him?' he added angrily.

'I don't know,' she said shakily. 'It all seems to come back to the fact that for some reason he believes the two of us are having an affair.'

'If I didn't know better I would say he was jealous,' Court frowned.

'Impossible!' Bryna gave a scathing laugh. 'If it weren't for the baby I would be out of his life and forgotten by now!'

'Hm,' murmured Court. 'It was because of Kate and Paul that he and Josey stayed together as long as they did.'

'Yes,' she acknowledged dully. 'Now he intends for us to have the same unemotional marriage.'

'It doesn't sound to me as if he wants you to take a lover,' Court derided.

She looked at him searchingly. 'You know about the relationship he and Josey had?'

'That they both had lovers?' he nodded. 'I think everyone knew except Kate and Paul. I can't believe that Raff would settle for that half-marriage again.'

'It isn't a question of settling for anything,' she told him heavily. 'He wants his child. And so do I!'

Court looked at her closely. 'You love him, don't you? Of course you do,' he said self-derisively. 'Why else would you have married him?' His hand covered hers comfortingly.

Bryna shook her head. 'Believe me, Court, if I had any choice I would never have become his wife. But he more or less threatened to take my child away from me if I didn't agree.'

'You——'

'Hello, darling,' greeted a smoothly controlled voice, and Bryna's stricken gaze raised to meet the coldly furious one of her husband. 'I told you I would try to get here, didn't I?' he added lightly.

Bryna knew that the last was added for their audience, that he didn't want anyone to realise his wife was having lunch with another man without his knowledge.

Oh God, she thought, how much of her conversation with Court had Raff overhead! Certainly the part about her having no choice but to marry him, if the angry glitter of his eyes was anything to go by, but he didn't look as if he had also heard Court claim she was in love with him, Raff.

Court sat back in his chair as he released her hand, relaxed and in control. 'Why don't you join us?' he invited politely.

'Unfortunately I'm with some business associates,' Raff bit out. 'Otherwise, believe me, nothing else would give me greater pleasure than to join the two of you and listen to some more of this fascinating conversation!'

Bryna swallowed hard. He *had* overheard the part of the conversation where she had expressed regret at having to marry him. And he didn't look in the mood to be convinced that it was the *having* to marry him that bothered her, not actually having him as her husband.

'Don't cause a scene, Raff——'

'Believe me, I'm very much in control,' he glared at the other man. 'If I wanted to cause a scene I would have punched you in the face and taken back my wife as soon as I came into the restaurant and saw the two of you together!'

Court's mouth twisted derisively. 'I thought I was supposed to be the one with the temper?'

Raff looked at him coldly. 'We all know that's my child Bryna is carrying,' he rasped. 'And I've warned her what will happen if she sees you again!'

She paled at the veiled threat. 'It's only lunch, Raff——'

'My wife of ten days lunching with my supposed best friend!' he scorned, his hands clenched at his sides, although for their audience his expression remained pleasant enough. 'Most people would say the honeymoon bed hadn't had time to cool!'

'The way I heard it it didn't even get lukewarm!' Court challenged, his own anger evident now, then he turned to give Bryna an apologetic look as she gasped. 'I'm sorry, Bryna, but——'

'That can easily be remedied,' Raff bit out

between clenched teeth. 'Starting tonight!'

'Raff, you can't mean that!' She looked up at him with haunted eyes, sure that to have him make love to her out of anger would be worse than the charity she had been imagining it would be.

'Oh, can't I?' he challenged, looking at her with disgust. 'Why don't we wait and see what I can or can't do!'

Bryna watched him as he strode across the restaurant to rejoin the people he had obviously arrived with, three men she didn't recognise, and Stuart Hillier; she wondered what they had all made of his abrupt departure seconds ago.

'I can't believe it,' Court said dazedly. 'I've never seen him like this before.'

She had never seen *anyone* as angry as Raff had been a few minutes ago. It had been worse than the night nine days ago, worse than all the days since; he had been totally out of control.

'I thought you said he wasn't violent.' Court looked troubled.

'He isn't—he hasn't been,' she amended, knowing that was no longer true. 'Oh, Court, what am I going to do?' she cried.

'Don't go back.' He clasped her hands. 'I have a spare bedroom at my flat. We could——'

'I couldn't stay with you,' she shook her head. 'The mood Raff is in, he would kill us both!'

He frowned darkly. 'Which is exactly why I don't think you should go back to him!'

She shook her head. 'He wouldn't hurt me,' she claimed shakily.

'That wasn't the impression I got just now,' Court said drily.

Or her! Raff had looked as if he would like to crush her with his bare hands! 'He'll have got over his anger by the time he comes home,' she said with more confidence than she felt. 'And then we'll be able to talk.'

Court still looked worried. 'If you're sure you'll be all right . . .?'

'Of course I will,' she dismissed lightly, all the time conscious of the man across the restaurant as he pointedly ignored her and Court in preference of charming his dining companions. And she didn't doubt that he was aware of her every move! 'I don't think I'll bother with lunch after all——'

'You and the baby have to eat,' Court told her firmly. 'Just ignore him, as he's ignoring you.' He signalled the waiter to come and take their order.

It was hard to ignore someone when their disapproving vibrations could be felt across the crowded room, but somehow Bryna managed to eat a small amount of the meal under Court's indulgent coaxing. The five men were still sitting at their table when she and Court stood up to leave a short time later, and she deliberately kept her face averted, although she sensed Court's movement as he gave a terse inclination of his head in parting.

She was trembling once they got outside. 'I'm so sorry you've had to be involved in this ridiculous situation,' she told Court shakily. 'I just can't seem to make Raff see sense.'

'Hm,' he looked thoughtful. 'I still wouldn't rule out jealousy. You know, he——'

'I would,' she scorned firmly. 'Jealous men don't look at a woman with hate in their eyes!'

'Maybe not,' he acknowledged slowly. 'But if he feels nothing for you why does he still doubt you when you claim our meetings have all been because of business?' he reasoned.

'Because I didn't tell him about them at the time,' she sighed. 'I hadn't been discussing my business with him for some time. You see, he always shut me out when it came to his business affairs, and so I thought if I stopped telling him about mine he would realise how shut out he makes *me* feel, and then perhaps open up to me a little,' she explained with a grimace.

'Oh, my God.' Court closed his eyes. 'I recognise my own advice there!' He looked at her apologetically.

'Yes,' she acknowledged ruefully. She and this man had become good friends during her relationship with Raff, and she had often confided in him, realising that he knew Raff much better than she did, than she ever would.

'I'll learn to keep my opinions to myself in future,' he groaned.

She squeezed his arm reassuringly. 'It was very sound advice,' she consoled him. 'Unfortunately, I think the man in question has to be in love with you and sensitive to your feelings for it to work!'

Court gave a grimace of regret. 'If you need someone to talk to again, just call me.'

Bryna had a feeling that was going to come sooner than she wished!

Raff didn't come home for dinner, and he didn't

telephone to say he would be late either, leaving her to wonder where he was and who he was with—and some of her conclusions were upsetting, to say the least.

She kept remembering how angry he had been to see her with Court earlier, remembered clearly the reckless glint in his silver eyes. And she knew he was with another woman. Probably the willing— and waiting!—Rosemary Chater.

The looks the other woman had shot at her during the wedding had been positively venomous. How she must be gloating now!

Bryna spent the evening alternating between anger and despair, waiting downstairs in the lounge for Raff to come home.

When he hadn't arrived shortly after eleven she decided she might as well go to bed; it didn't look as if he were coming home at all tonight!

She had only been in her room a couple of minutes when she heard the front door open and then slam shut, the sound of running feet on the stairs. Indignation and apprehension shone in her eyes as she turned to the door as it was flung open, her dress gaping at the front where she had just unbuttoned it.

There was a dark flush to Raff's cheeks as he slowly closed the door, the reckless glitter still evident in his eyes. 'Ah good, I'm just in time for the floor-show,' he bit out contemptuously, leaning back against the door to watch her with narrowed eyes, his arms folded across his chest.

Bryna pulled the edges of her unbuttoned dress

together. 'If you want to see a show go to a strip-tease club!' she snapped.

He shook his head. 'The thought of watching some woman I don't know throw off her clothes in front of a room full of people does nothing for me! Where did you spend the afternoon?' he suddenly rasped in a lightning change of mood.

She blinked at the attack. 'At my office,' she replied grudgingly; what right did he have to question her?—he was the one who had been missing all evening!

'I called there several times, but you weren't there,' he grated accusingly.

Her head went back in challenge. 'I was unavailable, that's hardly the same thing.' She had known of each of his calls and had told Gilly to tell him she was too busy to talk to him. Gilly had looked at her strangely at the request, but Bryna had offered no explanations for her behaviour. If she had even tried she would probably have broken down and cried. And once she started she wouldn't be able to stop.

She had no intention of breaking down; she intended going on with her life with or without Raff's love. She had survived the trauma of believing herself infertile, and now that she carried Raff's child she could surely survive not being loved in return by him.

But not if he continued to treat her with contempt, and demanded his rights in her bed!

'Unavailable to me only, I'm sure,' he bit out, moving away from the door to come towards her, the intent in his eyes unmistakable. 'You couldn't wait to get to your lover to tell him what a fiasco our marriage is, could you?' he grated.

'That isn't the way it happened,' she gasped protestingly. 'I met Court——'

'To discuss business?' Raff quoted the past excuses she had given him.

Colour darkened her cheeks. 'No. Not this time,' she added quickly as his eyes glittered silver. 'But in the past, yes,' she insisted firmly. 'Today I—I just needed someone to talk to!'

'And what better choice than your lover?' he taunted. 'What a pity neither he nor your secretary are here to tell me you're unavailable now!'

Bryna didn't fear his lovemaking, she knew that he could never hurt a woman in that way, but what she did fear was that she would respond to him— and that he would know she did!

She picked up her nightgown. 'A bathroom door will do as well,' she told him at the same time as she opened the door and then closed and locked it behind her, hastily moving to lock the other doors before leaning back against the wall, trembling in her apprehension, well aware that if he wanted to he could break the flimsy locks on any of the doors with one forceful kick.

Complete silence followed her escape, and she moved to the door, listening intently.

'We have all the nights of the rest of our lives, Bryna,' Raff murmured suddenly against the closed door.

He made it sound like a prison sentence!

CHAPTER EIGHT

DESPITE his threat, and her fear of it, Raff seemed to avoid Bryna more than ever during the next few weeks, always having left for the office before she got down in the mornings, rarely coming home for dinner, and when he did he asked for a tray in his study. The only time they had actually spent together had been her visit to the obstetrician.

Raff was adamant that he be involved in all aspects of her pregnancy, asking the doctor more questions than she did, some of them making her blush.

When she was sixteen weeks along in her pregnancy he insisted on coming along to the hospital with her while she had her scan, and the two of them watched in fascination as they saw the movements of their baby in her womb, every tiny part of it looking perfectly formed.

After they had shared such a moving experience the antagonism between them seemed completely unworthy of the occasion.

'I watched your face earlier,' Raff spoke gruffly on the drive home. 'You want this child very much, don't you?'

Some of her happy glow evaporated as she gave him a sharp look. 'Of course I do!'

'There's no need to be on the defensive,' he sighed. 'I wasn't being nasty.'

Bryna turned to stare out of the window beside her, blinking back the tears. She had been plagued with none of the morning sickness that such a lot of women complained of, she felt in extremely good health, but she was so emotional that she cried at the slightest thing; a sad programme on the television, a beautiful love story, watching small children with their parents in the park.

'As you looked at our baby your face glowed with pride,' Raff told her huskily.

'It's a miracle,' she told him with more feeling than he could ever understand. If they had been closer perhaps she would have been able to tell him of that operation in her youth and the years of emptiness afterwards, and he would have understood the wonder she felt at actually seeing the tiny baby inside her body. But they were further apart now than they had ever been.

'Bryna, is it too late for us?'

She turned to him frowningly, seeing the regret in his eyes before his attention returned to the road in front of them. 'What do you mean?' she asked suspiciously.

'We're married, in another twenty-four weeks we'll have a child of our own; don't you think we should try to make this marriage work?' he prompted huskily.

She wanted nothing else but for their marriage to work, but she didn't see how that was possible when he believed she was having an affair with another man. 'And Court?' she probed frowningly.

His mouth tightened. 'I can't change the way I feel about you and him, but I realise you're making an effort, that you haven't seen him since that day in the restaurant.'

She hadn't; she had felt it best not to aggravate the situation any further—but how did Raff know that? 'You've spoken to Court?' she said eagerly, willing the two men to be friends again.

'No,' he rasped harshly.

'Then how did you—Raff, no!' she cried as she shook her head, feeling suddenly sick. 'You haven't had me followed?'

His head went back arrogantly. 'How else was I supposed to find out what my wife has been doing with her life lately?'

'You could have asked me,' she groaned, hating the thought of some faceless person following her every movement. 'I hope he's entitled to boredom money,' she added disgustedly. 'Because watching a woman leave home for work, and then seeing her come home again and staying in for the evening, must be the most boring assignment he's ever had!'

'Bryna——'

'Don't touch me,' she avoided his hand as he reached out for her. 'Just take me back to my office, I have some work to do.'

He frowned. 'It's after five——'

'So I'll take a leaf out of my husband's book and "work late",' she snapped tauntingly, sure that working was the last thing he did on those evenings he arrived home late, even though Raff did always telephone now and give that excuse. 'I hope you've warned your latest lover that you're having her followed!' She and Court had been 'seen', he had said; he hadn't told her it was by a professional snooper!

'I don't have a lover,' he bit out grimly. 'And I've only had you watched since that day at the restaurant.'

'Why?' she groaned. 'Couldn't you trust me? Couldn't you——'

'Bryna, as soon as you got back to work you ran to him,' Raff grated. 'What was I supposed to think?'

She shook her head sadly. 'I don't think you've been doing much of that at all lately!'

He breathed raggedly. 'Bryna, I've been through one marriage where my wife took a lover——'

'You told me you both had lovers,' she protested the accusation.

'At first we did,' he conceded. 'And then I became sick of the lies—to the women involved, not to Josey. Oh, I still went to bed with a woman when I felt the need, but it was always only the one time, and always with a woman who expected nothing else from me. Josey's answer was somewhat different,' he added grimly. 'She found herself one lover and stayed with him, all the time refusing anything permanent with him because of the children.'

'How unhappy you must both have been,' Bryna sighed at the waste of it all.

He nodded. 'Which is why I don't want it to happen again with you. We were happy together once, Bryna, we could be again,' he added encouragingly.

'With you having me followed and personally avoiding me every chance you get!' she scorned.

'I've been working late because I had no reason to come home,' Raff told her quietly. 'But we could start again, tonight——'

'And your "employee"?' she bit out tautly.

He sighed. 'I'll get rid of him. Bryna,' he clasped her hand with his as it rested on her thigh, 'let's try!'

She was tempted, oh, so tempted; she still loved him in spite of the bitterness of their marriage. And maybe if they could become close she could convince him that there never had been anything between Court and herself. It still distressed her that she was the cause of the rift in the friendship.

'I'd like to——'

'Then let's do it!' he encouraged firmly.

She looked at him searchingly. 'And what happens the next time I have to see Court? I do want to do further business with him, you know.'

Raff's jaw clenched. 'I suppose I'll just have to learn to live with that. As long as you can assure me nothing is going on between you except business I'll believe you.'

'You haven't believed me so far,' Bryna reminded him wearily, wondering if this sort of truce between them could really work, but like him, doubting their marriage could survive as it was for much longer.

'My trust has taken a pounding the last few months, that's all,' he sighed. 'We'll learn to cope with that.'

His *trust* in her had been damaged. Not his love for her, or his need of her, only his trust. It wasn't much of a foundation for marriage. But what else did they have?

'I can't sleep with you, Raff,' she looked at him

unblinkingly. 'You see, although you doubt me when I say Court has only ever been a dear friend to me, I know the truth, and your lack of faith in *me* has badly shaken my trust in *you*!'

He gave an abrupt inclination of his head. 'I understand your reasons for choosing to keep your own room, but maybe in time even that physical closeness will come back again. For the moment, we're starting again from the beginning, like strangers.'

'I think our son or daughter might have something to say about that!'

Raff returned her teasing smile, the two of them sharing a brief moment of camaraderie. And as he smiled Bryna realised how strained he had looked until that moment, the leanness of his body and the lines about his eyes revealing that he was just as unhappy as she.

'Well, *almost* like strangers,' he mocked. 'Have I told you how much being pregnant suits you?' he added huskily.

They both knew he hadn't, that he had rarely spoken to her at all since her pregnancy began to show. Her blush of pleasure at the compliment added a glow to her cheeks, and a sparkle to her eyes.

She wasn't to know, as she smiled at him shyly, that Raff's trust in her would be tested sooner than she would have wished!

Their relationship didn't change overnight; there was still a strain between them that couldn't be banished no matter how much they talked and

laughed and spent time together. And they did a lot
of those things during the next few weeks, often
managing to lunch together as well as being
together in the evenings.

They were closer to being friends now than they
had ever been, having become lovers so quickly in
the first place that they hadn't really taken the time
to get to know each other as well as they probably
should have done. Now they had time to discover
the things they had in common, and surprisingly
enough they found that was quite a lot. Raff even
began to discuss his work with her, something she
had thought he would never do.

And yet that underlying strain persisted between
them.

It was physical rather than mental, Bryna either
withdrawing or trembling almost uncontrollably if
Raff should touch her, and she could feel his tension
if she should accidentally touch him in any way.

They wanted each other.

They had gone back to the beginning, started
again, had formed a sort of friendship, and now
they wanted each other so badly it was starting to
affect that very friendship they had striven for.

Bryna was more confused than ever; she had no
idea where it would all end.

But she was grateful that the two of them were at
least friends enough to be able to accept Kate's
invitation to dinner in the certainty that they
wouldn't cause any friction by their presence. The
young girl had given them a formal invitation to
what she called her belated moving-dinner-party,
and Raff had accepted just as formally.

'I just hope she's learnt to cook since the time she served up rice pudding and potatoes!' he said ruefully on the drive over to the flat. 'Together!'

Bryna laughed softly at the disgusting concoction. 'How old was she then?'

'Nine,' he grimaced. 'She was trying to act the "little mother" after Josey died, and Paul and I ate it because we didn't want to hurt her feelings.'

Bryna smiled. 'Well, I think she has more of an idea now; she was very helpful when we all cooked the Christmas dinner.'

'Let's hope so,' her father drawled. 'You look lovely tonight, Bryna.' He laced the fingers of her right hand with his.

So did he! He had always been handsome to her, but this last few weeks he had become even more so, so that she only had to look at him to feel her heart beat faster and her mouth go dry. And in an evening suit Raff could only be described as devastating! She knew she was suffering from frustration, that Raff could have been wearing patched denims and she would still have wanted him, but she couldn't help the way he made her feel breathless just to look at him.

And his compliment about her own appearance was very welcome. At nineteen weeks her pregnancy was almost halfway through, and her waistline had expanded to match that. None of her normal clothing fitted her any more, and although the maternity wardrobe Raff had insisted on buying her was very attractive she still didn't feel exactly glamorous in the flowing blue dress, and she needed Raff's compliment as a bolster to her flagging self-confidence about the way she looked to him and others.

Especially when she saw the dress Brenda was wearing! The tall redhead was very attractive, but even so the low-cut black dress seemed to be a little old for her eighteen years.

Kate gave her father and Bryna an apologetic grimace as she moved to pour them a drink. 'I only got it in for the occasion,' she hastened to explain at her father's raised brows.

'I hope so,' he murmured before turning to her flatmate. 'You're looking very sophisticated to-night, Brenda,' he told her smoothly.

Bryna watched ruefully as the young girl took the politeness as an invitation to flirt with him, knowing by the embarrassed flush to Kate's cheeks that she could cheerfully have strangled the other girl.

'I'll help you out in the kitchen,' Bryna offered gently, not at all perturbed about Brenda's obvious behaviour; the only thing she knew she could be sure of was that Raff wasn't interested in a college friend of his daughter!

'She's incredible!' muttered Kate as she banged about in the kitchen putting the finishing touches to the meal. 'I asked her to behave tonight, and she promised she would, and within a few seconds of Daddy's arrival she's throwing herself all over him!'

Bryna laughed softly at Kate's obvious disgust with her friend. 'I shouldn't worry about it, your father is only playing with her.'

'*We* all know that,' grumbled Kate, her pretty face flushed with anger. 'But Brenda doesn't know how to take no for an answer!'

Obviously the last weeks of sharing a flat with the other girl had opened Kate's eyes to Brenda's selfish nature. 'How's the flat-sharing going?' Bryna enquired casually.

'Oh, you know,' Kate turned away, shrugging. 'We get on okay together.'

Quite a turn-about from thinking Brenda was the most wonderful friend in the world, but Bryna wisely kept her thoughts to herself. She felt sure Kate felt badly enough about her father being proved right about the other girl without adding salt to the wound.

By the time they returned to the lounge Paul and his girl-friend, Lynn, had arrived with Kate's friend Roger and another young man known to them all as Flip, who appeared to be Brenda's date for the evening, although he certainly wasn't the same young man Bryna had seen emerge from Brenda's bedroom that day!

Bryna was sure Raff felt as out of place with these six youngsters as she was starting to!

The doorbell rang again shortly before eight, and Kate jumped up to answer it. 'Just so that you two wouldn't feel as if you'd been asked along to act as chaperons,' she told them teasingly before going to the door.

Bryna's sense of foreboding had warned her who the late arrival was even before Court came into the room at Kate's side. She looked pleadingly at Raff, knowing by the way he tensed that he was ready to demand that the other man leave—or he would.

Then he turned slightly and met her pleading

gaze, and some of the coldness left him as he followed her gaze to Kate's excited face. His daughter wanted both him and the other man here, and for either of them to leave would upset Kate. Raff relaxed slightly although his eyes remained dangerously narrowed.

'Look who's here!' Kate laughed her pleasure at this last arrival. 'Poor Uncle Court's date had a migraine and couldn't come,' she added sympathetically, her arm looped through his.

'And you couldn't come up with a replacement even though it was short notice?' mocked Raff, the hardness of his eyes telling of his intention to wound. 'You do disappoint me, Court,' he drawled.

Court met his gaze challengingly. 'I thought that with all the beautiful ladies here you gentlemen wouldn't mind sharing!'

Bryna winced at the barb. Court was angry at Raff's behaviour and he had a right to be, but the situation was rapidly spiralling out of control. Surprisingly it was Kate who smoothed the tense atmosphere.

'You can sit next to me, Uncle Court,' she told him lightly.

He gave her a wolfish grin. 'In that case you'd better stop calling me Uncle!'

Roger put his arm possessively about Kate's shoulders. 'She only said you could *sit* next to her,' he smiled.

Kate blushed at his obvious claim to her, glancing awkwardly at her father.

Bryna looked at Raff too, relieved to see that there was humour in his eyes now. Knowing how possessive *he* was of Kate she had feared his reaction to another man showing such proprietorial rights. But she should have known he didn't disapprove of the pleasant Roger Delaney. Tall and dark, with warm blue eyes, the younger man was studying to become a history teacher, and Raff obviously like him.

Bryna watched Raff now as he crossed the room to her side, stiffening a little as his arm curved possessively about her own waist to rest his hand against their child.

'You should have found a replacement, Court,' he drawled. 'None of us is willing to share.' He looked at the other man challengingly.

'Flip doesn't mind.' Brenda gave Court a glowing smile as she pressed against him.

Flip didn't have to mind, it soon became obvious. He was a quiet young man, obviously dazzled by the vivacity of his date, and it soon became apparent to all but him that Brenda had only invited him so that *she* wouldn't be the one without a partner for the evening. Now that Court had arrived alone she more or less ignored poor Flip, monopolising a bemused Court during the meal.

Bryna did her best to include Flip in the conversation, feeling the need to keep talking herself when, for the most part, Raff remained broodingly silent.

She knew he was angry about Court's presence here, but that for Kate's sake he was making an effort not to actually say anything in case he forgot this was supposed to be a happy occasion and insulted Court as he obviously longed to do. She

only hoped that he didn't think she had known of
Court's presence here tonight, because she hadn't;
she would never have willingly placed herself in this
tension-filled situation. The doctor was pleased
with her pregnancy so far, although her blood-
pressure's habit of fluctuating up and down did
cause him some concern. And she was sure tonight
couldn't be doing much to ease that situation!

The pity of it was that she and Raff had come so
far from the first cold weeks of their marriage.
There was true friendship between them now, a
sharing, something they had never had before. She
didn't want to lose all that now just because they
had been forced to endure an evening of Court's
company.

'I'm sorry.'

She looked at Court questioningly as he joined
her on the sofa during the brief time Raff left her to
get her a glass of orange juice, looking around
quickly to see if Raff were watching them now. Her
panicked gazed clashed with his unreadable one as
he stood across the room, and hers softened
pleadingly.

Court sighed. 'I should never have come here
tonight.' He was shaking his head as Bryna turned
back to him. 'I wasn't going to because I knew you
and Raff would be here too, but Kate was so
insistent.'

Bryna gave him a sympathetic smile, knowing
that if any damage were to be done to her new-
found relationship with Raff it would already have
happened; and she couldn't do a thing about it.
'How have you been?'

'Fine,' Court nodded. 'And you are obviously blooming.'

'Yes,' she gave a self-conscious laugh.

He looked at her searchingly. 'How are you really, Bryna?' he asked quietly. 'I've been worried about you since that day in the restaurant, but you didn't call me again . . .!' He shrugged.

'There was no need,' she dismissed the apprehension she had known that night as she waited for Raff, still believing he would never have physically harmed her.

'So you and Raff are okay now?' Court probed.

She gave a rueful shrug. 'About as okay as we'll ever be, I think,' she nodded.

He looked at her searchingly. 'And are you happy?'

Yes, she was happy. Not in an ecstatic way, but the new understanding she and Raff had come to in recent weeks had filled her with an inner tranquillity, an acceptance that he was giving her as much of himself as he was able, even if it wasn't the love she still craved from him.

She looked across the room at him anxiously now as she realised how long it was taking him to come back with her drink; he was deep in conversation with Roger Delaney, seemingly unaware of the two of them seated together on the sofa. And yet despite that Bryna knew he was very much aware of them.

'Yes,' she assured Court unhesitatingly.

'Hm. In that case, are you going to mind if I talk about Raff's suspicions concerning the two of us?' Court looked worried.

Some of the warmth left her eyes, but she shook

her head. 'If you have anything new to tell me I'd be glad to hear it.'

Court frowned. 'Well, the idea came to me when I saw him with Raff in the restaurant that day. I did notice him a couple of times while we were out together, and a few digs from him would——'

'From who?' she demanded impatiently.

'Raff's assistant. What's his name—?—Hillier,' he remembered. 'A couple of times when we were out together I noticed him at the same restaurant. I thought it was a coincidence, but you did say Raff had accused us of being *seen* together, and I suppose Hillier could have been the one spying on us.'

'Why on earth would he do that?' Bryna asked disbelievingly.

'I don't know,' Court shook his head. 'But he's the only one I can think of who actually saw us together.'

Stuart Hillier? She had never liked the man, but even so . . . !

Unless Raff had asked the other man to follow her? He had had her followed once, so why not then? He had denied having her followed then, of course, but surely it was too much of a coincidence to be one.

'You think he told Raff about us?' she said weakly, knowing by the compassion in Court's eyes that he had also guessed what she couldn't put into words, that Raff had *asked* his assitant to spy on them!

'Don't you?' he said gently.

'Yes.' She turned away, blinking back the tears, the trust and genuine liking she and Raff had built up in recent weeks crumbling as she knew it had been built on a lie. God, she felt ill when she thought now of the times she had ached to ask Raff to make their marriage a real one!

'I'm sorry, Bryna,' Court clasped her hand in his, 'I just thought it was something you should know.'

She was glad she did; she had wanted Raff so badly on the drive over here that she had been going to make the first move towards a normal marriage when they got home. Oh, what a fool she had been these last few weeks! Raff didn't want a friendship with her, he had just taken the doctor's advice that a 'happy and contented mother made for an uncomplicated pregnancy' so seriously he had been willing to forget their differences until at least her pregnancy was over. And then what? Would they go back to the coldness, the indifference?

'Here you are, Bryna.' Raff appeared back at her side with her drink after deliberately leaving her alone with Court, she felt sure; he had been testing her. 'Darling, you're very pale,' he added frowningly.

Darling. And the concern. *All false!* 'I think I'd like to go home now, if you don't mind,' she said bluntly.

He looked at the other man with narrowed eyes. 'Of course,' he agreed automatically. 'I'll tell Kate we're leaving.'

'I may be wrong, Bryna,' Court encouraged once they were alone. 'As you said, why would Hillier want to do something like that?'

They both knew why, because Raff had *asked* him to!

Bryna didn't remember saying her goodbyes and thanks to Kate, but she supposed she must have done, as she received no strange looks at their departure.

The easy camaraderie that had existed between herself and Raff on the drive over to Kate's flat was noticeably lacking on the journey back to their home; Bryna was lost in a sea of misery, and Raff's thoughts were grim, if his expression was anything to go by.

'Kate does seem to have more idea of what to serve at a dinner party now.' Raff's abrupt comment suddenly broke the silence.

The avocado with prawns, followed by chicken in white wine sauce, and then a delicious array of sweets, had been very enjoyable. 'It was very nice,' Bryna replied curtly.

'What did you think of Roger Delaney?'

'He seems very nice,' she shrugged.

'Yes,' he acknowledged tersely.

Bryna waited tensely for the question concerning her conversation with Court.

But it never came, Raff once again lapsing into silence.

Bryna went straight up the stairs to her room as soon as they got home, leaving Raff to lock up. She sensed his searching gaze on her as she walked up the stairs, her back ramrod-straight as she refused to turn around and meet that puzzled gaze.

She wasn't in the least surprised at his entrance to her bedroom minutes later after the briefest of knocks; she had probably been expecting it as she sat in her bedroom chair, still wearing her coat.

'Let me help you.' Raff stood her up to remove the coat and unzip her dress, turning her back to face him to slide the dress down her body. Bryna offered him no resistance, and he looked at her searchingly as he removed her silky underwear. 'What did Court say to upset you?' he finally rasped the question she had been waiting for.

She stood naked before him, and it didn't seem to matter, that intense awareness of him that had been with her in recent weeks had completely gone in the face of his deceit. 'Nothing,' she claimed flatly.

Raff's mouth tightened. 'He must have said something, you were all right until he spoke to you!'

'Was I?' she said dully.

'Yes, damn it!' He clasped her upper arms. 'Bryna, look at me!'

She raised lids that suddenly seemed too heavy. He looked the same as he always did, arrogantly handsome, totally in command. And for the first time since she had met him he left her cold.

'Bryna!' his voice deepened in desperation as he seemed to look into her eyes and see the complete vacuum of her emotions. 'I want you, Bryna,' he shook her slightly. 'I want you!'

'I'm not stopping you taking me,' she told him uninterestedly.

'God!' he groaned, his frown pained. 'Bryna?' He shook her again, giving a low groan as he bent his head to claim her lips as if by compulsion.

Emotionally he hadn't been able to reach her, but as the kiss went on and on, and his hands roamed almost desperately over the nakedness of her body, she felt her defences begin to crack, to crumble, and finally to be completely forgotten.

She was disgusted with her weakness even as she gloried in his lovemaking. It had been so long since she had known the ecstasy of his touch, and her body cried out for the fulfilment it knew only this man could give her.

She thought she would collapse completely as she felt his hand against the swelling of her body that was their child, feeling the baby stir in answer to its father's touch. The baby knew, as she did, that they were possessions of this man, to do with as he would. And if he chose to make love to her she couldn't stop him; she knew that she wanted him too.

His body was hard and yet warmly inviting as he moved above her as they lay on the bed, his clothes long ago thrown to the floor, and Bryna groaned her pleasure as they became one, arching her hips to meet his, needing to drive the demons of doubt from her mind even as she needed Raff's fierce thrusts inside her.

The weeks without each other took their toll on their control, and their pleasure was over almost before it had begun, although it was more intense than anything Bryna had ever known before. She revelled in Raff's release as he trembled above and within her.

Finally he found the strength to lie beside her, ever careful of their child. 'Now tell me what Court said to upset you,' he prompted huskily.

She had known, despite their lovemaking, that the question had only been postponed, not forgotten, and now that some measure of sanity had been returned to her she looked at him steadily. 'Was Stuart Hillier the one who told you I had been meeting Court?'

Raff frowned. 'What difference does it make who told me?'

'It matters to me,' she bit out. 'Was it him?' She sat up.

'I——'

'Oh, my God!' Dizziness swept over her as she looked at the bed between them, a dark red staining the cream sheet. 'I'm bleeding, Raff,' she looked at him with panicked eyes. 'I'm losing our baby!'

CHAPTER NINE

'THE doctor says about a week's rest here,' Raff told her grimly. 'And then you can probably come home. Also to rest,' he added determinedly.

Bryna voiced no complaint as she lay in the hospital bed. She knew she would stay here for the whole of the next twenty-one weeks as long as it meant her baby could be born healthy and safe at the end of it.

Raff had lost no time when he saw the truth of her distressed cry, dressing hurriedly before wrapping her in a blanket to carry her down to the car and drive her to the hospital.

They had been here almost two hours now, while the doctors stopped the flow of blood and established whether or not she had gone into premature labour. She hadn't, and the bleeding had also stopped, for now.

Raff had been beside her the whole time, and if the emergency staff at this prestigious hospital had found anything strange about his carrying his naked, obviously pregnant, wife in to them they hadn't shown it, but had worked quietly and calmly to make sure that she didn't lose her child.

And all the time that they had Bryna had known that before she made her horrific discovery she had seen the truth in Raff's eyes; Stuart Hillier *had* been the one to tell him she was meeting Court behind his back.

'I'm sorry.'

She looked up at Raff in surprise, startled by the anguish in his voice. He looked pained, under severe strain; the last few hours had taken their toll on him too. 'It's over now,' she dismissed distantly.

'God, I hope so!' He clasped her hand in his, looking strangely unreal dressed as he was in the evening clothes he had grabbed up off the floor to pull on before bringing her here. 'I should never have made love to you.'

For different reasons Bryna agreed with him. Making love with him had shown her that no matter how much he hurt her she loved him too much to ever say no to him. She had never believed herself to have masochistic tendencies, but surely loving Raff in the mindless way that she did had to be that!

'It wasn't that—the doctor said so.' She blushed as she recalled the embarrassingly intimate questions the young doctor had asked her; it seemed that when you had a baby privacy became a thing of the past! 'It's my blood-pressure,' she reminded Raff.

Raff shook his head. 'It was seeing Court again that did it——'

'It was knowing you would take the lies of a man you barely know over the truth of your wife!' she cut in on his angry tirade with one of her own, her eyes deeply purple.

Raff's jaw clenched. 'I don't think we should argue about this now——'

'I don't think we should argue about it all,' she bit

out caustically. 'You've already made your decision
about who's telling the truth, and I know you're
wrong. Stalemate. Now I believe the doctor said I
should rest . . .' she added pointedly.

Raff's cheeks became flushed at her dismissal. 'If
only you would let me explain——'

'I don't have to do anything but rest now,
remember?' She looked at him coldly.

He sighed his defeat. 'Bryna, I—I care for you. If
anything had happened to you——'

'You mean the baby,' she corrected harshly. 'But
don't worry, Raff, I probably want this baby more
than you do.' Because it was probably the only child
she would ever have. Conceiving had been difficult
enough, but now that she was pregnant her body
still seemed to be rebelling.

His eyes darkened. 'I doubt if that's possible,' his
voice was husky. 'Get some sleep now.' He bent to
kiss her brow, drawing back quickly as she
flinched. 'I want the baby to be all right,' he rasped.
'But God, how I wish you'd never become
pregnant!'

Bryna's chin went back defensively. 'Believe me,
if I'd thought there'd been a possibility that I *could*
conceive I wouldn't have chosen you as the father!'
As soon as she had made the heated statement she
regretted it, sure that Raff would twist her words in
some way so that he could think even more badly of
her. She had never meant to tell him that she had
believed herself barren, but her temper had got the
better of her.

Raff became suddenly still. 'What do you mean?'

'It doesn't matter——'

'*What do you mean!*'

She swallowed hard, meeting his gaze unflinchingly. 'I had an operation in my teens that made the doctors tell my parents at the time that I would never have a child,' she dismissed carelessly. 'I didn't use any form of birth control during our affair, Raff, because I didn't think I could become pregnant!'

He drew back to drop down into the chair drawn up beside her bed. 'I thought perhaps you didn't like children, that like actually living together, they were too much of a commitment. I never guessed . . .' He looked at her sharply. 'And instead it was Court who was sterile.'

'Yes, what a pair we would have made,' she acknowledged bitterly.

'Is that why——?'

'What?' she probed warily as he broke off abruptly, his jaw tight, his mouth thinned. 'Why what, Raff?' she pressured.

He drew in a ragged breath. 'Why you chose me that day and not Court.'

She could feel herself pale. 'I didn't choose you, *you* chose me,' she choked out hardly. 'And I was hardly likely to have asked Court if he was capable of fathering a child before deciding whether or not to go out with him, just *in case* the doctors were wrong after all and I could conceive!'

'No, of course not,' Raff accepted self-disgustedly. 'I don't know what's the matter with me. I——'

'I do,' she scorned. 'You're determined to think the worst of me, to believe I had some ulterior motive for going out with you at all, for marrying you. Well, maybe this will help,' she snapped. 'I never *would* have married you if I hadn't been frightened you would take my baby from me!' She was breathing hard in her agitation, glaring up at him.

A nerve pulsed in his cheek. 'I——'

'I'm sorry, Mr Gallagher,' a pretty nurse murmured smoothly as she entered the private room. 'But Mrs Gallagher should be resting now. You too,' she encouraged gently. 'It's two o'clock in the morning! And from my experience, fathers-to-be need as much rest as the mother!' She frowned when her teasing didn't even arouse a rueful smile. 'The danger is over now, Mr and Mrs Gallagher,' she comforted softly.

The danger was over, but so was her marriage; Bryna knew now it should never have begun, that instead of taking what she had believed was the only way, she should have fought Raff in court. She wanted to tell him so now, but as the nurse continued to hover pointedly in her room she knew it would have to wait until another time, when they were alone.

But they never were alone. She didn't think it was through Raff's design, but each time he visited her he had either Kate or Paul with him, the two of them very concerned about her and the welfare of their brother or sister. The scare had succeeded in bringing them closer to their sibling, at least.

She had plenty of other visitors too. Her worried parents came down from Scotland, several of the models and friends she worked with popped in for a few minutes, Gilly, and once Court arrived just before the regular visiting time, obviously so that he should avoid running into Raff.

'For you, because they remind me of your eyes.' He put a posy of violets on the bed.

Bryna stroked the delicate petals, blinking up at him tearfully. 'Thank you.'

'Hey, I came here to cheer you up, not make you cry!' He pulled up a chair and sat down, grinning amiably. 'What's the food like?'

'The food?' she laughed. She couldn't help it!

'I've always been told it's one of the first questions you should ask a person in hospital,' Court explained. 'I've heard that the food is atrocious in these places. I could have something exotic sent in——'

'The food is fine,' chuckled Bryna. 'How did you know where I was?' she asked curiously.

'Kate,' he supplied ruefully. 'She told me about the scare you all had. How are you feeling now?'

There had been no more bleeding, her blood-pressure had steadied, and the doctor seemed very pleased with her. 'I was a little scared when it happened,' she admitted 'But everything seems fine now.'

He suddenly looked older, his expression strained. 'I couldn't bear it if anything I'd said or done had caused you to lose the baby.'

'You haven't, and I didn't,' she reassured him, knowing exactly why he would be so upset if he should be the cause of harm coming to her child. Poor Court! 'Court, when—when the baby is born I would like you to be its godfather.'

His brows rose. 'And what would Raff have to
say about that?'

'Nothing,' her mouth firmed, 'because it will be
none of his business.'

His brows rose at the vehemence in her voice.
'You've left him?' he sounded puzzled.

'I—— Not yet,' she moistened dry lips. 'I haven't
had the opportunity to tell him yet, but I—I will.
And I want you to be the baby's godfather.'

Court looked at her searchingly, his eyes dark
with pain. 'He told you, didn't he,' he said flatly.

She had blundered and hurt him, and that was
something she had never meant to do. 'Court——'

'It's all right.' He stood up, his face strangely
expressionless now. 'Knowing what Raff believes
about us, and the existence of your pregnancy, I can
imagine under what circumstances he told you.' He
drew a ragged breath. 'I have to go now——'

'Oh, Court, no!' she pleaded with him, reaching
out to him imploringly. 'I'm so sorry. The last thing
I wanted to do was hurt you——'

'You haven't,' he told her abruptly. 'I came to
terms with my sterility years ago,' he added bitterly.

'Most women would be happy to adopt a baby
just to have you as their husband——'

'Most women!' he scorned. 'I think you're
overestimating the majority of your sex, Bryna.'

She swallowed hard. 'And so you've decided not
to marry at all,' she guessed, having made much the
same decision herself once she accepted how her
own infertility made her feel.

'I didn't make the decision,' Court rasped. 'It was
made for me.'

'But, Court, there are lots of women nowadays who don't even want children——'

'Selfish, egotistical women who don't want to ruin their figure or their careers,' he cut in disgustedly. 'I don't want a wife like that.'

She shook her head. 'They aren't all like that, some of them——'

'Am I interrupting anything?' Alyson stood hesitantly in the doorway, her eyes lighting up with pleasure as she looked at the man she had found so fascinating at Bryna's wedding, glowingly beautiful as she came into the room, her black-haired, green-eyed beauty making her very photogenic. 'You didn't call me after the wedding,' she flirted with Court.

Some of the tension left his body as he smiled ruefully at Bryna before grinning wickedly at Alyson. 'Tonight?'

'Lovely,' Alyson gave him an enticing smile.

He nodded, his expression sobering as he turned to Bryna. 'Take care of yourself and the baby.'

'You aren't leaving?' she realised in dismay; they still had so much to say to each other.

His mouth twisted derisively. 'I think I'd better go before Raff gets here.'

'Oh, but——'

'Goodbye, Bryna.' He bent to kiss her cheek. 'Be happy.'

It sounded like a final parting! 'Court, you——'

He turned briefly at the door. 'I really do have to go,' he told her gruffly. 'Don't worry about me, Bryna,' he drawled as she still looked upset. 'I get by.' He looked pointedly at Alyson before leaving.

Bryna sat back wearily. The last thing she had wanted to do was hurt Court. Between the two of them she and Raff had hurt Court very much.

'*Did* I interrupt something?' Alyson looked concerned as she sat next to the bed, placing the magazines she had brought with her on the bedside table.

Bryna shook off her mood of despondency with an effort, smiling at her friend. 'No, of course not,' she dismissed lightly.

'Only Court seemed a little upset,' Alyson still frowned. 'Not at all like the charming rake I was so attracted to at your wedding.'

Bryna gave a disbelieving laugh. 'You think he's a rake, but you still asked him to call you!'

'Of course,' her friend grimaced. 'He'll be a welcome relief after that self-opinionated creep I *did* get a call from,' she grimaced.

She and Alyson had begun their modelling careers together eight years ago, and unluckily for Alyson, there seemed to have been a lot of 'creeps' during that time.

Bryna shook her head. 'You always did choose the wrong men.'

'You could have warned me,' Alyson complained. 'Then I wouldn't have had to endure that disaster of a date with him.'

'How could I have prevented that?' mocked Bryna.

'Well, I know he only works for your husband, but you must have realised by now what a creep he is!' Alyson said with feeling.

Bryna had stiffened just at the mention of Raff,

but as Alyson's words became clear she felt herself pale. 'Stuart Hillier called you?' she gasped.

'Yes.' Alyson wrinkled her lovely nose tellingly.

He wouldn't, Raff *wouldn't* . . .! 'He didn't give any indication at the wedding that he was attracted to you.' Bryna said dully.

'That's what I thought,' her friend grimaced. 'His call came completely out of the blue. In fact, I had trouble placing him at first. Then I realised he was the one who was attracted to you——'

'Oh, I don't think so,' Bryna protested instantly.

'Well, he certainly couldn't take his eyes off you.' Alyson shrugged. 'But after all, it was me he called. And he's quite attractive . . . If only he weren't such a bore.' She wrinkled her nose again.

'He talked about himself a lot?' prompted Bryna, not wanting to hear how Stuart Hillier had watched her constantly at the wedding.

'He talked about *Raff* a lot,' Alyson grimaced. 'I find your husband as attractive as the rest of the female population,' she sighed. 'But he *is* your husband, and while I'm on a date with another man I'd prefer to talk about something a little more— personal.'

Bryna wasn't sure if she was breathing any more. 'And me, did Stuart talk about me too?'

Her friend frowned. 'A couple of times,' she replied thoughtfully. 'Nothing detrimental,' she hastened to add. 'I wouldn't have allowed that. He mainly asked questions I thought he had no right to. I told him to ask Raff if he was that interested in you, and that seemed to shut him up!'

Because he didn't need to ask Raff anything

when he was the one that had prompted Stuart to ask Alyson the questions in the first place!

Raff had gone too far this time. Challenging her with his nonsensical accusations was one thing, alienating his best friend was another thing he was going to have to live with, but persuading her friends to talk about her was something else entirely.

It couldn't go on.

She forced herself to give Alyson a bright smile. 'Believe me, Court is much nicer than Stuart Hillier.'

Alyson gave a smile of anticipation. 'I certainly hope so!'

The two of them were still chatting together when Raff arrived a few minutes later. And for once he was alone. Bryna didn't try to stop Alyson leaving when she excused herself a few minutes later, although she did thank her for the magazines and for finding the time to come and see her, knowing how busy her friend was running the agency in her absence.

Raff placed the books and box of chocolates he had brought next to the magazines. 'It was nice of her to come,' he said lightly.

Bryna looked at him coldly. He was thinner, his cheeks hollow, his eyes lacking their usual brightness; she only wished it were his guilty conscience making him look that way. But she knew it wasn't. Raff didn't have a conscience to feel guilty with.

'Yes,' she bit out.

'Kate and Paul will be along later; they went to buy you a present.' He stood awkwardly beside the bed, making no effort to sit down as her other visitors had done.

'There's really no need for them to buy me something every time they come to see me,' she shook her head.

'This one is a welcome home present.' Raff's eyes blazed his satisfaction. 'I've just seen the doctor, he said you can come home tomorrow!'

She knew all about her proposed discharge from the hospital; she had discussed it with the doctor herself when he had visited her this morning. 'Yes,' she confirmed unenthusiastically.

Raff frowned at her tone. 'You don't sound very pleased about it.'

'Being discharged means that the danger to the baby is over, and I'm very pleased about that,' she insisted evenly.

'Then what's wrong?' He looked at her searchingly.

Bryna drew in a deep breath, knowing this wasn't going to be pleasant, but determined to go through with it. 'I'm not coming home,' she told him flatly.

Raff looked taken aback. 'But the doctor said that you're well enough to leave, that there's been no more bleeding, that——'

'I know exactly what the doctor said,' she cut in firmly. 'When I said I wasn't coming home, I meant to *your* home.' She met his gaze challengingly as his head went back in protest.

'It's *our* home, damn you,' he finally bit out gratingly. 'And where else would you go?'

She shrugged. 'Back to Scotland, to my parents——'

'You aren't well enough to travel,' he rasped.

She knew that, but she had hoped Raff wouldn't. She should have known better! But she hadn't really had time to think all her plans through yet. All she did know was that she had to get away from Raff.

'Then perhaps my mother could continue to stay on here and we could get a flat——'

'You know your father is having difficulty coping at home without your mother, that it's a busy time of year for them,' Raff dismissed. 'Besides, you don't have a flat any more.'

Her cheeks flushed in her agitation. 'I could rent one——'

'You aren't strong enough to shop for furnishings,' he bit out grimly.

'Then I'll rent a furnished one,' she told him desperately. 'But I am not living with you!' she glared at him, breathing hard.

'Calm down,' he instructed authoritatively. 'Do you want your blood-pressure to shoot up again?'

'No,' she conceded tightly. 'But our marriage is over, Raff. I want nothing more to do with you.'

A nerve pulsed in his jaw, fury glittering in his eyes. 'Do you have to move out for that?' he demanded finally.

Puzzlement darkened her eyes as she looked at him questioningly.

He gave an impatient shrug. 'We managed to live together all right the last time we ignored each other's existence!'

Bryna shook her head. 'I'm not sure I'll be able to do that this time,' she snapped.

'Why not?' he rasped.

'Because I don't trust you,' she scorned.

Raff's mouth tightened. 'I'm hardly likely to risk the life of my child by upsetting you again!'

'We married because of the baby, we agreed that would be all it was, but you broke your promise almost as soon as we were married,' she reminded him tautly. 'I can't trust you,' she repeated flatly.

'You can!' he grated. 'I give you my word I won't come near you or try to touch you again. I just want to take care of you. Let me take care of you,' his voice gentled.

She didn't want to do it, she wanted to get as far away from him and his continuous spying on her, but she knew she never would. 'You said you would stay away from me!' She looked at him with narrowed eyes.

'I will,' he agreed heavily. 'But I have staff at the house who can look after you, make sure that you don't overdo things. And you know it would only worry your parents if you asked your mother to stay on any longer than she already has.'

Her parents had both come down as soon as they knew she had been admitted to hospital, but her father had had to return to Scotland after a couple of days. Having convinced both her parents that both she and the baby were fine now, she knew it would only upset them if she left Raff now.

'I don't even want to see you, Raff,' she told him coldly. 'And once the baby is born I'm finding a place of my own.'

His mouth tightened over the last, but he said nothing, nodding acceptance of her conditions.

CHAPTER TEN

SHE had only been back in the house a few days when Kate arrived with her suitcase in her hand.

Bryna put down the book she was reading to look anxiously at her stepdaughter as she dropped the suitcase down on the floor to run sobbing across the lounge. Bryna opened her arms to the girl, murmuring words of soothing comfort as she stroked the glossy black curls while waiting for the tears to stop.

Kate finally gave a last shuddering sob and moved back out of Bryna's arms. She looked so young and vulnerable that Bryna's heart went out to her.

'What happened?' she prompted gently.

Kate shook her head, wiping away the tears with her fingertips. 'I shouldn't be worrying you in your condition——'

'My "condition" at the moment is that of being your stand-in mother,' chided Bryna. 'I care about you, Kate.'

'I care about you, too,' the girl gave a watery smile. 'And I do think of you as my mother, but Paul and I decided you're too young to have us call you Mum. We thought you could be our big sister instead.'

Bryna wasn't upset that Kate and Paul had decided on the latter; the fact that her stepchildren had discussed the possibility of calling her 'Mum' and only vetoed it because of her age filled her with a warm glow. 'Big sisters are for confiding in,' she encouraged softly.

Kate grimaced. 'It's Brenda!' she said with feeling.

Bryna had an idea that it might be, in fact she was surprised Kate had lasted the two months that she had with the other girl. 'Do you want to tell me about it?' she prompted lightly.

Kate stood up restlessly. 'Why not?' she said disgustedly. 'I thought she was my friend,' her eyes blazed darkly grey. 'But she isn't,' she scorned. 'She doesn't know the meaning of the word friendship!'

The presence of the suitcase, and Kate's obvious anger, implied that the disagreement between the two girls was serious. 'Did Brenda do something you disapprove of?' Bryna probed.

'Oh, I could accept her untidiness, her selfishness, even the men she occasionally had staying overnight with her.' Kate blushed as she revealed the latter. 'But I can't, and I *won't*, accept her trying to seduce Roger!'

It was worse than Bryna had expected, knowing how much Kate liked Roger; her affection for him had been obvious on the occasions he had accompanied Kate to see her over the last ten days.

'Did she succeed?' Bryna asked reluctantly.

'Of course not!' Kate defended indignantly. 'Roger isn't interested in her, he lo— well, it's me he likes,' she amended blushingly. 'He's as disgusted by her behaviour as I am.'

Bryna could imagine that he was, but she had felt

the question had to be asked. She was glad, for
Kate's sake, that Roger's affection was as deep as
her own for him. 'What exactly happened?' she
frowned.

'I was late getting out of my class this evening,
and Roger thought I must have already left, and
went straight to the flat. I walked in just as Brenda
was trying to kiss him while he tried to fight her
off!' Her eyes glittered angrily with remembered
outrage. 'I watched them as he succeeded, wiping
the touch of her lips from his mouth with the back
of his hand while he told her to stay away from him,
that he wasn't interested. Of course, as soon as
Brenda saw me she claimed that Roger had
attacked her, but I'd *seen* them! I packed my case
and left. I'll get the rest of my things later. I just had
to get away from there.' She shuddered.

'And where is Roger now?'

Kate looked uncomfortable. 'He wanted to come
home with me, but I—I told him I'd see him later. I
think I should face Daddy alone,' she added with
obvious reluctance for the idea.

Bryna's mouth firmed as she guessed the reason
for Kate's reluctance was that she dreaded the idea
of her father saying 'I told you so'.

Raff had kept completely to his word this time,
spending his evenings in his study, not even
bothering to say hello to her when he arrived home
at night. And she liked it that way; she couldn't
have even borne a distant politeness from him,
feeling about him as she did now. But she was as
unsure as Kate about the way he would react to

Kate's news, and she didn't think the girl should face him alone!

They both gave a startled jolt as the front door was slammed closed, Kate turning pleadingly to Bryna. 'That will be him now,' she grimaced. 'I think I've changed my mind about seeing him alone!'

Bryna gave a rueful smile. 'Don't worry, I'm not going anywhere.'

They were sitting together on the sofa as Raff strode past the lounge door on the way to his study as he usually did. The same pattern had been followed on the last three evenings, and Bryna had known that he wouldn't vary his routine. Usually he didn't even glance into the room he knew she occupied, but tonight he frowned and then stopped, turning slowly, his eyes widening as he saw Kate sitting with Bryna, Kate's suitcase standing between them and him.

Bryna looked from father to daughter, Raff's expression questioning, Kate looking as if she might begin to cry again. 'Kate has decided to come back home for a while,' she informed Raff lightly.

His eyes narrowed, and then he relaxed slightly, strolling into the room, dropping his briefcase down into a chair. 'That will be nice,' he murmured. 'How long can you stay, darling?' He poured himself a drink as the two women shook their heads at his offer.

'I—er—I——' Kate looked helplessly at Bryna.

She gave the girl a reassuring smile. 'The truth is, Raff, Kate has decided she'd like to move back with us and help keep me company until the baby is born. Isn't that nice of her?'

'Very,' he drawled. 'I'm sure Bryna appreciates your kindness, Kate,' he told his daughter warmly.

Kate blushed at the unmerited praise. 'I—I think I'll take my things upstairs and change for dinner.' She gave Bryna a grateful hug before hurrying from the room.

Raff sighed as the door closed behind her, suddenly looking weary. 'What really happened?'

Bryna sat tensely on the edge of the sofa now that the two of them were alone. This was the first time thay had spoken together since the morning Raff had driven her home from the hospital, the first time she had really looked at him in that time too. If he had looked ill three days ago he looked ten time worse now, his face gaunt, his eyes bruised and sunken, the looseness of his suit telling of his loss of weight.

'Bryna?' he frowned as he received no answer.

She drew in a ragged breath, dismissing any feelings of compassion for him that might have reared their silly head. This man was invincible, he needed no one's pity, least of all hers. 'Brenda flirted with one man too many,' she drawled. 'Roger,' she explained at his puzzled look.

'Oh,' he rasped.

'I'm sure Kate intends telling you about it, as soon as she calms down a little,' she said distantly. 'At the moment she's just very disillusioned.'

'About Roger?'

'About Brenda,' she corrected drily. 'Roger very firmly repulsed the over-confident Miss Sanders.'

'Thank God for that,' grimaced Raff, standing

close to the fireplace, the warmth the fire emitted not seeming to bother him. 'I get the feeling Kate is in love with him.'

Bryna didn't miss the half-question in his tone. 'I think you would have to ask Kate about that,' she evaded.

He nodded abruptly. 'Thank you for—well, for being here when she needed someone to talk to.'

She looked at him searchingly. 'Why shouldn't I be?' she finally answered him. 'I like both your children, I always have.'

'It's just their father you can't stand to have near you!' Raff swallowed some of the whisky in his glass. 'You do realise that Kate's being here will have to change all that?'

'What do you mean?' she asked warily, her hands clenched.

He shrugged. 'We can hardly continue to act as strangers with Kate back in the house.'

The last three days of peace and sanity faded as she saw the truth of his words. The last thing she wanted to do was upset Kate any further, by letting her see the deterioration of her father's marriage to Bryna, when she had already suffered such a blow to her trust in people being what they seemed to be. But neither could she pretend this was a happy marriage.

'I'm willing to start taking my meals with you again if it will help,' she accepted stiffly.

His mouth tightened. 'You would do that for Kate but not for me?'

'You aren't vulnerable the way she is,' Bryna snapped.

'I'm not?' he rasped self-derisively. 'Then why am I clinging on to a wife who's just waiting for the time she can leave me to be with the man she really loves?' His eyes were narrowed.

Bryna gasped. 'Not Court again!' she sighed her angry impatience. 'I haven't seen him since——' she broke off as she realised how recently she *had* seen him, a visit Raff knew nothing about.

'Four days ago,' Raff put in, softly contradicting that belief. 'I saw him come into your room that night,' he explained at her startled look. 'That was why I came in late,' he added grimly.

'You told me you'd been to see the doctor——'

'I'd seen him earlier,' he bit out.

'If you knew Court was in my room with me why didn't you——?'

'Walk in on the pair of you?' he finished bitterly. 'I had no wish to see the two of you together. It was enough that you told me you were leaving me when I did get in to see you!'

'But that had nothing to do with my having seen Court, that was because——'

'Aren't you going to change, Daddy?' Kate bounced back into the room, her usual exuberance almost restored. 'I called Roger from upstairs and invited him over for dinner; he'll be here in a few minutes.'

Raff gave one last regretful glance at Bryna before smiling at his daughter. 'And when can I expect him to ask for my daughter's hand in marriage?' he teased her.

Kate blushed. 'We've already decided that we

aren't going to get married for a couple of years,' she told him awkwardly.

'I suppose I should be grateful you bothered to tell me even that,' her father said drily.

She grinned. 'I'm determined to wait until the baby is old enough to be either pageboy or bridesmaid!'

The laughter left Raff's eyes, although the smile remained on his lips. 'That may not be for some time,' he said drily.

Bryna knew from his expression that he doubted she or the baby would still be here then. But although she might have accepted banishment from his children's lives as well as his when their affair ended she had no intention of doing that now that she had been his wife and was having Kate's and Paul's brother or sister.

Kate shrugged, unaware of the tension of the adults. 'We have time. Do hurry up, Daddy,' she encouraged impatiently. 'I'm hungry!'

'You always were,' he shook his head ruefully. 'Maybe if I tell Roger how much you're going to cost to keep in food he'll change his mind about marrying you!' he teased before going upstairs.

Kate moved to hug Bryna a second time. 'Thank you so much for coming to my rescue like that earlier.'

'Your father guessed I wasn't telling the truth,' she grimaced.

'I knew he would,' Kate nodded. 'I'll talk to him about it later.'

For all that Bryna and Raff didn't exchange more than a couple of words it was a pleasantly lighthearted meal, Roger and Raff getting on just as well as they had in the past; Bryna was sure that when the time did come that Kate would have no difficulty at all in convincing her father of Roger's worth.

They returned to the lounge for coffee, Bryna pouring, glad to have something to do with her hands; the meal was a strain for her even if it had passed without incident.

'I'm so glad you and Uncle Court have resolved your differences,' Kate told her father happily. 'Whatever they were,' she added. 'You needn't look so surprised, Daddy, I'm well aware of the fact that the two of you haven't been the best of friends lately.'

That had to be an understatement, and Bryna looked questioningly at Raff; he hadn't given the impression earlier that he and Court were friends again.

He frowned at Kate. 'I didn't doubt your astuteness, I merely wondered what had given you the impression our "differences had been resolved",' he grated.

Kate's pleasure wavered a little. 'You mean they haven't?'

'No. Look, Kate,' he continued soothingly as her expression revealed her dismay. 'Arguments happen occasionally. We can't live happily-ever-after all the time——'

'I know that,' she dismissed scornfully. 'I just thought—hoped——'

'I don't know why you thought that,' he frowned. 'I haven't seen Court for a couple of weeks——'

'No, but Stuart has,' Kate cut in. 'And the only reason I could think of for him being with Uncle Court was if the two of you were setting up a business deal.'

Raff's eyes were narrowed. 'When did Stuart see Court?' he enquired quietly.

Kate shrugged. 'I saw them together a couple of weeks ago.'

Bryna had become very still. Court and Stuart Hillier? What possible reason could the two men have to meet if not on Raff's behalf? The only answer she could find to that made her pale.

'I don't—Bryna?' Raff looked at her with concern, coming down on his haunches beside her chair as he grasped her suddenly cold hands in his. 'Darling, what is it?'

He sounded so concerned for her. Could it be true? Had she trusted and believed the wrong man?

'Bryna?' Raff sounded desperate now. 'Kate, call the doctor——'

'No,' she managed to choke out. 'I—I think I'd like to go and lie down for a while.' She looked at Raff with darkly purple eyes. 'Would you please help me up the stairs?'

Pleasure blazed in his eyes before it was quickly brought under control. 'Of course.' He stood up to swing her up into his arms.

She didn't protest, not altogether sure her legs would support her weight if she had tried to stand up on her own. 'I'm just tired,' she assured Kate and Roger wryly as they watched her anxiously.

Raff gave them what could only be described as a wolfish grin. 'It's really just her way of dragging me off to bed to have her wicked way with me!' he teased, instantly easing their tension. 'I wish she would realise I'm not going to argue!'

His teasing had eased the atmosphere of worry, although his expression became grim again as he carried Bryna up to her room, placing her down carefully on the bed. 'What happened down there?' he asked gently.

She closed her eyes a moment, breathing deeply to calm her racing thoughts. She had to be wrong. But did she want to be—didn't she want all those horrific accusations that were crashing about in her head to be true so that she was free to love Raff again? She knew, no matter how painful it would be if what she suspected were true, that she *so much* wanted it to be right.

'Raff, who told you about my having an affair with Court?' She looked at him unblinkingly.

'Bryna——'

'Raff, please answer, this is very important to the future of our marriage.' She grasped his arm encouragingly.

'The future of . . .?' Suddenly he looked as vulnerable as he had claimed to be earlier. 'Bryna, don't play games with me!'

'I'm not,' she shook her head, still feeling ill. 'But I think someone has been playing a game with us, a sickeningly destructive game!'

'What are you talking about?' he groaned his impatience.

'Raff, did you ask Stuart Hillier to spy on me?'

Anger darkened his face. 'Of course not,' he rasped. 'I'll admit he was the first one to mention seeing you and Court together, but I certainly never asked him to *spy* on you!'

'Then who did?' she probed quietly.

'No one did,' Raff dismissed impatiently. 'You——'

'Then why did he?' she persisted.

'He didn't! He saw you in a couple of restaurants together and just happened to mention it to me——'

'Raff, how many restaurants are there in London?' she reasoned.

He gave a perplexed frown. 'I don't know, hundreds probably,' he shrugged.

'Then how is it that I've been seen so regularly with Court in *different* restaurants, by both you and Stuart Hillier?'

'Coincidence, I suppose——'

'That's exactly what he said,' she recalled flatly.

'He?' Raff looked totally confused. 'You mean Stuart?'

'No—Court.'

Kate said she had seen Court with Stuart Hillier a couple of weeks ago, and yet when Bryna had spoken to Court ten days ago he had trouble remembering the other man's name! She had nothing else to go on but the coincidence of the restaurants, the meeting Kate had witnessed, and Court's memory lapse about the other man's name, and yet suddenly she knew. She *knew*!

'But that sort of coincidence doesn't occur in a place as big as London unless schedules are known and shared,' she sighed. 'Court had been trying to drive a wedge in our relationship almost since it began,' she told Raff dully. 'It has to be him. I

thought it was you, but—but now I know it's Court.'
She swallowed hard, the pain of disillusionment
almost too much to bear. She had genuinely liked
Court, and he had tried to destroy her, had almost
succeeded in destroying her child.

Raff sat on the edge of the bed, frowning darkly.
'How do you know?'

She blinked back the tears. 'For now will you just
accept it if I tell you I *do* know?'

'Darling Bryna, don't you know I would accept it
if you told me black was white and white was
black?'

That was it. The day she had first met Court and
been introduced to Raff she had believed Court was
the light one, like the sun, and Raff was the dark
secretive one, like the moon. She had gone on
thinking of them in that way even after she fell in
love with Raff, and all the time she had had the two
men the wrong way around; Raff was her sunlight,
Court was the dark destructive one.

'He saw exactly what I thought,' she realised
chokingly. 'And that I loved you anyway. And he
used that love against me!'

'You—love—me?'

It was a strangulated plea that it be the truth, and
she looked at Raff with all her love shining in her
eyes for him. 'I've always loved you. I fell in love
with you that first night we went out together, and
it's continued that way. I would never have agreed
to have an affair with you if I hadn't loved you,' she
added ruefully.

He grasped her arms. 'And I never would have

settled for one if I'd known how you felt!' he groaned.

Bryna looked up at him uncertainly. 'What do you mean? The affair was your idea——'

He shook his head. 'Yours.'

'But——'

'We made love, and I was about to tell you how much I loved you and wanted to marry you when you started talking about how clever you'd been to choose someone as skilled as me as your first lover, how we both knew the rules—no ties, no commitment, how we would just enjoy each other,' he remembered bitterly. 'For the first time since my youthful love for Josey I'd been about to bare my soul and tell a woman how much I loved her, and before I could she told me she was only interested in my body! Talk about a reversal of the roles!' The pain he had known could still be heard in his voice.

'I thought it was what you wanted,' she pleaded for his understanding.

'I don't usually take a woman home to meet my children on a second date,' he groaned. 'I fell in love with you almost instantly, couldn't get you of my mind, and that day I returned from my business trip to America and you greeted me like a spitting tigress I knew I had to have you for my wife, that I always wanted you to be there when I came home. But I had other commitments in my life, and I thought it best if you met Kate and Paul so that you knew what those commitments were, if by some miracle I could persuade you to marry me.'

'I didn't know how you felt about me, Raff,' she squeezed his hands in her own. 'But he did. And he used our uncertainty of each other against us.'

'But why?'

'I don't know,' she sighed. 'I wish I did.'

'Bryna, do you really love me?' Raff still didn't look as if he really believed her.

'So very much,' she said with feeling.

'Then you must have been going through the same hell I have,' he groaned, his eyes dark with pain. 'Bryna, I love you. I love you so much!'

'Raff, make love to me,' she urged throatily.

He blinked. 'Now?'

'Don't you want to?' she teased huskily.

He gave her a look that told her just how much. 'But I don't want to hurt you or the baby. We've had one scare——'

'That had nothing to do with our making love,' she assured him quickly.

'You almost fainted downstairs just now,' he reminded her concernedly.

'Both I and the baby would like to be reacquainted with the man we love!' Her eyes shone, no more shadows on her love for him.

'If we have a daughter and she looked at me the way you do I'll never be able to deny her anything!' he groaned as he buried his face in her hair.

Bryna cradled his head lovingly, for the first time knowing herself loved in return by this magnificent man. 'I'll make sure it's a boy so that your authority won't be threatened,' she teased.

He didn't seem to care very much about that as he made slow love to her, touching every inch of her, his hands possessive against their child as he suckled against her, driving them both towards the edge of fulfilment.

When finally the silken shaft of him was encased inside her they were both so highly aroused that they just lay together as the waves of pleasure washed all the past pain away.

Raff lay damply against her breasts. 'Perhaps it's as well you're already pregnant, otherwise I have a feeling you would be after tonight!'

Bryna knew exactly what he meant. The first time they had ever made love had been so earth-shatteringly perfect, but although they had always found pleasure in each other's arms it had never ben quite that perfect again. Tonight, just now, it had superseded perfection, had been a vow to how much they loved each other. And she now knew why the first time and just now had been so different from all the others; on neither occasion had they tried to hide their love from each other. This time nothing would spoil that.

'I love you, Raff,' she told him softly. 'I'm proud to be carrying your child.'

'No more proud than I am,' his lips moved against her moistly. 'God, we've said some vicious things to each other in an effort to hide our love.' His arms tightened. 'I felt as if you'd twisted a knife inside me the night I had to rush you to hospital and you told me you would never have had *my* child if you'd realised you could ever have had one!'

'Because Court had just told me enough at Kate's dinner party to convince me you had asked Stuart Hillier to spy on me! And because you'd already told me *you* wished I weren't pregnant either!'

'Because of you,' groaned Raff, trembling slightly. 'I thought you were going to die and be taken from me now.' He picked up her left hand, kissing the eternity ring that sat so comfortably next to her wedding ring. 'I could see you were puzzled when I gave you this,' he told her huskily. 'But it means exactly what it's supposed to; I'll love you for eternity. And I can take anything but losing you!'

'You'll never lose me,' Bryna promised fervently. 'Although I can't guarantee that we will ever have another child,' she added uncertainly. 'This one is still a miracle to me.'

'I love the baby because we made it together,' he looked down at her with dark eyes. 'But it isn't something I planned either.'

She frowned. 'Are you sure you want another child in the house?'

'Sure?' he dismissed lightly. 'I'm looking forward to it. When Josey and I had Kate and Paul I was very young, believed it was a woman's place to take care of the babies while I went out and earned the money. I intend being involved in every aspect of this baby!'

'Oh, Raff, I didn't realise, not even once, that you loved me,' she groaned. 'You said you were only marrying me for the baby——'

'Because using the baby was the only way to make sure *you* would marry me,' he corrected. 'At first you seemed happy enough with the affair you asked for, and then you started to drift away from me. I took on Stuart Hillier in the first place in an effort to delegate my work and spend more time with you, showing you how much I needed you——'

'You only seemed to need me in bed, cruelly cut me out of any interest in your work or Kate and Paul——'

'Because I believed the commitment to my work and my grown-up family were part of the reason you only wanted an affair with me,' he shook his head. 'Kate and Paul seemed like a reminder of how much older and more experienced I was than you, and so I did my best to keep the three of you apart. I didn't always succeed, but after that first night when you seemed so lost in their company I certainly tried.'

'It was only that it seemed a little—strange, meeting your children. I *wanted* to share them as the months passed,' Bryna sighed her impatience with the misunderstandings that had kept them apart for so long. 'Your refusal to do so seemed a way of telling me you wanted me in bed but in no other part of your life. And then even that began to pall, be less intense. When you agreed so readily to my condition that we wouldn't sleep together during our marriage I believed you no longer wanted me.'

Raff gave a self-derisive groan. 'I only agreed because I had no intention of being married to you and yet living apart. But the only way I could get you to marry me at all was by using blackmail, and to have told you then that I intended it to be a normal marriage would have frightened you away. I stayed away from you until after we were married, but I never intended to live like that for the rest of our lives.'

'You told me those nights that you only wanted to touch the baby!'

'And you,' he smiled. 'I never intended to let you

go.' He gave a pained frown. 'Until it seemed you preferred Court to me. You told me you were leaving me after he visited you in hospital, and I thought——'

'Alyson visited me too that night,' she frowned. 'She told me she'd been out with Stuart Hillier and he'd asked a lot of questions about me, and I thought it was because of——'

'Me,' Raff realised grimly. 'I didn't put him up to it, so it must have been Court.'

'Raff, we have to talk about Court,' Bryna told him quietly. 'But first of all we have to understand that we love each other, that Court can never use our uncertainty of each other to hurt us again. I don't know why he wanted to hurt us, but I do think a little boy capable of attacking another little boy with a cricket bat and breaking his nose can't have just lost that temper because he's now an adult. He may be able to control it better, but not to lose it completely.

'Court told you about that episode when we were at school together?' Raff frowned.

'The first day we met,' she nodded. 'Oh, it's obvious he's a controlled man now, but that vindictiveness must still be below that surface pleasantness. We have to be sure of our love for each other before we challenge him on it, have no doubts, otherwise he'll still be able to find a way to drive us apart.'

'Darling Bryna, I swear to you I will never doubt you or your love again,' he looked down at her with dark eyes. 'It was only because I loved you so much and it didn't seem to be returned that I've been acting like a madman since we got married, throwing out accusations while still secretly hoping we could start again and make our marriage work. That day I saw you lunching with Court and made that threat to you about forcing our marriage to be a real one I was so disgusted with myself by the time I got back to my office that I felt too sickened to come home at all that night. I dreaded coming home to find that you'd left me, acted like an idiot again when I found that you hadn't.'

She could see that Court had been able to witness their weakness about each other all the time, and that he had used that to hurt them. But she didn't doubt Raff's love now; she knew that all his cruelty since they were married had been because his heart was breaking and he just didn't know what to do to hold on to her. He would never have *reason* to doubt her love for him again.

'Call Court and ask him to come over,' she said huskily.

'Now?' Raff's eyes widened.

'It isn't that late, and this can't wait any longer,' she insisted dully. 'We have to know *why*, Raff.'

He had barely had time to get out of bed and pull on his trousers before a knock sounded on the bedroom door.

Kate stood outside, her amused gaze going from her father's tousled appearance to Bryna's blushing cheeks. 'And I thought you were joking downstairs,' she mocked. 'I came to say goodnight, but that seems a little——'

'Kate!' her father warned.

'See you both in the morning. Or afternoon,' she

added cheekily. 'I guess the honeymoon isn't over!'

Raff gave a rueful smile as he closed the door behind her. 'She isn't going to let us forget this in a hurry!'

Bryna laughed softly, her eyes glowing with pleasure as she watched the ripple of muscles across his shoulders as he dressed. 'She'll have to get used to it.'

His eyes softened caressingly. 'God, I hope so!'

'You can be sure of it,' she promised huskily.

'I never told you, but I felt so damned grateful that I was the first man to make love to you,' long fingers caressed her cheek. 'I was going to tell you, but——'

'I started talking about rules and no commitment,' she realised ruefully. 'I thought it was what you wanted!'

'You were still a virgin because you were afraid, weren't you?' he said huskily. 'Afraid you were incomplete in some way?'

'Yes,' she nodded with remembered sadness. 'I'd like to say I saved myself for you, but the truth is——'

'The truth is that was exactly what you did,' he finished firmly. 'I'm sure I wasn't the first man to want to make love to you, and yet it was *me* you trusted to make you feel you were a complete woman.'

'I loved you,' she said simply. 'I needed you.'

'We'll always need each other, Bryna. I promise you nothing else will drive us apart!' he vowed fiercely.

When Raff telephoned Court the other man had

just got in, although he was obviously alone, but he agreed to come over straight away.

Bryna and Raff were seated together on the sofa when the doorbell rang a short time later. Raff went to answer the door himself, having dismissed the staff for the night, and Kate obviously having gone to bed and to sleep too.

Court was still wearing the evening suit he had obviously worn to go out in. He gave Bryna a friendly nod, refusing Raff's invitation for him to sit down. He turned to the other man. 'So what was so important it couldn't wait until morning?'

'Did you have a pleasant evening?' Raff enquired cordially, handing him a glass of brandy.

Court gave a puzzled frown. 'Very nice, thank you,' he answered distractedly. 'What——'

'See anyone we know while you were out, my assistant, for instance?' Raff added, silky-soft.

Court's eyes widened. 'Hillier?' he queried. 'Why should I have seen him?'

'Well, you look as if you've probably eaten out this evening, and with the coincidental meetings that have gone on at restaurants lately I wondered if the two of you might have met.' Raff quirked dark brows, his eyes icy.

Court glanced at Bryna's stony expression, and then back to Raff's accusing one, giving a choked cry as he dropped down into an armchair. 'I never meant it to go this far,' he groaned, his face buried in his hands.

Bryna looked at Raff in stunned disbelief; the last thing either of them had expected had been an instant confession from Court. In fact, she was sure that secretly they had both hoped they had made some terrible mistake. But that was impossible now, and some of the coldness drained out of Bryna as she saw how broken Court was.

'Why, Court?' Raff prompted gruffly, and Bryna wanted to go to him and comfort him because of the pain she knew he was suffering. But she sat completely still, having the feeling this was something the two men had to settle between them. The time to comfort Raff would be after Court had gone.

'Because I loved her and she wouldn't leave you!' Tears fell unashamedly down Court's cheeks. 'I was okay to go to bed with, even to love a little, but she wouldn't leave *you*!'

Bryna gasped. 'I never went to bed with you——'

'Not you,' Court shook his head. 'Josey!' he explained bitterly. 'We were lovers for five years before she died, and although I pleaded with her, *begged* her, to leave Raff, she never would.'

Bryna could plainly see what a shock this revelation was to Raff. Of course he had always known there was someone else in Josey's life, but not Court!

'I couldn't give her the children she wanted if she left you,' Court continued harshly. 'And she knew you would never let her take Kate and Paul away from you. I waited ten years for you to love someone the way I loved Josey,' his eyes glittered as he glared at Raff. 'And when Bryna did come along you were too damned arrogant to tell her how you felt.'

Raff drew in a ragged breath. 'And you used that to hurt me.'

'It was what I wanted—I wanted you to know

how I felt, loving Josey but unable to have her,'
Court rasped. 'Unfortunately Bryna got hurt too,
and I didn't plan on that happening, I really do like
her. When she almost lost the baby I knew I had to
stop. I could never hurt an unborn child, never hurt
any child!'

'And Hillier?' Raff frowned. 'Where does he
come into all this?'

Court's mouth twisted. 'I should get rid of him,
Raff—he can be bought!'

'I loved you like a brother, Court,' Raff groaned
his pain.

'I loved you the same way,' the other man
nodded. 'But as soon as I saw Josey I fell in love
with her. Remember the first time we saw her,
Raff?' he smiled. 'It was at a party given by my
parents. I thought she was the most beautiful
woman I'd ever seen. But she only saw you,' he
added flatly.

'I had no idea you felt that way about her . . .!'
Raff shook his head.

'Why should you?' Court gave a self-derisive
smile. 'You couldn't help the fact that women
always preferred you. And with the others it never
mattered,' he added grimly. 'I thought your relationship with her would run its usual course and
then I could help her pick up the pieces, only she
became pregnant before that happened, and I had
to resign myself to just being a friend to you all. But
the marriage never worked, did it, Raff, and after a
couple of years you were both looking around for
other people. I hung around until Josey eventually

turned to me. But I couldn't give her the children she so desperately wanted!'

'Maybe if the two of you had come to me, talked to me about taking Kate and Paul——'

'What?' challenged Court. 'You would have let us have them?' he scorned.

Raff drew in a ragged breath. 'Maybe,' he breathed huskily.

'You would never have agreed——'

'I might have done,' Raff protested. 'It would have been hard for me, but I knew how much Josey loved them, and that you loved them too.'

Court looked at him angrily. 'You can't bring yourself to hate me even now, can you?' he choked.

'I could try, if you really want me to,' Raff told him raggedly.

'I nearly drove you and Bryna apart, nearly killed your baby!'

Raff nodded. 'And if you'd succeeded in doing either of those things maybe I could hate you. But I've loved you as a brother too long to hate you for what might have been.'

Bryna loved Raff more in that moment than ever before, as she went to his side to clutch his hand tightly. They had both suffered because of Court, but Raff had suffered much more than she, would probably always suffer for the loss of a man he had felt so close to.

Court stood up in controlled movements. 'Since I went to see Bryna in hospital I've spent the time moving my head office to New York,' he told them tautly. 'I intended telling you what I'd done before I left, but as soon as my move has been completed I'll be going to the States myself. Unless you have other plans for me?' He looked enquiringly at Raff.

Raff's arm moved about Bryna's waist as he drew her close to his side. 'You've done nothing illegal. And even if you had I doubt I would want to do anything about it.'

Court sighed. 'Then I'll say goodbye; I doubt we'll meet again.' He looked regretfully at Bryna. 'I really am sorry you almost lost the baby.'

'I know you are,' she nodded.

As soon as the front door had closed behind him Bryna felt Raff sag weakly against her, turning towards him as he sobbed in her arms.

'If you don't stop picking him up every time he so much as squeaks he's going to be thoroughly spoilt!' Bryna scolded as she walked into the nursery.

Raff turned guiltily, the tiny baby held securely in his arms. 'I thought he was choking.'

Bryna firmly took the baby away from him and put him back in his crib, ignoring the indignant wails that followed them as she pulled Raff from the room. 'Correction,' she said sternly. 'He's already spoilt!'

James Rafferty Gallagher—the reversal of the two first names Bryna had originally chosen had come about because Raff had decided they couldn't have two Raffertys in the house—was almost seven weeks old, but he had known from the day Bryna brought him home five weeks ago that *he* was going to be master in this house. With his thickly curling dark hair and purple eyes he charmed on sight!

'He was crying——'

'He's been changed, fed, cuddled, and now he needs to sleep. He just doesn't think he does,' she added firmly as Raff went to protest. 'Honestly, I sometimes wish that new assistant of yours wasn't so good at his job that you don't feel the need to put in more than the odd day or so at your office!'

But they both knew she wished nothing of the sort. She and Raff were together almost continuously, and they loved it. Raff's new assistant really was very good, and after taking over again during the latter part of Bryna's pregnancy, Alyson was running the agency very smoothly too.

'Between you, Kate and Paul, I hardly ever get to hold James myself,' Bryna complained, knowing she was really pleased by the acceptance of *all* the family of the baby that could have been an intrusion. But Kate and Paul were always here to see James, and on the odd occasion when Bryna and Raff went out for the evening they usually argued over which one of them was going to come over and babysit. Kate had moved during the summer to share a flat with another girl from college, and fortunately it seemed to be working out this time.

Both Kate and Paul had been upset by their 'uncle's' move to America, and Bryna knew that Raff often thought of Court too. But from pieces of information Raff received Court seemed to be doing well in the States, and now that their own happiness was so overflowing they wished him well. Maybe one day he would even find a woman he could love as much as he had Josey.

'Stop trying to find reasons to pick an argument with me and tell me what the doctor said this morning,' Raff encouraged throatily.

After the way he had been storming frustratedly about the house the last couple of months she had been deeply disappointed at his lack of interest earlier in her visit to the doctor for her post-natal check-up. Looking at him now, his eagerness barely contained, she realised he had been trying to be tactful, not wanting to pressure her.

She gave him a seductive smile. 'As soon as your son is asleep I'll tell you,' she ran caressing fingers down his cheek, his face softened with love for her.

He listened in the direction of the nursery, giving her a triumphant look as silence greeted them. 'Who said he was spoilt?' he drawled pointedly.

She laughed softly, moving into his arms. 'Who insisted he be put back in his crib?'

'You planned this,' Raff groaned. 'Oh God, Bryna, I've missed your closeness, missed being a part of you!'

'You'll always be a part of me,' she looked at him lovingly. 'I love you.'

'I love you too!'

They told each other of their feelings all the time now, not just after the loving but before and during too. It would always be that way for them now.

Lucy Gordon cut her writing teeth on magazine journalism, interviewing many of the world's most interesting men, including Warren Beatty, Richard Chamberlain, Roger Moore, Sir Alec Guinness and Sir John Gielgud. She also camped out with lions in Africa, and had many other unusual experiences which have often provided the background for her books.

She is married to a Venetian, whom she met while on holiday in Venice. They got engaged within two days, and have now been married for twenty-five years. They live in the Midlands, with their three dogs.

Two of her books, SONG OF THE LORELEI and HIS BROTHER'S CHILD, won the Romance Writers of America RITA award in the Best Traditional Romance category.

Look out for WIFE BY ARRANGMENT
by Lucy Gordon
in Mills & Boon Tender Romance™, May 2001

HIS BROTHER'S CHILD
by
LUCY GORDON

CHAPTER ONE

'Is IT much further to Rome?' Donna asked eagerly.

'Another ten miles.' Toni glanced sideways to give her a glowing smile. 'You're beautiful, *carissima*. My family will fall in love with you at first sight—just like I did.'

'Darling, please keep your eyes on the road,' she begged nervously.

He laughed and obeyed. 'All right, madam schoolmistress,' he mocked.

'Don't say that. I don't really sound like a schoolmistress, do I?'

'Of course you do. My delightful, adorable schoolmistress, always telling me off. Toni, drive more slowly. Toni, don't be so extravagant. Toni, don't—'

'Oh, *no*!' she cried, half laughing, half dismayed. 'Now you make me sound like a dragon.'

'But I like it. You're very good for me. My brother Rinaldo will be grateful to you for keeping me in order. It's something he's never managed yet.'

He spoke with his usual cheery good nature, but to Donna it was a reminder that, at twenty-seven, she was three years Toni's senior. That was something she tried not to dwell on, but it was hard when Toni still had so much of the boy in him. She regarded his profile with affection. He had vivid Latin good looks, typical of the south of Italy, where he'd been born. She remembered how her friends had envied her when he'd started to pursue her!

She'd met Toni Mantini in the hospital where she was

a nurse, and where he'd been brought after his car had lost an argument with a lamppost. He'd described the accident to her with rueful humour. That was typical of Toni, she'd discovered. To him life was laughter and pleasure. His injuries were slight, the insurance would pay for the car. Why worry?

Just what there was in her serious nature that had attracted this careless Italian boy she'd never been able to work out. But when he was discharged from hospital he'd returned persistently until she'd agreed to go out with him. After that things had moved at a speed that left her breathless.

He told her that he loved her, often and passionately. The knowledge filled her with wonder. Toni was vibrantly handsome. Her own looks, she thought disparagingly, were those of a little brown mouse.

'But no,' he'd said when she'd voiced this thought. 'You look like a Madonna, with your calm oval face, your dark hair and your big eyes. Near my family's home in Rome there's a little church with a picture of the Madonna and child. I'll take you there one day, and you'll see yourself. Never change, *carissima*. You are beautiful just as you are.'

It had never occurred to her that she might be beautiful, and she loved Toni for showing her to herself in that new light. She loved him for so many things—his eagerness for life, his boyish enthusiasm that could make him reckless, his careless laughter. But most of all she loved him because he loved her.

It was early afternoon now, and the Italian sun was high.

'Does the heat bother you?' Toni asked as she mopped her brow.

'It's a bit overwhelming, after England,' she admitted.
'I shall be glad to get into the cool.'

'Poor darling. You can rest this afternoon. Tomorrow
we'll go out shopping and I'll buy you some new clothes,
and jewels. I'd like to see you in rubies.'

She laughed. 'What a dreamer you are, darling. You
know you can't afford rubies, even if I wanted them.'

'Who says I can't?'

'You're behind with the repayments on this car.'

His face was a picture of innocence. 'Behind? Me?
Whatever gave you that idea?'

She chuckled. 'I answered the phone to the finance
company, remember?'

'Oh, well!' He abandoned the pretence with a shrug.
'Just a little bit behind. Not angry with me, are you,
cara?'

'How can I be angry with you?' she asked tenderly.

How could she be anything but passionately grateful to
this young man who'd brought warmth and colour into
her lonely life? He wanted her. That was the glorious,
unbelievable fact that flooded the world with light and
gave her a happiness she'd never even dreamed of before.

It was so long since she'd been wanted by anyone.
When she was seven years old her father had left home
for another woman. After the divorce he'd kept in touch
with her sporadically, sometimes even taken her out. But
he'd never taken her home to meet his new wife and
child, and Donna had come to understand, without it actually being said, that there was no place for her in that
family.

Then her mother had died. Donna was ten. Now,
surely, her father would claim her? And he'd promised
to do so 'when things are a little easier'. But it had

seemed the time was never right, and at last she'd lost hope completely.

She'd spent the rest of her childhood in care. There had been two foster homes, one of which had broken up in divorce. The other family had simply taken on too many children. Donna was fourteen by then, old enough to help out. She hadn't minded. She'd liked caring for the little ones, and it was good to be needed. But her foster mother had made it clear that she was there to be useful, and it wasn't the same as being wanted for herself.

When she'd left care at sixteen she'd made determined efforts to stay in touch, sending cards at Christmas and on birthdays, and thinking of them as 'my family'. But the cards were never answered. One day, paying a surprise visit, she'd found strangers living there. The family had moved away without telling her.

With such a background it was hardly surprising that she'd found Toni irresistible. Everything about him was enchanting in her eyes, even his nationality. Italy had always been the country of Donna's dreams. She'd planned to take a holiday there, and had even learned the language in readiness. But on a nurse's pay her savings mounted very slowly, so the Italian holiday had been put off, year after year, while she continued to weave her bright dreams. She pictured Italy as a colourful, light-hearted place, full of warm families that clung together. She was sorry Toni's family wasn't larger, only a grandfather and an older brother. But the affectionate way he spoke of them made her eager to meet them.

And now, soon, she would do so. And soon she would no longer be lonely Donna Easton, but Signora Mantini, bearing a Mantini child.

The thought made Donna lay a hand reverently across her stomach. It was much too soon for anything to show, but already the baby was precious to her. It would be hers and Toni's, linking them for ever as part of a true family.

When she'd told him she was pregnant she'd half expected the worst. Surely this careless charmer didn't want to be tied down to a family at twenty-four? But Toni had been overwhelmed with joy, repeating, 'You're going to be a mother…' many times in an awed voice. He'd become even more loving and tender to her, and her love for him had grown.

He'd insisted that they marry 'as soon as you have met my family'. She never knew what was said in his phone call to his brother Rinaldo, but he'd announced that they must go to Italy immediately.

'I've said only that I'm bringing my bride,' he told her. 'We'll tell them about the baby when we get there.'

'I'll get leave of absence from the hospital,' she said.

'No, no! You don't go back there. Give them notice.'

'Toni, I don't think that's wise.'

'My wife does not work!' he announced with a lordly finality that made her lips twitch. He noticed her trying to suppress her laughter, and grinned. 'OK, OK! I get a proper job. Perhaps I go into the business with Rinaldo and we live over there.'

'In Italy?' she said excitedly. 'That would be wonderful.'

'Good. It's settled!'

Toni was like that. Donna could have sworn that five minutes ago he'd had no notion of working in Italy. But suddenly it was settled.

A few days later they'd loaded their things into the car and started the long journey across the Channel, through France, then Switzerland, and into Italy. They'd stopped overnight several times, because Toni didn't want to tire her, and had spent last night in Perugia. This morning they had started early for the final stretch of road that would lead to Rome.

'Tell me some more about your family,' she begged now.

Toni shrugged. 'Nothing much to tell. Rinaldo is all right, but he's a bit of a bore. Thinks about nothing but business, as though making money was the only thing in the world that counted.'

'Well, if you're in business you need to make a reasonable profit,' Donna said. 'Didn't you say he sends you an allowance?'

'Oh, if you're going to talk common sense I give up. All right, the business pays my allowance, but that's no reason for brooding on it night and day, the way Rinaldo does.'

'What exactly is the business? You've always been very vague about it.'

'Engineering. Machine tools. One of the factories makes medical equipment.'

'Factories? Plural?' Donna frowned. She'd had a vague impression of the Mantini family as modestly prosperous. It had never occurred to her that they were richer than that.

'Six factories,' Toni said. 'No, it's five now. Rinaldo sold one because it wasn't meeting its performance targets. He believes in cutting his losses.'

Donna wasn't sure why the suggestion of wealth should disturb her, but it did. For the first time she had doubts about her ability to fit in. Then she thrust them aside. Even the owner of five factories might not live luxuriously. He probably ploughed the profits back into the business and lived modestly. She began to feel more comfortable.

'Didn't you ever want to go into the business yourself?' she asked.

'Heaven forbid! All that dreary grind! Mind you, Rinaldo was always on at me to learn about machines. He'll be glad of you. He wants to see me married. He says it will 'steady' me. Also, he wants an heir to take the business over.'

'Why doesn't he have his own heir?'

'Because it would mean getting married, and Rinaldo's relationships with women are all very short-lived. He prefers it that way. He says no woman can be trusted.'

'But he wants you to do what he won't do himself?'

Toni chuckled good naturedly. 'The way he puts it, I'm bound to make a fool of myself one way or another, so it may as well be the married way. Then at least I'll be doing something useful.'

'He sounds charming—I don't think.'

'Well, he glowers a bit, and he's got a very nasty temper,' Toni admitted. 'It doesn't do to get on his wrong side. But don't worry. I told you, he'll like you.'

To Donna's relief they were coming to the end of the *autostrada*, the long motorway whose uninterrupted vista had tempted Toni to hair-raising feats of speed. There followed a series of turns too complex for her to follow, and then they were driving along a wide, grassy avenue lined with cypress trees.

'This is the Appian Way,' Toni told her. 'A lot of Italian film stars have villas along here.'

'How thrilling! Is it much further to where we're going?'

'No, we're about five villas along.'

'You mean—your family lives on the Appian Way?'

'Of course,' Toni said in a matter-of-fact voice. 'Here we are.'

He swung the car through a wide gate and Donna found herself in grounds that seemed to go on for ever. The road ahead curved in and out of trees and shrubs. Gradually a building came into view. At first sight it seemed a simple house, with yellow walls and a red tiled roof. But as they drew nearer Donna saw how large it was, and how it branched off into wings.

Trees surrounded it and baskets of flowers, filled with geraniums, hung from the balconies. Birds called, and from somewhere Donna could hear the soft plashing of water.

It was all incredibly beautiful, but Donna's pleasure was marred by a growing sense of unease. Only a family of great wealth could own a dwelling such as this, and she felt a shrinking inside her. What was she doing in this luxurious place?

Toni brought the car to a halt outside the big front door. There was no sign of life. The house might have been deserted.

'Let's go in and see who's about,' he said, offering his hand to help her out.

Donna's discomfort increased when they entered the house and she saw the marble floor and sweeping marble staircase. The hallway was like a large room in itself. Doors led off to unseen regions. Between the doors were niches housing small statues surrounded by plants. In the midday heat the hall had an air of spacious coolness.

'I'll go and find someone,' Toni said. 'Wait for me here.'

He vanished down a passage, calling, 'Is anybody at home?' leaving Donna to study her surroundings. She hoped Toni would return quickly, before strangers found her here.

Then she noticed something. To her left a narrow cor-

ridor led to an open door, through which she could see
daylight. She knew she ought to remain here until Toni
came for her, but something seemed to draw her, as
though by hypnotism, along the corridor to the light.

She found herself in a courtyard, surrounded by cloisters. Here the gleaming marble floor ended, and there
were rough flagstones underfoot. The cloisters were about
four feet wide, with the wall of the house on one side and
arches supported by decorated pillars on the other. In the
courtyard she could see a pool, with a fountain in the
centre. Flower baskets hung from the windows above, and
white doves cooed and fluttered around a dovecote.

The cloisters took up three sides. The fourth side was
a wall, against which a staircase ran to the upper floor.
Flowers trailed through the gaps between the supports of
the stone balustrade and hung down.

Donna regarded the scene ecstatically. The place had a
rustic, weather-beaten charm that spoke of centuries. Li-
chen grew over the stone. The walls were red, brown,
faded yellow. This was the Italy of her dreams.

On one wall a few words had been chiselled into the
stone. They said simply, *'Il giardino di Loretta'*.

'Loretta's garden,' Donna murmured to herself. Who-
ever Loretta had been she'd loved this place with her
whole heart. Her love still breathed through every plant,
every vista of beauty.

Wherever Donna looked there were flowers—jasmine,
clematis, bougainvillea, oleander—filling the air with
their heady perfume. Entranced, she began to wander,
feeling as if she was moving through a beautiful dream.

The fountain had the elegance of simplicity. There
were no ornaments, just a pool with one tall spray rising
directly from the water. Donna watched it, revelling in

the cool drops that just touched her. At last she turned aside to explore more of the garden.

Here and there were small statues in niches. One in particular caught her attention. It was about three feet high, depicting two boys, one about ten, the other little more than a baby. The older boy was encircling the child with his arm, watching over him with a protective expression. The little one looked out at the world, his arms thrown wide, the hands stretching eagerly to grasp life. Only the older child knew that life could be dangerous as well as beautiful, and his arm stayed firmly in place, warding off evil.

Donna found a shaded stone bench and sat down, glorying in the peace and beauty of her surroundings.

'Yes,' she murmured happily to herself. 'Oh, yes. This is so right, so perfect.'

She closed her eyes and sat a while, listening to the water and the sound of birds. When she opened them again she became aware that she was no longer alone. A man was watching her from the other side of the fountain. At first she had only a hazy impression of a shadow standing behind the huge spray, the details obscured by the cascading water, and the fact that the sun was behind him. He seemed to loom up, a menacing silhouette, perceived like a dream through the glittering droplets. She rubbed her eyes, but he was still there.

He came round the fountain and stood regarding her. There was a puzzled look in his eyes. At last he spoke in a cynical, drawling voice.

'Well?' he said in English. 'Is it as splendid as you'd hoped?'

Now she could see him properly. He was very tall and broad-shouldered. His face was an older version of Toni's, and she knew that this must be his brother, Rinaldo. The dark eyes were the same, so was the high fore-head—indeed all the features looked as if they'd come from the same mould, but then something had changed and hardened them. Toni laughed a lot. This man looked as if he never laughed. Toni's wide mouth was made for kissing. The same shape on his brother hinted at a sensuality that was almost cruel.

But one thing was clear to her with almost shocking clarity. Toni was a boy. This was a man.

His expression went with his voice—cool, appraising. 'I'm Rinaldo Mantini,' he said in the same tone. 'Toni's brother.'

'Yes—I guessed,' she said shyly. 'You're so like him.'

A wry grin twisted his mouth. 'Only in appearance, *signorina*. In nature we're not at all alike. Toni is an enthusiast who jumps into life without considering the consequences. As a result he often finds he's been taken in. I'm the opposite. Nobody and nothing fools me.'

She wasn't sure what answer he expected her to make to that. The only thing that was certain was that he wasn't in a welcoming mood. Donna held out her hand.

'I'm Donna Easton,' she said. 'I expect Toni has told you about me—'

He touched her hand for the briefest possible moment, and his features didn't soften. 'Toni has told me all about you,' he confirmed. 'In fact, he's told me far more than he realises.'

She frowned. 'I don't know what you mean by that.'

'Don't you? Well, never mind for the moment. You're here as my brother's bride, and naturally I extend you the welcome of our house.'

But although he spoke of welcome there was no warmth in his tone. Only cold irony.

Donna summoned up her courage and found an irony

to match his own. 'Your hospitality overwhelms me,' she said. 'I'd heard that Italians were famous for their kindness to guests, and now I see that it's true.'

For a moment she saw astonishment in his eyes, followed by something that might have been appreciation. Then it was gone. 'Not entirely true,' he said, 'since my brother seems to have left you alone.'

'I have no complaints about your brother's behaviour towards me,' she said firmly, emphasising the word 'brother' very slightly. 'He always treats me well.'

'I'm sure he does. Toni likes to give. He doesn't always give wisely, or to the right person. But his heart is good.' Rinaldo delivered the words with a wry twist of the mouth and a wealth of meaning that left Donna feeling uncomfortable. Her temper began to simmer.

'Toni's told me a great deal about you, as well,' she said. 'He said you were longing for him to marry, and he seemed to think you'd be delighted about us.'

'Toni has always believed what he wants to believe. Whenever he brings his fiancées here, he's always convinced that I'll be pleased.'

Donna stared. 'Fiancées? Plural?'

'You're the fourth—or is it the fifth? I've lost count. The procedure is always the same. He turns up out of the blue with some totally unsuitable female in tow and announces that she's the one. The lady and I have a short conversation, after which she departs a good deal richer than she arrived. My dear girl, you're one of a crowd.'

Donna's temper nearly boiled over at the blatant way he announced his manipulations. 'If you keep blighting his engagements it's no wonder he has so many,' she snapped. 'And if you're suggesting that I'm here to be bought off you can forget it. I love Toni, and he loves me. And we're getting married.'

'Good, good. Don't concede too easily. Put the price up. But there's a limit beyond which I won't go, so don't waste your time trying to push me beyond it.'

'You're mad,' she cried. 'You've got this obsessed way of looking at things, and you can't see the truth.'

'But I have seen the truth,' he replied coolly. 'I saw it on your face a few minutes ago. You surveyed your surroundings like a dealer checking a good investment, and you were delighted with what you discovered.'

'I was delighted with its beauty,' she said, outraged. 'That was all. This garden is one of the loveliest places I've seen. Or it was. Not now. Not with you in it. Now it's like Eden after the serpent invaded.'

He flinched, and she knew she'd said something that had hit home. 'I have to admit that your approach is original,' he said. 'In fact you're not at all like Toni's usual choice in women. The others have all been brazen young pieces, with their charms set out on the stall, ready to bargain. You're more subtle.'

His eyes raked her up and down in a way that made her conscious of her own deficiencies again. 'There's less to please the eye.' His voice was smooth as he uttered this casual cruelty, then added another to it. 'You're also a lot older than his usual girls. Much too old for Toni.'

'I'm three years older than he is, and I've never pretended otherwise,' she said deliberately. 'Maybe he's not the child you seem to think.'

He gave a harsh laugh. 'You mean he's matured? I doubt that.'

'What you think doesn't matter. If you imagine you can talk Toni out of marrying me, you're welcome to try.'

'Look, I've played this scene too often to be interested in the details. Just tell me how much it will take this time. I'll go as high as ten thousand English pounds. I may even go up to twelve thousand if you're reasonable, but the longer you try my patience, the less you'll get.'

His arrogance almost took her breath away. She recovered enough to say, 'You're wasting your time. I don't touch tainted money.'

'Fine talk, but my money is made honestly.'

'But you use it for a tainted purpose,' she flashed. 'You try to buy and sell love—'

'On the contrary. Love has nothing to do with this.'

'How would you know? You couldn't recognise love unless it came with an itemised invoice. I'm marrying Toni because I love him, and also because—' She stopped. This wasn't the moment to speak of the baby. She and Toni must do that together.

'Yes?' he enquired, his eyebrows raised sarcastically.

'I'm marrying him for love,' she repeated. 'His love and mine. And nothing you can do can touch that. You can threaten all you like. The bottom line is that you're helpless.'

In the silence a very ugly look crossed his face. 'You are very brave, *signorina*,' he said at last. 'And also very stupid. I don't allow people to cross me and escape the consequences. It's—bad for business.'

'This isn't business.'

'It's business all right. But I'm better at it than you. A moment ago you'd won a substantial sum. Now you've lost everything, as you'll soon discover.'

'No, *you* will discover that people's feelings can't be bought off so easily.'

'Don't be a little fool,' he said roughly. 'I could turn my brother against you in a moment.'

'If you really thought that you wouldn't have offered me ten thousand pounds.'

His mouth tightened. 'I was trying to conduct our nego-
tiations reasonably—'

'Oh, no, you were trying to bully me. But I can't be
bullied, so don't waste your time. Try turning Toni
against me. See how far you get.'

'You're very confident,' he said grimly. 'Arrogant
even. You'll discover that in this house only one person
is allowed to be arrogant.'

But the knowledge of the child she carried gave Donna
courage. Toni wanted their baby. He would never turn
against his child's mother. So she didn't answer Rinaldo
in words. She let her smile say it for her, and she had the
satisfaction of seeing the certainty drain away from his
face. Their glances met—on one side the timeless certainty of motherhood, linked to the earth and all things
eternal, on the other side a dawning unease, mixed with
anger and tinged with reluctant respect.

'You have made a very dangerous mistake, *signorina*,'
he said softly.

'And you have made a very foolish one,' she replied.

He drew in his breath sharply. But before he could
speak they heard a cry from the shadows of the cloisters.
The next moment, a very tall, elderly man appeared. He
too had the Mantini face, but in him it was thinner, and
topped off by a thatch of snow-white hair. Delight radiated from him as he hobbled towards them with the aid
of a stick.

'So this is my new granddaughter,' he said. 'Welcome,
my dear. Welcome, welcome to our home!'

CHAPTER TWO

A MULTITUDE of emotions warred on Rinaldo's face at this sudden interruption: annoyance at having his rejection of Donna undercut by his grandfather's welcome, the need to disguise his anger in front of the old man, confusion at not receiving support from one he respected. Donna read all these in his expression. In the end propriety won, but it took a huge effort.

'Nonno,' he said courteously, 'this is Signorina Donna Easton, from England. Signorina Easton, this is my grandfather, Piero Mantini.'

'Welcome to the Villa Mantini, my dear child.' The old man bubbled over. Instead of taking Donna's outstretched hand he put his arms about her in an exuberant hug. She hugged him back, overjoyed to receive a welcome at last.

'*Grazie, signore,*' she murmured.

'Why, she speaks our language already,' he beamed.

'Two words,' Rinaldo observed wryly.

'Oh, don't be so grumpy,' his grandfather reproved him. '*Signorina, e felice di essere finalmente qui con noi?*'

Donna just glimpsed the curl of Rinaldo's lip, as though he were saying that now her pretensions would be exposed. But she'd understood Piero's words, asking if she was happy to be there with them at last, and it gave her the greatest satisfaction to reply, '*Molto felice, signore. Desideravo tanto conoscere la familia di Toni.*'

Rinaldo's mouth tightened at her assertion that she'd

looked forward to meeting Toni's family. She met his eyes in silent defiance.

It was Toni, standing just behind his grandfather, who broke the tension. 'Donna isn't used to this heat. I'd like to get her inside.'

'Of course, of course,' Piero agreed. 'Maria will show you to your room.' An elderly woman, dressed entirely in black, appeared from the shadows. 'Maria,' Piero said, 'this is Donna who is going to be one of the family soon. Take her upstairs and make her comfortable.'

'I will have your bags sent up,' Rinaldo said formally. 'I hope you will find everything to your liking.'

The room Maria showed her to was enormous, with two tall windows overlooking the front of the house. At this time of day the shutters were drawn, making everything dark. Maria threw them open, giving Donna a view of the large bed, with the headboard made of beautiful polished walnut.

While Maria was displaying the cupboards and the bathroom, there was a knock at the door and a young man entered carrying Donna's bags. He was followed by a maid with a tray.

'Some food and wine for you,' Maria said. 'Rinaldo thought you would wish to have a good, long siesta after your tiring journey.'

She spoke with an air of finality that left no doubt that this was a royal command. Obviously Rinaldo wanted her out of the way while he talked to Toni. But Donna wasn't disposed to argue. She felt weary and hot, and slightly queasy. Also, her mind was disturbed by the discovery of how much Toni had concealed from her. She needed time and peace to think.

She showered and consumed the refreshments, then lay down on the bed for a nap. She woke to the feel of

Toni's lips on hers, and put her arms round him, holding onto him as the one point of safety in an alien world.

'My room is right up the other end of the house,' he said with a grin. 'Fancy that, when we're already proud parents-to-be!'

'Have you told anyone?'

'Not yet. I'm waiting for the right moment.'

'Toni, why didn't you tell me about all your other fiancées?'

'*All* my other fiancées?' he teased. 'You make me sound like Bluebeard.'

'Four or five, according to your brother.'

'Oh, they didn't count. Only you count.' His tone showed that he was bored with the subject.

'But you left me without any idea what I was walking into,' Donna protested.

He shrugged. 'Don't make so much of it. We're going to be married, and that's all that matters.'

'I wish you'd be serious for a moment.'

Toni pulled a sulky face. 'If you're going to be serious I shall think you're as bad as Rinaldo.'

'And that's another thing. You said he'd welcome the prospect of your getting married, but he just thinks I'm after your money, like the others. He won't believe that I didn't even know your family was rich. You should have warned me about that too.'

'Why, would it have made you love me better?' he teased.

'Of course not. On the contrary, it would have put me off.'

'Perhaps in my heart I knew that. Besides, I've never felt rich. Rinaldo makes me a beggarly allowance because he wants to force me to come home. I'm always in debt, you know that.'

'I almost can't blame Rinaldo for what he's thinking about me.'

'I can. We've just had a big row. When he saw he couldn't change my mind he got very angry. Nonno came to my rescue. He says there's to be no more arguing over supper tonight.'

'I'm not looking forward to that. Will there be an atmosphere?'

'Don't worry. Selina will be there. She's an old girlfriend of Rinaldo's. Thirteen years ago he was really crazy about her, and they got engaged. Everyone was against it. He was only twenty and she was eighteen, but Rinaldo was determined to have his own way—as he always is—just as soon as he was of age.'

'So what happened?'

'Selina was film mad. She was always hanging around Cinecitta, the film studio in Rome. Somehow she actually managed to meet a film star and get into his bed. The next thing we knew, she'd vanished. It was a month before Rinaldo's twenty-first birthday, and he was planning the wedding, but Selina went off to New York for a fling with this film star. Their pictures were in all the papers, along with the man's wife sobbing and pleading for him to return. Not that Selina would care about that. She thought he could get her into films.'

'And did he?'

'In a way. She thought she'd be a big international star, but she ended up with small parts in minor Italian films. She can't act, but she just had to look gorgeous and say a few words. Now her career's drying up. Her last part was over a year ago.'

'How did Rinaldo take it?' Donna asked. 'He seems like the kind of man who would smash things.'

'Oh, yes. Nonno said he'd never seen a man so much

in love, or so angry. I was only eleven at the time, but
I knew quite a lot because Rinaldo's rage hung over the
house like a black cloud. For a while he went a little
crazy. He had a fast car, which he drove at top speed.
I'll never know how he didn't have an accident. Then
suddenly he stopped. He's like that. Never quite out of
control. He sees the danger and says to himself, I won't
do this. And he stops.'

Donna gave a little shiver. 'I don't think I like the
sound of him. He sounds superhuman—inhuman—*not*
human, anyway.'

'His control is superhuman,' Toni agreed. 'When he
sets his mind to something it's like watching a laser
beam. He went back to work and got on with his life,
but no one dared mention Selina's name to him. On the
day we heard she'd married a producer everyone crept
around, even Nonno, and Rinaldo's face was as black as
thunder. Two years later she got divorced and it was in
all the papers, but no one said a word to him.'

'But she's here tonight, as a friend?' Donna said.

'Somehow she managed to reappear in Rinaldo's life
and they started seeing each other again. She has an
apartment on the Via Veneto where the glitzy people
live. In all your reading about Italy, have you come
across the Via Veneto?'

'Of course I have. *La dolce vita!*' Donna said dra-
matically.

'That's right. I used to think it was the most thrilling
place on earth: the sweet life, delicious wickedness and
glamorous sin. All with plenty of money. It's exactly the
right place for Selina. Rinaldo visits her, and I suspect
he's paying her rent. The producer went bankrupt and
her alimony dried up. So Rinaldo helps her financially
and she probably repays him in her own way. She's per-

suaded herself that he's stayed single all these years for love of her.'

'Do you think that's true?'

Toni gave a hoot of laughter. 'What, Rinaldo? Never. The only influence she had was to teach him that no woman can be trusted and most of them are for sale. He's had plenty of women. They throw themselves at his head, and he takes what he wants. But none of them have touched his heart. Rinaldo never makes the same mistake twice, and he doesn't forgive.'

'But he seems to have forgiven her.'

'Don't believe it. He's conducting this affair on his own terms.'

'You mean he sleeps with her and enjoys watching her angling to catch him?'

'It wouldn't surprise me. Maybe he'll marry her in the end, but you can't blame him for enjoying his revenge first.'

Donna shivered again.

When she dressed for the evening she worked hard on her appearance. She would never be glamorous, but she could be elegant. She smiled wryly as she recalled her worries over the cream silk cocktail dress she'd brought. It had once been a designer model, and she'd spent the last of her savings to buy it second-hand, worrying in case it would be too dressy. But in company with a film actress, even a minor one, she would be hard-pressed to hold her own.

Still, she was pleased with the result. The dress was cut away at the throat, without being immodestly low. Around her long neck she wore a single strand of pearls which had been Toni's gift. She tried piling her hair onto her head, but although she liked the more sophisticated

air it gave her she decided it would be unwise to un-
derline the fact that she was older than Toni.

He collected her and tucked her arm into his as they
went along the corridor. 'You're beautiful,' he said. 'But
tomorrow I'm going to buy you an olive-green dress.'

'Why olive-green?' she laughed.

'Because the colour will suit you. Don't argue. I'm
never wrong about colours. And I'll give you rubies to
go with it.'

'Dreamer!' she chided.

'No, truly. A ruby necklace and ruby earrings. You'll
look wonderful.'

Before she could answer Rinaldo appeared round the
corner. He nodded politely to them both and went on his
way without a word, but Donna realised with dismay
that he'd heard Toni's words, and that they would confirm his impression of her. Then her head went up. What
did she care what Rinaldo thought?

Downstairs Toni said, 'Let's wait outside, in my
mother's garden.'

'Was Loretta your mother?'

'That's right. The courtyard was bare before she
started work on it. It was her life's work. She was a
sculptress, but she gave it up when she married my *papà*.
He didn't want her doing things outside the home.'

'That's outrageous,' Donna said indignantly. 'He
sounds like a real tyrant.'

'*Sì*, just like Rinaldo,' Toni said with a laugh. 'So
Mamma made this garden, and all the statues in it.'

'I love this one,' Donna said, stopping in front of the
bronze of the two boys.

'I wonder if you can guess who they are?' he asked
significantly.

'You and your brother?'

'That's right. Rinaldo was ten and I was one when she made this.'

'It's beautiful,' Donna breathed. 'There's real love here. I think your mother must have been a wonderful woman.'

'She was,' Toni said instantly. 'I was only five when she died, but I remember her so well. She was very pretty, and she loved me. I always knew I was her favourite. Papà was an angry man, always losing his temper, but Mamma wouldn't let him be angry with me. Once I stole some *panettone* from the kitchen, and she told him that she'd eaten it so he wouldn't beat me.' Toni laughed at the memory, but immediately his face became shadowed. 'Then she died, and the world was cold.' Then his beaming smile broke out. 'But now I have you, *carissima*, and the world will never be cold again.'

Donna regarded him tenderly. Was this the secret of her attraction for him—the fact that she was a little older, that they'd met when he was her patient, and she was caring for him? She remembered how often he'd said she was like a Madonna, and his words when she'd told him about the child. 'You're going to be a mother...' spoken in a tone of reverence and delight.

And if this was the answer, did it really matter? They were fulfilling each other's needs, and that could be the basis of a very happy marriage. Silently she vowed to love and protect him all her life.

She jumped as a small furry body leapt between them and onto the ledge.

'Hello, Sasha,' Toni cried, stroking the cat. 'She belongs to Nonno Piero. See, she likes you.' Sasha was making her approval clear, rubbing herself against Donna and purring like an engine.

'But of course,' came Piero's voice. 'Everybody must like Donna.'

They waited as he descended the courtyard stairs towards them, and kissed Donna. 'You will let me take you in to dinner?' he said. 'Toni won't mind. It's one of the privileges of age, to be able to steal a pretty girl from the young men.'

Donna laughed and slipped her arm through his, grateful to have him on her side.

Rinaldo was in the salon that looked out onto the patio. He was dressed in a dinner jacket, with a snow-white shirt and a black bow tie. His handsome, imperious head towered above everyone else's, and drew Donna's reluctant admiration. Even Toni's good looks were thrown into the shade next to his brother's arrogant grandeur. But this was a man on his home ground, a panther defending his cave, and woe betide intruders!

Beside Rinaldo was a tall woman with long blonde hair and a skin-tight black dress. The neck was daringly low, the waist tight and the hem short, revealing long, lovely legs sheathed in black silk. About her neck hung a diamond necklace, diamond pendants swung from her ears, and more diamonds flashed on her wrists. She swayed towards them, wafting a very expensive perfume as she went.

'Toni, darling,' she cried, enveloping him in her embrace, 'it's so good to have you back here. We mustn't let you run away again, must we, Rinaldo?'

She appealed theatrically to the older brother, but he shrugged prosaically and said, 'Toni never takes any notice of anything I say.'

Toni disengaged himself. 'You must meet Donna, my fiancée,' he said. 'Donna, this is Selina, an old family friend.'

Only by the swiftest flash of her eyes did Selina betray that she disliked the description. The next moment she embraced Donna effusively.

'Why, Toni, darling, she's charming,' she cried, speaking over Donna's head, as if she weren't really there. 'I just adore that quiet, demure look.' She beamed a diamond smile at Donna. 'How clever of you not to attempt anything showy. One should know one's own style, don't you think?'

'Know my place, you mean?' Donna murmured.

Rinaldo was just close enough to hear. A tremor passed over his face, but he controlled it instantly. Their eyes met. Despite his antagonism Donna felt he'd been briefly on her side.

Toni gave a shout of laughter. 'Do you know, Donna calls herself a little brown mouse?' he said. 'But don't you believe it.' He tapped Donna's forehead lightly. 'She's got brains in there. More than me.'

'Anyone has more brains than you,' Rinaldo observed drily.

Donna smiled. 'At this moment I'd sacrifice brains if I could look like you,' she told Selina pleasantly. 'No one could mistake you for a little brown mouse.'

Selina made a self-deprecating gesture, honed and polished to perfection. 'Looks are nothing,' she declared gaily. 'It's all the effect of the diamonds. I tell Rinaldo he gives me too many, but he just won't stop.'

Selina turned her attentions onto Piero. Rinaldo regarded Donna with narrowed eyes, behind which interest gleamed. 'I'm not just empty words, you see,' he murmured. 'I know how to be generous.'

'Well, some men prefer to express themselves with money,' Donna said pointedly. She met his eyes. 'And some know no other way.'

'I dare say you could tell me about that.'

'Your brother is different, *signore*. He gives his heart.'

'*Signore?*' he asked ironically. 'If you're planning to become part of this family, shouldn't you be calling me by my name?'

'I doubt whether you and I could ever be part of the same family—not in any way that means anything. Toni, yes. Your grandfather, yes. But not us.'

'Showing your claws, eh?'

'You declared your enmity for me in the first moments,' she told him in a soft, angry voice. 'At least that's honest. Remain my enemy, *signore*. Then I know where I stand.'

'So you carry the fight into the heart of the enemy's camp,' he said. 'Courageous, but futile. I sympathise with a forlorn hope.'

'Perhaps not as forlorn as you think,' she riposted, smiling. 'How do you know I don't have a secret weapon?'

'I shall wait with trepidation.'

'Now are we all ready to go in to dinner?' Piero asked, shepherding everyone. With Donna on his arm he led the way into the dining room. It was a long room, one of whose walls was almost entirely given up to floor-length windows that opened onto the cloister. Light poured in from this side, throwing the rest of the room into shade.

After a while Donna's eyes grew accustomed to it, and she saw that the dining room was traditional, but quietly luxurious. The table and chairs were made of dark wood. The chairs had very tall backs, covered with tapestry, as were the seats.

The table was laid with silver and gleaming crystal. Three glasses of different sizes and shapes stood like soldiers beside each place. They looked so fragile—as if a breath might cause them to shatter.

Piero indicated her place and pulled out a chair for her. She found herself seated in the middle of one of the long sides of the table, with Rinaldo directly opposite her. To her relief Toni was beside her. Under the table he gave her hand a gentle squeeze, and she squeezed back, trying to convey how nervous she was.

Donna noticed that the chair on Piero's far side was unoccupied, and wondered who was to join them. Then Piero gave a little whistle, and his cat scuttled across the floor and leapt onto the chair.

'Sasha likes to eat with me,' Piero declared.

Selina tittered. 'What a sweet idea! But then, you're a very sweet pussy, aren't you, *carissima*?'

Sasha hissed at her. Selina quickly drew back the hand she'd held out to stroke the furry head.

Rinaldo eyed his grandfather with fond exasperation. 'Since everybody is now present, perhaps we can begin,' he said.

Maria appeared. She was still wearing black, but now her dress was of silk, indicating that she was going to supervise the serving of the meal.

'Maria has prepared a very special meal in your honour,' Rinaldo told Donna with a little inclination of his head.

'That—that was very kind of her,' Donna said awkwardly. The luxury was beginning to oppress her, and her poise seemed to have drained away through the soles of her feet.

Under Maria's direction two maids appeared, bearing bottles. They went down the table filling the largest glasses with sparkling mineral water and the next size with dry white wine. When Maria was satisfied that this had been done properly she gave them a brief nod and they scurried away, returning a moment later with trolleys bearing the first course, which she served herself.

Donna had often eaten in Italian restaurants, but this was her first experience of Italian food cooked on its home ground, and it was overwhelming. To start with there was aubergine salad—a mixture of diced aubergine, celery, olives and endives, served with slices of hard-boiled egg and flavoured with onion, garlic and something that tasted incredibly like bitter chocolate.

Toni laughed when he saw her face. 'Yes, it's chocolate,' he said. 'It's a special trick of Maria's to put a little in with the vinegar.'

'It's the most unbelievable taste,' Donna said. 'Maria must be a genius.'

When Maria appeared, to supervise the clearing of the plates, Piero repeated this, to her obvious pleasure.

'Grazie, signorina,' she said, smiling at Donna.

There followed a dish of tagliatelle with pumpkin, which was even more delicious. Donna began to wonder how she could eat any more, yet such was Maria's skill that the two previous dishes balanced each other, leaving her satisfied but not satiated.

'For the main course Maria has prepared roast leg of lamb, especially for you,' Rinaldo informed her. 'She believes the English cannot be happy without roast lamb.'

But this was like no roast lamb Donna had ever encountered on an English table. It appeared on a bed of garlic, celery, onions and carrots, and was lavishly spiced with rosemary and oregano. Somewhere, too, Donna detected the taste of wine. It was more than a meal. It was a work of art.

Red wine was poured to go with the lamb. Maria

frowned at the sight of Donna's white wine, which she had barely touched.

'You do not like wine, *signorina*?' Rinaldo asked.

'I prefer mineral water,' Donna said. In fact she normally enjoyed wine, but she avoided alcohol now she knew that she was pregnant.

'Signorina Easton wants to keep her wits about her,' Selina said with a touch of mischief. 'She probably feels that she's in the lion's den.'

'But how can that be, when she is the guest of honour?' Rinaldo enquired silkily.

'Perhaps, *signore*, because you remind me of a Roman emperor,' Donna replied. 'Didn't some of them used to invite their enemies to dine, treat them with honour, and then—' she made an expressive gesture with her hands '—the enemies were never seen again? Who knows what became of them?'

Toni grinned, and Piero shouted with laughter. 'What do you say to that?' he demanded of his grandson. 'A Roman emperor.' He turned to Donna. 'Now you must say which one. Nero? Caligula?'

'Neither of them,' Donna said. 'They were mad and stupid, and I'm sure that whatever Signor Rinaldo does is done with intention, and worked out beforehand to the last detail, with no concession to emotion.'

'Then who?' Piero begged eagerly. He was enjoying himself.

'Augustus, perhaps?' Donna suggested.

Piero nodded. 'A chilly, unfeeling devil. There, Rinaldo. She has you to perfection. But how do you come to know so much about our history?'

Rinaldo's smile was deadly. 'I think you'll find, Nonno, that Signorina Easton has also worked out everything to the last detail—with no concession to emotion.'

'You speak as if you know her well,' Selina said, her glance flashing, cat-like, between them.

'I think perhaps I do,' Rinaldo agreed.

The look in his eyes seemed to reach across the table and scorch Donna. But she wasn't afraid. The knowledge that she could take this man by surprise was like heady wine.

'But she's a stranger to all of us,' Selina complained. 'Tell us about yourself, *Signorina*.'

'There's very little to tell. I'm a nurse. I met Toni when he crashed his car and was brought to the hospital where I work.'

'But how romantic!' Selina exclaimed. 'And did you fall in love instantly?'

'Yes,' Toni said. 'Donna is my own private angel of mercy.'

'And your family?' Rinaldo asked. 'How do they feel about your marriage?'

'I have no family to speak of,' Donna said abruptly. 'My mother is dead. My father left home years ago. These days I hardly know him.'

'She wouldn't even take me to meet him,' Toni said with a laugh. 'I think he must be some kind of ogre.'

Selina's eyes glinted. 'Well, we all have relations that we don't want people to meet.'

Donna's mouth tightened. It was true that she'd refused to take Toni to visit her father. She couldn't face him seeing how uninterested her own father was in her. But Selina's words had implied something else, something shabby.

'That's perfectly true,' Piero announced. 'None of my

relations ever want people to meet me. I'm the family skeleton. Have been for years.'

In the general laugh that this evoked the moment passed. Piero fed Sasha another titbit, apparently oblivious to having defused the tension. Donna saw Rinaldo frowning, and realised that another black mark had been notched against her. A woman without family, who would gain honour from her marriage but bring none to her husband.

The maids appeared and cleared the plates. Maria served chilled zabaglione, made of egg yolks whisked with Marsala wine, and decorated with amaretti biscuits. Like everything else in the meal it was perfectly prepared, and precisely calculated to set off what had gone before.

Then there was coffee in tiny porcelain cups, and brandy for those who wanted it. Piero stood up. 'And now I want to propose a toast,' he said.

Rinaldo looked puzzled. Selina fixed a smile on her face, but Piero gave no sign of noticing them. He beamed at Toni, then at Donna.

'This is a happy day,' he said. 'Our Toni has brought home a bride who will truly be worthy of this house. It will be our pleasure to make her a part of the family.' He raised his glass. 'I drink to my new granddaughter.'

The others all drank. Toni smiled at Donna.

'And there is one more thing,' Piero added to Donna. 'I have a special gift for you.' He reached into his pocket and brought out a tiny object, which he held up.

'This ring has been in the Mantini family for generations. I gave it to my wife, and it stayed on her finger until the day she died. Traditionally the eldest son has given it to his bride, but since Rinaldo refuses to marry

I give it to you, dear child, to show that you will be a true Mantini.'

He took her right hand and slipped the ring onto the third finger. It was a beautiful thing, made of emeralds and rubies, with an exotic design. Donna gasped with delight, less at its obvious value than at its symbol of welcome. For a moment tears blurred her eyes. When they cleared she saw Rinaldo's face, a mask of fury. She understood. She'd not only stolen his brother, but also part of his inheritance.

But after the first moment of anger he concealed his feelings, smiling and congratulating her. Selina did less well. Her mouth made the right movements but her eyes were cold, and Donna guessed she'd seen the ring as one day belonging to herself.

The rest of the evening passed uneventfully. Selina departed in a cloud of perfume and blown kisses. Rinaldo escorted her to her car. Toni poured his grandfather another drink, and Donna slipped out into the courtyard.

It was blessedly cool outside, besides being a relief to escape from the house. High up, trapped in the oblong of the buildings, the moon gleamed, illuminating everything below in silver. By its light Donna wandered over to the fountain and sat on the side, listening to the falling of the water and looking into the depths. Now and then a curious goldfish broke the surface, gazed at her and disappeared. She waggled a finger in the water, laughing softly as the goldfish darted in all directions.

Some changed quality in the air made her look up suddenly. Rinaldo was watching her, his face hidden in shadow. She wondered how long he'd been there.

He came towards her. He had a brandy glass in each hand, and he offered one to her.

'No, thank you,' she said instantly.

'It's good brandy,' he said, seating himself by the side of the pool, so that he could see her. 'The best. I don't offer it to everyone.'

'I'm honoured, but I never drink spirits,' she said firmly.

'You're a most unexpected woman. I'll admit that you've totally taken me by surprise.'

'But not enough to make you trust my motives?'

'On the contrary, I distrust you more than ever now I know how well you've prepared yourself to become part of this household.'

'But I didn't— Oh, why bother, when you don't believe me?'

'True, why bother? If it comes to that, why does a woman like you bother with a boy like Toni?'

'Because he's kind and sweet-natured,' she said, looking him in the eye. 'And because he wants me.'

'And you? What do you want?'

'I want—' her voice wavered suddenly '—I want to belong.'

Why had she said that? she wondered. She didn't know, except that there was something in this man's force of personality that compelled the truth.

He was looking at her curiously. 'And you think you will belong here?'

'If you will let me.'

'But I will not let you. You don't belong here as Toni's wife, and I won't allow you to fool yourself, or him.' He seized her hand suddenly. 'Listen to me,' he said in a low, urgent voice. 'If it's security you want, I'll give it to you. You can have an apartment in the most luxurious part of Rome, jewellery, clothes, anything you want—at my expense. I have friends who will give you a job to pass the time. All I ask is that you always be ready for me when I want you.'

She stared at him in horror. 'I don't believe what I'm hearing.'

'I only half believe it myself,' he said grimly. 'But I'll do anything to prevent the tragedy you're planning.'

She pulled her hand free. The physical contact with him unnerved her. 'And what about Toni's feelings? Don't you care about them?'

'It's because I care about him that I'm going to stop this marriage.'

'I belong to Toni.'

'You'll never belong to him in a million years,' Rinaldo said fiercely. 'And you know it. You've known it from the moment we met.'

'You arrogant—'

'Don't waste time calling me names because of what neither of us can help.'

'It's not true,' she said fiercely.

'Isn't it?' he asked, looking deep into her eyes. The next moment he lifted his hand and trailed his fingertips gently down the side of her face.

The sensation shattered her. His touch was feather-light, but it sent tremors through her in a way Toni's touch had never done. The whole world seemed to spin.

'Toni is a boy,' Rinaldo said softly. 'And you're not a girl but a woman. You need a man.'

'But not you,' she said, speaking with difficulty. 'Never you.'

'Why not me? Why not a man who can appreciate you, instead of that sulky child who wants you to mother him? Toni will forget. But we—we won't forget.'

Through the roaring in her ears she clung to one thought—that this was an unscrupulous man who'd stop at nothing to separate her from his brother. Even if it meant seducing her himself. But when the break was final he would toss her aside.

She fought to remind herself of this while his touch delighted and tormented her. She tried to pull away but his eyes held her in a hypnotic trance. His fingertips moved to her mouth, and slowly he began to trace the outline of her lips. The sensation was overwhelming. She hadn't known her flesh could experience such feelings. He was making her discover desires that she knew she should shun, forcing her to acknowledge that behind their mutual antagonism lay another feeling, far more dangerous than hostility.

Her mouth burned with the longing to feel his mouth against it. She couldn't breathe. She wanted this to stop. She wanted it to go on for ever.

'Only say yes,' he whispered, 'and I will do whatever is necessary. I'll take you away from here tonight and you need never see Toni again.'

She drew a long, shuddering breath, trying to still the mad pounding of her heart. The mention of Toni's name had the effect of reviving her courage. Toni loved her. He would be broken-hearted at what his brother was trying to do to him.

'Take your hands off me,' she said deliberately.

She saw the shock in his face. He'd thought he had her in his trap, and the discovery that she'd escaped brought a flare of anger to his eyes.

'What would Toni say if he knew the truth about you?' she demanded.

'And what, in your opinion, is the truth?'

'That you're the kind of man who tries to seduce his brother's woman.'

He flinched and his face became cruel. 'See if you can make him believe it.'

'Of course you'd deny it?'

'Of course. There's nothing I won't do to protect my family from danger—*nothing at all*. You've been warned. I would have played fair if you'd been sensible. You'd have had your apartment, and all the rest—as long as it suited me. But you chose to be clever. Well, we'll see who's cleverest.'

He rose abruptly and strode back to the house. Donna remained where she was, shaken. For a moment the look in his eyes, and a certain vibrant note in his voice, had transfixed her. She could almost have forgotten everything else. She shuddered with horror at herself.

Toni came to find her. 'Are you all right?' he asked anxiously. 'Has Rinaldo been making himself unpleasant?'

'No, I'm fine,' she said. 'But I would like to go to bed. I'm very tired.'

Toni took her indoors. Piero kissed her goodnight, and even Sasha came to rub herself against Donna's ankles. There was no sign of Rinaldo.

In her room she closed the door firmly behind her and stood for a moment leaning against it. The shutters were open, and the moonlight revealed something lying on her bed. She put on the light and examined it.

It was a large envelope, stuffed with English money. Appalled, Donna tipped it onto the bed, realising that there was a full ten thousand pounds. There was also a note that said simply, 'For God's sake, take this and go. R!'

CHAPTER THREE

EVEN at night the heat was stifling. Donna tossed and turned before throwing off all the bedclothes, but still there was little relief. She couldn't sleep. A fierce resentment at Rinaldo's behaviour seethed within her, destroying all peace.

Her dreams of being welcomed in Italy, of finally belonging somewhere, were shattered. One cruel, prejudiced man had ruined everything. She hated him.

Then the memory of that moment in the garden came over her again, causing the blood to throb in her veins. The sheer force of Rinaldo's masculinity had made her recognise, for the first time, that she'd tied herself to a young man who hadn't fully grown up, who might never grow up. It made no difference that she hated Rinaldo. Hatred could be as thrilling as love. In fact, more so. Had there ever been one moment when Toni's love had truly thrilled her? She felt gratitude and tenderness towards him, but not the searing awareness that had swept along her nerves in that shattering instant with his brother. She'd told herself that gentle affection would be enough, and she'd believed it, but that was before she had known...

She sat up in bed, shaking her head to clear it of the tormenting vision. She mustn't allow herself to think like that. She loved Toni. No matter that it was the wrong kind of love. It was too late to think of that. He was the father of her child. She forced herself to remember his tender kindness, his pride in her, the way he made her

41

feel cherished. But why hadn't he told the family about the baby?

The thought flickered across her mind that he'd kept silent for fear of Rinaldo. She dismissed the idea, but it left a footprint of unease. Toni feared Rinaldo as a youngster might fear a stern father. It was a troubling thought.

She got up, as oppressed by her own fears as by the heat, flung open the windows and drank in gulps of air. The night was in its last hour of darkness before dawn began to break.

She pulled on her thin cotton dressing gown and slipped out of her room. Somewhere there must be a way out of the house so that she could walk in the garden and grow really cool. She groped around uselessly for a while, before seeing a thin crack of moonlight under a door. Opening it, she found to her relief that she was on the stone staircase that led down into the cloisters. She descended halfway, then sat on the stairs and leaned against the wall, closing her eyes and letting the air waft gently over her. It was blissful.

She almost dozed off in that position. Then she heard the sound of angry Italian voices, deep in the house. In another moment a door was flung open and Toni came storming out into the courtyard.

Rinaldo was close behind him. 'Don't walk away when I'm talking to you,' he snapped.

'I've listened to you for hours,' Toni said.

'I haven't even started yet.'

The brothers had come to a halt near the fountain. Peering through the balustrades, Donna could see them clearly limned by the moonlight. They were still in the clothes they'd worn for dinner, as though they'd fought all night, with neither winning. Rinaldo had taken his jacket off, and torn open the neck of his elegant white shirt. His chest was rising and falling with the force of his anger.

'There are things I'm going to say, and you're going to listen,' he said in a quieter voice.

'I've heard them all before,' Toni said wearily. 'I know I've been a fool in the past, but Donna is different.'

Rinaldo gave a short, scornful laugh. 'You think every girl is different.'

Donna glanced wildly up the stairs whence she'd come. If only she could creep back to her room without being seen. One half of her wanted to stay here and listen while Toni defended her, but the other half shrank from eavesdropping. Besides, suppose she was caught? She shivered at the thought of Rinaldo's contempt if he found her here.

Moving slowly, she began to slide backwards, but her slippers made a faint scratching noise against the stone, and she froze.

'What was that?' Rinaldo demanded, looking round.

'What?' Toni asked impatiently.

'I thought I heard a noise.'

The brothers stood in silence for a moment, while Donna's heart thumped so hard she was sure they must discover her. But at last Toni said, 'The night's full of noises. It was probably Sasha hunting mice. Never mind that.'

'Yes, let's return to this woman who's cast a spell over you,' said Rinaldo in a hard voice. *Dio mio*, I've never seen you so stupid and obstinate before.'

'Because she's different,' Toni said. 'Can't you see that?'

'I can see that she *looks* different,' Rinaldo conceded.

'She's not flashy, but don't be taken in by her demure appearance. She's clever and shrewd. There's an educated brain working behind that pale face.'

'That's it!' Toni rounded on his brother. 'You can't imagine that an educated woman could be interested in me—'

'I find it hard,' Rinaldo admitted grimly. 'In a short life you've made yourself notable for many things—fast cars, expensive tastes, brushes with the law. But brains—never!'

'Think what you like. Donna loves me.'

'She loves your family's money, that's all. You heard her tonight. A woman with no background, three years your senior. You must have seemed like a golden chance, and she seized it. Then you brought her down here and she caught sight of the real goodies. I wish you'd seen her face as she surveyed this garden. She thought she'd found her crock of gold at last.'

'You think the worst of everyone,' Toni said.

'The worst is usually true.'

Toni gave a sudden crack of laughter. 'She stood up to you. That's what you don't like.'

'I've never denied that I think her intelligent, but I tell you this—you two could never be happy together. Now be sensible. You've made a fool of yourself, but it can be made right; I can get rid of her quickly and discreetly.'

'Damn you! Stop trying to pull my strings like a puppet!' Toni said furiously. 'It's always been the same. Toni, do this, do that, until I couldn't breathe.'

'It was as well one of us had a sense of responsibility,' Rinaldo said grimly, 'or your life would have been a disaster by now. I promised our mother that I would take care of you, and that's been a sacred trust to me.'

Toni's voice suddenly went up a pitch, as though Rinaldo had touched a raw nerve. 'Don't speak of our mother,' he shouted. 'Leave her sacred memory out of your dirty scheming.'

'I must speak of her,' Rinaldo snapped. 'It was she who made this family a *family*, who warded off danger and evil from her children. What would she say now if I stood aside while you ruined your life?'

Toni flung his glass away and it shattered against the stone. 'She would know that I'm not ruining my life but saving it,' he shrieked. 'She would be glad for me.' His voice rose again as though he were lashing himself into the courage to speak. 'She would say I was doing the right thing *because a man should marry the mother of his child.*'

In the terrible silence that followed, the words seemed to hang in the air. Donna inched her way along the stair until she could look between the banisters, and saw Rinaldo. Now she understood why Toni was frightened of him. His face was black with anger.

'Did I understand you correctly?' he said at last in a voice of cold menace.

Toni took a step back and his voice shook. But he'd come too far to stop now. 'Donna is pregnant,' he said huskily.

Full of tension, Donna waited for what Rinaldo would say next. But the sound that came from him wasn't made up of words. It was simply a bellow of fury, frustration, and thwarted will. She read all these things in the noise, and in the way he slammed his fist down on the stone.

'You *fool*!' he raged. 'You gullible, credulous fool! She's taken you in with that old trick. I thought even you had more sense. You don't imagine it's yours, do you? How long did it take your angelic Madonna to get pregnant?'

'W-well—almost at once,' Toni stammered, 'but—'

'Of course! She wasted no time once she'd lured you into her bed.'

'She—she didn't lure me—' Toni faltered. 'It took all my pleading before—'

'Oh, maidenly reluctance as well. My God, I underestimated her!'

'You certainly did,' Donna agreed, in English.

Both men swung round to face the stairs, from which Donna rose like an avenging fury. She ran down and faced Rinaldo, too angry to be afraid of him.

'My child is Toni's,' she cried, 'and that's true, no matter how you try to dirty it.'

'I might have known you'd go creeping about my house, eavesdropping,' he sneered.

'I never meant to. I came out here to get cool, and I'm glad now that I did. I think you must be an evil man. You know nothing about me, but you assume the worst, because you prefer to believe the worst of people. Yes, I slept with Toni, because I love him. Now I'm going to have his child. That's something that you can't take away from either of us.'

Emboldened by her defiant spirit, Toni had come to stand beside her, his hand on her shoulder. Rinaldo looked from one to the other, and his face grew ugly. 'Very pretty words,' he snapped. 'But they mean nothing. I don't believe you.'

Donna confronted him head-on. 'To hell with what you believe,' she said simply.

He drew his breath in sharply. His eyes glittered and she could almost feel his fury vibrating in the air about her. Then he muttered an oath and slammed one fist into the other. The next moment he turned on his heel and strode off into the shadows. They heard the crash of a door slamming.

Toni breathed out. 'Oh, Santa Maria!' he muttered. 'I was afraid of how he'd take it, but I didn't think it would be as bad as that!'

'What does it matter?' she pleaded. 'We don't need him. We don't need anyone. The sooner we're away from here the better.'

Without waiting for him to say any more she ran back up the stairs, hurried to her room and began to toss her things into suitcases. She had to get away from this house where she was treated like an enemy.

Toni appeared. '*Cara*, what are you doing?' he asked in dismay when he saw her.

'I'm doing what I said I'd do. Leaving,' she said tersely.

'But you can't leave me!' he cried. 'I need you—'

'Look at this!' She held up the money. 'He tried to pay me off. And look what he dared to write to me!'

Toni stared at the note, then at the money. Dazed, he counted it. 'Do you see how much is here?' he breathed.

'What difference does it make how much it is?' Donna demanded angrily. 'Did you think I'd let him buy me off?'

'Of course not, but—'

Donna didn't wait for him to finish, but began stuffing the notes back into the envelope. She wrote Rinaldo's name on the outside and put it down on her pillow.

'The maid will find that and take it to him in the morning,' she said. 'Now I'm going. I don't want to see him again.'

He seized her hands. 'You're right. We'll both go.'

'I don't want to come between you and your family—'

'But you are my family,' he insisted. 'You and our little *bambino*. We'll go together. Wait while I pack some clothes.'

He vanished, and Donna sat down on the bed, suddenly tired. She'd been in such a temper that she hadn't stopped to think how she would manage if Toni didn't come too.

She felt as if she'd been through a wringer. She had to get away from this cruel place, but most of all she had to get away from Rinaldo Mantini.

Toni was back in a few minutes with a hastily packed bag. 'Ready?' he asked.

'There's one final thing,' she told him. 'Please, darling, try to understand. I can't take your grandfather's ring.'

'But of course you can. He wanted you to have it.'

'It's a family ring—'

'But he gave it to us,' Toni said sulkily.

'I'm sorry, I just can't take it.' Donna slid the beautiful ring off her finger and looked about her. 'Where will it be safe to leave this?' she mused.

'Put it in the envelope with the money,' Toni suggested. 'Here, I'll do it while you check the bathroom.'

'I've checked it.'

'Better do it again. Women always leave something behind, like hairspray or nail polish.'

'All right, all right. But we must be quick.'

In fact Toni's instinct was correct; she'd left her sponge bag by the basin. While she was gathering it up and having a final glance round she heard him say urgently, 'Hurry, I think the house is beginning to stir.'

She emerged from the bathroom. 'Is everything—?'

He grabbed her hand and drew her to the door. 'Listen,' he said softly.

She listened, but could hear nothing.

'Let's go while we can,' he murmured.

Donna followed him out into the corridor. Quietly they crept to the head of the stairs and began to go slowly down the broad steps, holding their breath. To her relief there was no need to go out by the front door. Toni led her to a side door that opened directly into the garage. In a few moments they'd loaded up his car and he had the garage doors open.

Dawn was beginning to break as they drove slowly down the long path to the front gate. Donna kept looking behind her, certain that any moment she would find Rinaldo in pursuit. But nothing happened, and at last they were on the road. Toni promptly gunned the car into life, and in a few seconds they were streaking away. Donna was devoutly thankful to put the Villa Mantini behind her. She hoped she would never have to see it again.

They drove for a while in silence, while the land about them grew lighter by the minute.

Toni gave a sudden shout of laughter. 'Rinaldo's face when you rose up from the stairs and he realised you'd heard everything,' he said in a shaking voice. 'I've never seen him knocked sideways like that.'

'He wasn't too startled to insult me, though, was he?' Donna asked grimly.

'Oh, he didn't mean anything by it,' he said carelessly.

Donna felt dizzy at Toni's mercurial moods. The relief of escape seemed to have blown his cares away, and it was as if the past hour had not existed. 'Toni, he accused me of trying to pass another man's child off on you,' she said, with more of an edge to her voice than she'd ever used with him before.

'So what? I didn't believe it.'

'But he had no right to say it. Is he going to throw more mud at me at our wedding?'

'He won't get the chance. We'll marry first and tell him afterwards.'

'We'll do no such thing,' Donna said. 'He'd love that. A hole-and-corner wedding, so that he could tell everyone I'd proved his worst fears. We'll marry in the face of all the world, and send him an invitation. Let him do his worst.'

Instantly Toni's mood changed. The carefree look vanished from his face. '*Cara*, you don't know what Rinaldo's worst is,' he said in a hollow voice. 'He can't bear being defied. He'll do anything to get his own way.'

'What *can* he do?'

'Lots of things. Kidnap me from the church, probably.'

'Be serious.'

'I *am* being serious. Rinaldo has friends who'd do it, for a price.'

Donna stared at him. Toni was watching the road ahead, but she could see by the troubled frown on his face that he wasn't joking. She'd known that Rinaldo was an imperious, arrogant and unscrupulous man. Now she realised that he was also a frightening one. Toni was afraid of him. That much was clear.

'Which way are we going?' she asked.

'I'm heading for the *autostrada*. We're going home.'

'Home? But this is your home.'

'I mean England. We'll vanish where he can't find us.'

'Toni, you don't mean that.'

'Oh, yes, I do! I thought things were going to be so different. I thought Rinaldo would like you, and welcome you into the family. It would have made things so much easier—'

'You mean I could have protected you from him?' Donna asked shrewdly.

Toni just shrugged.

She felt a little stab of dismay. It didn't matter, she told herself. She'd known that Toni was immature. But it *did* matter. That was the truth.

'I'd better fill the tank first,' he muttered, with his eye on the gauge. 'There's a petrol station just up here.'

He swung in and pulled to a halt. While he was filling up Donna got out of the car. Her mind was in turmoil, and she knew she couldn't travel any further with Toni until they'd had a serious talk.

'I need some coffee,' she said. 'There's a little café just opening up over there.'

'All right, but don't let's be too long.'

Like many Italian men Toni liked to carry his immediate possessions in a leather bag worn on a long strap from the shoulder. He pulled this from the car now and followed her into the café.

'Sit there while I get you something,' he said.

Donna sat down and closed her eyes, feeling shaken by everything she'd been through. It didn't seem possible that only yesterday she'd travelled this road full of joy and hope for the future. Now everything was ruined.

No, not everything. She placed a gentle hand over her stomach. She still had her baby, even if she'd become disillusioned with its father. For the sake of her child she would do anything.

Toni returned with coffee and rolls, and gave her his old charming smile. She tried to remind herself that he was still the dear, warm-hearted boy that she loved. When they were away from this place everything would be all right again.

She put a hand out to steady his shoulder bag, which he'd dumped carelessly on a chair. But she was too late and the bag went spilling onto the floor. Toni made a nervous grab at it, but he wasn't fast enough.

'Oh, heavens!' Donna breathed, picking up something that had fallen out. 'How could you do this?'

'Look, *cara*, I was going to explain—'

'This is the money Rinaldo tried to force me to take, isn't it?' she said in disbelieving anger. 'I told you I didn't want it, but you picked it up when my back was turned.'

'Come on, don't make a fuss—'

'A fuss? You knew how I felt about taking his money—'

'Well, we're going to need money.'

'Not *his* money,' she said fiercely. 'Anyone but his.'

'What's wrong with his money? It's as good as anyone else's. He's my brother. Why shouldn't he help us?'

'Because it's deception, can't you understand that?'

But looking into his eyes she saw that he didn't understand at all. It was Toni's nature to take the easiest way. Donna began to feel sick again. She clutched the envelope hard, trying to decide what to do, and felt another pang of dismay as her fingers detected a small, hard bulge.

'What's this?' she asked in dawning horror.

But she knew what it was even before she pulled out Piero's ring. She closed her eyes. 'I explained why I couldn't keep this,' she said desperately.

'Well, I don't see why you shouldn't have it,' he said sulkily. 'Nonno gave it to you.'

'To welcome me into the family, but we're running away. Besides, he should have given it to Rinaldo. He's the eldest son.'

'He could do what he liked with it,' Toni said with an exasperated sigh that showed clearly how all this moralising was getting him down. 'He gave it to us. Can't you see that we're independent now?'

'Independent? With Rinaldo's money and Piero's ring, neither of which we're supposed to have?'

'Well, I think it's rather a good joke to use Rinaldo's money, when he thought he was buying you off. How I wish I could see his face when he finds out!'

'No, you don't,' Donna said with bitter realisation. 'You wouldn't like to be anywhere near when he finds out. Your kind of courage is in secret. You tricked me into checking the bathroom just to get me out of the way while you took all this. Oh, how could you?'

'I was only looking after you,' he said, aggrieved. 'We'll need money to live on until we're married. Then I'm sure Nonno will make me an allowance.'

'An allowance?' she echoed. 'Are you going to go all your life supported by someone else? Toni, I can't live like that.'

'Oh, don't make a fuss,' he said irritably. 'What's wrong with it, anyway? It's family money.'

'It's a family firm, but you're not working in it, are you?'

He shrugged. Donna stared at him in a kind of horror.

They drank their coffee in silence. Her mind was seething with miserable thoughts. 'What did Rinaldo mean about brushes with the law?' she asked after a while.

'Why bring that up now?'

'Because I never heard of it before. What happened?'

'It was nothing. I got followed by a police car when I was speeding and it became a chase. The police car crashed.'

'Good God! Was anyone hurt?'

'No, I promise you. The police got out, swearing at me, but their car was a write-off.'

'How long ago was this?'

'About six months, just before I went to England.'

'You mean you escaped to England before you were charged?' Donna asked. The pieces were falling into place quickly now.

'Rinaldo said I should lie low while he made it all right. He called about a month later and said it was safe to go home, but by that time I'd met you, *cara*.' He gave her his old winning smile, but she'd seen the weakness behind it and it didn't touch her heart as it once had done.

'No wonder Rinaldo was against me from the start,' she murmured.

With sudden resolution she drained her coffee, stuffed the envelope into her bag, and got up. 'Come along,' she told him, and began to walk towards the car, Toni trotting obediently after her.

'Hey, I'll drive,' he protested as she got into the driver's seat.

'I'll drive,' she said. She didn't want an argument about what she was going to do. She started the engine and swung the car round.

'Where are you going?' Toni yelped. 'This is the wrong way.'

'It's the right way. We're going back.'

'*What*? Are you crazy? Do you know how mad he'll be?'

'Toni, can't you see that we have to go back and

return the money and the ring? They're not ours. I won't keep them under false pretences.'

'OK, OK, we'll send them back through the post the next time we stop. Now turn the car round.'

'We can't send such valuable things through the post. Besides, I want to see Rinaldo's face when I hand them over and tell him what he can do with his money.'

'His face is just what I don't want to see,' Toni groaned.

Donna spoke instinctively. 'Don't worry, I'll look after you.'

Instead of being indignant at the suggestion that he needed her protection Toni groaned again. 'You think you will, but you haven't seen Rinaldo when he's in a really nasty temper. For God's sake, turn round!'

'No!'

'Look, we'll get married, then we can go back and see him.'

'*No*,' she repeated stubbornly. And even as she spoke she knew that there would be no wedding. Even for her child's sake she couldn't marry Toni. There would be no peace, always wondering what this overgrown infant was lying about or evading. She would let him see his child as often as he wanted, but it would be madness to chain her life to his. She should have seen it long ago.

She focused on the road ahead, longing for the moment when she would return to the Villa Mantini, hurl Rinaldo's money at him and depart, a free woman.

'Donna, you've *got* to turn back.'

'I'm going to face him,' she said determinedly. 'There's nothing he can do to us.'

'Oh, God!' he almost wept. 'You don't know what you're talking about. You don't know what he's like.'

When she didn't answer Toni stared at her, wild-eyed,

and, with a sudden spurt of determination, grabbed the wheel. She slowed, trying to push him away and keep a straight course, but Toni was fighting her now, desperately trying to wrench the wheel aside.

The car slewed violently across the road and went into a spin. Donna struggled to recover control, crying out to Toni to release the wheel, but his hands were clamped on it in a frenzy and she couldn't get them off.

'Toni!' she screamed. *'Toni, please—'*

It was too late. The world was beginning to whirl about her as the car rose in the air and turned over and over.

That was the last thing Donna saw. But she heard everything: the screech of tyres, the crash as they landed, Toni crying her name again and again, until his voice faded away into silence.

Through her pain and anguish she understood the meaning of that silence. She whispered Toni's name, but she knew he couldn't hear her. He would never hear her again.

She was lost in red-hot darkness. It swirled around her, jabbing her body with knives, making every breath an agony. At last she opened her eyes. It took time for them to focus, but then she made out that she was in a small white room. The walls were white, and the ceiling, and the bed in which she lay.

There was a dark shadow beside the bed. Slowly she turned her head, and saw Rinaldo Mantini. His eyes were fixed on her, and her heart almost failed her, for never before had she seen a look of such total hatred on any human face.

CHAPTER FOUR

FOR a long moment they looked at each other, until at last Donna whispered, 'My baby?'

'Your child is safe,' Rinaldo told her in a distant voice. 'You were lucky.'

'And Toni?'

'My brother is dead,' Rinaldo said flatly.

'Oh, God!' she whispered in horror. In her heart she'd known it. The fading of Toni's voice in her delirium had had a final quality that told her the truth, but it was still terrible to hear it confirmed.

'How long have I been here?' she asked huskily.

'Two days. At first the doctors thought that the shock would kill you too. But you lived.'

'And you wish I was dead, don't you?' she asked, frightened by something cold and bleak in his face.

His expression didn't change. 'I'll tell the doctor you're awake,' he said, rising. 'We'll talk later.'

He disappeared. Nurses came. Donna drifted back into sleep. Her whole body ached and her heart was sick with misery, but she clung to the thought that her child was still alive.

She drifted in and out of consciousness for several days. Rinaldo was always there, watching her, his eyes unyielding. Through her troubled dreams she could feel the force of his hate. At last she woke, clear-headed for the first time. And he was still there.

'I didn't imagine it, did I?' she asked. 'You told me Toni is dead.'

'Dead,' he confirmed in a flat voice. 'His funeral was yesterday.'

She began to weep. 'Oh, God! Poor Toni!'

'Yes, weep for him,' Rinaldo said in a voice that was almost a sneer. 'Weep for the man you killed, but expect no pity from me.'

'I didn't kill Toni,' she protested weakly. 'It was an accident.'

'Yes, an accident caused by your greed,' he told her. 'Your determination to seize all you could and escape as fast as possible.'

'No—no—I was coming back to the Villa Mantini— Toni didn't want to return—he tried to stop me—'

'Don't make it worse by lying.'

'I'm not—'

'You took the money I offered you, and my grand-father's ring, and persuaded Toni to escape at night. Did you give one thought to what you were doing to those he loved? When Toni's grandfather heard of his death he collapsed. He was brought to this hospital with a stroke, and has lain at death's door ever since.'

'*No!*' Donna gave a scream of protest. So much death and misery was more than she could bear right now. She turned away from Rinaldo and buried her face in the pillow, shaking with anguish.

The noise brought a nurse hurrying into the room. 'Please, *signore*, the patient must not be agitated,' she said urgently.

'Never fear!' Donna heard Rinaldo's voice. 'This one has no heart. She causes destruction wherever she goes, but she escapes unharmed.'

The impact of the crash had knocked Donna uncon-scious, broken her ankle and two of her ribs, but miraculously her child was unharmed. She soon began to notice her surroundings, and to realise that she was in a luxurious private ward. A middle-aged nurse, called Alicia, seemed to be assigned exclusively to her care. When she asked questions Alicia said, 'Signor Rinaldo said you were to be brought here at his expense.'

'How kind of him,' Donna murmured.

'He's a very generous man,' Alicia confirmed. 'He's a patron of this hospital, and has made it many gifts.'

But Donna knew that kindness had nothing to do with Rinaldo's apparent concern for her. He'd had her brought to a place where he could give orders. Alicia's next words confirmed it.

'The police wish to speak to you about the accident when you are well enough to talk,' she said. 'But they've been told that won't be for some time. Don't worry. No one will get in here to trouble you.'

She said it as reassurance, but it made Donna understand that she was a prisoner—Rinaldo Mantini's prisoner, to be kept apart until he'd decided what to do with her. She shivered.

She disliked the feeling of helplessness. The time had come to see if she could walk, and when the nurse had left she threw back the covers and gingerly set her undamaged foot on the ground. Her broken ankle was in plaster, but by holding onto the end of the bed she managed to rise slowly. When she was standing she paused and took a deep breath.

She began to put one foot in front of the other. Her legs were shaky but they supported her for a short way. There was a small mirror on the wall, and she managed to get close enough to see what had happened to her.

She looked dreadful, she thought. Her face was pale and two livid bruises marked it. She gave herself a wry smile and began to turn back, but suddenly her head started to swim and a feeling of nausea attacked her. She stretched out her arms, groping wildly for some support, but there was only empty air. Just as she was on the point of collapse she heard the door open, a harsh voice muttering a curse, and the next moment a man's hands seized her.

'What the devil do you think you're doing?' Rinaldo demanded.

'I just wanted—' She broke off and gasped as sickness swept over her. Without realising what she was doing she rested her head against his shoulder, glad only for the strength she found in him. He put his arm about her, careful of her damaged ribs, and supported her back to the bed. There he laid her down and drew the covers over her. 'I'm calling the nurse,' he said, grim-faced.

'No, I'm all right,' she gasped. 'There's some glucose by the bed. If I could just—'

He raised her with an arm under her shoulders and held the glass to her lips while she sipped. When she'd finished he laid her back. His movements had been gentle, but there was no gentleness in his face as he spoke.

'I forbid you to do such a thing again,' he said. 'If you can't be sensible I'll have a nurse posted in here all the time to keep an eye on you.'

'What does it matter to you what I do?' she demanded rebelliously.

'You're carrying my brother's child—or so you would have me believe.'

'But you *don't* believe it, do you? So why not just let me go?'

'When I'm sure about you, then I'll know what to do.'

The words had an ominous ring. Donna lay back

tiredly against the pillows. Although he'd ministered to her needs there was nothing yielding about Rinaldo. He was doing what needed to be done, until he was 'sure about' her. It was suddenly very clear to Donna why Toni had had to escape his brother's shadow.

'When are you going to let the police talk to me?' she asked.

'When I've talked to you myself. Although, God knows, it's hardly necessary. The truth is plain enough.'

'And what do you think the truth is?'

'I offered you money to give Toni up, but you got greedy. You persuaded him to leave with you that night, and you took the money with you, also Piero's ring.'

'It's not true,' she said desperately. 'I left the money and the ring behind. Toni took them. I didn't find out until we stopped for petrol. I was furious with him. I said we must come back. I was looking forward to throwing your filthy money back at you.'

'Oh, please!' he said contemptuously. 'Surely you can do better than that! The car was found facing north. You were going away from Rome, not towards it. You must have been driving very fast to have such an accident.'

Her head swam, but she fought for the strength to speak calmly. 'I'm telling you the truth. I started to drive back to the villa. Toni tried to change my mind. When I wouldn't budge he grabbed the wheel. That was what made the car skid out of control. I know we went into the air and turned over...' She stopped, shuddering at the visions that fleeted through her head. 'That must have been...how the car...came to be facing the other way...'

'A very neat story to put the blame on Toni,' he grated.

'Surely someone must have seen what happened?'

'There were no witnesses. The road was empty but for you. How could you have an accident on a straight, empty stretch of road?'

'I've told you—Toni—'

'Ah, yes! How convenient for you that he's not here to defend himself. Why should he be so anxious not to come back?'

Donna leaned back against the pillows. Her strength was almost at an end, but she wouldn't let this man intimidate her. 'Perhaps he'd had enough of you steam-rollering over him,' she said quietly. 'Look into your own heart, Rinaldo, and ask yourself why he was so desperate not to face you again.'

Rinaldo's face was livid. If he'd been her enemy before, he was doubly so now. After a long moment he left the room.

She slept, woke, slept again. When she next opened her eyes it was morning. When she'd washed and eaten something Rinaldo appeared.

'I can't hold the police off any longer,' he said coolly. 'They'll be here in a minute. I must know what you're going to say to them.'

'The truth.'

His mouth twisted. 'You mean you're going to stick to your story.'

'I'm going to tell the truth,' she said wearily. A moment ago she'd been feeling strong, but suddenly the weakness had started to creep over her again. It was the effect of this domineering man's presence. Nothing and nobody could stand up to him, but somehow she must try.

Ten minutes later a young policeman was shown in.

'The *signorina* is still very unwell,' Rinaldo said. 'I hope this won't take long.'

'I only wish for a simple description of the facts, *signore*,' said the policeman. Despite his uniform he spoke with a hint of deference, as everybody did to Rinaldo.

He turned back to Donna. 'Who was driving the car?'

'I was.'

The young man's face became grave. 'Where were you heading for?'

'I was going towards Rome and the Villa Mantini,' she said firmly.

He frowned. 'We found the car facing the other way.'

'So I've been told.'

'And I believe you had left the villa not long before.'

'We left it in the early morning and drove for an hour. We stopped at a service station and decided to return. At least—I wanted to return. Toni disagreed, but I was in the driver's seat. I headed back the way we'd come and he—he yanked at the wheel to stop me. The car swerved and—' She closed her eyes.

'Why did you turn back so soon after your departure, *signorina*?'

'I discovered that I'd brought something with me that I hadn't meant to bring. I wanted to return it before continuing the journey,' she said, choosing her words carefully.

'And Signor Mantini did not agree with this?'

'No, he wanted to keep travelling. We had an argument and—and he pulled at the wheel.'

'So you maintain,' the policeman said in an expressionless voice, 'that the accident was the fault of Signor Antonio Mantini.'

She sighed. 'Yes, I do.' It felt dreadful to be blaming poor Toni, who was dead, but she had no choice.

'It's a pity he can't be here to confirm your statement,'

the policeman murmured, and she could sense his disapproval. 'I'll have this prepared for you to sign.'

Rinaldo ushered him out. After a few minutes he returned, closing the door firmly behind him.

'So now you've saved yourself at the expense of my brother,' he said with contempt. 'Are you pleased with yourself?'

'I didn't lie,' she pleaded. 'Why can't you believe me?'

'Why should I? Can you imagine how you look to me? A few days ago all was well in my world. Then you arrived, with your greed, your deceit, your ruthless determination to mow down all who got in your way. And now my grandfather is near death, and my brother lies cold in the earth. Because of *you*.'

'Stop it!' she cried, burying her face in her hands.

'Does the truth hurt?' he sneered. 'Well, you'll just have to live with it.'

'And you?' she said, forcing herself to face him. 'What's the truth that *you're* afraid to face, Rinaldo?'

'The truth holds no terrors for me.'

'Doesn't it? Do you dare to admit that Toni was afraid of you? That's why he didn't want to come back.'

'That's enough,' he snapped. 'You know nothing, *nothing*. Isn't it enough that you blackened my brother's name to the police, without trying to blacken it to me too?'

'But perhaps it's not *his* name that the truth blackens,' she said defiantly. 'Why are you so afraid to look at yourself?'

He turned dreadful eyes on her. 'Don't make me hate you more than I already do.'

'I think you hate very easily. It's love you know nothing about. I loved Toni, or I wouldn't be having his child. I made him happy. He wanted to be with me. He ran away from you, towards me. That's the true reason why you hate me.'

He didn't answer in words, but he brought his fist down on a small cabinet. His whole body was trembling with the force of his emotion. When he lifted his head Donna saw that his face was ravaged. 'Stop tormenting me,' he said hoarsely. 'Why did you ever come into our lives?'

'Because Toni wanted me,' she cried.

'And you wanted what he had to give.'

'Yes,' she said boldly. 'I wanted what he had to give—love and tenderness. When he knew I was going to have his child he made me feel like a queen, and no one had ever made me feel like that before. But if I'd known about *you*, Rinaldo, I'd never have come near you. The sooner I'm away from here the better, and I hope I never have to see you again.'

'That's easily arranged,' he said, very pale.

'Let me see your grandfather, just once—'

'Never!' The word was like a whiplash.

'Then I'll have to go without seeing him. And you can forget I exist.'

'If only I could,' he said bitterly. 'But there's an empty place in my home, a place that will never be filled because of you.'

'I'm sorry,' she said in a softer voice. Even through her dislike of him she could sense that his anguish was real. 'But it's no use talking. You'll always think the worst of me. You'll find it easier when I'm out of your sight.'

'And your child? This baby that I'm supposed to believe is Toni's?'

'Forget me. Forget the baby. It's better that way. Also—I want you to take this.'

She pulled out her bag from the bedside table. Inside it were the possessions that had been retrieved from the accident, including the envelope containing the money and the ring.

'I found that I still had this,' she said. 'I thought you would have taken it.'

'While you were unconscious?' he said bitterly. 'I'm not a sneak thief. I wouldn't go rummaging through the possessions of a sick woman. Besides, I wanted the satisfaction of taking it back before your eyes.'

'Then you can do so now.' She held it out to him. 'Please take it. I want nothing from you.'

'How will you support your child?'

'That doesn't concern you.'

'Answer me,' he said angrily.

'I'm a nurse. I can always earn a living.'

'And who'll care for your baby while you do? Childminders? Babysitters drawn from God knows where because you have to hire the cheapest?'

She looked at him steadily. 'You've said that my child isn't Toni's. Why should you care what happens?'

He snatched the envelope from her and hurled it to the floor. 'Admit it,' he said, seizing her shoulders. 'Say that this isn't Toni's baby and I'll see you have enough to live on. *But for God's sake, admit it*!'

She knew a strange stirring of pity for him. He didn't know what to believe, except that, whatever the truth, he was faced with pain and misery. But her anger too was roused, and she refused to yield to softer feelings.

'I want nothing from you,' she said huskily. 'Can't you understand that?'

'Admit it! Say it isn't Toni's baby, and you can have anything you want.' His face was tortured.

'The only thing I want is to be free of you,' she cried. 'My child was fathered by Toni but it will carry *my* name, not his, because I'm finished with the Mantini family. I'll leave here as soon as I can, and I never want to see or hear from you again. Now please leave. I'm tired and I want to be alone.'

He stared at her for a moment. Then he walked out.

It was late at night, and Rinaldo was sitting in the garden, staring at the moonlight glittering on the fountain, when the maid came to tell him that a police officer had called. She had to speak to him twice before he came out of his unhappy dream. He pulled himself together and told her to show the man in. The officer was Gino Forselli, a man of Rinaldo's age whose rank proclaimed him far beyond making this kind of call. But the two men had been at school together, and greeted each other cordially.

'It was good of you to come yourself, Gino,' Rinaldo said, speaking with an effort, as though it had been a struggle to return to the world.

'I'm sorry to call so late, but I thought you'd be glad to hear the news.'

'About what?'

'A witness has come forward who saw the accident.'

Rinaldo slammed down his glass with an exclamation of triumph. 'At last! Now the truth will come out. No more lies! Why hasn't this witness spoken up before?'

'He was afraid to. He'd been visiting a lady in her husband's absence.'

Rinaldo grunted.

'He slipped out at dawn and was walking along the

road when he saw a red, open-topped car approach. Everything in his statement confirms Signorina Easton's story. He says the car was travelling south, towards Rome—'

'What?' Rinaldo's voice was full of incredulity. He stared at Forselli, tense with baffled rage. 'Are you sure?'

'Completely. According to him the driver was a woman, with a man beside her. He saw the man grab the wheel, then the car began to slew across the road until the movements became so violent that it spun into the air, overturned twice and came to rest facing in the opposite direction. He ran back to his lady friend, called the police on her phone, and vanished.

'I must admit, I thought Signorina Easton's story sounded highly unlikely. After all, why should Toni seize the wheel like that? It would mean—'

'Never mind,' Rinaldo said harshly.

Gino Forselli coughed and added cautiously, 'There'll be no charges. Since I understand that this woman is— shall we say—close to your family, I wanted to be the first to tell you the good news.'

'Yes,' Rinaldo said heavily. 'Good news.'

Donna worried constantly about Piero. He alone had smiled and welcomed her, and she had brought him grief. Nurse Alicia said that Piero was 'as well as can be expected'. But she refused to reveal any more, and Donna had the feeling she was obeying Rinaldo's instructions.

She had better luck with her night nurse, Bianca, who had a chatty disposition, and let slip that Piero was at the far end of the building, on the next floor up. Donna didn't allow her interest to show in her face, but at dawn she slipped out of her ward and made her way towards the stairs that led up to the next floor.

She passed down corridor after corridor, studying the names on each door, her heart thumping with apprehension. She wasn't sure what would happen when she found Piero. She only knew that she must tell the kindly old man how sorry she was.

At last she reached a door bearing the card 'Signor Piero Mantini'. Now she was here her nerve nearly failed her, but she pulled herself together and softly turned the handle.

The room was almost dark, but she could just make out Piero's frail figure on the bed. He was lying with his eyes closed, pain and weariness written on his face. Tears stung her eyes as she remembered him as she'd last seen him, full of life and jollity. Now he looked as if the will to live had gone, and she had helped to do this to him.

Suddenly Donna felt that she'd done a terrible thing in intruding on him. Why should he want to see her? She turned and almost collided head on with Rinaldo. She gasped, for she hadn't seen him.

'What the devil are you doing here?' he snapped. 'Is nowhere safe from you?'

'I wanted to tell him how sorry I am,' she said desperately.

'And will your crocodile tears make any difference?'

'My feeling for him is real,' she insisted in a low, hurried voice. 'And if—if he understood that, it might ease his pain.'

'You don't know what you're talking about. Get out before I throw you out.'

There was a faint movement from the bed. Rinaldo swiftly went to Piero's side. 'It's all right, Nonno,' he

said in a voice whose gentleness fell strangely on
Donna's ears after the harsh way he'd spoken to her.
'Everything's all right. I'm here.'

Piero was trying to say something, but Donna could
see that the stroke had left him paralysed. She looked at
him in helpless pity, and began to back out of the room.
But he saw her and all at once he was transfixed. His
mouth contorted and frantic, frustrated sounds emerged
from it. At first she thought he was distressed, but then
she saw that he was fighting to raise an arm from the
bed, reaching out to her.

Ignoring Rinaldo's displeasure, she went forward and
gathered his hand between hers, smiling at him in reassurance. 'I've been worried about you,' she said softly.
'When they told me you were ill I had to come and see
you—'

Tears threatened her. She fought them back and continued in a choking voice, 'I know how much you loved
Toni. I loved him too.' She spoke without deception. At
this moment her feelings for the dead boy came rushing
back, and the final moments, when she'd turned against
him, were forgotten. 'I wish it could all have been different,' she said huskily. 'I wish you hadn't had to be
hurt—I wish—' She couldn't go on.

Piero answered, not with his mouth but with his eyes,
which softened and told her that he didn't hate her. After
the verbal battering she'd suffered from Rinaldo, Piero's
gentle forgiveness was balm to her soul.

'You should go now,' Rinaldo said, speaking quietly
but with an inflexible hardness in his voice. 'My grandfather is tired.'

'But he's trying to say something,' Donna said. She
hadn't taken her eyes off Piero's face.

With a terrible effort he fought to speak but only the

vague shapes of words emerged. Donna thought she made out the sound of 'baby'.

'The baby's fine,' she said, and knew by the glow in the old man's eyes that she'd said the right thing. Inspired, she placed his hand over her stomach. 'Still there,' she said. 'It would take more than an accident to finish off your great-grandchild.'

She felt Rinaldo stiffen beside her. She knew the words 'your great-grandchild' were provocative but she didn't care. She was speaking the truth.

Piero's eyelids drooped and the brightness died out of his face, leaving his skin grey. Donna felt Rinaldo's touch on her arm and looked up to find him indicating the door with his head. Impulsively she leaned down and kissed Piero's cheek before following Rinaldo out of the room. Outside the door she turned to face him, expecting condemnation. But his expression was blank and unreadable.

'Come with me,' he said.

When they were back in her own room Rinaldo said quietly, 'I don't understand anything about you. My grandfather was like a dead man. Then you appear, the woman who injured him, and suddenly he returns to life. It makes no sense.'

'It does to me,' Donna said. 'He has a loving heart. He isn't filled with bitterness as you are, Rinaldo. And I'm carrying Toni's child. He knows that, even if you don't, and it calls him back to life.'

She turned away, trying to escape the sensation of being overpowered that she had whenever she was near him.

'And when you've gone?' Rinaldo demanded. 'What will call him back to life then?'

'You'll have to do that.'

'I have no power to do so,' he said sombrely. 'It was always Toni with him.'

'I'll bring the baby to show him, if you'll let me. I know you think I'm lying, but I swear—' She stopped, for he had put up a hand.

'I had a call from the police last night,' he said. 'There was a witness to your accident.'

'And?' she asked tensely.

'I didn't believe you were telling the truth. Now it seems that I must. He confirms that you were driving back to Rome, and also—the other things you said.'

Donna sat down on the bed. The suddenness of the news had knocked her off balance. After a moment she looked up at Rinaldo, and found no softening in his expression. A rigid sense of honour had forced him to admit what he knew, but his hostility to her was unabated.

'So there's nothing to stop me going,' she said.

'There's everything to stop you going,' he said harshly. 'You're carrying my brother's child. I suppose I have to accept that now.'

'Because you've discovered that I was telling the truth about the accident?' she asked angrily. 'There's no connection.'

But there was a connection, and they both knew it. His picture of her as devious and deceitful had taken a knock, and he was no longer so convinced of his own judgement. She should have felt a sense of triumph. Instead she longed to get away from him, back to the safety of her own country. Once she'd dreamed of coming to Italy, but its stormy passions had defeated her. Now she only wanted to escape.

'I'm glad you believe me,' she said. 'But it makes no real difference.'

He stared at her. 'Of course it makes a difference. Do

you think I'll allow my brother's child—perhaps his son—to be born out of wedlock? Such a thing is unthinkable; a dishonour.'

'Toni is dead. I can't marry him.'

'Of course not,' he said coldly. 'It is necessary that you marry me.'

She stared at him in outrage. 'If that's a joke, it's the unfunniest joke I've ever heard.'

He looked at her as though she'd said something in a foreign language. 'I do not make jokes,' he said flatly.

'Then you must be mad.'

'I was never more sane. It's the only possible solution.'

'Oh, no, it isn't! I've told you, I'm going back to England.'

His face tightened and she thought he would argue, but instead he relaxed again and merely said, 'In your present condition? How do you expect to travel?'

'Not now, but in a few days—'

'Very well. In a few days we'll discuss the matter again. I advise you to give my suggestion serious consideration.'

'Was it a suggestion?' she asked ironically. 'It sounded more of a diktat to me.'

'Well, I can't force you, can I?' he replied smoothly. 'I can only suggest and ask you to consider. Once we're married your child will be born legitimate. Your own life will be comfortable. Why should you refuse?'

'Why?' she echoed, scandalised. 'Because you've been my enemy from the first moment. Because there could never be peace between us. Because I dislike you intensely.'

He shrugged. 'I too have no liking for you. This is a matter of propriety. I don't wish Toni's child to be born a bastard. This is Italy, *signorina*. Such things matter here.'

'But I shan't be here,' she reminded him firmly.

He sighed impatiently. 'Very well, let's drop the subject. But don't be in too much of a hurry to leave. Your visit did my grandfather some good. Perhaps if you return often he'll start to improve. You owe him that.'

'Yes, I do,' she agreed instantly. 'I'm happy to do anything I can for him. He was so kind to me.'

'Good. I'll leave now, but I'll return later.'

He departed, leaving Donna's head aching. The discovery of Piero's condition, his warm response to her through the devastation of his illness, the knowledge that a witness to the accident had cleared her, and finally Rinaldo's shattering, outrageous proposal—all these had left her too shaken to think.

The worst of all was the suggestion that she should marry her enemy. For he was still her enemy. He'd made no bones about that. And her own hostility to him was so sharp that it pervaded her whole being. Marriage to a man she hated? No! Not for anything in the world.

But her indignation was pierced by a treacherous memory that returned insistently, despite her attempts to shut it out. That first night, they'd sat together by the fountain and he'd told her that she would never belong to Toni.

'You've known it from the moment we met.'

He'd touched her face with his fingertips, sending flickers of fire through her body, murmuring words she'd feared yet longed to hear.

'You're not a girl but a woman. You need a man.'

'Not you,' she'd protested.

But it could have been him. This was the man who

might have brought her heart and body to life. If only things had been different…

She gave herself a shake and came back to reality. It was too late. It had been too late even before they met. Now they were foes, and the brief, treacherous attraction was consigned to the limbo of might-have-been. She belonged to Toni, who had loved her in his own way, and whose death lay on her conscience more than she would admit to Rinaldo.

It was he who'd caused the accident, but perhaps if she'd handled the situation better he might not have panicked. Or if she'd never come into his life at all he would be alive now. That was the burden she carried. And the weight of it would crush her again whenever she looked at Toni's brother.

CHAPTER FIVE

SOON after breakfast Alicia came in with a wheelchair. 'I've come to move you,' she said. 'You've been assigned a different ward, next to Signor Piero.'

Donna didn't have to ask who'd ordered that. It made perfect sense, but Rinaldo's high-handedness annoyed her. She seethed in silence as she collected her things and let Alicia settle her into the wheelchair.

Her new room was pleasant, especially when her possessions had been delivered. Donna immediately limped next door. Evidently the nurse had been warned to expect her arrival, for she ushered her in with a smile. It seemed that any arrangement made by Rinaldo went smoothly.

Piero was lying asleep. Donna sat quietly by the bed, and stayed without moving. 'How bad is he?' she asked the nurse.

'At first we thought he would die, but he's held on. I think he'll live, but it will only be a half life. He's mostly paralysed, and he can't speak except to make a few sounds.'

Once he opened his eyes and smiled at Donna, but he went back to sleep straight away, and she returned next door.

In the evening Rinaldo visited his grandfather, then came to see her. 'Is this to your liking?' he asked, looking at her surroundings.

'It's a nice room, but it would have been more to my

liking if you'd mentioned it to me first, instead of just having me fetched like a parcel.'

'It didn't occur to me that you would object.'

'I only object to not having been consulted. And what about the person who was already in here?'

'I assure you it was very easily fixed.'

'You mean you gave your orders and everyone jumped,' she said crossly.

'That's usually how I manage my affairs,' he replied, with a touch of surprise. 'Why not?'

'Why not indeed? But not me. I'll do all I can for Piero, because I like him. But as soon as I'm well enough I'm going.'

He gave a slight shrug. 'Have I said otherwise?'

'As long as we understand each other.'

'How are you feeling?'

'I'm improving very fast, thank you.'

'And the baby?'

'The baby is doing well.'

'Take good care of him.'

That made her very angry. 'Do you think I need you to tell me to care for my own child?'

'But it's not only yours, is it?'

'Legally it is.'

'You mean to shut Toni's family out completely?' he asked in a voice that might almost have been indifferent.

'Let's just say I won't let you interfere. I thought I'd already made that plain.'

'Yes,' he said. 'You did. Very plain. But I hope your dislike of me won't make you leave hospital too soon. You should remain here for another couple of weeks, for your child's sake.' His voice was coolly ironical. 'Am I allowed to suggest that, or am I being unbearably high-handed?'

'This is a private hospital, isn't it? I don't like the fact that the expense falls on you.'

'I do it for Toni. Can't you find it in your heart to allow me that?'

'If you put it that way, I have no choice.'

'You are all graciousness. And if the expense worries you repay me by caring for Piero.' A wintry look came over his face. 'Your company does him more good than mine. I'll trouble you as little as possible.'

Slightly to her surprise, he kept his word over the next fortnight. He visited Piero each day. If Donna was there she would slip away to leave them alone. He would look in for five minutes before his departure, and enquire politely after her health. His manner was coolly civil, and he uttered no barbed words.

Once, while Donna was sitting with Piero, holding his hand and talking to him gently, she looked up to find Rinaldo regarding her with a dark expression. He'd entered the room unheard. Now she'd caught him off guard. Unhappiness shadowed his face, but for once there was no anger there, and when he realised that she was looking at him he took a deep breath and seemed to come out of a dream.

'Is he any better?' he asked her.

'He's getting stronger every day. He still can't talk, or move very much, but he speaks to me with his eyes.' She rose from her seat. 'I'll leave you now.'

'There's no need.'

'No, you'll want to be alone with him,' she said, slipping quickly out of the room.

That was how it was between them—restrained courtesy, not meeting each other's eyes, except by accident, as though each was secretly afraid of what they would find there. In this way the time slipped away peacefully. The only agitation was Donna's discovery that she couldn't find her passport, but this soon reappeared, having been mislaid during the move, and later found in a locker.

With a shock she realised that over three weeks had passed. Soon she must move on, and the thought that troubled her most was how to tell Piero. He was almost well enough to go home. Rinaldo had briefly informed her that the preparations were in train—his room had been adapted for a disabled man, and the nurses engaged. And on the day he left the hospital she would say goodbye to him.

She tried to prepare his mind one day. 'We won't be able to talk like this much longer,' she said gently. 'You'll be going home in a few days and—well, everything is going to change.'

He smiled. Donna took a deep breath. This was going to be harder than she'd expected.

'It will be different for me too,' she said cautiously. 'You see—' She stopped as she became aware that Piero was trying to move his hand. At last he managed to point to Donna's left hand. With dismay she realised that he was indicating her wedding finger. Indistinct sounds came from him as he struggled to enunciate a word.

'*M-m-moglie*—' he managed at last.

She was astounded. *Moglie* was the Italian word for wife, but she wasn't going to be a wife. Could Piero's mind be wandering? Had he not, after all, realised that Toni was dead?

'Piero,' she said gently, 'I can't be Toni's wife...'

'R-Rinaldo—' he managed.

She stared at him as some glimmer of the dreadful truth got through to her. But her mind refused to accept

it. Surely even Rinaldo wouldn't dare do such a dicta-
torial, outrageous thing?

But the question answered itself. Of course he would
dare. Why not? He was used to getting his own way,
simply riding over the opposition if necessary. Her refusal had been merely a temporary inconvenience.

Her anger was so overpowering that she knew she
must get out at once. Piero mustn't be upset.

'I'll—be back soon,' she said, and left quickly.

Once in her own room she sat on the edge of the bed,
shivering with her inner turmoil. It wasn't just anger that
consumed her, but a kind of shocked awe at the lengths
to which Rinaldo was prepared to go. For the last few
weeks he'd let her think he'd forgotten his incredible
proposal, and all the time he'd been making plans to
brush her opposition aside as something of no importance.

Someone was coming along the corridor and going
into Piero's room. After a while Rinaldo entered her
room, closed the door behind him, and stood looking at
her.

Donna returned his gaze.

'I didn't misunderstand, did I?' she snapped. 'Piero is
expecting us to marry. You've been arranging a wedding
all this time, even after I made it clear that I'd have
nothing to do with it?'

'I have.'

'Is that all you can say?'

'There is nothing else to say. I hadn't planned for you
to find out like this. I didn't know Piero could communicate enough to tell you.'

'I wonder when you did plan to tell me?' she demanded indignantly. 'Halfway to the church?'

'Look, I understand that you're annoyed—'

'I hope you understand my annoyance rather better than you understood my refusal. Has nobody ever said no to you before, Rinaldo? Is that why you don't recognise the word?'

'I was sure you'd come to your senses when your health had improved. It was sensible to set things in train. So I did.'

'Including telling your grandfather? That was utterly unscrupulous.'

'It's given him something to live for. It would break his heart if I let you leave.'

'What do you mean, "let" me leave? I don't need your permission. I shall just go.'

'That I will not allow,' he said simply.

'*You* won't—? Who are you to allow me or not allow me? I don't take your orders.'

His dark eyes flashed and for a moment she saw a glimpse of the imperial authority that had once made Rome great. 'Donna, it's time we understood each other. I'm not asking you for your consent to this marriage. I'm telling you that neither of us has any choice. This is something we have to do—'

'I don't have to do it,' she said desperately. 'There's always a choice—'

'Very well, then,' he said impatiently. 'It was my decision and I've made it for the honour of my family and the welfare of my brother's child. You cannot refuse.'

'Try me.'

'Toni wouldn't want you to refuse. He loved you. He'd want you and his child to be safe.'

She drew a swift, painful breath. 'How could you sink so low as to use Toni as a weapon?'

'I'm not using him as a weapon,' he said harshly. 'I'm reminding you of your obligation to him. He'd be glad that I'm going to protect his family. In this country family counts for a lot.'

Donna turned away, covering her ears with her hands, trying to shut him out, but it was in vain. This man's power was hypnotic. He could make the most outrageous demands sound reasonable. There was no escape from him.

He moved swiftly, turning her towards him, pulling her hands down, forcing her to listen to him. 'Listen to me. The wedding is set for the day after tomorrow. There's no point in arguing.'

She stared at him in outraged disbelief. '*The day after*— How could even you arrange that? Aren't there formalities—?'

'Of course. But in view of your state of health the officials didn't insist on your being personally present. Your passport was enough.'

'My—*you stole my passport*?'

'Borrowed it, since I believe it has now been returned to you.'

'So that was why it disappeared. How dare you?'

'It was necessary,' he said impatiently. 'I couldn't make the arrangements without it.'

'Then you should have spared yourself the trouble. I'm leaving tomorrow, and that's the last you'll ever see of me.'

Instead of repeating his insistence Rinaldo studied his nails for a moment. When he lifted his head his face was unreadable. 'Perhaps you're right,' he said. 'It was foolish of me to think you would submit to force. I admired your spirit the night we met.'

She breathed a little more easily. 'I'm glad you understand.'

He gave her a strange look. 'You and I understood each other from the beginning, didn't we, Donna?'

'I—don't understand you.'

'Don't you? Was it all in my imagination, then?'

His eyes held hers, reminding her of things she would rather forget.

'Have you never wondered,' Rinaldo went on, 'what would have happened if we'd met some other way?'

She gave a little sigh. 'We'll never know. It doesn't matter now. There are too many barriers between us. I was Toni's woman.'

'But you wouldn't have been—if I'd met you first.'

Suddenly she saw the danger and backed away from it. This was another of his unscrupulous schemes. 'You're a clever man, Rinaldo,' she said. 'Luckily for me, I know how clever you are.'

He gave a wry laugh. 'I didn't take you in, did I?'

'Not for a minute. I know there are no lengths you wouldn't go to to get what you want.'

He shrugged. 'Well, I'd better tell my grandfather that the wedding is off.'

'Will he mind very much?'

He stopped at the door. 'Yes, he'll mind very much. But that's no longer any concern of yours.' He went out.

Donna stayed where she was, racked by feelings that pulled her in ten directions at once. She knew she'd done the right thing, but the thought of Piero's pain hurt her.

After a few minutes Rinaldo reappeared. 'He wants to see you.'

The old man gave a crooked smile as she entered. 'How did he take it?' Donna asked in a low voice so that Piero couldn't hear.

'I haven't told him,' Rinaldo said. 'You're going to tell him.'

She gasped and tried to pull away, but Rinaldo's hands were firm on her shoulders, blocking her escape. He'd outmanoeuvred her again.

'Say it,' Rinaldo repeated with soft vehemence. 'Break his heart. Tell him that the dream that's kept him alive is over.'

'How could you do this?' she breathed.

'Because our marriage *has* to take place. Haven't you understood that yet?'

He urged her to the bed. His grip was superficially light, but she could feel the steely strength in the arm about her shoulders. Donna took a deep breath. She must tell Piero the truth now, before another moment passed.

But the words died before the shining look in his eyes. She had done this to him, and she couldn't hurt him more.

Feebly Piero stretched out his good hand to her. She took it and dropped to her knees beside the bed. He was struggling to speak.

'Figlia,' he said at last, softly.

Despite her turmoil her heart leapt at the word. *Figlia.* Daughter. Not even granddaughter, but daughter. It was years since anyone had called her that. Suddenly she was shaken by sobs. She lifted the frail hand in her own and laid her cheek against it, wetting it with her tears. She knew she couldn't fight any longer. Rinaldo had trapped her, just as he'd always meant to.

'He's trying to say something else,' Rinaldo said.

Donna looked up and released Piero's hand so that he could point. He indicated her and then Rinaldo, and whispered, *'Bene.'* Good. Piero had given them his blessing.

His lips continued to move, and Donna thought he was repeating, *'Bene.'* Then she realised that he was saying another word that began with B. At last she made it out, and to her horror realised that the word was '*bacio*'. Kiss.

'What is he saying?' Rinaldo asked. 'I can't hear.'

'It's nothing,' she said hastily.

'Let me be the judge of that.'

Piero managed to raise his voice a little. '*Bacio,*' he repeated huskily.

Donna rose and moved away from the bed, but Rinaldo detained her with a hand on her arm. 'My grandfather wants us to kiss,' he said.

'*No,*' she said, speaking quietly with her face averted. 'I couldn't. *I couldn't.* How can he ask such a thing when he knows—?'

'You misunderstand. What Piero wants from us is a kiss not of passion but of tenderness. He knows that we're marrying for Toni's sake, but he needs to feel that there can be peace between us.'

'Peace?' she whispered, looking at him out of stormy eyes. 'Peace between us?'

'You're right,' he murmured. 'Such peace was never meant to be. But we can pretend for his sake.'

She didn't try to resist as he drew her closer and placed his fingers under her chin. 'Look up at me,' he murmured.

Unwillingly she did so. His eyes were dark and they seemed to draw her in. Rinaldo bent his head and laid his lips gently against hers.

His mouth barely touched her, and yet she felt as if a burning brand had seared her. She wanted to escape from him, but she couldn't move. Her senses were reeling from the feel of him. His lips were warm and firm. Once again the thought would not be denied. This was a man, not a boy. There was strength and purpose in the way he held her, one hand on her shoulder, the other behind her head.

She should never have agreed to this kiss. Marriage to Rinaldo would only be tolerable if she could shut out all awareness of him as a man she might have loved, in another life. But how could she ignore such things when his lips were on hers and she could feel the power of his body against her own? Her pulse was racing, and her whole body seemed to be caught up in the hot, insistent rhythm.

If only he would stop, she thought wildly. But she didn't want him to stop. She wanted this kiss to go on for ever, thrilling her with the sweet, new sensations. They possessed her utterly, revealing depths of awareness within herself that she'd never dreamed of before. And it was all too late. Now, in the very moment that she'd agreed to marry him, she knew that the barriers would always be between them.

He released her. Donna looked up into his face and saw on it a dark look that she couldn't understand. Was he as shaken as herself? Or was he merely angry? Perhaps he'd sensed her reaction to him, and despised her for it. She pulled away from him, trying to get command of herself.

Piero was smiling contentedly. His lips shaped Rinaldo's name.

'Yes, Nonno,' Rinaldo said at once.

With his eyes Piero indicated the little table at his bedside, on which stood a tiny box. When Rinaldo opened it he discovered the emerald and ruby ring that Piero had given Donna the first night.

'He wants you to have this again,' Rinaldo said.

Donna nodded. She was beyond words. Rinaldo took her hand and spoke softly.

'There's no guard on the door, Donna. Despite what I've said, if you really refuse to marry me, no one will stop you leaving. Now is the time to say.'

'You know I can't,' she whispered.

He gripped her hand. 'Let me hear you say that you will marry me.'

'I'll marry you.'

He slipped the ring onto her finger, and she knew that now there was no turning back.

The next day—the day before the wedding—both she and Piero left hospital and returned to the Villa Mantini. Rinaldo had engaged two nurses to care for Piero, but Donna stayed with him until he was comfortably settled in his room. He seemed happier when she was there.

He was not to attend the wedding in the town hall. Normally this would be followed by a religious service, but Rinaldo had decreed that a civil ceremony would be enough, and Donna was glad. To have entered this incongruous marriage in church would have felt like sacrilege.

To her surprise Selina had insisted that the honour of attending the bride should fall to her.

'She does this as a gesture of friendship,' Rinaldo explained. 'It means a great deal to her.'

'What have you told her?' Donna asked.

Rinaldo looked surprised. 'The truth, of course. I couldn't hope to deceive her. She knows you were engaged to Toni.'

'What about the rest of the world?'

'The rest of the world won't dare to ask.'

'But surely they'll wonder?'

'At first. With luck, in time the details will fade and people will assume the child is mine.'

'Unless Selina entertains them with the truth,' Donna said a little sharply.

'I don't know why you've taken against her,' Rinaldo said, annoyed. 'She's a friend of mine and she wants to show you nothing but kindness.'

'But it isn't natural,' Donna protested. 'Toni told me she wanted to marry you herself.'

'Toni had to dramatise everything,' Rinaldo said impatiently. 'If Selina wanted to marry me she could have done so thirteen years ago.'

'But you *were* in love with her?'

'Madly, desperately,' Rinaldo said in an indifferent voice. 'In love as only a boy of twenty can be in love. She turned me down to take up a film part. She was perfectly right. Our marriage wouldn't have been a success. She said I was possessive—which I was. She wanted to follow her star. Those days are over. Now she's my friend, and I ask you to treat her civilly. Is that too much to ask?'

'Of course not,' Donna said. 'And after all—it's none of my business.'

'That's true,' Rinaldo said after a moment.

On the wedding day Selina arrived early, all smiles, and embraced Donna with every appearance of warmth. She insisted on doing her hair, and did it expertly. But the style was fussy and didn't suit her. Selina herself was dressed in cream silk and pearls, with a large hat. Her face was flawlessly made up, and radiant, as though she were the bride.

Enrico drove the three of them to the town hall. He was Maria's nephew, a big, cheerful man whom his aunt usually referred to as 'that idiot'. He did gardening, driving and odd jobs.

When they arrived Rinaldo went away to complete

some formality. Donna and Selina were left awkwardly together. Donna caught a glimpse of herself in a mirror. As she'd suspected, the fussy hairdo was unbecoming.

'I wish I'd had more time to work on your appearance,' Selina sighed. 'You should have had a proper dress.'

'I appreciate all you've done,' Donna said, trying to be polite. 'But I'd rather everything was kept very simple. This isn't—quite like other weddings.'

'Of course. Rinaldo has explained everything to me. He marries you because he must. Otherwise he and I—' She broke off with a shrug. 'I'm a realist. And so—I hope—are you.'

'What do you mean?'

'Oh, come. We're both women of the world. Rinaldo is a man with a strong sense of duty and family honour. It makes him do what otherwise he wouldn't have dreamed of doing. After all, you're as indifferent to him as he is to you, but you're marrying him for the sake of your baby. I admire you for it.' She gave her a dazzling smile. 'I think you have the soul of a good mother. You know what they say. Some women are born to be wives, and some to be mothers.'

'And some to be mistresses?' Donna added lightly.

Selina beamed at her. 'I knew we'd understand each other. But then, you're much brighter than you look, aren't you?'

'I'm certainly brighter than you think I am,' Donna said firmly.

There was no more chance to talk, and no need for it, Donna realised. Everything had been communicated in those few minutes. Now all that was left was for her to walk to her meaningless wedding to a man who cared nothing for her, and try to come to terms with the shocking feelings that had destroyed her peace.

Donna moved through her wedding day in a dream, and afterwards could recall nothing clearly. At some time in her uneasy trance she and Rinaldo stood before civic officials and spoke the words that made them husband and wife in the eyes of the law. Donna thought of Toni, who should have been there with her. Would their marriage have stood any more or less of a chance of success than this strange, incredible union?

Throughout it all she was conscious of Selina, radiant in her beauty, a stark contrast to Donna's pallor and unease.

Then came the journey home in the car, with the three of them trying not to be self-conscious; Selina chattering away while the bride and groom avoided each other's eye.

At the Villa Mantini they went through the semblance of a marriage feast, but Donna escaped as soon as she decently could, using Piero as an excuse. She saw him settled for the night and stayed talking to him for a while. He indicated for her to return downstairs, but she shook her head.

'I'd rather stay with you,' she said simply.

She wondered what the other two were talking about. Was Rinaldo looking at Selina and contrasting her with his dull bride? Suddenly Donna was too tired to care. It had been a full day, and she was four months pregnant.

With a blinding sense of revelation it dawned on her that she had the answer to her stormy feelings. How many times had she advised newly expectant mothers about this very thing?

'There are so many hormone changes going on inside you just now,' she'd said to them, 'that it'll probably make you more emotional than usual. Don't worry about it. You'll settle down eventually.'

Of course. That was it. The sudden riot of her feelings really had nothing to do with Rinaldo. It was an illusion brought about by her pregnancy. To think that she'd been afraid that she might fall in love with him! And all the time it had simply been a clinical phase. The relief was so great that she nearly laughed out loud.

From down below she could hear noises. Looking out of the window, she saw Rinaldo's car, which Enrico had brought to the front door. Selina stepped inside, and Enrico drove her away. A few minutes later she heard Rinaldo mounting the stairs.

'I said goodbye to Selina for you,' he told her as he came into Piero's room.

'Thank you.' Donna kissed Piero. 'I'll go to bed now. I'm very tired.'

Rinaldo held the door open for her, and she returned to her bedroom. His own sleeping arrangements hadn't been mentioned between them, and it occurred to her how few things they had actually discussed. But one didn't discuss things with Rinaldo. One listened while he laid down the law. To her relief there was no sign of his things in her room.

Half an hour later there was a knock on her door, and Rinaldo's voice called, 'May I come in?'

She was in her dressing gown, and had pulled the elaborate hairdo down. 'Yes, come in,' she replied.

He too had undressed for bed. He was wearing a silk dressing gown over pyjamas whose open edges revealed the thick hairs on his chest. Donna felt a jolt of pleasure before she could suppress it. However much she disliked Rinaldo, he was an attractive male animal. She was glad that she'd remembered in time that the attraction wasn't real, but merely the result of her turbulent hormones.

'Are you all right?' he asked. 'The day hasn't tired you too much?'

'I'm perfectly well, thank you,' she said politely.

'Is there anything you need?'

'No, thank you.'

'Then I'll bid you goodnight.'

'Goodnight.'

She had a feeling that he wanted to say something else, but after hesitating for a few moments he went away.

CHAPTER SIX

DONNA was woken by the chiming of bells. She rose and went to the window, throwing open the shutters on a magical scene. Her view was over the countryside. Far away rose the seven hills of Rome. Nearby there were winding roads, and villages with little churches whose bell chimes were carried to her in the clear dawn air. A soft light lay over the countryside. Donna was silent, awed by so much beauty.

From here she could see the Mantini land. Close by the house, shaded by trees, lay some ground that had been separated from the rest by railings. This was the family burial plot. It was here that she would find Toni.

She dressed quickly, noticing that the clothes she'd worn before her spell in hospital were tighter. Before she left the room she took her little wedding posy from the vase where she'd placed it the night before.

It wasn't hard to find the plot. There were the head-stones of Giorgio and Loretta Mantini, and a few others who appeared, from their dates, to be grandparents, aunts and uncles. And there, flat on the ground, was a square marble slab, newer than all the rest.

Beneath it lay all that remained of the vital boy who'd filled her life with love and laughter, however briefly. She no longer imagined herself in love with him, but she was torn with pity for his fate. Toni had been irresponsible, and weak. But he'd also been kind and generous in his careless fashion. He'd deserved better than this.

Donna held the posy against her face for a moment, and when she laid it on the tomb it was wet with her tears.

'I'm sorry,' she whispered. 'I'm so very sorry.'

She had an overwhelming awareness of another presence, and when she glanced up she saw Rinaldo, watching her. But he moved back into the shadows before she could speak, and when she next looked he was gone.

They met properly at breakfast. Rinaldo was there first, seated at the long table in the dining room. He rose and courteously pulled out a chair for her, opposite him.

'We won't usually eat together in the mornings,' he said. 'I leave for work very early, before the day becomes too hot. I'll be home at about eight o'clock in the evening, and we should be seen to dine together. You need have no fear of my troubling you at other times.'

She wasn't sure how to respond to this last remark, but Rinaldo didn't seem to need an answer. He was telling her how he'd arranged her life, and there was nothing for her to do but acquiesce.

'I have something here that requires your signature,' he said, pushing papers towards her. 'I've opened a bank account for you. The money will be available to you tomorrow.'

She stared when she saw the amount. 'I shan't need that much,' she protested.

'Nonsense, of course you will,' he said with a brusqueness that robbed the words of any amiability. '*My wife* is expected to dress well, and that takes money. Please don't argue about this.'

'Very well.'

'You'll also need to buy things for the baby. Just sign there, and then I must be going. You'll find a parcel in your room. It arrived from England this morning.'

He stuffed the signed papers into his briefcase, and

departed. Donna had a light breakfast of coffee and rolls, then hurried upstairs, eager to investigate the parcel.

As she'd suspected, it came from a friend who had a key to the flat she'd recently shared with Toni. He'd gathered up some letters that had arrived there, and sent them on.

There were a couple of minor items for herself, and several credit card statements for Toni. The amounts gave her a shock. She'd always known that her lover was a spendthrift, but she hadn't imagined anything like this. His debts were at least three times what he'd admitted to her, and in addition there was a letter from the finance company about his car. Toni had fallen behind again with the repayments, and now the whole amount was due.

She couldn't think straight at the moment. She thrust everything back into the big envelope and went along the corridor to Piero's room. He was dressed, and sitting in a wheelchair by the window, Sasha purring on his lap. His weary face lit up at the sight of her. His love was the one bright spot in a lonely world, and it was going to have to be enough to help her endure the next few months.

She spent the morning with him. While she was eating a light lunch Maria told her what she was planning for the evening meal. Did the *patrona* approve?

'It sounds lovely,' Donna said.

'Grazie, patrona.'

Maria vanished at once, leaving Donna puzzled by the feeling that she'd wanted to escape. When she'd first come here she'd thought she had Maria's goodwill, but now the old woman seemed very anxious to get away from her. Did she too blame her, and regard her as a schemer?

Most of the afternoon was spent writing to her neighbour, and taking a nap. In the evening Rinaldo returned. When he'd visited Piero husband and wife dined formally together downstairs. He was polite, but nothing more. It was a relief when he asked her to excuse him, as he'd brought work home.

That first day set the pattern for the others that followed. Occasionally she would see Rinaldo at breakfast. More often she would hear his car leave early, and eat alone. She spent as much time as possible with Piero. His nurses were at first inclined to regard Donna as a well-meaning amateur. But when they learned of her professional qualifications and, more importantly, saw her with Piero they relaxed. Soon they were deferring to her.

She set herself to improve his condition, but the stroke had been a massive one, leaving him almost entirely paralysed. Sometimes he could force out the rough semblance of a word, but the effort tired him, and the odd word wasn't enough to put him in touch with the world. He was a man with a subtle brain and complex thoughts, and the frustration of not being able to communicate properly was terrible for him.

Donna read to him, talked to him, or just sat with him listening to the radio or watching television. To Donna's dismay, he showed no signs of regaining his abilities. He had stabilised but that was all. It seemed as if he faced a lifetime entombed in his own unresponsive body.

One evening she was sitting with him, listening to music and contentedly scratching Sasha's ears. It was late but Rinaldo was still not home, and soon she would go to bed. She looked at Piero, who was lying with his eyes closed, wondering if he'd gone to sleep. Then she noticed that the fingers of his left hand were softly beating time to the music.

The sight riveted her. Piero had been able to move his arm a little, but not individual fingers. But now the fingers were making clear, separate movements, and it gave her a flash of inspiration.

'Piero,' she said urgently. He opened his eyes. 'Look.' She took his hand and placed it in her own. 'Can you draw a letter—any letter?'

Instantly his eyes were alert. Slowly, with infinite concentration, he shaped a letter in her palm with the tip of his forefinger. It was a D.

'Another,' she said excitedly.

He shaped an O. Then, without waiting for her to urge him further, he drew an N, and another, and an A. Donna.

'You can talk,' she said, thrilled. 'You can say anything you want.'

He began to write in her hand again. When he reached the third letter she said, 'Yes, it will be slow. But we can *talk*. That's what matters.'

He began to draw again. *You're clever.*

'No, you're the clever one. Oh, I can't wait for Rinaldo to get home and hear about this.'

Let's talk now.

When Rinaldo returned an hour later he was astonished to hear laughter coming from his grandfather's room. He opened the door on a scene of merriment. Donna was sitting by the bed, raising a glass of orange juice. As Rinaldo watched she clinked it against the glass that Piero was just managing to hold, with her help.

'Here's to us!' she cried. 'We're brilliant.'

'What's happening?' Rinaldo asked.

Donna turned a smiling face on him. 'Piero can talk

again,' she said. She removed Piero's glass, leaving his
hand free. 'Watch.'

Slowly he spelt into her palm, *Thank you, my dear.*

Rinaldo stared for a moment, before raising his head
and looking her directly in the eye. He seemed thunder-
struck. When she stood back he took her place at the
bed. Donna slipped out of the room and left them together.

It was late, and the concentration had tired her more
than she'd realised. She went straight to her room and
lay down, wondering if Rinaldo would come and talk to
her. But soon her eyes closed, and she drifted off to
sleep.

When Rinaldo left his grandfather's room he hesitated
in the corridor. He knew how much Piero's new skill
was due to Donna. Piero himself had told him so, and
expressed his heartfelt relief that she'd stayed with them.
What would we do without her? he'd asked. And Rinaldo
had given a forced smile and said, 'I don't know.'

Now he felt he should see Donna, and thank her, but
he was torn by conflicting feelings. It had been simpler
in the days when he'd felt only hostility towards her, he
reflected. But then disturbing memories came flooding
back, and he knew that there'd never been a time when
his feelings about her had been uncomplicated.

There was no answer to his tap on her door. He turned
the handle and looked in. Donna was lying on the bed,
still with the small table lamp on, as though she'd meant
to stay awake, but couldn't manage it.

Rinaldo moved quietly to the windows and closed the
shutters. Before turning off the lamp he stood for a moment looking down at her face. It was as soft and defenceless as a child's, and for a desperate moment he

wished she would stay one thing or the other, so that he could know what to think about her. But that day might never come. He felt as if he could only see her through distorting filters, which constantly altered.

He switched off the light and left without waking her. Downstairs he wandered out into the grounds, to where the burial plot lay. Pain twisted inside him as he reflected that on the first day after their wedding she'd come to lay her wedding bouquet on his brother's grave. She'd come every day since, with fresh flowers plucked from Loretta's garden. This morning's offering lay there now, its white petals gleaming in the moonlight. He lifted one flower, holding it against his face, and it seemed to him that it was wet with her tears.

Donna spent the next day talking with Piero. Through his new method of communication he was able to tell her why he didn't blame her for the accident.

Toni—bad boy. Charming, lovable, but always in trouble. He said many things—not true—whatever was easiest. Why—crash?

Donna hesitated, unwilling to hurt him with the details, but he wrote in her hand, *Tell me.*

She related the story simply, and when she'd finished he gripped her hand.

I thought—something like that. Not your fault. He always ran away from difficulties.

'Yes, I began to realise,' she said sadly.

You must raise his child to be stronger. Rinaldo will help you. He's a strong man, a good man.

'And a very unforgiving one,' Donna mused. 'Why must he be so unyielding all the time?'

Because he doesn't dare to look into his own heart. You must help him. You loved Toni. Now you must love

Rinaldo—not an easy man to love—but needs love very much.

Something stirred inside her. Would it be so very difficult to love Rinaldo? If she'd met him first, before Toni—

She wouldn't let herself think any more. What was the use? Rinaldo's attitude towards her was still mostly one of distrust and hostility. He'd learned to have some respect for her, but there was no softening in him.

He'd thanked her gravely for helping Piero find a way to 'speak'. 'It means everything to me to see him find some interest in life again,' he'd said the next day. 'You have all my gratitude.' But he'd been full of tension as he'd spoken.

Now that a method had been found, Donna sought other ways to make it easier for Piero. She bought a set of children's alphabet bricks, thinking that he might point to the letters he wanted. But Sasha, convinced that this was a new toy, kept pawing the bricks and confusing everyone. At last the idea was abandoned and Sasha was made a present of the whole set, whereupon she immediately lost interest.

Although Rinaldo loved his grandfather his nature was too impatient for him to sit while letters were spelled out one by one. His contribution was a word processor with a specially enlarged keyboard, upon which Piero could tap out letters. But the keyboard seemed to confuse him. Or perhaps he just preferred people to machines. So this idea too was abandoned, and he continued to write in Donna's palm.

One evening, about a month after their marriage, Donna sat preparing herself for dinner. That afternoon Piero had repeated his insistence that Rinaldo needed love. It was something he told Donna often, watching her closely, as if trying to decide whether it was too soon for her to love him. Despite the difficulties, the words gave her a strange feeling of hope and expectancy. She waited eagerly for his return.

But when he entered the house she knew at once that something was wrong. There was an extra constraint in his manner, and his eyes held an odd glitter. During the meal she several times found him regarding her cynically.

'Is something the matter?' she asked at last.

'Yes. I thought we could wait until later, but since you ask I want explanations from you, and they have to be good.'

The glitter in his eyes had grown more pronounced. There was no doubt of it. This was a man in a furious temper.

'I don't know what I have to explain,' she said.

'Indeed? Well, let's start with the dress you're wearing. It's been cleverly let out, but you never bought it in Italy. In fact I recognise it from our very first meeting. And I'd like to know why you're altering clothes when I gave you money to buy new ones.'

'I—it seemed a waste to buy new clothes before I get much bigger,' she stammered.

'For God's sake!' he exclaimed in disgust. 'Why don't you tell me the truth? You've been sending money to England. I only found out today. Practically every penny I gave you has been passed on to a man called Patrick Harrison. You have ten seconds to tell me who this man is, what he is to you, and why you've given him money from my pocket.'

These days her moods were growing increasingly volatile, and within seconds her temper had risen to match his own. She faced him furiously. 'To pay Toni's debts,' she said bluntly.

'What do you mean?'

'I thought I could do it discreetly. I never meant you to know anything, but I'm not going to stand for being spoken to like that. Wait here.'

'I'm not going anywhere,' he said ironically as she jumped up from the table.

She was back in a couple of minutes with some papers that she tossed onto the table in front of him. They were the letters that had reached her on the first day of their marriage.

'You knew what Toni was like better than I did,' she said. 'I'm surprised this possibility never occurred to you. He left an avalanche of debts behind him. Not just credit cards. He owed a lot on the car.'

'Surely the insurance covered that?'

'There was something wrong with the insurance. Toni hadn't told the truth on the forms, and that gave them the excuse not to pay up. Patrick was our next-door neighbour. We left him the key. He sent all these on to me, and I sent money to pay them.'

Rinaldo's face was full of chagrin. 'You should have told me.'

'I preferred not to.'

'It was my job to settle his debts.'

'You did settle them,' she pointed out.

Rinaldo threw the papers onto the table and took a ragged breath. 'I apologise for the way I spoke to you.'

'Please don't mention it,' she said sharply. 'In due course Patrick will send me the next statements, showing everything paid, and I'll pass them on to you.'

'There's no need. I accept your word.'

She gave a wry smile. 'You accept my word when I

can produce the paperwork to prove it. I wonder if we'll ever see the day when you'll accept my unsupported word?'

He was silent and she thought he didn't mean to answer, but at last he said, 'I was wrong about a good deal. I've admitted that.'

'Very reluctantly.'

'I don't like being wrong.'

'Isn't that a little illogical in our situation?'

'What do you mean?'

'You thought me a devious schemer without a single honest feeling. Would you rather have been right?'

He grimaced. 'If you put it like that, no. You're a disconcerting woman. I never know where you're going to come from next.'

'Maybe I shouldn't have kept all this from you, but—' She made a helpless gesture. 'I suppose you're not the only one with a lot of mistaken pride. I was trying to protect Toni's memory.'

She jumped as his hand slammed down on the table. 'For the love of God, why?' he shouted. 'Why should you protect him? Then or now?'

'Because he needed it,' she cried.

'Was that what you loved about him?' Rinaldo sneered. 'His foolishness? His weakness?'

'Perhaps. I like caring for people, and he needed looking after. He needed *me*. I have to be needed. It's the only way I can live.'

'Is that the kind of man you want, Donna? Not a man at all, but a chick sheltering under your wing? A child in a man's body, clutching your skirts for protection?'

'It's a kind of love.'

He looked at her through narrowed eyes. 'For some

women it's the only kind. Must a man be a weakling before you can love him?'

'He must need me before I can love him,' she said fiercely.

'Some men would sooner be dead than have a woman on those terms.'

'Some men know nothing about love,' she flung at him.

The air between them was jagged. This wasn't about Toni. Donna knew she should end the conversation quickly. She could scent danger, not in him for once, but in herself. She'd been unpredictable moody and emotional for the last few days, and now she could feel her control slipping away.

'And my brother knew about love?' Rinaldo asked cynically.

'In a way, yes, he did. He was kind and affectionate, and gentle. I loved his gentleness.'

'You loved his weakness,' Rinaldo said contemptuously.

'What if I did? Doesn't a weak man have the right to be loved too?'

'And how would it have been in a few years? How attractive would his weakness have seemed when you'd grown tired of having to run to me for help whenever he let you down?'

'I would never have run to you for help,' she said flatly.

'You think you wouldn't.'

'Never. And I wouldn't have let him do it either.'

'How would you have stopped him? It was what he'd done all his life. Do you think you would have made all that much difference?'

Something in her snapped and she flung her next

words at him, never minding what she said if only she could remove the hateful, cynical look from his face. 'Yes, because he'd have clung to me instead of you. He wouldn't have needed you any more, Rinaldo. That's what you really blame me for, isn't it? The fact that *when he died he was trying to escape you.*'

Before the words were out she knew them to be monstrous, unforgivable. She hadn't meant to be cruel, but he'd lashed her with his own cruelty until she'd lashed back. Now she knew she'd done something terrible. Rinaldo looked like a dead man.

'Get out,' he said softly.

'Rinaldo, please—'

'Get out.'

Horrified, she fled the room.

It was two o'clock in the morning. Donna lay awake, listening for Rinaldo climbing the stairs. For hours now he'd been down there, alone with whatever terrible thoughts she'd left him with.

She blamed herself bitterly for what she'd said. It made no difference that she'd merely responded to his own attack. It was her nature to protect and care, and she knew she'd inflicted another wound on an already injured man.

At last she heard him coming upstairs, moving slowly, as if he had to drag himself under the weight of a crushing burden. She sat up as she realised that his footsteps were coming towards her door. There they stopped. Donna waited in the darkness, her heart beating rapidly.

But then the steps moved away again, and a moment later she heard his door close. She lay still, her thoughts going this way and that, giving her no rest. When she couldn't stand it any longer she got up and threw her dressing gown on.

There was still a light under his door. She tapped gently and after a moment heard him say, 'Come in.'

He was standing by the window, a glass of wine in his hand. A bottle stood nearby, and she realised that he'd drunk a good deal. His eyes glittered when he saw her.

'Come to tell me some more unpleasant truths?' he asked softly.

'No, I came to say I'm sorry. I shouldn't have said that.'

'Why not? It's true, isn't it? He was trying to turn the car so that he wouldn't have to come back and face me. You, on the other hand, were determined to face me, and hurl your victory in my face. You've got courage, I'll admit.'

'Nothing's ever that simple,' she said desperately.

'On the contrary. Some things are exactly that simple. I should have acknowledged it before. You told me the facts weeks ago. Somehow I managed to avoid them— which isn't like me. But you have a way of showing a man the ugly truth about himself—' He drained his glass.

'Rinaldo, please—I don't know the truth about you— any more than you know it about me.'

'The truth is that I'm far more to blame for my brother's death than you are,' he said savagely. 'Let's have it out in the open. I crush everyone I care about because I don't know how to do anything else.'

'I don't believe that,' she said.

'Don't you? It's what you've been saying about me from the start. Why should you have changed your mind?'

She didn't know, except that the sight of him in pain appalled her. It was like seeing a lion brought low, and in spite of everything some part of her wanted him to become himself again: arrogant and domineering, even unlikable. A man who had to be fought. But a man, all the same.

He refilled his glass and sat on the bed. 'Why don't you go away?' he growled.

'Because we can't leave it like this,' she said. 'We're both doing our best in a difficult situation, but it's impossible if we're going to attack each other all the time. We have to call a truce. Can't you see that?'

When he didn't reply she sat down beside him. He looked at her, wary, mistrustful.

'Why did you have to come into our lives at all?' he said slowly. 'Why did he have to fall in love with you?'

'I don't know,' she said helplessly.

He set down his glass and put his hand up, touching her hair, studying her face. *'Why?'* he breathed. 'You're not beautiful—passable, but he dated a hundred women prettier than you. None of them turned our lives upside down as you have.'

He stroked her face, tracing the outline of her cheek, her lips. Donna watched him, unable to tear her eyes away. Rinaldo was in a dangerous mood. His usual steely control had slipped, or rather he'd chosen to let it go. There was no knowing what he'd do now. She knew she should break free quickly, but somehow she couldn't move. His movements, and the strange caressing murmur of his voice, held her transfixed. Her heart was beginning to beat hard, its slow rhythm inducing a sense of drowsiness. All this was happening in a dream.

'What are you?' he whispered. 'Are you human or a

cruel spirit sent to torment me? What do you have that makes a man want to—?' He drew a shuddering breath.

Suddenly his hand tightened in her hair, pulling her hard towards him. His other arm came round her shoulders, holding her against his chest while his mouth descended crushingly on hers.

There was no tenderness in his embrace. It was an assertion of authority, of ownership, brooking no refusal. With a movement of alarm she tried to fend him off but he held her tighter while he covered her face with kisses.

'Rinaldo—' she pleaded.

She wasn't sure he heard her. He was murmuring again, looking down into her face with feverish eyes. 'What are you?'

'Just an ordinary woman,' she said hazily. 'Doing her best—floundering a bit—'

'No, you're no ordinary woman. That's just the mask you wear to fool men. Underneath—a devil—a witch—a Madonna—'

She sighed. 'Madonna. Toni said—'

'Don't speak of Toni!' he said fiercely. 'Forget him. He's not here. I am. It's my arms that hold you, my mouth that kisses you. Why can't I—?'

He traced his fingers over her cheek, then down to her breasts, now swollen and voluptuous. She knew he must be able to feel the heated pounding beneath.

He drew her close again. This time his kiss was gentler, his lips caressing hers with soft, teasing purpose. The feeling made her sigh. She must stop him—but not yet—it was so sweet. She whispered his name and immediately his arms tightened, pushing her down onto the bed while he kissed her face, her neck, her breasts. The sensation made her wildly ecstatic. She put her hands behind his head, pressing him closer.

'You should have come to me that first night,' he murmured.

'Too late,' she whispered. 'Always—too late—Toni—'

'Toni is dead.'

'Not dead—not while his child—'

Rinaldo stopped as if something had turned him to stone. Donna could feel him become rigid, then begin to shake, as though with a mighty effort.

'Dio mio!' he whispered. 'What am I doing?'

Slowly he released her and drew back. Donna felt herself come out of a dream to find that he was looking at her with horror. She pulled herself up on the bed and moved away. Rinaldo stayed completely still. He seemed transfixed.

Then he moved suddenly, seizing his wineglass and hurling it through the window. They heard it smash on the stone below.

'Go,' he said hoarsely. 'Go, and lock your bedroom door. For both our sakes, *go!*'

CHAPTER SEVEN

THE next morning, when Donna paid her usual visit to Toni's grave, she found Rinaldo there before her. His face was dreadfully pale, and he spoke with an effort.

'I've been waiting for you,' he said. 'Don't worry, I shan't keep you long. I want to apologise for last night, and to assure you that it won't happen again.'

'Rinaldo—'

'Please, just forget everything. You were right about a truce. It's what we have to do, of course.'

He looked ill. There were dark circles under his eyes and his face was taut with strain. But he was in perfect command of himself.

'I'm sure we'll find a way,' she said gently.

He nodded. He suddenly seemed awkward. 'Forget what I said about locking your door. There's no need. I'll never trouble you.' He looked at Toni's grave. 'I'll leave you alone with him now.'

Within a couple of days the money she'd sent to England had been replaced in her bank account. She also had an account at Racci, a gown shop in the Via Condotti in Rome. Donna stared when she saw the address. The years when she'd eagerly read everything she could find about Italy had taught her that this was the most exclusive and expensive street in the city. But when she queried it Rinaldo merely looked surprised.

'My mother had her clothes made there,' he said. 'It's the best.'

'Will you take me?' she asked cautiously.

'No, I'm too busy. Enrico will drive you. He has orders to be at your disposal whenever you wish to go into Rome.'

A few days later Donna was chauffeured to a dark, narrow street in the heart of the city, where most of the shops were so expensive that they didn't bother to display the prices. At one end the road widened suddenly into a piazza out of which climbed a flight of broad steps which looked as if they were covered with flowers. The steps were a gathering point for traders, calmly selling their wares in the shadow of Trinità dei Monti, the huge church at the top that towered over everything.

'The Spanish steps,' she breathed. 'I've always wanted to see them. They're beautiful.'

'They're not really Spanish,' Enrico said with a grin. 'They're Italian, and Trinità dei Monti is French. But that's Italy for you. Nothing is quite the way it seems.'

'Yes,' she murmured. 'I know.'

'Here's Racci,' Enrico said, pulling up outside a small, discreet shop. 'I'll park the car. When you're ready to leave, the shop will send someone to fetch me from the usual place.'

Donna thanked him and got out, wondering about 'the usual place'. Who did Enrico normally bring here? Selina, perhaps? Did Rinaldo pay for her clothes as well as her flat? There was no time to ponder more, for the door was already being pulled open for her.

Inside Racci she was simply taken over. When Donna ventured to suggest that too many expensive clothes would be a waste of money just now, as she was swelling by the day, her protests were waved aside.

'Elegance is of the first importance at all times,' Elisa Racci stated politely but finally. She was a tiny woman in her fifties.

'Of course,' Donna said, trying not to feel intimidated. 'It's just that I don't want to squander my husband's money.'

Signora Racci shrugged. Whether she meant that Rinaldo could afford it, or was simply expressing a general indifference for the problems of husbands, wasn't clear. 'Signor Mantini said that money was no object,' she observed.

Then an assistant produced a draped, olive-green dress that almost made Donna weep with joy. After that she pushed her scruples aside. By the time the session had finished three dresses were being packed up in large boxes and a fitting had been booked for three more that were being specially made.

'Do you want to go straight home?' Enrico asked as he drove her away.

'No, I'd like to see something of Rome first.'

'OK!' Even as he spoke a horn blared at them. Enrico swerved the car expertly and hurled some splendid-sounding Roman curses at various other drivers. 'Your godmother was a cow and your father was a donkey,' he bawled. 'Why don't you put your—?' The rest was lost in more shrieking of horns.

'That's one of the best sights of Rome,' he said cheerfully when it was over. 'Roman drivers. Anything special you want to see?'

It was on the tip of Donna's tongue to say, St Peter's, or the Castel Sant'Angelo, or the Trevi Fountain. But for some reason the words that came out were, 'The Via Veneto.'

Enrico promptly swung the car right, cutting up a goods van, whose driver responded indignantly. After a ritual exchange of pleasantries he said, 'The Via Veneto's a terrific place. Bright lights, exciting people.'

Before long they were in a wide, tree-lined avenue whose shops were as expensive as those in the Via Condotti, but more glittery. There were also luxury hotels and bars, whose tables spilled out onto the broad pavements.

'I'll stop for a coffee,' Donna said.

Enrico glided to a halt beside one of the pavement cafés. 'Shall I return for you in half an hour?' he said.

'Why not have a coffee with me?'

He winked. 'I have a little friend in the next street,' he said conspiratorially.

'In that case,' she said, laughing, 'we'd better make it an hour.'

It was delightful in the shade, and Donna leaned back, enjoying the idyllic setting and the music wafting from the three-piece orchestra, both of which were reflected in the price of the coffee. Three tables away there was a television celebrity whom she'd watched on the screen only the previous night. Women who might have been models strolled past. One especially caught her eye, her figure honed to perfection, her fair hair gleaming in the sun. Then she turned and Donna recognised Selina.

After the first moment there was no surprise. Wasn't this really why she'd come here? She watched as Selina sashayed out of a jewellery shop, carrying the shop's distinctive black and silver bag. Donna wondered what the bag contained, and whose account it had swelled.

Selina approached the kerb, not even glancing at the cars. Donna had already learned that Roman traffic stopped for nobody, whatever the lights might say. But Selina was at ease, almost insolent in the consciousness of her own beauty as she stepped out. Brakes screeched and vehicles came to a sudden halt, curses dying on the drivers' lips as they saw her. They waited with a kind of reverence as Selina crossed in front of them. Then the bedlam resumed.

Selina approached an apartment block and entered the main door. So that was where she dwelt in the flat that was paid for by Donna's husband.

She tried not to dwell on the thought, but her eyes insisted on covering the building. A window opened on the third floor, and behind it she was sure she could make out a flash of blonde hair.

It was a relief when Enrico collected her.

Before long Donna realised that Maria was avoiding her. The old woman seemed to scuttle away if she approached. If she had to talk to Donna she was clearly uneasy, and escaped as soon as possible.

One evening she heard voices coming from Rinaldo's study. The door stood slightly ajar, and she could hear Rinaldo, then Maria. Maria seemed to be weeping, and Donna thought she heard her own name.

She decided that the time had come to take the bull by the horns, and walked inside. Maria was seated on a small sofa, mumbling tearfully, and Rinaldo was beside her in an attitude of comfort.

'I think if I've done something to offend Maria she ought to tell me,' Donna said.

Rinaldo rose and came to her. 'You haven't offended her,' he said. 'She's frightened of you.'

'But why?'

'Because you're a nurse, and Maria is afraid that she has something terribly wrong with her. Her fear has made her avoid doctors, but she thinks you'll know what's the matter, and give her bad news.' He added in a lower voice, 'She has a growth on her hand. Her brother died of an illness that started with a growth, and she's scared out of her wits.'

'Is that why she's been avoiding me?' Donna asked, aghast. 'But—' She checked herself. It was useless asking why Maria didn't seek help. Terror couldn't be reasoned with. Instead she raised her voice and spoke loudly in Italian so that Maria could hear her.

'Maria looks healthy enough to me. Perhaps she's worrying about nothing.'

Tears poured down Maria's face and she shook her head vigorously.

'Well, why don't you let me see?' Donna said firmly. She sat on the sofa and took hold of Maria's hands. The old woman tried to protest. *'Basta!'* Donna said firmly. Enough.

In the face of her calm authority Maria yielded. At once Donna felt the lump on the back of her left hand. Touching it gently, she discovered that it was soft. Maria had given up all resistance, and now hung her head, expecting the worst.

There was a low table near the sofa, with a few books lying on it. Donna laid Maria's hand palm down on the table, took one of the books and put it over the back of the hand. Then, too fast for the others to know what she was doing, she slammed her fist down hard on the book.

Maria screamed with shock rather than pain. Donna calmly removed the book and saw what she had hoped for. The lump had gone.

Maria screamed again and crossed herself, murmuring, *'Santa Maria!'*

'What did you do?' Rinaldo demanded in astonishment, reverting to English.

'It was just fat,' Donna explained. 'I broke it up. It was perfectly harmless.' She put her hands on Maria's shoulders and said gently in Italian, 'But tomorrow we're going to the doctor together, and he'll tell you the same thing.'

'No, no.' Maria was still reluctant, but through her babble of words it became clear that she now regarded it as near sacrilege for anyone to question Donna's word.

'Yes,' Donna said firmly. 'Maria, you call me *patrona*, so treat me as the *patrona* and do as I say. Tomorrow I'm taking you to the doctor.'

'*Sì, signora,*' Maria said meekly.

Later that night Rinaldo asked, 'Are you quite certain of your diagnosis?'

'Almost entirely,' Donna said. 'I'd like a doctor to confirm it, but I'm not expecting any surprises.'

'I'll drive you myself.'

He was as good as his word, arriving home in the middle of the afternoon and escorting them both to the doctor. Maria held Donna's hand tightly all the way, as though there lay her only safety.

As Donna had expected, Dr Marcello, a stout, middle-aged man with a friendly smile, confirmed what she had said, and reproved Maria for not coming earlier. She smiled happily, and looked at Donna with a kind of triumph, as though they shared a secret.

Before going home Rinaldo took them to one of the bars that in Italy sold not only alcohol but also tea, coffee, ice cream and cakes. He bought Maria a huge chocolate sundae. When she'd finished it he promptly bought her another one—'to celebrate'.

His eyes were tender as he regarded the old woman. Now that the weight had been lifted from her shoulders Maria was like a child released from school. She chattered non-stop, said everything three or four times, and couldn't keep still. Rinaldo listened to her with a loving smile, and showed no impatience, no matter how often Maria repeated herself.

Donna watched him with a kind of aching delight. She hadn't known that this harsh, domineering man could show so much affection and gentleness. But then, he had many different aspects, she realised. Toni had been one man, always the same, whichever way you looked at him. But Rinaldo was many men in one, infinitely fascinating as one vista after another opened up in his character. She listened to him exchanging silly jokes with Maria, and was sad to think that none of this was for her. But perhaps one day...

Then he caught her looking at him, and the laughter faded from his face, leaving only the courteous mask that he normally wore.

But that night before they went to bed he said, 'I must thank you for what you did for Maria. She means a very great deal to me.'

'It was nothing,' Donna said. 'I only wish I'd known before. It's terrible to think of her suffering so much needlessly.'

'Yes, indeed. But it wasn't just your medical skill. You were kind to her.' He paused, and said awkwardly, 'You know how to treat people in distress.'

Seeking a way through to him, she said, 'That was how I met Toni, in hospital. Not that he was in distress. In fact he thought it was all a big joke. You know how he was...' She faltered to a standstill.

'Yes, I remember,' Rinaldo said. 'It's late. You must be tired. Let me escort you to bed. Then I have work to do. And accept my thanks again for your excellent work.'

The brief moment of warmth had gone. The mention of his brother had made him retreat behind a film of ice.

It wasn't in Donna's nature to fret. From then on she concentrated on preparing a nursery for her baby. It led to a clash with Rinaldo, because the room she chose was Toni's. 'It's lovely and sunny,' she explained. 'The perfect place.'

'But it's Toni's room,' Rinaldo said in a hard voice.

'What better place for Toni's child?'

Rinaldo looked about him at the pictures on the wall, the football trophies, the pennants, the little personal knick-knacks. 'You would just sweep all this away?' he demanded.

'Rinaldo, we can't keep Toni alive by making a shrine. Only the dead have shrines. A living baby in here—*Toni's* baby—will make it a place of life again. Can't you see that that's the best way to keep him with us?'

He was silent, brooding.

'Toni will always be alive for us,' Donna persisted. 'He's alive here.' In her fervour she took his hand and placed it over her stomach. For a moment their eyes met and Donna felt something stir in her heart at what she saw. The man was there before her, vulnerable in all his pain and misery. His unhappiness seemed to be one with her own. Now she knew that she could reach him. If only…

The next moment Rinaldo snatched his hand away. 'I'll have his things moved from this room,' he said. 'After that you can do whatever you like with it.'

Within a few hours the contents had vanished and Donna had taken over not only this room but also the one next door, which she meant to make her own. It was smaller than the one she now occupied, but it had a connecting door with the nursery. She wanted to be near her baby at all times.

Rinaldo raised his eyes at the move, but said nothing. He left everything in her hands now.

But he reacted strangely when the olive green dress was delivered from Racci's. His mouth tightened as she lifted it from the box and held it against her. Maria cried out in delight at the perfection of the colour against Donna's warm skin, but Rinaldo left the house without a word.

The mystery was explained that evening when he returned with a small package that he thrust into Donna's hand. Opening it, she gasped at the sight of a ruby necklace.

'You bought this for me?' she said, amazed. 'How lovely! Help me put it on.'

But he didn't come near her. 'It's a gift from Toni,' he said. 'The one he promised you.'

'The one he—?'

'The day you came here, he promised you an olive-green dress. He said the colour would suit you, and he was never wrong about things like that. It's charming that you bought the dress in his honour. In giving you the rubies I'm merely his deputy.'

Now she remembered the conversation she'd had with Toni that first evening, as they'd gone down to dinner. Rinaldo had overheard it. She hadn't bought the dress in Toni's honour. She hadn't even remembered. But Rinaldo had.

'These are really beautiful...' she began.

'They'll suit you, and that's what matters. I should like you to wear them when Selina comes to dinner. She has a gift for the baby that she would like to give you

in person. I said you'd call her to settle the date. Here's
her number. Now I have some work to do, and I'd prefer
not to be disturbed.'

Donna was left turning the rubies over, thinking that
she'd never had such a lovely present, given so coldly.
She slipped the jewels back into their box, noticing that
it came from an address on the Via Veneto, and was
black and silver, like the one she'd seen Selina carrying.

She called Selina that evening, and found the other
woman all sugar and sympathy.

'*Carissima Donna,*' she purred. 'How are you feeling?'

'Extremely well, thank you.'

'Rinaldo tells me that you've been decorating the
nursery, and doing far too much of the work yourself.
He keeps saying how worried he is about you.'

Donna didn't miss the significance of that 'keeps saying', with its suggestion of constant contact. And she
was shrewd enough to realise that Selina had slipped it
in on purpose. She replied brightly, 'No one could ask
for a more concerned or attentive husband than Rinaldo.
I reassure him that I'm strong and healthy, but you know
what he's like.' She gave a conspiratorial chuckle.

'Yes,' Selina said slowly. 'Yes, I do.'

'Anyway, the nursery is finished now,' Donna said.
'I'll look forward to showing it to you when you come
to dinner. Shall we say tomorrow night?'

'I simply can't wait,' Selina purred.

If Selina had been more likable Donna would have
felt some remorse for having taken her man. As it was,
she couldn't make herself feel bad. Selina struck her as
a proud, vain, self-absorbed woman, who'd counted on
snaring a wealthy husband when her career began to

fade. The things she'd said on their wedding day showed that she hadn't given up hope.

Rinaldo's feelings for Selina remained a mystery. If he'd longed to marry her he would surely have done so before now, but he obviously found her a satisfying lover. Why should that have changed now that he was bound in a marriage of duty? He'd saved his brother's woman and his brother's child from lives of hardship, but did duty go further?

And what, after all, did she care if he still shared Selina's bed? Every line of his body bespoke a man of lusty appetites. Once he'd briefly shown that Donna could inspire him with desire, but he hadn't been himself that night, and it had never happened again.

He was to collect Selina in his car, her own having apparently broken down. Donna dressed for the evening with great care. The olive-green silk dress made her look elegant, despite her increasing bump, and the rubies went with it perfectly.

But she knew she might as well not have bothered when Selina walked into the house, attired in a scarlet satin, figure-hugging dress. It had a short skirt that revealed Selina's lovely long legs, her feet adorned with silver sandals. The top was low, revealing a magnificent bosom, and the sheen on the satin emphasised every movement of her curves. Donna, who'd felt reasonably good about herself a moment ago, knew suddenly that she looked like a frump.

The meal was a triumph. Maria had put forth her best efforts to ensure that the new *patrona's* first dinner did her credit. Donna flashed her a smile of gratitude, and began to relax.

As they ate, Selina begged for their advice. 'I don't know what to do,' she said. 'I've been offered another film role. It's a wonderful part, but I'm not sure if I should take it.'

'Why not?' Donna asked.

'Because it means acting with—' She named a notorious B-rank Italian film actor. 'In fact I'm sure he made them offer it to me.'

'Don't touch it,' Rinaldo said at once. 'The man's filth. You know his reputation.'

'But it would be such a wonderful chance for me to get back.'

Her meaning was clear. Having lost Rinaldo, she was trying to revive her career via the casting couch. And she was making sure that he knew about it. Donna resisted the temptation to look at Rinaldo to see how the news affected him, but his arguments showed that he hated the idea.

At last Selina said, 'Ah, well, enough of my problems. I simply must show you my gift.'

She'd brought with her two large suitcases. The first one was full of little garments, all in white. Everything a new-born baby could possibly need was there, several times over. Matinée coats, trousers, mittens, bootees, bonnets, all the best, the most exquisite, the most costly. The centre of the collection was a long christening robe of white satin and lace, with tiny pearl buttons down the front.

To some people this might have seemed enchanting, but Donna felt anger begin to well up inside her. She'd looked forward to buying these things herself, but now there was no need. This tinselly woman, who tried to behave as though she owned Donna's husband, was now acting in a proprietorial way towards her baby.

But none of this could be said. With a huge effort at

self-control Donna smiled and said, 'They're beautiful. You—you seem to have thought of everything.'

'I tried to,' Selina cooed. 'Look—' She began to lift the little clothes out of their tissue paper. 'I just know he's going to be the prettiest baby in the world, and he deserves only the best.'

'Or she,' Donna remarked.

'Or she.' Selina's tone admitted the technical possibility, but no more.

Rinaldo had begun taking some of the clothes out, exclaiming over their beauty. The little frown he threw Donna made it clear that he thought she should show more appreciation. Donna pulled herself together and began to say the right things in what she hoped was a suitably enthusiastic voice. But inwardly she was furious.

There was more to come. Selina opened the second case and produced a set of dainty bedclothes, satin-trimmed blankets and soft sheets with embroidered tops. 'I bought these for the nursery,' she said.

'How kind,' Donna said with difficulty. 'After all, I might easily have forgotten.'

Rinaldo scowled at her. Selina's eyes flickered this way and that, seeing everything. 'Do let me go up and see what you've done.'

Before they left the room Selina took a tissue-wrapped object from the second case. It was very large and shapeless, and seriously hampered her as she climbed the stairs. Rinaldo was forced to take her arm and guide her.

'What on earth have you got there?' he asked with a grin.

'Wait and see. It's a surprise. Whoops!'

'Steady,' he said, putting his arm about her waist to

help her. Donna walked on ahead, determined to see nothing.

At last Rinaldo threw open the door to the room on which Donna had expended so much love and care. The carpet was a pale biscuit colour, and the walls pale cream with a light green border round the top. Large white cupboards ran along one wall. Donna walked in ahead of the other two, surveying her domain with pardonable pride. Selina exclaimed over everything, but her eyes were cold and shrewd.

'It's beautiful, Donna. Just beautiful,' she said, a wide smile on her face. 'I wonder if—? But of course, you're English. You've created an English nursery, haven't you? And it's charming—charming...' She left the implication hanging in the air.

'I don't think my baby will be troubled about what's English and what's Italian,' Donna said with determined affability, and just the tiniest emphasis on 'my' baby. 'Why don't you show us the big secret in that parcel? We're dying to see it, aren't we, Rinaldo?'

'Of course. Shall I help you open it?'

He assisted Selina to tear off the mountains of wrapping, revealing a huge furry mouse.

'It can sit on the cot, waiting for the baby,' Selina said. 'Let's put him in place.'

Donna stood back as Rinaldo helped her to adjust the mouse. She might have been an onlooker, watching as two proud parents prepared their child's cradle. Somehow Rinaldo and Selina looked right together.

'What shall we call him?' Selina cooed.

'How about Max?' Donna said, trying to be civil.

'Oh, no, that's not a nice name. I know. We'll call him Jojo. Don't you think that suits him, Rinaldo?'

'Anything you like,' he said, grinning.

'Jojo it is, then,' Donna said with a forced smile. 'Thank you, Selina. Excuse me, I think I'll just go and have a word with Maria.'

She stayed away as long as possible, calming her annoyance. When the coffee was ready she carried it in herself. Rinaldo and Selina had returned to the dining room. As she approached the door she could hear Rinaldo talking in an urgent voice.

'You mustn't work with that man. I forbid it.'

'But what else can I do, *caro*? My career is all I have left.'

'Don't say that. I hate to think of you—'

'Here we are,' Donna said, walking into the room with the tray. She smiled at them brightly. 'I'm sorry it took so long.'

CHAPTER EIGHT

DONNA lay awake, counting the minutes in the darkness. It was five hours since Rinaldo had driven Selina home, and still there was no sign of his return. She knew the other woman would have asked him up to her apartment—*their* apartment—and presumably he'd agreed. But what then? Five hours!

Was he with her at this moment, running his hands over that perfect body? A *slim* body, not one thickening with child. Were they using words and caresses whose meaning only they knew?

Donna buried her face into the pillow, trying to shut out the images that tortured her. Her whole body was full of treacherous desire for him. She'd fought it, blaming it on the mood swings of pregnancy. But the memory of his kiss wouldn't be so easily banished. She'd felt as if she was going up in flames. Nothing she'd felt in Toni's arms had equalled that sensation of ecstasy, and now she couldn't forget it. She wanted Rinaldo with every part of her. But he was hers in name only.

Unable to stand it any longer, she rose and put on her dressing gown. The house was silent as she crept downstairs and out into Loretta's garden. She sat by the fountain and scooped up some water to put on her burning brow. It cooled her skin, but it didn't help with the real fever that tortured her.

At last she heard the car draw up outside the house, then his footsteps, coming towards the cloisters. He must have seen the door to the garden standing open, and come to investigate.

'Is anyone there?' His voice came from the darkness. 'Donna?'

He moved towards her, through the moonlit garden. 'What are you doing here at this hour?'

She tried to restrain the words but they burst from her. 'You're late. I thought you'd be home hours ago.'

He looked at her with surprise. 'I thought *you* would have been asleep hours ago. Is it your concern where I go and what I do?'

'I think it is, especially when you're with Selina until the small hours. Everyone knows what she is to you.'

'Indeed.' There was a dangerous note in his voice. 'And just what is she to me?'

'A woman you're keeping,' she flung at him. 'A woman whose rent you pay.'

His mouth twisted. 'I suppose Toni told you that.'

'Is it true?'

'What if it is? If I choose to help out an old friend, that's my business. I won't tolerate your interference in what doesn't concern you. Let that be understood.'

'And I won't tolerate being made a fool of,' she said vehemently. 'You and I know why we made this marriage but the world doesn't. How do you think I'll feel being laughed at because you went straight back to your mistress?'

'My mistress? You take a lot for granted. I've told you, she's an old friend.' There was a steel edge to his voice. 'You'd be well advised to leave it there.'

'And suppose I don't choose to leave it there?' she said angrily.

His voice was soft and dangerous. 'I strongly suggest that you do, Donna.'

'Suggest? Or order?'

'Whichever you like, as long as you do what I say. Don't argue with me, and don't try to dictate to me. A jealous scene is hardly appropriate in our situation.'

'Jealous?' The colour flew to her cheeks, making her glad the darkness hid her. 'How dare you say that? It's nothing to me who you sleep with.'

'Indeed?' he said cruelly. 'No one who'd heard you this last few minutes would have thought so.'

'I told you, I don't like you making a fool of me.'

He regarded her strangely. 'And that's all it is?'

'Of course.'

'So, as long as I'm discreet I can have a mistress with your goodwill. Is that what you're saying? Visit her during the midday siesta, and as long as you don't know there'll be no arguments?'

She gave a shaky laugh. 'I wonder how you'd feel if I took the same attitude.'

The irony vanished from his face to be replaced by thunder. 'That's entirely different.'

'Only for the moment. Once my child is safely born, what's to stop me acting as you do?'

'*I* will stop you. I will not permit it. You'll behave yourself properly as my wife, because I will tolerate nothing else. You'll never so much as look at another man.'

'You're medieval,' she said fiercely. 'You want to be free to do as you please, but keep me in a loveless desert.'

'I *am* free to do as I please. I will not explain myself to you, or account for my actions. As for the desert— why should it come to that? When the child is born we can consider the terms on which our marriage is to be lived.'

'*Your* terms,' she said angrily.

'Of course my terms. This is Italy. I'm not some docile Englishman saying, ''Yes, dear,'' and, ''No, dear.'' I say yes and no as it pleases me.'

She was silent, hating him. But her eyes told of her rebellion, and he stepped closer to her. 'Think what you like of me, Donna,' he said softly. 'But you belong to me. Now and in the future. That's the bargain you've made.'

'Never,' she said furiously. 'Our bargain is a formality. I never agreed to be a piece of property.'

He didn't reply, but she read in his face that a reply was unnecessary. She might rail as much as she pleased. He was master here.

'I think you must be a devil,' she said bitterly.

'No, just an Italian, with an Italian sense of family. A woman from England would hardly understand that, but I told you once, here family counts. You're a Mantini wife, bearing a Mantini child, and you'll behave as a good wife and mother.'

'I'll be a good mother, Rinaldo. You can be sure of that. But you and I aren't husband and wife in any sense that means anything.'

'But we will be, when the time comes. What else were you proposing? To keep to your solitary bed, leaving me to other women? Do you think I'll let you?'

His hands were on her shoulders, drawing her towards him. She made a last-minute effort to struggle free but he had her in a grip of iron, covering her mouth with his own, holding her fast in a crushing embrace.

'Is that the kind of marriage we'll have, Donna?' he whispered against her lips. 'Keeping our distance?'

His mouth was on hers again before she could answer,

silencing all protest, kissing her with fierce purpose. 'Do you really think that's how it will be?' he murmured.

'I won't share you,' she said fiercely. 'I won't be a docile Italian wife, turning a blind eye while you do what you please.'

He laughed. 'Then you'll have to find a way to keep me at home, won't you?'

'Stop this,' she begged. 'Let me go. You have no right—'

'You're my wife. You'd be surprised what rights I have. But why should we fight now? Let's save the fight for after the birth—when we might both enjoy it.'

'Let me go.'

'Not yet,' he whispered, bending his head again. 'You belong to me,' he said against her lips. 'Whether you like it or not, you belong to me.'

'No—' She tried to protest but he muffled the words with his mouth. Donna struggled against the violence of her desire, pitting her anger against it. She wanted him but not like this, not on his terms.

'Say it,' he commanded her. 'You belong to me. *Say it.*'

'Never. Not now or ever.'

'Ever is a long time, Donna. Do you think I couldn't make you mine?'

She looked at him steadily, in control of herself again. 'You'll never make me admit it,' she said in a voice that challenged him.

A shadow of anger passed swiftly across his face. 'You have a genius for knowing where to attack, *mia piccola strega*. Of course. Admitting it is everything. Go to bed now. Keep me at a distance while you can, while you can use Toni's child to fend me off. But remember—I'll be waiting.'

*   *   *

Strangely enough, after that Donna found herself settling into a life of peace and contentment. As she grew larger her mood swings disappeared and a pleasant calm pervaded her.

She was popular at the villa. Piero openly adored her, and the servants had been won over by her care of him, and what she'd done for Maria. They loved her too for her constant attendance at Toni's grave, and the attention she showered on Loretta's garden. When Maria found her there one day, and confided, 'The mistress would have liked to see you here,' Donna's success with her household was assured.

She had time to study the garden in detail, and came to realise that every one of the statues was of Rinaldo or Toni. Toni was the fat, laughing baby whose hands constantly reached up to the flowers, and Rinaldo was the young boy, serious too soon, whose eyes stared ahead at something that troubled him. Donna wondered if Loretta had been aware of trouble. Had she understood her son that well, or had her clever fingers worked it into the bronze unknowingly?

The man himself behaved punctiliously. He never again stayed out late with Selina, and if he visited her at the noon siesta, as he'd half threatened, Donna had no way of knowing. He was always home on time, his manner invariably courteous and gentle. But he lived just apart from her, in a place she couldn't reach.

But this troubled her less now that all her attention was for her coming baby. Increasingly the household came to revolve around her. For the first time in her life she was cocooned by the affection and approval of a family—a huge family that encompassed everyone in the Villa Mantini.

She moved into her new room with the connecting

door to the nursery. Now she was more than ever aware of Rinaldo's movements, for his room was just across the corridor. She knew when he came to bed, which was usually very late. She knew also that he sometimes paused outside her door. But he never came in.

Their truce held. When he discovered that she loved opera he took her to a performance at the Caracalla Baths, the huge open-air theatre created from the ruins of an ancient Roman sauna. Donna had a vivid imagination and she could picture the building as it had been two thousand years ago, not just a bathhouse but a meeting place for the rulers of the Roman empire.

The programme gave a brief description of Caracalla in its great days, with illustrations. One of them was a profile of a Roman general, fresh from conquering provinces, his hair adorned with laurels. His face was clean-cut, arrogant, full of the certainty of superiority—the classic Roman profile.

Then she glanced sideways at her husband, and saw a profile so similar that she almost gasped. There was the same arrogance and certainty, transmitted down two thousand years. Rinaldo was born of a race of men who'd once subdued the whole world. And the signs were still there. It might be fanciful, but she felt she understood him a little better.

She understood other things too. The Italy she'd dreamed about, the brightly coloured, merry country, full of sun and wine, was only one facet. There was another Italy, a place of dark, fierce passions. They were there in the violent drama on the stage. *Sangue, morte e vendetta*. Blood, death and vengeance. The Italians wrote operas about these things because they were deep in the Italian soul.

But the stormy passions in the music destroyed her

calm, and that night she was haunted by a dream that had troubled her recently. She was back in the car. It rocked violently. She fought to keep control of the wheel, but Toni was there, screaming at her that he didn't want to go home. He seized the wheel…she tried to fight him off, but he held onto her and her puny strength was useless against the power of the arms about her.

'No,' she screamed. 'Toni, no!'

'Hush now.' The voice was strong and reassuring in her ear. 'Donna, wake up! It's all right.'

She couldn't struggle any more. She collapsed, sobbing helplessly, and felt Rinaldo's arms tighten about her.

'It's all right,' he said. 'It was only a dream. It's over now.'

'No,' she wept. 'It will never be over.'

He switched on the bedside lamp, throwing a mellow glow into the room, then gathered her to him again. Donna leaned against him while tears rolled down her cheeks.

'It was the accident,' she whispered. 'It was happening all over again.'

'I think you have that dream often,' he said.

'Yes. How did you know?'

'I hear you calling in the night. Usually you only cry out once or twice, but tonight it went on and on, and I had to come to you.'

'Sometimes I'm afraid to go to sleep. Toni's there…but when I call him he vanishes, and there's only his grave.'

'You still miss him?' Rinaldo asked heavily.

She was too weak and weary to think of putting on a

brave front now. She could only hiccup like a child, and say forlornly, 'He was always kind to me.'

Rinaldo was silent, and she became aware that she was leaning against his bare chest. It was smooth-skinned and muscular, rising and falling with the power of his emotion. He was wearing only pyjama trousers made of silk, and through the thin material she could clearly see the lines of his taut hips and long thighs. A pleasant, warm smell came from his brown skin.

'Yes,' he said at last. 'He was kind. He never thought of tomorrow, any more than a child does. But he laughed and sang and made the house bright with his warmth.'

'I keep half expecting him to come back, and then I won't be so lonely,' Donna said huskily. 'I wait, but he doesn't come, and I feel alone again.'

He pushed her a little away from him and stared down into her face, astonished. 'That's exactly how I feel,' he said in an incredulous voice. 'I look up, thinking I'll see him, laughing in his old merry way. But he's not there, and the empty space is terrible.' He sighed. 'He'll never be here again, for either of us. We both have to live with that.'

He rocked her slowly back and forth. 'There's no need for you to be lonely,' he said. 'You have all of us here to care for you.'

'For the mother of Toni's baby,' she said softly. 'Not for me. Toni cared for *me*; that's why I loved him.'

He looked down at her in surprise. 'That was why?'

'Yes. Just that. I know you thought it was money, but it wasn't. He wanted me so much. No one ever wanted me before.'

Once it would have been impossible to speak this way to Rinaldo, but while he held her so tenderly she suddenly found she could open her heart to him, without fearing his scorn.

'But surely you had a family?' he asked.

'Not really. My father left when I was seven. There was a divorce and he married his other woman. When my mother died I thought he'd take me to live with his new family, but he never did. He made all kinds of excuses, but the fact was that I didn't fit in.'

'*Dio mio!*' Rinaldo said with soft violence, tightening his arms about her.

'I grew up knowing I didn't belong anywhere. But then there was Toni. He made me feel beautiful, and loved. He talked about his Italian family, and it sounded the most wonderful thing in the world. I dreamed of being part of a real family at last—' She broke off, partly because Rinaldo had brushed his fingers across her mouth.

'Don't,' he whispered. 'I'm to blame. I should have tried to be more understanding.'

'And then I got pregnant and he was thrilled. I thought, Now I've got my family—and then—'

'Hush,' he said fiercely. 'No more. I can't bear it.'

She looked up in wonder at the new note in his voice. His face was haggard. 'It should have been different,' he said. 'Everything was his, and I took it away from him—I killed him—'

'No,' she said swiftly. 'No—that's not true.'

'It is true. We both know it is. It'll always be there. How can we forget?'

'*Aagh!*' she said suddenly.

'What is it? Is the baby—?'

'No, it's not coming. Just kicking. He's done that a lot recently.'

'He?' Rinaldo asked, with the nearest approach to teasing she'd ever heard from him.

'Got to be a he,' she gasped. 'He's going to be a footballer, from the feel.'

'Can I do something for you?'

'I sometimes make myself some tea during the night—'

'Stay here. I'll go.'

Slightly to her surprise he was back quickly, with a pot of tea that had been properly made.

'This is delicious,' she said, sipping it.

'Can you sleep now?' He saw the wary look that passed over her face. 'What is it? The dream?'

'Yes. Sometimes it comes back.'

'Don't worry. I'll stay with you.' He pressed her gently back against the pillows and pulled the sheet up over her. 'If you seem troubled, I'll wake you.'

'Are you sure?'

'Quite sure. I won't go away. Go to sleep now. I'm here.'

She was already feeling drowsy. It was nice to be able to relax, knowing that she had nothing to fear. He slipped into bed beside her and put his arms about her. Her last conscious thought was of him, solid and reassuring, keeping her safe.

But when she woke in the morning the sun was high in the sky, and Rinaldo had left for work an hour ago.

CHAPTER NINE

As THE year drew on Donna discovered that another of her preconceptions about Italy had been wrong. Although the summer months were scorching hot, winter was just like England, except that possibly the weather was colder. She woke one morning to find Loretta's garden a magical place of frozen beauty, with everything covered by a dusting of sparkling frost. A few days later the snow came, an endless stream of soft white flakes. Icicles hung from the fountains, and everywhere was silent.

The week before Christmas Piero developed a nasty lung infection.

'There's no cause for alarm,' Dr Marcello told them. 'But I'd like to have him back in hospital for a while.'

The day after Piero returned to hospital Rinaldo said, 'We'll visit him tonight, if you feel up to the journey.'

She was eight months pregnant and had recently been feeling tired, but she immediately agreed. By the evening she was beginning to wish she'd said no. Her head was aching and she longed to go to bed early, but she wouldn't disappoint Piero.

Snow had fallen and the air was bitterly cold. She shivered as they left the house, and drew the edges of her coat close.

'Be careful,' Rinaldo said sharply. 'The path is slippery.'

They found Piero in a cheerful mood. The antibiotics were working and his colour had improved. These days his left hand was noticeably stronger and he enjoyed flexing it for their appreciation. He smiled as Donna poured tea for him. But when the smile died his face was full of anxiety. He pointed at Donna, frowning in Rinaldo's direction, then indicated the door.

'I think he wants us to go,' Rinaldo said. Piero gave a grunt of agreement. 'Are you tired, Nonno?'

Piero managed a slight shake of the head and drew a D on the counterpane.

'Donna's tired?' Rinaldo asked, and Piero nodded.

'Are you?' he asked her abruptly.

'A little, yes.'

'Then I'll take you home.'

She kissed Piero, and they left. As they descended the steps she felt Rinaldo's hand under her arm. He never failed in such little gestures of courtesy.

He drove fast, his tense gaze fixed on the road. He was a skilled driver, and despite the treacherous conditions Donna felt no alarm, until he braked sharply and cursed at something he'd seen on the road ahead.

'Traffic jam!' he said. 'I'd forgotten how easily the roads clog at this time of year. It's blocked solid.'

'Oh, no! We could be hours getting home,' she said in despair.

'No, I can take another route.' He wrenched the wheel, turning the car down a side street. 'We'll have to cut across country this way. It's longer but the roads should be free and there'll be less delay.'

Donna couldn't follow the twists they took in the next few minutes, but soon they were out in the country. The lights had disappeared and when she peered out of the window she could only make out fields, stretching into the distance.

'I don't know where we are,' she said. 'Is this any-where near home?'

'We're almost—*Santa Maria*!' The words were torn from him as the car suddenly skidded on a patch of ice. He fought with the wheel, trying to keep steady, while waves of horror engulfed Donna. She'd lived through this before. The car out of control, the frantic efforts to stabilise it, and the end approaching… She screamed into the darkness.

They stopped with a thunderous impact. Donna sat shivering, trying to grapple with the dread that possessed her mind.

'We've just lurched into the ditch,' Rinaldo said in a shaken voice. 'Are you all right?' Receiving no answer, he looked closely into her face. 'Donna…'

'Over and over…' she whispered. 'Over and over…and he called my name…until there was si-lence…'

'Donna,' he said firmly, gripping her hands, 'listen to me. It's finished—that other time—we're not turning over. We're just in a ditch. I'm going to get you out and— *Ouch*!' he finished with a small grunt as her nails dug into his hands sharply enough to hurt. She turned to him, wild-eyed.

'The baby,' she gasped. 'It's started.'

'What? It's not due for another month.'

'The shock—'

'My God! I've got to get you back to hospital. All right. Hang on.'

He tried to start the car, but the engine whirred with-out sparking into life. Donna clutched her stomach, wait-ing for the next pain, praying that her baby wouldn't be born like this.

Rinaldo got out and placed his shoulder against the

front of the car. Donna felt the vehicle rock as he strained to push it out of the ditch. Another pain tore through her. Horrified, she realised that it was only a few minutes since the last. The shock of the impact had sent her into premature labour, and there wasn't much time.

Rinaldo got back in beside her. 'I can't get it free,' he said grimly. 'How are you?'

'Not good. It's coming fast.'

He snatched up the car phone. 'It'll have to be an ambulance, then,' he said, dialling furiously. In a few moments he was talking to the hospital, describing what had happened.

'For God's sake get here quickly,' he said. 'I'll describe where we are.'

But pinpointing exactly where they were in the darkness of the countryside was almost impossible. At last he said, 'Look for a vehicle slewed into the ditch with all the lights on. And try to hurry.' He replaced the phone. 'It may take them half an hour, but babies don't come that fast, surely?'

'Not normally,' Donna said in painful gasps. 'But this is different.' She arched her back. 'If only I could lie down.'

'I can make it flat in the back,' he said.

She heard him thumping seats and pulling levers, then her own seat was eased gently backwards, and he said, 'Slide over. I'll help you.'

Using his hands to steady her, she eased herself sideways and half crawled, half slid until she was lying down in the back of the car. A sharp pain seized her while she was moving and she gasped, biting her lip so as not to cry out. He drew her against him. 'Hold onto me,' he said through gritted teeth.

She did so, digging her nails into his arms until the contraction had passed, and taking deep breaths. Looking into his eyes, she saw a reflection of her own alarm that the baby might be born like this.

'Is there anything I should do for you?' he asked. 'You'll have to tell me.'

'Give me some support on the left side,' she said. 'The car's sloping a little.'

He retrieved the cushions that he'd pushed aside from the flattened back seats and wedged them in beside her. Before she could thank him another pain tore her apart. She forced back a groan.

'Scream if you want to,' he said desperately. 'With any luck the ambulance driver might hear and find us sooner.'

It made sense but she couldn't force herself to do it. Pride forbade any show of weakness in front of Rinaldo. She gritted her teeth as another pain came. She'd attended births in the past, some of them emergencies, but always in hospital, surrounded by machines to help, and with painkillers available. Nothing had warned her of this terrible raw agony with nothing but her husband's strength to rely on.

She turned to that strength now, burying her face against him as the pain racked her. Somehow she must hang on and help her child to be born safely.

'I'm cold,' she whispered.

Instantly Rinaldo was tearing off his overcoat and laying it over her, tucking it up to the neck. He cradled her in his arms, looking anxiously into her face, but she didn't see him. She'd closed her eyes, trying to gather her energy for the next contraction. The world was dark and full of agony. It seemed impossible that she should survive. A long, mysterious tunnel opened up in her consciousness. Perhaps Toni was waiting for her at the end of it, she thought wildly.

'Rinaldo,' she gasped.

'Yes—yes, I'm here.'

'If—anything happens to me—'

'Hush,' he said quickly.

'But if—if I don't—you won't hate the baby because of me—will you?'

'Donna—'

In her pain-crazed state she barely registered that he'd spoken her name—something he rarely did.

'Promise me—'

'Stop talking like that,' he said roughly. 'It's nonsense. You're not going to die.'

The far end of the tunnel was clearer now. She could see him...

'Toni's waiting for me...' she whispered. 'He needs me. He always needed me...'

'And *I* need you. Donna, he isn't there. It's an illusion. Open your eyes. Look at me.' She lay still in his arms, breathing softly. *'Look at me!'* he cried in sudden dread.

At that moment the pain attacked her again with terrible force. She arched against him, reaching up mindlessly to put an arm about his neck. Rinaldo bent his head to her, murmuring words she barely understood.

'It's all right, *carissima*, it's all right—they'll be here soon—'

'No, just you—' she gasped. 'I only want you—'

'I'm here. Hold onto me.'

Their enmity was forgotten now in the space of this greater power that possessed them both. Toni's image vanished. Through the delirium of pain she was conscious only of Rinaldo, holding her close, letting his strength flow into her.

The contractions were coming faster. With terror she realised that the time was only moments away. 'It's coming,' she gasped.

'*Dio mio*! I'll see if there's any sign of the ambulance.'

'No,' she cried, and held him tighter. 'Don't leave me.'

She braced herself against the front seat and felt her baby fight its way into the world. Rinaldo was there to help its journey, and no sooner was it in his hands than he tore off his jacket and wrapped it around the tiny body.

'It's a boy,' he said in wonder. Then his tone changed to one of horror. 'He's not breathing.'

'Give him to me.' Donna held out her arms and took her son into them. She breathed into his mouth, gave him a slight tap on the rump, and the result was all she could have wished. A cry broke from the child, showing that the lungs had started to work.

She felt exhausted, light-headed and triumphant. This was her son, around whom there had been so many storms, born at last, and safe in his mother's arms. He was beautiful.

'Toni,' she whispered. '*Mio piccolo Toni*, after your father.'

Suddenly she was swept by grief for Toni, who'd fathered this beautiful child, and who would never see him. She'd wept before, in sadness for the loss of him, but now her feeling was all for what *he* had lost. He was there in her unsettled mind, smiling as she'd so often seen him, and it seemed intolerable that his smile would never shine on his son. He'd loved life, and passed it on to his child, but his own was silenced for ever beneath a cold marble slab.

Now she could only perceive him dimly at the far end of the tunnel. He wasn't beckoning to her any more, but waving farewell. Sobs choked her as she understood that this had a finality greater even than his death.

Possessed by her grief, she didn't notice Rinaldo watching her closely. He took in everything—the protectiveness of her arms enfolding the baby, the look in her eyes as she gazed down at the little face, the tears on her cheeks. He was waiting for her to look up at him, and include him in the magic circle.

'Donna,' he whispered.

But she couldn't hear. She was saying goodbye to Toni for the last time. 'Toni,' she wept. 'Oh, Toni— Toni—'

Rinaldo listened in silence. Then he turned away and put his hand over his eyes.

There was a flash of light through the car window. Rinaldo came back to life and looked outside, to where the ambulance was just drawing up. Pulling himself together, he climbed out.

After that the medical machine took over. In moments Donna was on a stretcher, being carried to the ambulance, her child held against her breast.

'Are you coming to the hospital with us, *signore*?' the nurse asked.

Rinaldo hesitated. With all his heart he longed to go with his wife and son—no, not his son! Hers and Toni's. She'd called for Toni. Had she been aware of him— Rinaldo—for one moment? She'd cried, 'Don't leave me!' and clung to him. But her eyes had been closed. Who had she really been talking to?

'I'll stay with my car,' he said heavily. 'I must call for help.'

'Very well, *signore*.' The nurse entered the ambulance

and slammed the rear door. Rinaldo stood watching as the vehicle's tail-lights vanished into the darkness. Then it was gone and there was only silence and the frozen fields surrounding him. It was hard to believe that just a few moments ago he'd been at one with Donna in the closest experience that could unite a man and woman. At least, that was what he'd thought. But it had been an illusion. He'd helped her bring Toni's child into the world, and now she had no further use for him.

As soon as they reached the hospital baby Toni was whisked away to an incubator.

'But he's going to be all right, isn't he?' Donna pleaded. How often had she reassured mothers in such situations? But this was different. This was her Toni. It was desperately important to make them understand that he was different from all other babies.

But it seemed that they did understand. The nurse spoke to her gently. 'He's going to be fine, but the accident caused him to be born a month early, so we'll take no chances.'

'Will you tell my husband—? Where is he?'

'He stayed with his car.'

'Oh—oh, yes, I see,' she stammered. 'It's an expensive car—I'd forgotten.'

A dark cloud had settled over Donna's heart. In those few dramatic minutes during the birth she'd felt close to him. When the pain had torn through her she'd reached out and he'd been there for her. But the closeness had been an illusion. He'd cared about the child, not about her. Now that Toni's son was born, Rinaldo had no more use for her.

She wished the world would keep still. It was normal to feel weak after giving birth, but this terrible exhaustion was new to her. The nurse's face was swimming and she couldn't see it clearly, but she could make out its sudden look of concern.

While he waited for the garage to send a truck Rinaldo tramped up and down the road. He'd retrieved his overcoat, but his jacket had stayed in the ambulance, protecting the baby, and now it was hard to keep warm. He wished he'd listened to his first instincts and gone with Donna. She neither needed nor wanted him. She'd made that clear. But mightn't that have changed if he'd been with her?

He called the hospital on the car phone, and was alarmed to discover the baby was in an incubator.

'It's a normal precaution when a child is born prematurely,' the nurse reassured him.

'How is my wife?'

For the first time she hesitated. 'Signora Mantini is as well as can be expected in view of what happened.'

'What the devil does that mean?' he asked sharply.

'She began to haemorrhage soon after arriving. Luckily her blood is a common type and we were able to give her an instant transfusion…'

The words swam together. Rinaldo gripped the phone. 'Is her life in danger?'

'There's no need for undue alarm… Hello? Signor Mantini?'

The nurse was talking to empty air. Rinaldo left the keys in the ignition for the mechanic, jumped out of the car and began to run towards the main road. It took him a long time on the icy path, but at last he made it and stood staring into the distance, willing something to come along.

When he finally saw headlights he placed himself in

front of the approaching vehicle and waved madly. The driver didn't see him for a long time, but Rinaldo stood his ground. At the last minute the van stopped. The driver leaned out and delivered a stream of highly colourful curses.

'Yes, I know,' Rinaldo said urgently. 'You're right, but I've got to get to the hospital quickly. My wife's just had a baby…'

The driver opened the door at once and cleared some debris off the front seat. The vehicle smelled strongly of garlic, and the driver—a middle-aged man with a heavy moustache and a loud voice—confided that he was a dealer in vegetables. From this he passed on to talking about his wonderful family: his five children, his wife—even his mother-in-law was wonderful.

'Your first?' he demanded.

'First? I—oh, yes, our first child.'

'Our first was born at Christmas too. Wonderful. Like no other Christmas. You'll enjoy it.'

He continued talking like this all the way, cheerfully unaware that he was subjecting his passenger to a form of torture. At the hospital he set him down, demurred at the money Rinaldo pressed into his palm, finally accepted it, and drove away, calling, 'This is the best time of your life.'

Donna was lying with her eyes closed, her face dreadfully pale, her arm attached to a drip. He sat beside her, hurling reproaches at himself. How could he have let her go without him for no other reason than his damnable pride? He fixed his eyes on her face, willing her to wake up as he'd willed the car to come. But this time his will failed. She couldn't hear the silent messages he was sending her. She'd gone somewhere where he was not invited to follow.

Perhaps Toni was there with her, and she didn't want to return to reality. Jealousy, shocking in its violence, possessed him. It was the same feeling that he'd experienced the first night she'd come to the Villa Mantini, when he'd looked at her and known that she was a woman like no other, and that his callow, puppyish young brother had secured her for himself.

His frustrated rage had made him cruel both to her and to Toni. He'd sought any way to prise them apart. Once he thought he'd found the key. For a scorching moment in the garden he'd known that she could be his. She'd known it too. He'd seen it in her eyes. But then she'd snubbed him, accusing him of being willing to seduce his brother's woman.

Her pregnancy had come as a stunning blow. His bitter resentment of the fate that had sent her to him too late had made him lash them both with terrible words. He'd driven them to flight. But for him…

Rinaldo buried his head in his hands, unable to bear his own thoughts.

He rose and walked to the window, trying to break the spell by stretching his limbs. But the spell wouldn't be broken. It carried him remorselessly back to that first evening, when he'd seen her through the spray of the fountain, revelling in the beauty of Loretta's garden, instinctively at home with his mother's artistry. He'd challenged her, and she'd challenged him back, unafraid. So many people were afraid of him, but not her. She belonged at the Villa Mantini. Toni had seen it. Piero had seen it. But to himself the knowledge had brought only torment.

He returned to the bed and knelt down with his lips close to her ear.

'Donna,' he whispered urgently. 'Donna, can you hear me?'

But she lay still and quiet, in a secret world that he could not enter.

CHAPTER TEN

EVERYWHERE was safe and warm: just a soft, comfortable slipping into nothingness.

But Donna couldn't quite take the last step. Someone was preventing her. Someone spoke her name, calling her back to life. Strong fingers clasped her hand, refusing to let her go.

'I need you—Donna, I need you—stay with me—'

She couldn't see his face. There was only the firm clasp of his hands, refusing to be gainsaid, and his voice speaking urgently in her ear. 'I need you—I need you—don't leave me—'

Then she opened her eyes to find that the world had settled back into place. She was in a quiet hospital room, surrounded by machinery, a drip attached to her arm. Standing by the wall was Rinaldo, watching her.

As soon as he saw that she was awake he went to the door and called for the nurse. She came in, smiling.

'That's better. You gave us all a fright.'

'My baby,' she whispered at once.

'Your baby's fine. We put him in an incubator as a precaution, but he didn't need it, and he'll be coming out of it today. We had more worries about you. It took three transfusions to stabilise you.'

'What happened?'

'You started to haemorrhage badly. You lost a lot of blood, and it was quite a struggle to hold onto you.'

Rinaldo came closer to the bed. His eyes were dark

and sunken from lack of sleep, but they held an eager expectancy that Donna was too drowsy to notice.

'I feel as if I've been a long way away,' she said.

'You have,' he answered gently. 'You've been in a coma for two days. I thought you weren't coming back.'

'I think I nearly didn't,' she said slowly. 'It was very strange—as though everything was ready for me—and then I couldn't leave. Two days? Have you been here all that time?'

Something that might have been hope died in his eyes, as though a light had gone out, leaving his face as unreadable as before.

'Yes, I've been here,' he said. 'Where else would I be when my wife and son were in danger?'

'Of course—and Toni's really all right? Have you seen him?'

'Several times. He's very well now. The circumstances of his birth don't seem to have troubled him.'

'The circumstances of—? Oh, yes, he was born in the car, wasn't he?' She remembered now that Rinaldo had chosen to stay with his car, rather than come to hospital with her. She wondered how long he'd had to stay there before the recovery van had arrived, but she felt too tired to ask.

A sudden feeling of desolation swept her. This should have been a wonderful moment, one that perhaps might have brought them closer. But the memory of him letting her go to hospital alone had destroyed it. How stupid of her to imagine that the voice and the hands that had drawn her back from death might have belonged to him. Wearily her eyes closed again.

Rinaldo watched her in silence. He felt drained and utterly exhausted. In the two days since he'd ridden to the hospital in the vegetable van he hadn't closed his eyes for a moment. He hadn't dared, in case she slipped away while he wasn't there to hold onto her. He'd stayed with her, exerting all his force of will to keep her alive, pleading, praying, *commanding* her to stay with him, until lack of sleep had made him a little crazy.

He wondered now what it had all been for. She hadn't known him, and he had a heartbreaking suspicion that she'd returned against her will. What had she really wanted during those dark hours when she'd wandered in the valley of the shadow? To whom had her heart turned?

One thing he was sure of with increasing bitterness. It wasn't himself who'd given her the will to live. It was her love for her baby. He might as well not have been there.

For Donna the following days were a mixture of joy and anguish. There was the moment, on Christmas Day, when her baby was first laid in her arms. Once she'd dared to hope that it would be Rinaldo who brought little Toni in and gave him to her, and that they could share the perfect moment. But he held back while a nurse gave her the baby, and she was conscious of him watching her from a distance.

But the next instant all this was forgotten in the feel of her child nestled close to her. Nothing in her whole life had been as sweet, or as beautiful. Her arms closed around him naturally, and he fitted against her breast as though they were still one.

'Has Piero seen him?' she asked.

'Not yet,' the nurse said.

'Let's take him now.'

They helped her into a wheelchair and settled Toni in her arms. Rinaldo would have kept apart then too, but

Donna insisted that he wheel her along the corridor, knowing that the sight would please Piero.

The old man's joy would have been compensation for a thousand griefs. 'This is Toni,' she told him, holding the baby close to him. 'He's come back to us. Happy Christmas.'

Their eyes met in perfect understanding. Rinaldo watched them, saying nothing, and Donna found herself feeling the same sadness for him as she'd felt for his brother, both of them cut off from the joy that filled her life.

She remained in hospital for another fortnight. She could have returned home earlier, but she stayed the extra days to be with Piero, knowing that seeing the baby often did him more good than any medicine. They returned home together on a cold day in January.

Donna spent most of the first few nights in the nursery, watching over her child. When he woke she breast-fed him, and changed him, and when he settled again she sat beside him, watching like a miser gloating over treasure. To her he was pure gold. She couldn't have enough of him. It was a kind of pain to think he was no longer physically a part of her, but the pain vanished when she held him to her breast.

'You're not getting enough sleep yourself,' Rinaldo said one night. He was standing in the doorway watching her as she suckled little Toni, her head bent over him.

She glanced up briefly, but immediately returned her attention to the child, who was concentrating furiously on the task in hand.

'I sleep during the day,' she said. 'With two nurses and Maria fussing about me, what is there for me to do?' She smiled down fondly. 'He really is like Toni, isn't he? What I said to Piero was true. He hasn't really gone away at all.'

She said this to comfort Rinaldo, on whom she knew the loss of his brother weighed heavily. But it didn't seem to please him. Instead, he looked at her awkwardly for a while, before saying, 'There's something I've been meaning to tell you. I have to visit some of the factories that I haven't seen for some time. I should have gone before.'

'Will you be away for long?'

'Perhaps three months. They're in the south, in Calabria. I'll need to spend several weeks in each place. I should be back mid-April.'

Three months without seeing him, she thought. But then Toni gave a little belch, and she laughed with pleasure, revelling in the feel of the little warm body.

'You'll be all right,' Rinaldo said. 'As you say, there are so many people here to look after you—you won't need me.'

But I do need you, she thought. I wanted us to share the first few weeks of Toni's life. It might have brought us closer. Now I know you don't care.

'I'm sure your work is very important,' she said politely. 'Don't hurry back on our account.'

He left the very next morning, and it seemed to Donna that he was glad to be gone. He'd made sure she had the number of his mobile phone.

'There's no point in my giving you the factory numbers because I don't know where I'll be at any one time.' He'd hesitated. 'Take care of yourself,' he'd said gruffly, and had got straight into the car.

At first it was lonely without him, but little Toni absorbed her. There was no chance to feel very lonely while this tiny life depended on her utterly. She breast-fed him whenever possible, occasionally supplementing this with formula.

Everything revolved around the baby. The servants adored him, even the men sneaking away from their work to take 'just a little peep'. Enrico made faces until Toni responded with a small but distinct raspberry, which made him roar with laughter. Maria was never happier than when Donna allowed her to change or bathe the little deity of the household.

Donna could have delegated almost every job to someone else, but she only wanted to hug him to herself. She resisted the temptation, and let everyone have a share in him, but though she smiled and thanked them for their efforts she was always secretly waiting for them to be gone. Then she could take him in her arms and murmur, 'My love—my darling…'

Night was her favourite time, when she could have him all to herself for hours on end, gazing at his tiny sleeping body with silent, passionate adoration.

She talked to Rinaldo most days, sometimes calling him, but mostly waiting for him to make the call. Their talks never lasted long. She described Toni, how he was growing by the day, beginning to smile at her—at least, *she'd* thought it was a smile, though Maria had said it was wind. He responded politely, and they were both relieved when it was time to finish.

The cold of January and February passed away. Rain fell, bringing Loretta's garden back to life for another year. Donna enjoyed standing in the cloisters, watching the showers, with the sun close behind them.

She came in one day to find Maria just putting down the telephone. 'It was the police,' she said. 'They've found Rinaldo's car.'

'You mean he's had an accident?' Donna asked quickly.

'No, not the new one—the one that was stolen.'

'I didn't know he had one stolen,' Donna said blankly. 'Come to think of it, when he left he wasn't driving his usual car, but it didn't really register.'

'The other one was stolen on the night Toni was born,' Maria said.

'But he stayed with it.'

'Not all the time. He called the hospital and they told him you were very ill. So he left the keys in the car for the recovery people, and got a lift from a vegetable van. When he called the recovery firm they said they'd never found the car. Someone must have taken it. Now it's been found, but the police say it's in a bad way.'

Donna hardly heard the last part. Only one thing stood out. 'Rinaldo came to the hospital?'

'You didn't know?'

'I know he was there when I woke up but—he came that same night? In a vegetable van?'

'You think he'd stay away when you were ill? I took him in some clean clothes, and I saw him there. He never left you for a moment, day or night.'

'But why didn't he tell me?' Donna cried.

Maria regarded her with fond exasperation. 'It seems to me,' she said severely, 'that you two never tell each other anything. Best you start, quickly.' She waddled away.

'What do you think of that?' Donna asked Toni as she cuddled him that night. 'It was him all the time, holding onto me. What do you suppose it means?'

Toni gave a little grunt.

'You think he cares about me? So why doesn't he just

tell me? Of course, he's a very difficult man. He'll be home soon. And then we'll see...'

Toni didn't answer. He'd fallen asleep.

As exercise and sensible eating returned her figure to normal Donna began to consider a new wardrobe. Signora Racci was eager to help, and Donna spent a satisfying morning in the Via Condotti, being measured.

'I don't think I should order any more,' she said at last, with a touch of guilt.

Elisa Racci appeared to consider the matter judicially. 'Signor Mantini placed no upper limit on your account,' she mused.

Donna chuckled. 'That might be very unwise of him.'

'But of course you wish to celebrate the recovery of your figure. It's understood.'

'In that case, let's see if we can make him wish he'd set an upper limit,' Donna said resolutely.

She wondered at the change that had come over her. At one time she would never have thought of spending so much money on herself, but the birth of her son had given her confidence. In this fertile country, a mother had status, especially if her child was a son. It might be old-fashioned, but it was true. The warmth and approval that surrounded Donna at home had pervaded her with its message, and now she was sure of herself.

Only Rinaldo's return was needed to make that assurance complete. She was a woman who knew where she stood with her child and her household. Soon she would know how she stood with her man.

Her man. She'd called him that instinctively, although he wasn't hers. But in the light of what she'd learned it was easy to believe she could fight for him and win. She gave the shop a mountain of orders, and left wearing a new red dress that had simply demanded to belong to her. Red was one colour she could wear better than Selina.

She'd left Enrico behind today, preferring to travel by taxi. The weather was still cool enough to make walking pleasant, so she went up the Spanish steps, which looked oddly bare before the arrival of the azaleas and the tourists. From here it was no more than a reasonable stroll to the Via Veneto, where she would have coffee before returning home.

She found the little restaurant where she'd been before. Just across the way she could see the apartment block where Selina lived, and she wondered what Selina was doing these days.

A terrible temptation came over her. In her bag were some photographs of Toni—the perfect excuse, if she needed one, for a visit.

Why not drop in on Selina and subtly let her know that war had been declared? She rose and crossed the road to the entrance to the apartments. There was a row of bells with a little label beside each one. Selina lived on the third floor—as Donna thought. She was about to ring the bell when someone came out, and she took the chance to slip in through the open door.

The lift took her to the third floor, and in a moment she was knocking on Selina's door. It was opened by a maid in uniform.

'I'm Signora Mantini,' she said. 'I've called to see Selina. Is she in?'

'No, *signora*. She is away for several weeks.'

'Oh, dear. Do you know where she's gone?'

'She couldn't say exactly, only that she was going south, and might be moving around.'

An uneasy feeling began to creep over Donna at these

words, so close an echo of Rinaldo's. 'Do you—know when she'll be back?' she asked.

'Mid-April, she told me.'

'Thank you,' Donna said, hardly knowing what she uttered. She turned blindly and made her way out of the building. Rinaldo and Selina were both absent at the same time, both moving around, both expected back in mid-April. A little mocking voice inside her called her a fool for not having foreseen this. She tried desperately to believe it might be simply a coincidence, but her new-found confidence had run away out of the soles of her feet.

Rinaldo returned home early one evening, without telling anyone he was coming. Unseen, he walked through the house and into Loretta's garden. Donna was there, sitting by the fountain, with the cradle on a bench beside her. She was looking down into the cradle, totally absorbed. Rinaldo couldn't see the baby, but he saw one tiny, starfish hand waving about. Donna chuckled softly and seized it, kissing the fingers one by one. Her face was alight with joy.

He'd seen her with her baby before he left. There had been love in her face, but nothing like this. Then she'd been cautious, always on her guard because he was there. But now she thought herself unobserved, and Rinaldo caught his breath at her look of total, defenceless adoration. Mother and child existed on another plane, where there was only love. There was an ache in his heart that he'd known once before.

He'd been nine when he'd come home from school one day and found his mother cradling his new-born baby brother, looking down into his face with an expression that Rinaldo had thought reserved for himself.

He'd lived all his short life in the knowledge that he was Loretta's darling, superseding even his father in her heart. It had made him feel like a king. In a moment everything had been snatched from him. He was displaced, set aside for the infant whose helplessness could call forth that look of devotion on his mother's face.

It hadn't been exactly like that, of course. Loretta hadn't stopped loving him. She'd gone on listening to him when he wanted to confide, interesting herself in his concerns, and her pride in him had been immense. But he'd had to compete for her time, which had been a shock to a boy who'd believed that the world revolved around him. Suddenly he was no longer first, and it had hurt.

He could still remember how that moment had ended. His mother had glanced up, discovered him watching, and smiled. 'Come and look at little Toni. Isn't he beautiful?' she'd said. And when he'd gone hesitantly towards them she'd laid the baby in his arms.

He could always win her approval by being a good brother, he'd thought. But in time his pretend interest in the baby had turned into the real thing. From the start Toni had possessed charm and a beaming smile that had melted all hearts. Even Rinaldo, serious before his time, couldn't resist it. Often he'd put himself between Toni and trouble, and where Toni was there was usually trouble.

On her death-bed Loretta had whispered, 'Take care of Toni. Protect him…'

And he'd said, 'I promise, Mamma.' He'd waited for her to say something for himself, but she'd sighed as if he'd removed her last care, and slipped away.

Rinaldo had loved Toni and he'd tried to protect him, even though at the very last he'd failed. But beneath the

brotherly affection there had been a barely acknowledged resentment that the love he'd wanted had always
gone to Toni. He'd thought those days were over. Until
now.

But this was different. In a moment Donna would notice him. She'd say how much she'd missed him, how
glad she was that he'd come back. Anything. But it
would be about just the two of them, and would tell him
how their marriage was to start.

Then she looked up. For a moment it seemed as
though she would make a joyful move towards him, but
instead a cloak of reserve seemed to settle over her.

'Come and look at little Toni,' she said. 'Isn't he
beautiful?'

CHAPTER ELEVEN

SOMEWHERE in her dreams Donna could hear Toni crying. It went on and on, and she struggled to wake, but the tentacles of sleep clung to her insistently. She was so tired…but her baby needed her.

At last she managed to open her eyes, and realised that the crying had stopped. For a moment she wondered if it had just been part of a dream, but her instincts told her that Toni had really been calling, and now he was silent.

Then she noticed the door to his room. She'd left it slightly ajar, but now it was closed, and there was a faint sliver of light coming from beneath it.

She moved quietly to the door and listened. From the other side came the sounds of movement, and the faint murmuring of a voice. Donna wondered if she was still dreaming, because the voice sounded like Rinaldo. Softly she nudged the door open.

Rinaldo was there, with Toni, whom he was just laying down on a small table covered with a towel. He held the baby easily, with a hand beneath its head, like a man who was used to babies, and he spoke softly.

'You're surprised to see me, *piccolo bambino*? You thought it would be your *mamma*. But you've worn her out, so we shall let her sleep tonight.'

Donna watched, astounded. In the two weeks since he'd been home Rinaldo had taken no more than a polite interest in the baby. But now he was talking to him as though they instinctively understood the same language.

Toni regarded him intently, his eyes wide and curious. Rinaldo went on speaking in a soft murmur that only just reached her.

'Don't be afraid that I don't know what I'm doing. I've done this before, although not for many years. When my brother was little my mother taught me how to look after him.'

Donna couldn't see Rinaldo's face as he moved around, getting a fresh nappy, but she could hear the smile in his voice as he said, 'I didn't want to do it. I was nine years old. I protested, ''Mamma, babies are for girls.'' But she said, ''Every man should know how to look after a baby.'' And she was right.'

He began to fix the nappy into place on the tiny body, his fingers moving dexterously. 'Is that all right?' he asked at last, speaking seriously, as if sure that Toni could understand him. And perhaps he was right, for Toni gave a small, contented grunt.

'I'll have to get used to these modern nappies,' Rinaldo told him. 'When I last did this, a nappy was a triangle of towelling and you fixed it with a pin. It took practice to become handy with the pin. Once I pricked your fa—my brother, and he yelled the place down.'

Toni made a sound that might almost have been a chuckle. To Donna's incredulous delight Rinaldo grinned. In the soft light from the lamp Donna could just make out the warmth in his eyes as he looked down on the infant. He'd finished now, but instead of returning Toni to bed he gathered him up and sat down with him in his lap. The child lay there contentedly, his tiny arms and legs stuck out in front of him like flippers, his wide eyes fixed on Rinaldo's face.

'Is that better now?' Rinaldo asked. 'You don't mind that it's me? It's time we got to know each other, man to man, and we can't do that when there's a pack of women around.'

Donna gave an involuntary giggle and he looked up quickly, grinning ruefully when he saw her. 'I guess that's it for tonight,' he told Toni. 'Another time.'

He laid him gently back into his cot. 'Do you want to check that I've done everything right?' he asked Donna.

'No, I can see you're a real expert.'

Rinaldo looked around. 'What became of that mouse Selina gave us?'

Donna's face was bland. 'I'm afraid Sasha got it. He's a mouser and no one explained the difference to him.'

He regarded her cynically. 'You didn't happen to shut that cat in here, did you?'

'No, but I gave him the very best fish for supper the next day,' she admitted.

They laughed together. Donna's heart swelled with happiness. Rinaldo switched off the bedside light.

'Thank you,' she said. 'I was a little tired.'

He touched her face. 'Are you tired now?'

Suddenly her heart was racing. 'No,' she whispered. 'Not now.' She reached up and touched his face in return, and his arms slipped around her.

His kiss was gentle, almost tentative. They stood close for a moment, arms about each other, sharing body warmth.

'You smell of baby talc,' she murmured.

'You smell of sleep.'

Nothing was the way she'd feared. Instead of insisting on access to her bed, the way he'd once threatened, he held back until she took his hand.

A few moments later her nightdress fell to the floor, revealing a figure that was still slightly voluptuous. He ran his hands over it with pleasure, caressing her subtly, not demanding but asking. Her flesh responded with a joyful *yes*.

Stripped of the silk pyjamas his own body was lean and hard, enticing her to run her fingers over it. She could feel the steely strength beneath the skin, but it was leashed back now as he slowly incited her to passion.

Of the two, it was she who was the more demanding. Her whole being ached to be one with him. In the four months since the birth she'd regained her health and strength. Her fulfilment as a mother had put a glow in her eyes and a sheen on her skin. Now she was ready to be fulfilled as a woman. It was her right. She loved this man, and tonight she would not be denied.

She gave herself up joyfully to his touch, revelling in the warmth of his body, the hot, masculine odour of his arousal, and the anticipation of love. She was ready for him long before he moved over her, and when he entered her she gave a long, satisfied sigh of completion. It was all so easy. Why had they spent months as strangers when this answered all questions? She gave a soft moan as he thrust slowly deep inside her. She moved her hips in rhythm with his, letting him make the pace now, content only to be in his arms, to be united with him, to be his.

Pain and loneliness melted away. She was doing what she'd been born for, expressing her love for her man. The problems could be dealt with later, but they'd be dealt with more easily because of this perfect experience.

She saw his face, and wondered if she'd imagined his astonished look. Then thoughts faded in the joy of the flesh. She was being carried to heights she'd never dreamed of before, and when the blazing moment was over she found she was drifting down gently into the safety of his arms—and sleep.

She woke to find Rinaldo standing at the window, his body touched by the first light of dawn.

'Come here,' she said blissfully, holding out her hand.

But though he came to her he didn't join her in bed, but stood holding her hand, as if unsure what to do next.

'What's the matter?' she asked, puzzled.

'Nothing—that is—we need to talk, Donna—about many things. I'd meant to talk to you before this—last night took me by surprise.'

'Me too. But does it matter?'

He smiled uneasily. 'Let us talk first,' he said. Stooping, he kissed her lightly and left the room.

What sixth sense warned Selina to call that day? Perhaps it was the instincts of the cat that made her scent danger and pounce while there might still be time.

Donna was in the garden when Maria came to tell her crossly that Selina was in the house and had gone straight to the nursery 'as though she was the mistress here'.

Donna hurried upstairs. In the doorway of the nursery she stopped, her mouth tightening at the sight that met her eyes.

Selina was standing there, with Toni in her arms. She was smiling at the baby in a way that disturbed Donna. There was no fondness in it, only possession and satisfaction. Toni seemed to recognise something wrong, for he was making feeble struggling movements and giving little squeaks of displeasure.

'I'll take him,' Donna said, holding out her arms.

But Selina turned away from her. 'Oh, we're just getting to know each other, aren't we, my little one?'

'I said I'll take him,' Donna repeated.

Selina's grip tightened. 'You really shouldn't be so possessive, Donna. He isn't just your baby, you know.'

'As far as you're concerned he is,' Donna said in a hard voice. 'Give him to me.'

Selina laughed. 'I don't think he wants to go to you. I think he wants to stay with his other *mamma*, don't you, my precious? Yes, of course you do. We've got to get to know each other.'

'Give him to me at once,' Donna said in a voice as quiet as it was deadly.

That got through to Selina at last. Her head shot up and she looked straight into Donna's eyes. What she saw there seemed to decide her, for she shrugged and handed the baby over. Toni relaxed as soon as he was in his mother's arms. She held him against her shoulder, stroking his back and soothing him, and looked at Selina.

'Don't ever speak of yourself as his mother again,' she said.

Selina laughed. '*Dio mio*! You *are* possessive. I know new mothers have strange moods, but this is ridiculous. You ought to get psychiatric help.'

'You're no kind of mother to Toni, and you never will be.'

Selina's green eyes narrowed. 'Well, I wouldn't be too sure of that if I were you.'

'What is that supposed to mean?'

'Oh, really, Donna, hasn't this gone on long enough? Rinaldo only married you to secure his brother's child. It was a sacrifice because he and I were lovers. You knew that, unless you've been too stupid to notice, which wouldn't surprise me.'

Donna's heart was hammering with a kind of fear, but

she wouldn't let it show. She faced Selina with her head up and gave back insult for insult.

'I know you've wanted to marry Rinaldo ever since your career began to slide out of sight,' she said. 'It never was much of a career, was it, Selina? Just bit parts where you could flaunt your shape. But there are lots of actresses with nice shapes, and film directors prefer them in their teens rather than their thirties.'

'I'm twenty-seven,' Selina snapped.

'Of course you are. You've been twenty-seven for the last five years, haven't you? I don't blame you for trying to make your assets last, since they're all you've ever had. But their day has been over for some time now, so you decided to try to recapture the prize you threw away thirteen years ago. Do you think Rinaldo hasn't seen through you all the time? You're fooling yourself.'

Selina's face was dark with rage, but she kept it in check, and her voice was a smooth purr. 'No, I think it's you who are fooling yourself, *cara*. Rinaldo and I understand each other. I came back to him because he begged me to, and I turned down a dozen parts to do it. The poor darling was still so desperate for me that he'd have taken me on any terms.'

'I don't believe you,' Donna said, fighting to keep her voice steady.

'Don't you know how often he's shared my bed since he married you? No, I suppose you've buried your head in the sand. But while you were swelling like a sack Rinaldo and I were making love anywhere and any time. Sometimes he came to my apartment, sometimes I slipped into his office. He has a bedroom there, you know.

'But we didn't always have each other in bed. Rinaldo is a man who likes a great deal of sexual variety, but I don't suppose you've ever had the chance to discover that. Or have you? Was he kind, just once? I really don't mind. I told him to do whatever was necessary to keep you quiet for a while.'

'Rubbish!' Donna said, more confidently than she felt. 'If Rinaldo had wanted to he could have married you before I came on the scene.'

'*Cara*, he begged me to marry him. I was the one who said no. You sneer at my "assets" but I've put in a lot of work on them, and I didn't want them ruined with child-bearing. But you've taken care of that problem for me. As soon as he told me you were pregnant I told him to marry you. He took a little persuading but—'

'Wait a minute,' Donna whispered. 'Are you saying that *you* suggested our marriage? Because I'll never believe that.'

'What difference does it make what you believe? Rinaldo wanted that baby and I showed him the way to get it.'

'Y-you're lying,' Donna stammered.

'Am I? Then where was he in the three months after Toni's birth? Not here looking after you, that's certain.'

'He had business—'

'Business—just then? There was nothing his assistants couldn't handle. You don't even know where he was.'

'He was in Calabria—'

'You telephoned him there, did you?'

'Of course I did—' Donna fell silent as she realised that she'd called him on a mobile phone. He could have been anywhere. Watching her face closely, Selina saw every thought reflected, and her feline smile grew broader.

'In your heart you knew we were together, didn't you? Especially after you called at my flat. We had a won-

derful time. After months of your moods and crotch-
etiness he was ready for a real woman. Desperate in
fact.' She laughed out loud. 'Once you even called us
when we were actually—'

'That's enough!' Donna screamed.

'Our plan was for him to marry you and divorce you
when you'd outlived your usefulness.'

Donna pulled herself together. 'Rinaldo will never divorce me.'

Selina gave a nasty little laugh. 'Why do you think
he only married you in a civil ceremony? It makes the
divorce so much easier. He's making the arrangements
now. You'll be paid off decently, and you'll leave the
country and never come back. Toni, of course, will stay
here.

'I'm a little surprised that all this comes as a shock
to you. I'd have thought Rinaldo would have prepared
your mind by now, but he tells me that it's difficult.
You're so set in your own way of looking at things that
nothing gets through. But truly, hasn't he dropped a hint
recently? Never mind. You'll give in at last. You know
what he's like when he's determined to have his own
way.'

'Get out of my house,' said Donna coldly. 'And never
try to set foot in it again.'

Selina raised her eyebrows and a little smile played
around her beautiful mouth. 'Oh, yes, of course,' she
murmured. 'It's your home, isn't it? For the moment.
But soon it will be my home. For years Rinaldo has
dreamed of bringing me here. You've just been the
lodger.'

Something snapped in Donna. She laid Toni in his cot,
then turned back to Selina. The other woman just had
time to read the purpose in her eyes, but no time to get

out of the way. She put up an arm to defend herself, but
Donna reached past it to close her finger and thumb hard
on Selina's ear. Selina shrieked.

'You're leaving,' Donna said firmly. She moved out
of the room, forcing Selina to go with her. The beautiful
Italian burst into a stream of invective, struggling and
trying to free herself.

'Let me go,' she screamed. *'Let me go!'*

'When I'm ready,' Donna said. 'Mind how you go
down the stairs.'

Drawn by the noise, servants began to gather in the
hall below, witnessing Selina's humiliating descent.
Some of them covered their mouths with their hands.
Others didn't bother. Two of them pulled open the front
doors and actually saluted, grinning. None of them liked
Selina.

'Thank you,' Donna said, and marched through, keeping her grip on the writhing woman.

When they reached the car she released her. Selina
turned on her. The struggle had disturbed her heavily
lacquered hair, which fell forward in stiff chunks, giving
her the air of a drunken woman. Her face was red and
blotchy and tears poured down her cheeks.

'You'll be sorry for this,' she raged.

'Not nearly as sorry as you'll be if you ever dare come
near my husband or my baby again,' Donna informed
her.

'*Your* husband—?' Selina began, but stopped as she
met Donna's eyes. Something in them made her scram-
ble into the car and start the engine hurriedly.

Donna waited until the vehicle had vanished around
a curve in the drive before hurrying back into the house.
Her mind was in a turmoil of misery. With all her heart
she longed to disbelieve Selina's spiteful accusations,

but too many of the details fitted. Rinaldo's absence so soon after Toni's birth, his insistence on giving her only the number of his mobile phone, Selina's disappearance at the same time.

Most ominous of all were his words last night about needing to talk to her. What did he want to say? Had he been, as Selina had said, trying to prepare her mind for an infamous plan?

If there was the slightest chance of that she couldn't risk staying here a moment longer. Even now Selina might be on the phone to him, warning him to get home quickly.

She began to throw clothes into suitcases. She was working from the surface of her mind, refusing to look at the torment that lay below. Despite their unpromising beginning Rinaldo had won her love. Sometimes it had seemed to her that he even wanted it. His unexpected vein of tenderness had delighted her. And all the time he'd been making a fool of her with Selina, his true love. The evidence was all around her, and she'd been a blind fool not to see it.

This was his country, where he had power and she had none. She couldn't risk a battle on his home territory. She had to get back to England before he could stop her.

There was a second car in the garage that she occasionally used. She hurried downstairs with her suitcases and threw them inside. But before leaving she knew there was something she had to do. With Toni in her arms she pushed open the door to Piero's room.

He was alert as soon as he saw her, trying to reach out his hand to her.

'I came to say goodbye,' she said softly. 'I have to go. I'm sorry—I'll miss you—but I *have* to—'

'No—no—' He whispered the words in distress.

It was harder to do this than she'd thought. 'Tell Rinaldo—' she struggled for words '—tell him—just tell him goodbye.'

She leaned down to press Toni's little face against Piero's. Then she dropped a light kiss on the old man's cheek, and hurried out. His words floated after her. 'No, Donna—don't leave…'

For a couple of hours the house existed in an uneasy limbo. None of the servants knew what to think, except that her departure must be connected with the extraordinary scene with Selina they had witnessed. Everyone was relieved when Rinaldo returned, but relief turned to apprehension when he enquired after the whereabouts of his wife and child.

'You just let her go without knowing where?' he demanded angrily of Maria.

'Don't be angry with me,' Maria said crossly. 'She is the *patrona*. None of us has the right to question her.'

'I thought you liked her,' Rinaldo flung at Maria furiously.

'I do like her,' Maria said. 'And I tell you this: if it weren't for the other thing that happened I'd say she'd gone to escape your nasty temper, and good luck to her. And don't glare at me. I knew you when you were a baby, and I'm not scared of you, even if the others are.'

'What do you mean?' Rinaldo demanded. 'What "other thing that happened"?'

'Selina was here. I don't know what was said between them, but the *patrona* threw her out.'

Rinaldo stared. 'She told her to go?'

'No, she threw her out.'

'You mean—literally?'

'She hauled her down the stairs by her ear,' Maria said with relish. 'Not before time too.'

Before Rinaldo could answer they heard Piero's bell ringing. There was something agitated about the sound. 'I must go to him,' he said quickly.

Upstairs he found Piero sitting up in bed with a look of terrible anxiety on his face. 'It's all right, Nonno. I'm here,' he said, taking the frail hand gently between his own. 'Everything's all right.'

In his heart he had a dread that everything was far from all right, but he hid his alarm.

'Donna…' Piero whispered. *'Donna…'*

'She'll come to see you soon,' Rinaldo said. 'But first we— *Dio mio!* What is that noise?'

The commotion was coming from downstairs. Rinaldo hurried out to the landing and was in time to see Selina reach the foot of the stairs.

'Rinaldo,' she shrieked, seeing him above. 'Oh, thank God you're home.' Her hair and make-up had been repaired, and she presented a beautiful picture as she flew up the stairs and collapsed at his feet in a passion of sobs. Rinaldo seized her arms and hauled her to her feet with an absence of gentleness that should have warned her to be careful.

'What are you hysterical about?' he demanded.

'Donna—she's gone mad—she attacked me—'

'I heard she threw you out. Why, Selina? What did you do?'

'I didn't do anything, I swear it.'

'Have you been playing off your tricks?' he asked. 'Donna wouldn't have gone for you without some reason.'

'I just picked up the baby to cuddle him, because I love him so, and she—she just seemed to go crazy. She's so possessive with that child. She doesn't want to share him with anyone, not even you.'

'She's Toni's mother,' Rinaldo said. 'There's a bond between mother and baby—it's natural.'

'Is it natural for her to be so selfish that she doesn't care how she treats other people?'

'What do you mean?'

'Why do you think she married you?'

Rinaldo gave a grim laugh. 'Because I forced her to.'

'You think you did. After that little show of reluctance she grabbed her chance with both hands. She wanted the family name, for herself and the baby. Now she's got it, all she cares about is getting a divorce and a nice fat settlement.'

'Where did you get these wild ideas?' he snapped.

'She admitted it. She's always known I'm the one person she can't fool. That's why she hates me—because she knows I love you and will fight for you. Today she let the mask slip and I saw the real Donna: selfish, hard and grasping. Why don't you bring her here and make her face me—if she dares?'

'Donna isn't here,' Rinaldo said. 'She left, with Toni.'

Selina's hands flew to her mouth. 'Don't you see? That proves it. Once she'd admitted everything to me she had to go quickly before I warned you.'

'But you didn't warn me,' Rinaldo said coldly. 'You could have telephoned me instead of waiting and giving her a head start.'

'I—I was afraid of her,' Selina said quickly. 'You don't know what she's like—mad, evil—'

'All the more reason for warning me before she took Toni,' Rinaldo said. There was something implacable about his face that Selina couldn't mistake. She gave a little scream.

'Why are we wasting time? If she gets the baby out of the country you'll never see him again.'

Maria had come up the stairs and stood listening to Selina, scowling. Rinaldo swung round to her. 'Did you hear any of this?' he demanded.

'I've told you what I heard,' she retorted. 'There was a fight and the mistress threw her out.' Without favouring either of them with another look, she passed on into Piero's room.

'She attacked me like a madwoman,' Selina protested.

'I doubt that,' Rinaldo said. 'I haven't been married to Donna all these months without learning something about her. And I haven't known you for years, Selina, without knowing how you get your own way. I'm not the gullible boy I used to be. I told you that when I ended our relationship, but you wouldn't listen.'

Selina covered her face with her hands, and when she spoke again it was in trembling, heartbroken tones. 'Think what you like about me. Reject me. Perhaps I've deserved it. All that matters now is little Toni's safety. She's stolen him away from you.'

Aghast, he realised that she was right. Donna had taken Toni and departed without a word to him. However much he distrusted Selina, that was the hard fact he had to face. He felt as if Donna had punched him in the stomach.

He tried to thrust the pain aside, to override it with anger, which was how he'd coped with pain all his life. That had been his magic talisman, his way of coping with all hurt from his mother's death onwards. It had helped him show an indifferent face to the world when his brother had spurned his protection, and had somehow brought him through the horror of Toni's death. Anger was good. It was positive, it conquered weakness, and he dreaded weakness most of all. So now he called on anger to help him again.

At first it was easy. Donna had no right to vanish with the baby. But there were ways of dealing with that.

'Wait for me downstairs,' he said curtly to Selina, and turned to walk away. He was forestalled by Maria, who'd just emerged from Piero's room.

'He wants to talk to you,' she said.

'Not just now. Try to reassure him and say I'll come as soon as possible.' He strode away.

In the bedroom he made a phone call to Gino Forselli, describing Donna's car. 'She's probably driving north to the border,' he said.

'If she only left a couple of hours ago she won't be anywhere near the border yet,' Forselli reassured him. 'I'll put out an alert for her. Do you want her arrested?'

'No,' Rinaldo said explosively. 'Just keep her in sight and let me know.'

He slammed down the phone and sat there, shocked to find that the talisman had failed to work. The anger was there, but instead of smothering the pain it made a bitter counterpoint to it. Donna had deceived him, defied him, made a mockery of him. But all that was as nothing beside the fact that she had rejected him.

CHAPTER TWELVE

MARIA appeared in the doorway. 'You must come to Signor Piero now,' she urged. 'It's very important.'

He found Piero sitting up in bed, with a heightened colour and an agitated manner. 'Calm yourself, Nonno,' he said. 'Everything will be all right.'

'No—no—' Piero struggled to speak, but the more agitated he grew, the harder it was for him to form words. He managed to say, 'Donna—' before collapsing back against his pillows.

'What about Donna?' Rinaldo asked.

But Piero could say no more. Looking into his eyes, Rinaldo sensed uneasily that there was something important here, something he was missing.

'What is it?' he asked. 'Try to tell me.'

He felt the old man's left hand move in his own. 'Show me,' he urged.

Using his forefinger, Piero managed to trace a D in Rinaldo's palm.

'Donna?' Piero gave a grunt of agreement. 'What about Donna?'

Piero traced more letters. At first Rinaldo couldn't understand. The letters were clear enough but his mind wouldn't accept them. But Maria, who'd followed him into the room, had no such inhibitions.

'Love,' she said robustly. 'Donna loves you. That's what he's saying.'

'It seems like it, doesn't it?' Rinaldo said bitterly. 'Look, I appreciate what the two of you—'

'Basta!' Maria snapped. Rinaldo's head went up in surprise. Maria hadn't spoken to him like that since he was a baby and she his nurse.

'Basta!' she repeated. 'When you were young you knew how to listen. Now you're a man you never hear anyone else. Otherwise you'd have heard what your wife has been trying to say all this time. She loves you. I know it. Signor Piero knows it. Even that idiot Enrico knows it. Everyone except you. Because you don't listen.'

And he replied meekly, 'All right, Maria. I'm sorry. But I can't believe it. Why should she run away from me if she loves me? Tell me that.'

'I can't. He can,' Maria said, pointing to Piero.

'What is it, Nonno?'

Slowly Piero traced an S, then an E.

'Selina?' Rinaldo guessed, and Piero grunted. 'What about her?'

This time the letters were traced more strongly, and Rinaldo got the word quickly. 'Lies? Selina tells lies? What lies?'

Slowly it came out. Piero had been close enough to hear everything Selina had said. *Selina. Mistress.*

'Selina my mistress?' Rinaldo said. 'Well, yes, at one time. But that's over. I ended it before my marriage.'

She told Donna no.

'She told Donna that she and I were still—? Are you sure?'

Heard her. Calabria—you and her—she said.

'She told Donna she was with me in Calabria?' Rinaldo said, his eyes narrowing.

True?

'No, of course it's not true,' Rinaldo said explosively. Piero made more signs in his palm. Rinaldo was on his wavelength now, picking up the ideas before they were fully spelt out.

'She told Donna that our marriage was her idea? That I planned to divorce my wife—marry Selina—and keep the baby?' he asked in a tone of outrage. 'You heard all that?'

Piero managed a faint derisive grin. *Selina stupid. Thinks I can't speak. But—for Donna's sake—*

'Yes, she is stupid,' Rinaldo breathed. 'But I've been even more stupid to be taken in by her. And now my wife is running away because she thinks I'm planning a monstrous trick like that. How could she believe that of me, whatever Selina said?'

'Why should she think well of you?' Maria demanded. 'How have you treated her?'

'I've done my best. It hasn't been easy for either of us.'

Maria made a sound that was perilously like a snort. Rinaldo scowled at her, but she was sharing a smile with Piero and didn't see him. Rinaldo strode out of the room and went searching for Selina.

He found her in Loretta's garden, sitting on the edge of the fountain. She turned to him, with a look of angelic suffering. But it died when she heard his first words.

'You will leave this house and never set foot in it again,' he said bluntly.

Her smile wavered. It was less Rinaldo's words than the expression on his face that made his meaning plain.

'Why—? Rinaldo—'

'Shut up and listen, because this is the last time you and I will ever talk. Two years ago, when you reappeared in my life hinting about the old days, I made it very clear to you that there would never be any question of marriage. I took you into my bed because it suited my pride to get you back on my own terms. I'm not proud of my behaviour now, but I never lied to you.

'I should have finished with you altogether when I married, but you pleaded so convincingly. "Just let us be friends," you said. To save your face, and stop people laughing at you. Like a fool I listened. I even made a parade of our friendship because I was sorry for you. And all the time you've been scheming to turn my wife against me. I know the lies you told her today. Piero heard them and told me.'

'I don't believe you,' she said quickly. 'Why, he can't even get two words out.'

'He found a way, because he loves Donna. I wouldn't have believed such things even of you.'

Selina began to weep beautifully. 'How can you talk to me like this?' She gulped. 'I don't understand.'

'True,' he said ironically. 'You don't understand anything important. You never did. You know nothing about people except in one very narrow sphere. Outside that sphere you're like a blind idiot stumbling through the world. A woman like Donna would be impossible for you to comprehend: her inner beauty, the way she can make everyone love her. And of course love is what you understand less than anything else.'

Selina gave a soft hiss, like a cat. 'Oh, if you're going to say that you love her—'

'My feelings for Donna are something I won't discuss with you,' he said coldly. 'Just talking to you would pollute them. Now leave this house at once. And think yourself lucky I'm not throwing you out the same way my wife did.'

The little farmhouse was well off the beaten track, and didn't normally accept guests. That was essential, because a hotel would have asked to see Donna's passport. The details would have been recorded and routinely passed on to the police. Then she'd have been apprehended, for Rinaldo was bound to have put out a police alert.

She'd parked the car behind some bushes and approached the farmhouse on foot, her baby in her arms. The farmer and his wife had apparently accepted her story of being stranded. They'd offered her a bed for the night, cooed over little Toni, and fed her a huge meal. She'd had little appetite, but had forced herself to eat to keep her strength up.

She retired to her room early, saw Toni settled, and sat beside him, brooding. She'd pulled the shutters tight, so that no light from her room could be seen outside. She was as safe as she could be in the circumstances, but she wouldn't be easy in her mind until she was back in England.

She knew she ought to try to sleep, but that was impossible. Her mind was full of turmoil. Despite the room's warmth she was shivering. The discovery of her husband's duplicity had shattered her. She'd never really known or understood him, but she'd come to believe he could be trusted. Now she saw that she'd believed it only because she'd wanted to, foolishly letting herself fall in love, and blinding herself to reality.

He was a hard, domineering man who'd go to any lengths to enforce his will, no matter who he had to crush. And he'd never pretended otherwise.

But there were other memories that wouldn't be kept out: moments when he'd shown her unexpected tenderness. Her heart cried out at the thought that they had only been part of a cruel trick to dupe her, but she had to accept it.

Toni woke, and she attended to his needs. He drifted off to sleep again, and she held him close, feeling the sweet warmth of the precious little body. For her baby she would take any risk, face any fear, endure any pain.

But her mind was unruly. It persisted in remembering how Rinaldo loved little Toni, how gently he'd tended him, as loving as any father. He'd lost one Toni, and now he was losing another. It was terrible to do that to him. And yet she had no choice.

When she was sure her baby was asleep she laid him gently back in his travelling cot. 'Goodnight, my darling,' she whispered. 'We'll soon be safe.' Then she leaned her head against the cot and let the tears come. It was the last time she would allow herself the luxury of weeping, but the tears couldn't be denied.

There was a light tap on the door. She dried her eyes and moved across cautiously to open it a crack. What she saw there made her try to slam it shut, but she was too late. Rinaldo had his hand through the gap. Horrified, she backed away and stood between him and Toni.

'You!' she said in a shaking voice. 'Oh, God, I might have known you'd find me.'

Rinaldo shut the door behind him and stood looking at her. His face was strained and his eyes looked sunken, as if with suffering.

'It's a pity you don't know me better than you seem to,' he agreed. 'How could you be taken in by anything Selina said?'

So that was going to be his first approach, she thought wildly. Persuasion, to lure her back into his trap.

'It's no use, Rinaldo,' she said. 'It won't work. I'm not going back, and you can't force me.'

'Have I said I want to force you?'

'It's your way. Force is the thing that works, isn't it?'

'Perhaps in the past,' he said gravely. 'But I know it won't be any use to me now. I want to take you back, but only willingly. If you refuse—'

'I refuse.'

'If you refuse when you hear what I have to say, I'll take you to England myself.'

'No,' she cried. 'That's just another of your tricks. I won't be deceived again.'

He grew pale. 'You really do think I'm a devil, don't you? And perhaps I have only myself to blame. But I swear you can trust me. I only want what will make you happy. Maybe you can be happy with me, but if not—' His face tightened as though the thought gave him pain.

'We can't make each other happy, Rinaldo,' she said. 'Let's end it now, and forget each other.'

'I could never forget you, and I never will,' he said slowly. 'I love you.'

'*No.*' She covered her ears with her hands.

'I can't blame you for not believing me. I've behaved badly because I've been in hell. From the first evening when I saw you in the garden I've known you were the woman nature made for me. I didn't trust you. I didn't even like you. But I wanted you and I'd have done anything to get you. You know how far I was prepared to go that first night, trying to take you away from Toni. And all the time I hated myself for coveting my brother's woman.

'I wasn't just being selfish. I knew you didn't belong with him. It would have been madness for you to marry him. When I learned you were pregnant I wanted to smash things because it meant I'd lost you. I tried to believe the child wasn't his, but I knew the truth in my heart. When he died—' He broke off and closed his eyes.

'We can't forget that,' she cried. 'Whatever else is true, that would always be between us.'

'It mustn't be,' he said fiercely. 'We've come through too much to lose each other now. If you can't love me, say so. But I warn you I won't believe it. Not completely.'

Despite her turmoil she couldn't resist a faint smile at this flash of the old, domineering Rinaldo. 'Of course, you always get your own way, don't you?'

He gave a short, mirthless laugh, mocking himself. 'I thought so. Years ago I determined that in future I'd wrest life to my will, that no woman would ever have it in her power to drive me mad again. But then there was you. I had part of you, but the other part belonged to Toni. In the end I had to face the fact that you really loved him.

'He was always there between us. When the baby was born I thought you'd turn to me, but it was his name you called. I've been wild, crazy with jealousy. I went away because I couldn't stand to watch you looking at the baby and thinking of his father, when it should have been *me*.

'If I could really have got my own way I'd have wiped my brother from your mind. But I couldn't. Nothing I could do—' A shudder possessed him. Donna stood looking at him in wonder, trying to believe what she was hearing. It was impossible, and yet…

'I believe you love me,' he said at last. 'Maybe I only believe it because I want to, because I can't face losing you. And I know you'll never love me as you loved him. I accept that. I'll take—whatever is left. Whatever you feel you can give me. But I have to believe there's *something*.'

It was true. This proud man had humbled himself for her love.

'You fool,' she whispered through her tears. 'There's everything—*everything*—all my heart—all my love.'

He was very pale. 'Don't say it if it isn't true, Donna. Don't say it just to make things right. I'll take you home and make you happy. You can have anything you want. Just be there and love me a little. I can live on crumbs, but I can't live on kindly lies.'

She walked over to him, took his face between her hands and spoke to him very simply. 'You could have had my love long ago—if only you'd wanted it.'

'If I'd *wanted* it! I've always wanted it, but I couldn't get past your love for Toni—' He stopped, for Donna had laid her hand over his mouth.

'That was over long ago. The morning of the accident I'd already decided not to marry him. I'd realised how weak he was, and I knew I couldn't live with it. But when he was dead I forgot the bad things. I could only remember how nice he could be, and I pitied him so much. But you were right. He and I could never have been happy, especially after I met you. I knew you were the one that first night, but I tried not to face it.'

'If only I'd known!' He pulled her into his arms and laid his face against her hair. 'I've been in hell, wanting you, thinking you loved Toni, hating you, hating him, hating myself…'

'I thought you still loved Selina.'

'I haven't loved Selina for thirteen years,' he said emphatically. 'After the lies she told you I never want to see her again. I can't forgive myself for putting you in that position.'

'How do you know what she said?'

'Piero told me. He heard everything. She thought no

one could give her away, but I know she told you that our marriage was her idea—that she'd been with me in Calabria—that I planned to get rid of you and marry her. Not a word of it was true. My darling, my love, how could you believe such monstrous stories?'

'But I didn't know what to believe. You forced her on me at every turn.'

Rinaldo groaned. 'I was trying to save her face by staying friends. She begged me to do that. I didn't take her to Calabria. I don't know where she was then. I imagine she vanished for your benefit, so that you'd find her absence suspicious, but she wasn't with me.'

'She made it sound so plausible,' Donna said. 'She said that was why we'd only had a civil ceremony.'

'I wanted to delay the church service until you were really mine. When we make our vows they'll be real vows, not some legal formality in the town hall. The night we made love I dared to hope that you were ready to become my wife in truth. But I'd meant us to talk first.'

He gave a twisted smile. 'It was all planned, everything I was going to say to you. I had some crazy idea that we must talk before we made love, forgetting that love finds its own moment. I wanted you to come to my arms willingly, not just because I'd surprised you.'

'I've always been willing,' she said softly. 'And I always will be.'

He touched her face gently. 'You've been weeping,' he said. 'Love me, and I swear I'll never give you cause to weep again.'

Her mouth was against his before he'd finished speaking. He picked her up and carried her to the bed, lying down with her and holding her against his heart in a gesture of protection.

'Tell me that you belong to me,' he begged, not for the first time.

'Fair exchange?' she murmured. 'Gift for gift?'

'Yes, *I* belong to *you*, *mi amore*.'

'*Strega?*' she teased.

'No, not witch. How could I ever have called you that? Heart of my heart. Love of my life. Let me hear you say the words.'

'I belong to you,' she whispered, and his kiss silenced all further talk.

There was far more, and better, to come. Their marriage would be full of passion and tenderness, fights, reconciliations, and sometimes even laughter, when she'd taught this too serious man how to laugh. But that was for the years ahead. For now it was enough that they'd found each other.

In his cot Toni stirred, grunted, and went back to sleep.

MILLS & BOON®

Makes any time special™

Mills & Boon publish 29 new titles every month. Select from...

Modern Romance™   **Tender Romance™**

Sensual Romance™

Medical Romance™   **Historical Romance™**

MAT2